The rider sli[...] [...]ned to the saddle and t[...] [...]hair, dark eyes, and high cheekbones spoke of Indian heritage. She could picture him on the front of a dime Western novel: horse rearing, guns blazing.

"I really appreciate your help. They would have taken my car and left me stranded here."

"Maybe not. They might have taken you with them."

"They'd a had a fight on their hands," Kathleen said spiritedly.

"I reckon they would've." *Her eyes were the color of his denim britches after they had been washed a hundred times.*

He smiled, and she realized that he was very attractive in a dark and mysterious sort of way. It hadn't occurred to her to be afraid of him.

"Well ... . thank you."

"You're very welcome." He tipped his hat.

Kathleen got in the car, waved, and drove away.

Johnny Henry chuckled as he watched the car disappear. Not many women would set out alone to drive more than two hundred miles across country. Miss Kathleen Dolan had spunk to go along with that red hair.

A sudden burst of happiness sent his heart galloping like a runaway horse.

Turn the page for praise for Dorothy Garlock's previous 1930s novels . . .

"Ms. Garlock just gets better, and in this era she is exceptional! Splendid! Four and a half stars!"
—*Bell, Book & Candle*

"Garlock writes with an uncanny ear for the nuances of this era, and bravo to her for bringing forth this uplifting love story."
—*BookPage*

"More than just the poignant love story of Henry Ann and Tom, *With Hope* is the complex, gripping, and rich story of an entire community during the Great Depression."
—CompuServe Romance Reviews

"A master of the Western genre, Ms. Garlock now turns her talents to the 1930s."
—*Romantic Times*

"Ms. Garlock doesn't forget to make the romance believable. She lets the reader know that even when things aren't easy 'with hope' there is love."
—*Belles & Beaux of Romance*

"Dorothy Garlock takes her gritty Westerns straight into the 1930s seamlessly. . . . I am definitely looking forward to the next installment of the series."
—*Interludes*

"There is some mighty powerful writing going on here. *With Hope* is a no-holds-barred journey—not a trip to Walton's Mountain; but you're traveling with a master writer . . . and that makes all the difference in the world."
—June Folk, Bookbug on the Web

Books by Dorothy Garlock

Published by WARNER BOOKS

ATTENTION: SCHOOLS AND CORPORATIONS
WARNER books are available at quantity
discounts with bulk purchase for educational,
business, or sales promotional use. For
information, please write to: SPECIAL SALES
DEPARTMENT, WARNER BOOKS, 1271 AVENUE
OF THE AMERICAS, NEW YORK, N.Y. 10020

DOROTHY GARLOCK

With Heart

A Time Warner Company

WARNER
VISION
BOOKS

A Time Warner Company

WARNER BOOKS EDITION

Copyright © 1999 by Dorothy Garlock

Cover art and design by Tony Greco

Warner Books, Inc.
1271 Avenue of the Americas
New York, NY 10020

Visit our Web site at
www.twbookmark.com

 A Time Warner Company

Printed in the United States of America

First Printing: November 1999

10 9 8 7 6 5 4 3 2 1

Dedicated with Deep Gratitude to the

TIME WARNER TRADE SALES GROUP

Bruce Paonessa	Harry Helm
Suzanne Abel	Peter Mauceri
Christine Barba	Karen Torres
Cassandra Murray/Mulligan	Catherine Wisniewski
Martin Conroy	Judy DeBerry
Conan Gorenstein	Christopher Austin
Paul Leahy	Bob Levine
Tom Walser	Dick Van Zile
Jerry Simmons	Richard Efthim
Monica Bartolone	Suzanne Crawford
Mark Gustafson	Michael Heuer
Linda Jamison	Jerry Jensen
Mark Lee	Cassandra Leoncini
Steve Marz	Jennifer Royce
Tom Rusch	Rich Tullis
Jill Yngve	Alan Fairbanks
Diana Frerking	Shawn Foster
Barry Broadhead	Rick Cobban
Paul Kirschner	Carol Lovercio
Judy Rosenblatt	Sandor Szatmari
Anne Zafian	Rose Cola
Anita Hennessey	Joarvonia Skipwith
Brian Tinson	Norman Kraus
Luis Rivera	Louis Kotsinis
David Leftwich	Lynn Sutherland
Mark Nichols	Traci Brandon

INSIDE STORY

Extra! Extra! Read about it!
Murder Solved! Black headlines shout it.
Find details you want to get
On Page One, *Rawlings Gazette*.

New reporter's Kathleen Dolan,
She will keep the presses rollin'.
Brains inside that head of bright red curly hair.
She's a lady, folks will find, is hard to scare.

Nearly victim of hijackin'
Till Johnny Henry sent thieves packin'.
She very kindly thanked him, never cried.
Got inside her little car and continued on her ride.

Now the girl who knew no fear
Trembles, with love, when Johnny's near.
But Johnny thinks her far above him,
Is sure that she can't love him.

Take a chance with her, John-boy.
Don't let false fears deny your joy.
You rode a steer on rodeo day.
Grab life's horns! See what she'll say.

—F.S.I.

With Heart

Imogene

Chapter One

Tillison County, Oklahoma—1938

"Bury me not on the lone prair . . . ie
    where the coyotes howl and the wind blows free.
In a narrow grave—just six by three,
    Oh, bury me not—"

Kathleen stopped singing abruptly when she rounded a bend in the lonely stretch of Oklahoma highway and saw a dilapidated old car sitting crossways in the road. Her hands gripped the wheel of her old Nash as her feet hit the clutch and the brake at the same time.

"Oh Lord! Hijackers!"

She had read about them, had even written about them while working for a year at a small paper in Liberal, Kansas. Now a hijacking was happening to her! She put the car in reverse and started backing up. Out of the brush beside the road a man sprang up and ran toward the car. Afraid to look away from him and watch where she was going, she began to zigzag. Then, to her horror, the back wheels of the car sank into the ditch beside the road.

Quickly shifting gear into drive, she gunned the motor in an attempt to go forward. The wheels spun, digging deeper into the sandy soil.

The door beside her was flung open, and a big hairy hand gripped her wrist.

"Stop it! You'll strip the gears."

"Let go!" Kathleen jerked on her arm and tramped hard on the gas pedal. The engine roared.

"Stop or I'll break your goddamn arm!"

She looked into a flabby, whiskered face. The man's lips were drawn back showing tobacco-stained teeth. He twisted her arm cruelly.

"All right! All right!" she shouted.

"Get out!"

She took her foot off the clutch. The car jerked and the motor sputtered and died. When she was pulled from under the steering wheel, she fell to her knees next to two pairs of run-down boots planted in the red dirt beside her.

"What she got in there?" The second man peered into the back window of the car. "Jesus! It's loaded with stuff."

"We gotta get this thin' outta the goddamn ditch. You stupid-ass woman! I never met one a ya that had the brains of a suck-egg mule." He reached into the car and snatched Kathleen's purse off the seat. "Got any money?"

"No."

"Liar." He pulled two ten-dollar bills out of her purse. "This all you got?"

"No! I've got a dozen gold bars in the bottom!" Anger was replacing her fear. She had lost one of her shoes when she was pulled from the car. She reached down to get it.

"Watch her!" The first man snarled and gave her a push that sent her reeling backward. He poked the two ten-dollar bills into his shirt pocket, tossed aside the thick pillow Kathleen used on the back of the seat so that her feet could reach the pedals, and slid under the wheel. "Get back there and push. Both of you."

"If you think I'm going to help you steal my car . . . you're crazy as a cross-eyed mule!"

"And if ya know what's good fer ya, you'll shut yore mouth and do what yo're told."

"Lippy, ain't she?" The second man was shorter and had a big belly. He wasn't much taller than Kathleen, who was five feet and four inches. He leered at her. "She ain't hardly got no titties a'tall, but she shore does have pretty red hair." When he reached out to touch her breasts, Kathleen's temper boiled over. She balled her fist and swung, hitting him square in the mouth.

"Ouch! You . . . bitch!" He dabbed at the blood on his mouth with the sleeve of his shirt and lifted his hand to hit her back. She drew back her fist; too angry to notice her sore knuckles, she prepared to fight.

"Touch me again and I'll . . . knock your head off!"

"Whapsy-do! If I had time, I'd take the fight outta ya."

"Goddammit, Webb." The man in the car turned the key, and the motor responded. "Stop messin' with 'er and help me get this thin' outta the ditch. Push, goddamn it! We've got to get out of here 'fore somebody comes."

The gears were shifted into drive and then into reverse to rock the car. The spinning wheels sent sand and dirt flying out behind. The wheels almost reached solid ground, then rolled back into the hole.

"*She's* not pushin'," Webb shouted, his face splotchy with anger and exertion.

Kathleen moved up onto the road and searched the horizon for something or somebody. The only movement in all that vast landscape was a few white clouds drifting lazily. A dozen scattered steers grazed on the sparse dry grass. There wasn't a car in sight.

Then she saw something coming over a small rise. At first she thought it was another steer; seconds later, she recognized a man on horseback riding across the prairie toward the steers. After a quick glance back at the two men arguing beside her car, she lifted both arms and waved wildly to the horseman and pointed toward the car. The rider gigged the horse and was less than two hundred feet away when Webb came back to the rear of the car.

"Shit!" he shouted. "Somebody's comin'."

The other man got out and looked over the top of the car. The cowboy's horse jumped the ditch and trotted toward Kathleen. She hurriedly got between it and the hijackers.

"They're stealing my car!" she exclaimed, without even looking at the man's face. Anger made her voice shrill.

In the brief silence that followed, the man who had jerked Kathleen from the car eyed the rifle that lay across the rider's thighs.

"Ah . . . naw. We is just a helpin' the lady get her car outta the ditch."

"You . . . lyin' son of a jackass!" Kathleen yelled.

"You're stealing it. Make him give back my twenty dollars." She looked up at the rider and almost groaned. He looked to be not much more than a boy.

"Give it back." Young he might be, but he spoke with quiet authority.

"I don't have her damn money."

"It's in his shirt pocket." The rifle, more than the boy, gave Kathleen courage. "Two ten-dollar bills. I was trying to get away from them when I went into the ditch. See. Their car is blocking the road."

The end of the rifle moved. "Toss the money on the seat."

"She gave it to me. It's pay for getting her out of the ditch."

"Liar! You took it out of my purse."

"I'm not telling you again," the cowboy warned.

"Good thing you got that gun, boy." The hijacker threw the bills on the seat.

"Both of you move out and stand in back of the car."

"Make them help me get my car out of the ditch. It's their fault I'm stuck."

"Get under the wheel." The end of the rifle stayed on the two hijackers. Before Kathleen started the motor, she heard the boy say, "Take off your shirts and put them under that right wheel, then lift and push when she guns the motor."

"I'm not puttin' my good shirt under that wheel."

"No? Would you rather I put it under there with you in it?"

"It'll be ruint."

"Don't look like it would be much of a loss to me."

"Don't I know you?"

"Maybe. Are you going to help the lady, or am I going to see if I can shoot the button off the top of that cap you've got on that bump on your shoulders?"

A few minutes later the Nash was up on the road, and the hijackers were putting their shirts back on.

"Which way are you going, lady?" the cowboy asked.

"Rawlings." Kathleen left the motor idling and stood beside the car.

"You two stupid clods get in your car and head back up the road."

"Are you letting them go? I want them arrested."

The cowboy glanced at the girl. Her fiery red hair, thick and curly, was a halo around her head. It was what had drawn his eyes when he first came over the hill to see about his steers. There were not many redheaded women here in Indian country. Her blue eyes sparkled angrily. He noticed the heavy sprinkling of freckles across her nose. Lord! It had been a long time since he'd seen a girl with freckles on her nose.

Ignoring her question, he walked his horse behind the men until they reached their car.

"We got a flat tire," Webb complained.

"Don't you have a tire patch, you lazy son of a bitch? It's easier to steal the lady's car than sweat a little. Is that it?"

One of them muttered something about a blanket-ass. Any other time the cowboy would have made him eat the words. Now he just wanted to get rid of the two of them. He glanced in the car to make sure that no guns were on the seats, then motioned for them to get in. He waited while they got it started and watched as the car bounced along the road on the flat tire. When it passed the Nash and headed away from Rawlings, he went back to Kathleen and spoke as if there had not been a ten-minute interruption in their conversation.

"How do you suggest we get them to the sheriff? I know who they are. I'll see that he knows about this." He slid his rifle into the scabbard attached to the saddle and tilted his hat back.

He was considerably older than Kathleen had at first thought. Inky black hair, dark eyes, and high cheekbones spoke of Indian heritage. He was tall, judging by the length of his stirrups, and lean. She could picture him on the cover of a dime Western novel: horse rearing, guns blazing.

"I really appreciate your help. They would have taken my car and left me stranded here."

"Maybe not. They might have taken you with them."

"They'd a had a fight on their hands," she said spiritedly.

"I reckon they would've."

Her eyes were the color of denim britches after they've been washed a hundred times.

He smiled, and she realized that he was very attractive in a dark and mysterious sort of way. The thought entered her mind that she was out here on this lonely stretch of road with this cowboy, and he had a gun. It hadn't occurred to her to be afraid of *him.*

"Well . . . thank you."

"You're very welcome." He tipped his hat.

Kathleen got in the car, waved, and drove away. She

glanced in the rearview mirror and saw the cowboy still sitting his horse in the middle of the road.

Johnny Henry watched the car until it was out of sight. Why hadn't she told him who she was? Probably she saw no need to introduce herself to a cowboy out here in the middle of the prairie, even if he had saved her pretty little hide from a couple of no-good hijackers. He had known the minute he saw that red hair and the Nash car that she was Kathleen Dolan and that she was on her way to Rawlings to work at the *Gazette*.

A week earlier Johnny had gone over to Red Rock to visit his sister, Henry Ann, and her family. Her husband, Tom, had had a letter from his brother, Hod, in Kansas telling him that their niece, Kathleen, would be coming down to Rawlings. She had been working for a year in Liberal, and for some reason known only to her, had decided to use some of the money left to her by her grandparents to buy into the paper at Rawlings.

"She wants to see and do a lot of things before she settles down," Hod had written. "She's twenty-six years old. Guess she's old enough to do as she pleases."

She didn't look to be that old, Johnny thought now. That would make her a year older than he was. She had looked to be about twenty-one or -two.

Tom had told Johnny that Duncan Dolan, the eldest of the Dolan boys, had gone to Montana when he was a youth and married a widow from Iowa. He'd had a fierce love for the woman and their child. Many of his letters were lovingly centered on his little girl whose red hair had been inherited from her mother. After Duncan was killed in an accident, his daughter and wife had gone back to Iowa to live with her parents, and for a while the Dolans had lost track of Kathleen. Several years ago she had written that her mother and grandparents were gone and she wanted to know her father's family.

Johnny had not given her more than a thought or two . . . until today. Now he wondered if he could ever get her out of his mind. He chuckled as he watched the car disappear. Not many women would set out alone to drive more than two hundred miles across country. Miss Kathleen Dolan had spunk to go along with that red hair.

A sudden burst of happiness sent his heart galloping like a runaway horse.

Rawlings, Oklahoma, was like most other towns in 1938. Jobs were scarce, farm prices had risen only a little since the bottom price for wheat had been twenty-five cents a bushel, oats ten cents and cotton five cents a pound back in 1932. Most of the cotton farmers were allowing their fields to go to grass to keep the soil from blowing away in the dust storms and were trying to make a living raising cattle. Some of them were packing up and following Highway 66 to the "promised land" in California where fertile fields provided a better prospect of jobs.

A steady stream of hobos looking for work or a handout came through Rawlings daily, seeking the community soup kitchen. The town had survived partly because a hide-tanning plant had opened several years ago and now employed more than fifty people. Hides were shipped from the meatpacking plants in Oklahoma City and Wichita Falls.

There was dissatisfaction among some in town, however, because white men who needed jobs believed that too many Indians were working at the plant. Miss Vernon had written that the tanning plant was owned by an oil-rich Cherokee Indian, who was not only wealthy, but smart, and wouldn't stand for any interference in the way he handed out jobs.

During the past two months, Kathleen had learned quite a bit about Rawlings, Oklahoma. Miss Vernon had sent her every issue of the *Gazette* since she had answered the advertisement for a business partner in the Oklahoma City paper. The first *Gazette* had been published in 1910, just three years after Oklahoma became a state. The family had held on to the paper during the worst years of the Great Depression. Now, without an heir to take over, it was in danger of being put to rest.

As Kathleen drove slowly along the street, her heart pounded with excitement. The town was quiet beneath the hot September sun. A dust devil danced down the middle of Main Street, where only a few cars were parked along the curb, and only a few people strolled along the walks.

She stopped at an intersection and sat there viewing the buildings that made up the business part of town. A number of them were vacant, but no more than in other towns she had passed through. The sidewalks on both sides of the street were new, no doubt paid for by President Roosevelt's recovery program. The new school she had passed was another WPA project. Even the water tower had a fresh coat of paint. The district evidently had a hardworking congressman.

Most of the three thousand residents of Tillison

County resided there in Rawlings, the county seat. The two-story, solid redbrick courthouse building sat in the middle of a square. An arch made of deer antlers and steer horns spanned the walk leading to the entrance. Kathleen smiled at that.

Her bright interested eyes took in everything. Rawlings was not as big as Liberal, but then she had been aware of that. It did have a good-sized business district because it was the only town of any size for fifty miles around. The Hughes department store was on the corner. Next to it was the Piggly-Wiggly grocery and at the end of the block the Tillison County Bank and Trust. "Bank and trust" she thought was kind of ironic when most folks had little trust in banks since so many had gone broke.

She passed the Rialto Theatre and saw that the movie *Hell's Angels* with Jean Harlow would be shown on Wednesday and Saturday nights. Claude's Hamburger Shack was across the street. Wilson's Family Market had a choice location on the corner across from the bank, and next to it was Woolworth's five-and-dime. Two grocery stores meant advertising money for the paper. Then, there it was near the end of the block between Corner Drugstore and Leroy's Men's Wear—the *Gazette* building, two-story redbrick, narrow, with one large window and two recessed doors; the second door led to a flight of stairs. RAWLINGS GAZETTE was painted in gold letters on the window.

Kathleen was not disappointed. Here she would invest her five hundred dollars and be part owner of a real live newspaper. Her duties would be gathering news and writing editorials for the weekly paper. Miss Vernon would take care of the society news, obituaries, and bookkeeping. Both would work on advertising. Kathleen's only concern was that she might not have time for her *other* writing, the writing that didn't bring in enough money for her to live on . . . yet.

She angle-parked the Nash in front of the building and sat for a few minutes to allow her heartbeat to slow. *Thank you, Grandma and Grandpa Hansen, for making this possible for me.* Several people passed while she sat there. An Indian woman with two black braids hanging over her ample bosom and moccasins on her feet came out of the *Gazette* office. The screen door banged shut behind her and she shuffled down the street.

Kathleen climbed out of her car. The late-September wind blew her hair across her face and wrapped her full skirt around her legs. She looked through the window before she entered and saw a heavy oak desk littered with papers. A typewriter sat on a pullout shelf at one end of the desk. The swivel chair was empty. Coming out of the bright sunlight, she waited beside the door to allow her eyes to adjust. The familiar clanking of a linotype machine came from the back room. No one was in sight.

The newspaper office had an odor she knew well: a combination of melting lead, ink, and paper. The clutter was also typical. As she wasn't being observed, Kathleen let her eyes wander over the office. A few framed front pages of the *Gazette* hung on the wall; Armistice Day, November 11, 1918, the stock market crash in 1929, Roosevelt's election in 1932.

The *Gazette* might be a weekly, she thought with owner's pride, but it had style.

Between the well-scarred desks were two four-drawer filing cabinets. Along the opposite wall on a waist-high counter, a thick book of advertising illustrations lay open. Suspended on long rods from the high ceiling, two fans turned gently.

Then she noticed a leg and a foot jutting out from behind one of the desks. Shock kept her still for a second; then she rushed over to the woman who lay on the floor between the desk and the wall.

"What . . . in the world—?" Kathleen knelt down for a closer look. *This must be Miss Vernon!* There was blood on her forehead. "Help!" Kathleen yelled as she ran toward the back room and the clattering linotype machine. "Help! Come quick!"

The man who sat at the machine continued to type, then dropped the line of lead and started another. He appeared not to hear Kathleen's call for help. She ran to him and put her hand on his shoulder. He jumped and turned. She backed away.

"Help me!" She took a few steps toward the front, then looked back. The big, shaggy-haired man was still standing beside the machine with a stupefied look on his face. "Can't you understand? I need your help!" she screamed. *Oh, dear Lord! He's either deaf or he can't hear me over the racket of that damn machine.*

Kathleen turned, ran back to the office and grabbed the phone. She flipped the receiver holder several times when the operator didn't answer immediately.

"Hold your horses, Adelaide." The voice came at last.

"Operator, we need help at the *Gazette* office," Kathleen said breathlessly. "Miss Vernon's had an accident."

"Adelaide? What's the matter with her?"

"She's unconscious and has blood on her head."

"Is she there in the office?"

"Yes, yes. Get a doctor."

"I'll see if I can find him."

By the time she had hung up the telephone, the man from the back room, still wearing his heavy leather apron to protect him from the hot lead, was kneeling beside Miss Vernon. Kathleen hurried to a large tin sink she had seen in the printing area of the building. When she returned with a wet towel, he had lifted the woman out from behind the desk and was holding her head and shoulders off the floor. Kathleen pressed the towel into his hand. As he dabbed at the blood on the woman's forehead, Kathleen got her first good look at her new partner.

In her letters to Kathleen, Miss Vernon had not mentioned her age. Her dark hair was streaked with gray at the temples, and the creases fanned out from the corners of her eyes. She was slender; almost fragile. Kathleen judged her to be in her middle or late forties.

Little moaning noises came from the man holding her. He was in anguish. He wasn't her husband; Miss Vernon had said she had never married. Kathleen couldn't see his face, but her first impression when she had seen him in the back room, was of a big, strong man, considerably younger than Miss Vernon.

The screen door slammed behind a large woman in a white nurse's uniform. A starched white cap was perched on top of her head. She was six feet tall or more and she looked to be a no-nonsense person who would be able to handle almost any situation. The nurse dropped a bag on the floor and knelt.

"What the hell has Adelaide done to herself now?" Her voice was loud and brisk. "Move over, Paul. Let me have a look."

The man lowered Adelaide gently to the floor and stepped back. As he looked up from the woman on the floor, Kathleen was startled by beautiful amber-colored eyes deeply set in his worried, homely face. His dark lashes were thick and long, his brows smooth and straight. The large nose looked as if it had been flattened in a hundred barroom brawls. A deep scar in his upper lip extended almost to his right nostril. He was broad-shouldered and thick-necked. His arms were heavily muscled. He reminded her of a gentle gorilla, if there was such a thing.

"Wake up, Adelaide." The nurse waved an open vial of smelling salts beneath Miss Vernon's nose. Adelaide sputtered and rolled her head. "Wake up," the nurse commanded briskly. "You're all right. You've just had a little crack on the head."

"Maybe not," Kathleen said. "She may have had a stroke . . . or something." The quelling glance the nurse gave her would have sent a more timid person running. Not Kathleen. She looked the nurse in the eye and said, "Shouldn't she be examined by a doctor?"

"Who are you? Her long-lost daughter?"

"No, but—"

"She's awake," the nurse said, ignoring Kathleen. "Help her into the chair, Paul."

With his hands beneath Adelaide's armpits, Paul easily

lifted her into the chair. Her eyes were glazed as she tried to focus on the man kneeling beside her. She flinched when the nurse dabbed at the cut on her forehead with a pad saturated in alcohol.

"You'll not need any stitches if I put a tight tape on it. What happened, Adelaide? Did you drink a little too much of that rotgut whiskey and fall out of the chair?"

Kathleen could tell by the snort that came from Paul that he didn't like the nurse's comment. Kathleen didn't like it either. She thought it very unprofessional. Adelaide continued to try to focus on Paul and said nothing.

"Don't get so huffy, big fellow," the nurse continued. "You know as well as I do that Adelaide is fond of the bottle."

"I didn't smell anything," Kathleen said.

"Who are you?" the nurse demanded again.

She was a very intimidating figure when she stood up, almost a foot taller than Kathleen and *big*, rangy big, like a roustabout who handled heavy machinery. Bangs, cut straight across, hung to the middle of her forehead and straight, henna-colored hair formed loose swirls, Clara Bow style, on her cheeks. Arched high above lashes, heavy with mascara, her brows were a thin line drawn by a reddish brown pencil. She had applied lipstick to her small mouth to make her lips appear fuller. It was smeared at the corners.

"Kathleen Dolan."

"You're new in town." Strong, quick fingers pressed the tape in place on Adelaide's forehead.

"You might say that."

"How long are you staying?"

"A long time."

"I see. Then you're the one who is taking over the paper."

"No. I'll be working with Miss Vernon on *our* paper."

"Here in Rawlings we don't butt into other people's business. You've got a lot to learn, girl." The nurse picked up her bag. "And for your sake, I hope you learn it fast." With that, she left the office, letting the screen door slam behind her.

Watching her leave, Kathleen had the feeling that she had just met an enemy. She was certain of it when she looked down to see the scowl on Paul's face.

"What put a bee in her bonnet?"

"She doesn't like Adelaide."

"Why not?"

"She thinks that Adelaide may know too much." Paul spoke very softly and smoothed the hair back from Adelaide's face with ink-stained fingers.

"Too much about what?"

"'Bout that clinic she and Doc run."

"Paul!" Adelaide tried to look up without turning her head. "Shhh . . ."

"It's all right," he said soothingly. "She's the one from Kansas."

"You sure?" she whispered.

"Looks like the picture she sent."

"Kathleen Dolan?" Adelaide turned her head slowly and painfully so that she could see Kathleen.

"Yes, I'm Kathleen. I just got here."

"Oh, Kathleen, I've been thinking that . . . that bringing you here may be the biggest mistake of my life."

"Why is that, Miss Vernon? Are you doubting my ability to help you run the paper?"

"No! No, it isn't that. It's just that—"

"—You can tell her later," Paul said. "Come on upstairs and lie down. You've got a partner now. She'll handle things down here for a while."

Chapter Two

Kathleen was sure that she would never forget this day for as long as she lived. Being hijacked was frightening enough without being thrust into the position of having to take over the office. She had no more than said hello and good-bye to her new partner when Paul took Adelaide up the back stairs to her rooms, leaving Kathleen with the explanation that *maybe* Adelaide had fallen out of her chair and with an apology for needing to leave her to cope alone.

Within an hour she had answered a dozen questions from curious townspeople about why the nurse had been there, taken a classified ad and several items for Adelaide's "Back Fence" column.

"Miss Jeraldine Smothers of Randlett spent Sunday afternoon with her aunt, Miss Earlene Smothers. They attended church and had dinner at the home of Miss Earlene Smothers's sister-in-law, Mrs. Willard F. Smothers." Kathleen read aloud the item she had written, based on the information given to her by the woman who had come panting into the office.

"Be sure you spell Jeraldine with a *J*. Jeraldine hates it

when her name is spelled with a *G*. Oh, my!" She fanned herself with her handkerchief. "I had to hurry. I was afraid the office would be closed."

"I'll be sure to spell Jeraldine with a *J*."

"You're new here. Where is Adelaide?"

"She's upstairs resting."

"I heard that Louise Munday was here this afternoon."

"The nurse? She didn't mention her name."

"Why should she? Everyone knows Louise. Anything serious?"

"No, I don't think so. I'll give the item to Adelaide for her column."

"Did she hurt herself?"

"She got a little bump on the head."

"Bullfoot. Must have been more than a little *bump* if Louise was needed."

"I wouldn't know."

"You sure do have red hair."

"I can't argue with you about that."

"Well—" The woman waited for Kathleen to say more. When she didn't, she said, "That boy better bring my paper before four-thirty. If not, he'll hear from me. I pay extra for delivery, you know."

"Yes, I know."

"Last week it was almost five o'clock."

"The sign on the window says that the papers are available at four on Wednesdays. That doesn't give him much time."

"P'shaw! That boy dawdles around and don't pay attention to what he's hired to do. He's lucky he's got a job when men are walking the streets every day, looking for work."

"I'll ask him to get it to you as soon as he can."

When the woman left, Kathleen pressed her fingertips to her temples. A few more like that one and she would have a splitting headache.

The next person to come into the office was the owner of the men's store. He was quite proper and introduced himself as Leroy Grandon, president of the Chamber of Commerce. He was aware that she was Adelaide's partner and invited her to a Chamber meeting. Kathleen sold him a two-column-by-three-inch display ad. She quickly sketched the ad for his shoe sale. At the top she printed, WALK IN MY SHOES. He was pleased and decided to run it in the next two editions. He lingered in the office until a woman came in with another item for the "Back Fence" column.

By six o'clock Kathleen was tired and hungry. She still had to find a place to spend the night. In her correspondence, Miss Vernon had said that there were several good boardinghouses in town. Paul was still at the linotype machine. If she could get him to turn it off, she'd ask him to direct her to one.

The screen door opened as she was on her way to lock up the office for the day. A tall, lanky man came in. *The cowboy.* He lifted a hand and pushed his hat back off his forehead.

"I was just about to close," Kathleen said.

"Adelaide didn't waste time putting you to work. I came by to see if you'd made it here all right."

"I made it. Did you tell the sheriff about the two crooks who tried to steal my car?"

"Yup. He knows about 'em."

"How did you know that I was coming here?"

"You might say that a tumbleweed told me."

"I might, but I won't."

"I saw your car out front. You've not unpacked it."

"I haven't had time. Miss Vernon had an accident—fainted, I guess. Anyway she got a bump on the head that knocked her out."

"Is she all right?"

"I think so. Paul took her upstairs to rest."

Johnny's eyes roamed Kathleen's face. He liked the way she looked and talked. She was a woman, yet she was a girl, too.

"Where are you staying? Can I give you a hand unpacking your car?"

"Thank you, no. I'm not sure where I'll be staying. I need to talk to Paul, or Miss Vernon if she's able." She looked at him with wide, clear eyes—waiting for him to leave so that she could lock the door.

"I should have introduced myself. My brother-in-law, Tom Dolan, would skin me alive if I didn't help his niece settle in. I'm Johnny Henry." He held out his hand, and she put hers into it.

"Glad to meet you. I'm Kathleen Dolan, but I guess you know that." *So this is the Johnny Molly told me about.*

"Yes. I also know your Uncle Hod and Aunt Molly. I was just at the post office and picked up a letter from Hod. He said that you were on your way and for me to look out for you. 'Course, I'd already had instruction from Tom."

"It was good of them to be concerned for me. You more than did your duty today by helping me with the hijackers." Kathleen pulled her hand from his.

"It wasn't a duty, it was a pleasure. The sheriff may ask you to sign a complaint."

"I'll do that gladly. Now if you'll excuse me. Paul has turned off the linotype, and I've got to talk to him."

"Hi, Johnny." Paul came out of the back room and placed a sheet of newsprint on the counter. "Adelaide proofs this before I lock the type into the frame."

Kathleen glanced at the headline: Lead stories were, BRITAIN IS PLEDGED TO FIGHT and AMERICANS TOLD TO RETURN HOME. Despite her being so tired, Kathleen's interest was piqued. This was heavy stuff for a small-town paper out here on the edge of nowhere.

"Does it have to be done tonight?"

"In the morning. The press starts rolling at noon."

"Is Adelaide all right?"

"Seems to be." He said it in a way to cut off any other inquiry.

"I was going to ask her to recommend a place to stay. I'll stay at the hotel tonight and talk to her tomorrow."

"Mrs. Ramsey has a room for you. Adelaide spoke to her this morning." The big man's amber eyes went from Kathleen to Johnny.

"I'll take her there, Paul."

"I'd be obliged, Johnny. Adelaide's worried about her—"

"There's no need for her to worry. Tell her I'll be here in the morning."

Kathleen glanced at Johnny. When she had time she would try to remember everything Hod and Molly had said about him. For now she welcomed his help.

Paul pulled the shade and closed the door behind them. Out on the sidewalk, Johnny's hand gripped her elbow.

"Have you eaten?"

"Did you hear my stomach growling?"

"Is that what I heard? I thought it was thunder." He smiled down at her, and both of them were suddenly embarrassed. His hand dropped from her arm and he stepped back. "How about one of Claude's hamburgers?"

"Sounds heavenly."

They walked the block to the well-lighted diner that had been converted from an old streetcar. Kathleen was thankful for the tall, broad-shouldered presence beside her in this unfamiliar town. She cast a glance up at him; and into her fertile mind sprang the image of a perfect male hero from one of her stories: strong, handsome, a champion of the underdog, yet gentle with his woman.

Music from the jukebox blared through the open windows of Claude's diner. Kathleen recognized the familiar voice of Gene Autry, the Oklahoma cowboy, singing a song he had made popular. *"In a vine-covered shack in the mountains, bravely fighting the battle of time, is a dear one who's weathered life's sorrows, that silver-haired daddy of mine."*

Several people sat on the stools at the counter that ran the length of the eatery. Behind the counter was the grill, a stove, shelves of dishes and tin Coca-Cola and Red

Man chewing tobacco posters. A man in a white apron, a striped shirt, and a black bow tie yelled out as they entered.

"Hi, Johnny. Come right on in and set yourself down." The man's voice reached them over the sound of Autry's singing.

"Hi, Claude." Johnny placed his hat on a shelf above the row of windows, ran his fingers through his hair to smooth it, and ushered Kathleen to one end of the counter. He waited until she was seated on a stool beneath the overhead fan before straddling a stool beside her.

Claude, wiping his hands on his apron, came down the counter. His round face was flushed and his bright blue eyes twinkled. Long strands of dark hair were combed over the near-bald spot on his head.

"Howdy, ma'am."

"Hello."

"This is Miss Dolan, Claude. She'll be working with Adelaide over at the *Gazette*. Claude White, the chief cook and bottle washer at this greasy spoon."

"Glad to meet ya, miss. Adelaide's been needin' somebody to give her a hand over there. Paul's good at printin', but ain't never heard that he was worth a tinker's dam at writin' up a story. Well, now, that's said, what'll ya have?"

Kathleen looked at the menu board above a shelf of crockery, then at Claude, and smiled.

"I'm hungry enough to eat everything up there, but I'll have a hamburger and a piece of raisin pie."

"What will you have on your hamburger?"

"Everything but onions."

"I'll have two hamburgers and a bowl of chili," Johnny said.

"Onions, Johnny?" Claude lifted his bushy brows.

"No."

"You usually have extra onions. Guess that tells me what I wanted to know." Claude winked at Kathleen and turned back to his grill.

Kathleen glanced at Johnny and saw his eyes narrow, his lips press into a firm line, and knew that had the deep suntan not bronzed his face, it would be flushed with embarrassment. A muscle jumped in his clenched jaw. He looked even younger without his hat. Hair as black as midnight sprang back from his forehead and hung almost to the collar of his shirt.

"Claude's quite a joker," Johnny murmured.

"Does he always wear a bow tie when he cooks?"

"Always. I don't think I've ever seen him without it."

Claude brought a bowl of thick, fragrant chili and placed it in front of Johnny.

"Sure you don't want one, miss?"

"It smells good, but I'll wait for my hamburger and pie."

Claude dashed back to the grill, flipped over meat patties with a long-handled spatula, while placing open buns on the grill with the other hand. No wasted motion there. He kept his eye on the door and greeted each customer who came in by name.

"Hi ya, Allen. You're late tonight. How ya doin', Herb? Take a seat. Be with ya in two shakes. You want anythin' else, Jake?" Claude rolled a nickel down the counter. "Put this in the jukebox, Allen. Play 'Frankie and Johnny' for my friend Johnny who has brought me a new customer to brighten up the place. Once she's eaten a Claude hamburger, she'll be back."

"He'd make a good politician," Kathleen murmured.

"That's what I've been tellin' him," Johnny grinned at her. "He takes a backseat to no one once his mouth gets goin'. He's got his fingers in most every pie in town." Johnny said the last loud enough for Claude to hear as he put the hamburgers on the counter in front of them.

"Here ya are, miss." Claude winked at her again. "Don't pay no mind to what this long drink of water tells you. He only comes to town when he gets tired a talkin' to hisself."

"I knew I shouldn't have brought her here. After hearing you spout off she'll probably head right back to Kansas."

"Not on your life." Kathleen chewed and swallowed her first bite of her hamburger. "I'll hang around just for this."

"Smart lady you got here, buster—"

"Hey, Claude. Stop flirting with the pretty redhead and get me some catsup."

"Hold your horses, Jake. I'm making sure she knows that this kid ain't the only single man 'round these parts."

By the time Kathleen finished her meal, Johnny was done with his. When she reached into her purse to pay, he put his hand on her arm to stop her. Not wanting to embarrass him, she waited until they were back out on the walk in front of the diner before she spoke.

"I never intended for you to pay for my supper. Please—" She opened her purse.

"No," he said, his tone so firm that it stopped her protest.

"Well . . . thank you."

"My truck is across the street from your car. I'll lead you to Mrs. Ramsey's. It's only a few blocks."

"Thank goodness for that. I'm about out of gas. I got so excited coming into town that I forgot to stop and get some."

They walked down the darkened street to her car without speaking; then she followed a truck as dilapidated as the car the hijackers had used to block the road. The bed of the truck, without sides, held a piece of machinery lashed down with ropes. A block off Main Street, they left the paving and drove onto a hard-packed road of red clay. Kathleen followed Johnny's lead and dodged the potholes. He stopped in front of a one-story bungalow with a porch that stretched across the front. A dim light glowed from a lightbulb between the two front doors. Johnny came to her car as she was getting out.

"Do you want to meet Mrs. Ramsey before we unload the car?"

"Are you thinking that I may not want to stay here after I meet her?"

"It isn't a fancy place."

"I'm not used to a fancy place. I'm used to a clean place, but I need to know—about Mrs. Ramsey."

"She's decent, if that's what you mean. Adelaide Vernon wouldn't have recommended her if she wasn't. She's a good hardworking lady who hasn't had an easy time of it."

Kathleen was keenly aware of the cowboy who stood close beside her on the darkened road. He looked confident and dangerous . . . yet she felt perfectly safe with him.

"I'll take your word for it." She walked beside him to the porch. As they stepped upon it, one of the doors was flung open and a small girl rushed out.

"Hi, Johnny? Is that her?"

"Hi, Emily."

"Emily, for goodness sake!" The woman who came out to take the girl's hand had snow-white hair and a sunbrowned, weathered face. She was short and very plump. "Excuse Emily, miss. She's excited."

"She's pretty, Granny, and she ain't fat. You said she'd—"

"—Well, aren't you smart to see that she's pretty." The woman pulled the little girl's head to her side, hugged her to shut her up, and smiled at Kathleen. "Adelaide sent word this morning that you'd be here sometime today."

"Thank you for the compliment, Emily." Kathleen smiled at the child, who had suddenly turned shy and hid her face against her grandmother.

"Come in. I'll show you the room."

"Mr. Henry was kind enough to show me the way here."

"Go on into the front room, Johnny." The top of the woman's head came to Johnny's armpit. She indicated the door that she and the girl had come through.

"Thanks, but I'll wait out here and help Miss Dolan with her things before I go."

Mrs. Ramsey opened the door and led Kathleen into a room that had the smell of recent cleaning: lye soap, vinegar, and linseed oil. The only furniture was a bed, a dresser, and a wardrobe. The bedcover was a white sheet with a spray of appliquéd flowers in the middle. A colorful rag rug lay beside the bed on the scrubbed wooden floor. Curtains that Kathleen recognized as having been made from white flour sacks and embroidered with yellow-and-green cross-stitch along the hems hung at the windows.

Kathleen glanced around the room, then at the small woman who clutched her granddaughter's hand. There was an anxious look in her eyes. She hurried to open a door revealing a bathroom with a clawfoot tub, a sink, a toilet with the waterbox near the ceiling, and a door leading to another room.

"The water is . . . a little rusty, but I catch rainwater—" Her words trailed.

"I love to wash my hair in rainwater," Kathleen said to fill the void. "Do you rent by the week, or by the month?"

"By the week, if that's all right. Two dollars . . . or four if you want breakfast and supper. Ah . . . nothing fancy, but plain eatin'. We have meat on Wednesdays and Sundays."

"That'll be fine."

"You're takin' it?"

"Oh, yes. This is just the kind of place I like." Kathleen opened her purse and took out one of the ten-dollar bills Johnny had made the hijackers return. "I'll pay for two weeks."

The woman's hand was shaking when she reached for the bill, and Kathleen was sure she saw mist in her eyes.

"But . . . I don't have change."

"That's all right. I'll owe you two dollars for the third week."

"I'll do my best to make you as comfortable as I can."

"Is she stayin', Granny?"

"I plan on it, if you want me, Emily." Kathleen patted the little girl on the head. "Will you help me bring in my things?"

"Uh-huh."

"You can park your car behind the house if you want to get it out of the road." Her new landlady's voice was raspy.

"Thank you, I will."

Kathleen, Johnny, and Emily made several trips to the car before Johnny carried in her heavy typewriter. He looked around for a place to put it.

"Just set it on the floor. My trunk is coming down on the train. I can use it as a table."

"I thought a reporter did her writing at the newspaper office." Johnny divided his glance between her and the near-new machine.

"I do . . . most of it," she said, not wanting to tell him that she used the typewriter almost every night and most always on Sunday afternoon.

"I have a small table out at my place. I'll bring it in, if you like."

"Oh, would you? I'll buy it from you."

"I'd have to have fifty or sixty bucks for it."

"Fifty or sixty—" Her eyes questioned. Then, "Oh, you!" she exclaimed when she saw him trying to keep the grin off his face. "Johnny Henry, you're a tease." His smile would give a charging bull pause for reflection, Kathleen thought, and wondered why it was that he was so "at home" here.

"That's everything out of the car. Do you want me to move it around back?"

"I would appreciate it. I probably won't use it much. Rawlings is about half the size of Liberal."

"Be right back."

When she was alone, Kathleen looked around the room that would be her home for a while. The door leading to the front porch had new screen on the bottom. The one going into the opposite room stood open, and she could see a couch and a library table. The third door led into the bathroom. The rooming house where she'd stayed in Liberal had six boarders, all on the second and third floors, and they shared one bathroom. This was almost like having one all to herself.

She heard Johnny when he came in the back door and paused to talk for a while with Mrs. Ramsey and Emily. She could hear the murmur of their voices but not what they said. She was taking things out of her suitcase and placing them in the drawers when he appeared in the doorway of the connecting room.

"Here are your keys."

"Thank you." Her gaze was drawn to his like iron to a magnet. Occasionally, Kathleen was attracted to men, mostly professionals or businessmen who wore suits and ties and were well versed on world affairs. She never expected to be attracted to a cowboy, a young one at that. The dark eyes that looked into hers were deep-set, and even though they gleamed with a friendly light, they looked to be as old as the ages.

"Welcome," he said after the long silence between them. "I'll bring in the table the next time I come to town."

"I feel that I'm imposing. You've already done so much."

"My pleasure." He slapped his battered hat down on his head. "Good night."

" 'Night, Mr. Henry."

Kathleen heard the squeak of the screen door and went to the porch. He was going down the walk to his truck.

"Thanks again," she called.

"Don't mention it." His voice came out of the darkness.

He ground the starter several times on the old truck before it started. The lights came on, and it moved on down the street. Kathleen watched until it turned the corner and was out of sight.

Damn, but she was pretty.

Johnny hadn't been especially interested in meeting Tom's niece from up north after Tom had told him that she was a newspaper reporter who had written stories that had been sent out on the wire to the big papers, that she was investing money she had inherited in the Rawlings paper, and that she was bold enough to drive across country by herself. He couldn't imagine a woman like that needing any help from him.

Well, she had needed him today with the hijackers. He had done what any decent man would have done under the circumstances.

When he had seen her car sitting, still loaded, in front of the *Gazette,* he had stopped before he had given it much thought. If he hadn't stopped, Paul would have seen to it that she got to Mrs. Ramsey's. But no, old dumbbell that he was, he had to stick his bill in, take her to Claude's, help her unload and then further complicate matters by offering her a table for her typewriter. She had been nice, but she probably was uneasy with the feeling that she owed him.

He wasn't usually uncomfortable around city women, but when he'd first seen Kathleen Dolan he'd been stunned. She was lovely and warm, with a smile that would melt the coldest of hearts. Her hair, and there was plenty of it, was the color of a sunset, her skin creamy white, and those damn freckles— Her looks hadn't matched the image he'd had of her. He'd thought she'd be more hoity-toity with her education and ability to *buy* into a newspaper. He couldn't imagine being able to write down things that hundreds, maybe thousands, of people would read.

She was far beyond his reach, and he'd best stop this silly thinking about her and keep his distance. Everyone in town knew he came from Mud Creek trash and they wouldn't let him forget it. Almost all of them knew him as the offspring of a whore and a redskin. It was true. He had grown up knowing that and also knowing there was nothing he could do about it.

Johnny had made a niche for himself out on the Circle H. In addition, during off-seasons, he made a little money working for the Feds on special jobs. No one around here knew about that, and that's the way he wanted it. He had been content until two o'clock this afternoon when he had come over the rise and seen the sun shining on a head of bright red hair. The damn woman had disturbed him, had made him want to be with her and want to try to interest and impress her.

"Horse hockey!" Johnny pounded the steering wheel with his fist.

The presence of Kathleen Dolan angered him because suddenly his niche no longer seemed enough for him.

Chapter Three

"Come eat, Miss Dolan. Granny's made chocolate gravy." Emily, dressed for school, stood anxiously beside the kitchen door.

"Chocolate gravy?" The thought made Kathleen's stomach queazy.

"You girls sit down." Hazel Ramsey opened the oven door and took out a pan of golden brown biscuits. "Do you drink coffee, Miss Dolan?"

"If you have it made. Don't make it especially for me. I usually drink tea, a taste I acquired from my grandparents in Iowa. I'll get a box while I'm in town today. I'll leave some at the office and bring the rest home. I like tea hot when it's cold and cold when it's hot."

"Can I have some?" Emily asked.

"Sure."

"You don't drink tea, sugar."

"I will if Kathleen does."

"You don't call grown-ups by their first names," Mrs. Ramsey chided gently.

Kathleen buttered a biscuit and helped herself to the peach jam. Mrs. Ramsey split a biscuit, placed it on

Emily's plate, and covered it generously with the light brown gravy.

"Don't you want some?" Emily asked.

"Well . . . I've never had chocolate gravy."

"It's good."

"Then I'd better try it. I may be missing something." Kathleen placed a spoonful of the gravy on a biscuit half and tentatively took a bite. "Humm, it is good. I can't taste the chocolate at all."

"Told ya." Emily glanced at her grandmother and beamed, showing a missing tooth.

Kathleen walked part of the way to town with Emily, who was in the second grade. The little girl cast proud glances up at Kathleen when they met her curious schoolmates and, at one time, reached up and took her hand. She chattered happily about her school activities, making sure the children walking ahead of them were aware that Kathleen was her special friend.

"'Bye, Miss Dolan. See ya tonight," Emily shouted when they parted.

"'Bye, Emily." She watched the little girl go slowly down the walk, making no attempt to catch up with the other children.

It was five blocks from Mrs. Ramsey's to the downtown area. Many heads turned to watch the pretty redhead, not only because she was a stranger in town, but because Kathleen walked with the confident grace of a woman who knew who she was and where she was going. She approached the *Gazette* right at eight o'clock, wishing with all her heart for a cup of tea to help fortify herself for the first day at the *Gazette*.

"Good morning." Adelaide rose from behind the desk as soon as Kathleen walked in.

"Hello. Are you feeling better?"

"Oh, yes. I'm sorry you had such a poor welcome yesterday."

"I'm glad I was here to carry on. Did I make too big a mess of things?"

"Not at all. By the way that was a clever ad you laid out for the men's store. How did you get Leroy Grandon to buy *two* ads? He's usually as tight as the skin on an onion."

Kathleen laughed. "I don't know."

"I do." Adelaide looked pointedly up and down Kathleen's trim figure.

Adelaide Vernon was a sweet-looking woman: small-boned and thin. Beneath thick brown hair, gray at the temples, her face was pale, and her expression conveyed her anxiety as she met her new partner. Her fragile looks belied her toughness, a legacy from her father that had allowed her to run this weekly paper alone since his death. She wore a blue print dress with a white collar, a white belt, and large white buttons down the front to the hem.

"Did you find the 'Back Fence' items I put on your spindle?" Kathleen went to the other large desk in the office where she had worked the day before.

"I found them. Too bad you had to be introduced to Earlene Smothers on your first day."

"I knew right away that she was a pain. I assured her that you would spell Jeraldine with a *J*. It was very important to her. She was extremely curious as to why the nurse was here."

"She would be. She's next to the paper when it comes to spreading the news. Did you take the room at Hazel Ramsey's?"

"Yes. Thanks for arranging for me to go there. She's very nice, and the room is comfortable."

"I was hoping you'd stay there. Hazel is having a hard time. She takes in ironing and anything else she can do to support herself and Emily."

"Where are the child's parents?"

"Emily is one of those unfortunate children without a father. I doubt that even Clara, her mother, knows who he is. Clara comes and goes. Hazel and Emily are better off when she stays away." Adelaide put a sheet of paper in her typewriter. "The press starts rolling at noon. Paul proofed the front page and made up the ad you took from Leroy. We're in pretty good shape for press day."

"What's the press run?"

"We're down to twelve hundred. Five hundred are delivered to the towns around. We have correspondents in Deval, Grandview, Loveland, and Davidson. They send in news. Most people like to see their names in the paper. A hundred and fifty go out in the mail. A hundred and fifty are delivered here in town, and the rest go to the stores and are sold here at the office."

"The paper in Liberal didn't do much better than that."

"We need new ideas, Kathleen. It's what we must talk about. But first let's get this edition out."

"Sounds logical. What shall I do first?"

Kathleen was amazed at the amount of work Paul was able to do. She noticed that he was surprisingly fast on his feet for a big man. She had found very few mistakes when she proofed the stories he had set on the linotype machine.

The press was old and printed only four pages at one time. This week's paper would be eight pages, which would require two runs. The front of the paper would be printed last. When it came off the press the first run would be inserted.

At noon Paul locked the columns of type into the page frame and the frame to the press. After inking the type with a roller, he turned the big iron wheel by hand to print sheets for Adelaide to look over before he started the press.

Kathleen was familiar with the procedure even though the press was much older than the one in Liberal. Every available hand was needed once the press began to roll. She wished she had thought to bring a smock to protect her dress from the wet ink while she helped insert the first run into the second one when Adelaide came to her, with a big loose shirt to put on over her dress.

"Thanks. I'll bring something next week."

"Hello, Woody."

When Adelaide spoke, Kathleen turned to see the man who had come in through the back door. He wore a cap and overalls. She couldn't see his face clearly, but from the way he hurried forward to help Paul lift a large roll of newsprint to the press, she realized he was young and strong.

"Woody helps us on press day," Adelaide said. "He'll take the papers from the press and stack them on the table, then help insert them in the final run. He delivers the papers to the stores. I start addressing for the mail as soon as we start the second run. We have to have the papers at the post office by five o'clock if we want them to go out tonight."

Kathleen nodded and glanced at Paul. He had not said one word to her all morning, and very few words to Adelaide. The two of them worked together as if speech were not necessary. The next few hours flew by for Kathleen. She loved the clank, clank of the press, the smell of the ink, and the rush to get the papers stuffed and out.

Paul left his position by the press, where he watched continuously for a tear in the paper that would clog the flow and cause the press to be shut down, to tell Adelaide quite firmly that she should go sit down.

Kathleen heard her say in a low voice, "I'm all right, Paul. Don't worry."

Kathleen added to the suggestion by saying, "I can handle this back here, Adelaide."

"All right. I'll go up front and start addressing the mailing. Usually a dozen or so people stop in to get papers hot off the press." Adelaide went to the office with a stack of papers, then returned to speak to Kathleen over the clatter of the press. "Hazel came by to find out what time you'd be there for supper. I took the liberty of telling her that I'd like for you to have supper with me tonight so that we could talk. I hope you don't mind."

Kathleen smiled, nodded, and continued to stuff papers.

When the press was shut off at last, Kathleen washed the ink from her hands at the sink, using the harsh Lava soap, then went to the front office where Adelaide was busy with a tray of subscriber plates, stamping the papers, making them ready for the post office.

Three paper boys came in. Each picked up his bundle of papers.

"I have two "stops" on your route, Gordon." She gave the boy a slip of paper. "If either of these flags you down for a paper, tell them to come see me. I have three for you, Donny, and one for you, Ellis. Get going now and, Gordon, try to get to Mrs. Smothers as soon as you can. She's been complaining again."

"But . . . Miss Vernon, I deliver to her . . . almost first."

"I believe you. Just try to get along with her."

"I hate to stop papers," Adelaide said when the boys were out the door. "But those six subscribers haven't paid for several months."

While they were stamping papers, the nurse, Louise Munday, came into the office. Her starched uniform and cap were immaculate. She carried a small black bag.

"Well, well. I see you're up and about. Of course, you'd have to be dead not to be down here on the day your little gossip sheet comes out." She marched over to the counter where Adelaide was working as if she was going into battle, took her chin between her fingers, and turned her head toward her so she could look at the cut on her forehead.

"I'm all right." Adelaide jerked her chin to free it.

"You don't look all right. You looked washed-out."

"Thanks for the compliment, Louise." Adelaide took the tray of address plates to her desk. "Have you met my partner, Kathleen Dolan?"

" 'Fraid so. How did you get that bump on the head?"

"Dammit, Louise. It's none of your business."

"She said you fell out of your chair." The big woman turned accusing eyes on Kathleen.

"I didn't say that," Kathleen said sharply, and wondered how long it took the nurse to put all that mascara and paint on her face.

Louise ignored Kathleen's retort and fixed her eyes on Adelaide.

"Where's that big ugly galoot that's always hovering over you? He knows you fell out of your chair." Louise looked toward the back room. "Isn't he a little young for you, dear?"

"Why don't you ask him, *dear*?"

"It isn't any of my business if you make a fool of yourself and set the tongues to wagging."

"That's right. It isn't any of your business."

"Better go slow on that rotgut whiskey, Adelaide. You might fall down out in the street and get run over." She picked up the bag she had set on the desk and headed for the door.

"And you'd cry at my funeral."

"Don't count on it." Louise turned, her eyes narrowed and her small red mouth puckered as if she were going to throw a kiss. "Doc told me to come by and see about you. Guess I can tell him you're still full of piss and vinegar."

"You do that. Don't bother to make another house call."

"I'll be back if Doc tells me to."

She walked out and let the screen door slam behind her.

"What a disagreeable woman," Kathleen said into the silence that followed. "Does she carry so much weight in this town that she can come in here and be rude to the editor of the paper?"

"She thinks she does."

"I could see that. I'm glad you stood up to her."

"Dr. Herman is county commissioner, medical officer, on every board in the county, besides being mayor of Rawlings. He runs things to a certain extent here in Tillison County."

"So when his nurse comes around threatening people, she is speaking for him?"

"I guess you could say that. She's not rude around him. Butter wouldn't melt in her mouth," Adelaide said with a sniff.

"If she's afraid that you'll print something she won't like, it isn't very smart of her to antagonize you." It was an opening for Adelaide to explain the animosity between the two, but the older woman failed to step into it.

Instead she said, "I wasn't drinking, Kathleen." Adelaide waited to speak until after a small boy put a nickel in the cup and took a paper. "Paul and I have a drink sometimes in the evenings, but I never take a drink during the day. My father was a fall-down drunk. Louise likes to think that I inherited his weakness."

"Have you known her long?"

"She came here about fifteen years ago to work for Doc. She was mouthy even then. Doc's wife died soon after that. I think she thought she was going to be Mrs. Doc. It didn't happen, but they're still as tight as eight in a bed."

"He sleeps with her?"

Adelaide rolled her eyes and said drily, "Who knows?" Then she laughed and her eyes lit up, showing a hidden sense of humor. "He'd have to be careful or she'd crush him. She's a head taller and must outweigh him by a hundred pounds."

"Maybe she's interested in Paul and sees you as her competition."

"He's one of the few men in town who's her size." Adelaide continued to smile. "About a year ago, she started flirting with him. A fat lot of good it did her. He dislikes her as much as I do."

"Is she disagreeable to everyone in town?"

"I don't know. You'll find out that folks here know when to keep their mouths shut. One of them might need a doctor for one of their kids one night and would be told that he's out of town."

Kathleen wanted to ask about the "what she knew" that Paul had referred to last night as causing Louise to dislike her, but decided that Adelaide would tell her when she was ready.

"I'm the one who called her," Kathleen said. "I was so scared when I came in and found you on the floor that I called the operator for the doctor. She came."

"I bet that she thought, 'Oh, boy. I've got her this time,' and trotted right over here."

Kathleen laughed. "It didn't take long, but at the time it seemed like hours. By the way, when I drove up and parked out front, an Indian woman came out of the office and walked off down the street. I would have thought that she'd have seen you lying on the floor."

Kathleen was waiting for Adelaide's comment about the Indian woman when Paul and Woody came from the back room.

Paul had taken off his ink-stained apron, had washed, and had combed his hair. He had a terribly homely face, but nevertheless, was such a large, well-built man that he made an impressive figure.

Woody politely removed his cap and tucked it under his arm when he came into the office. While working with him at the press, Kathleen had become aware that he was a light-colored Negro. Now, looking him full in the face, she saw how nice-looking he was. His dark eyes were large, his features fine. It was hard to tell his exact age.

Both men avoided looking directly at Kathleen.

"We're almost finished," Adelaide said. "My, it goes faster with two working. It's just now four-fifteen."

Woody was pulling a big red coaster wagon loaded with bundled papers. He stacked them beside the door.

"They're for the bus," Adelaide said. "The driver drops off bundles at Deval, Loveland, Grandview, and Davidson."

"Do you get any advertising from those towns?"

"Some."

When the mail subscribers' papers were all stamped, tied, and loaded in the wagon, Adelaide gave Woody the necessary papers for the post office and held the door open for him. He eased the wagon over the threshold and took off down the street.

"That's done." She sighed.

"I'll take care of things down here. Why don't you and

Miss Dolan go on upstairs? I know you've got things to talk about."

Out of the corner of her eye, Kathleen saw Paul's hand sliding up and down Adelaide's back. *They are more than friends. He's very protective of her. If they are lovers, they must have more of a reason for hiding it other than because he's younger than she is.*

"You'll come up after you close?"

"I hadn't planned on it. You two need—"

"—I'll have supper ready. Like always." Adelaide placed her hand on his arm and kept her eyes on his face.

Kathleen felt like an intruder and busied herself clearing off her desk.

"You're tired and you don't need to cook. I'll go over to the store and bring up some meat for sandwiches." He spoke softly just to her.

"I invited Kathleen for supper. I'm going to fix salmon patties and fry some potatoes. Nothing fancy."

"Don't go to any trouble for me," Kathleen protested. "I can go to Claude's for a hamburger."

"We usually have a sandwich or eggs on press day. Sometimes we're almost too tired to eat."

"I don't see how you two got this paper out all by yourselves. There were six people working at the paper in Liberal."

"Paul does as much work as a dozen people," Adelaide said proudly. "There's nothing he can't do from writing editorials—he'll be mad at me for telling this—to fixing those two monstrous machines we have in the back room. He tunes in to Eastern radio and takes down the news . . .

like the headlines we had today: 'Chamberlain Off by Plane to See Hitler.' "

"I wondered how you got that. Pretty clever."

Kathleen watched color flood the big man's face and heard Adelaide's soothing words to him.

"She had to know, Paul, that I couldn't write this entire paper by myself." With her hand on the big man's arm, she turned to Kathleen. "Most of the people here have no idea what it takes to get out a paper. They think that because a man gets greasy working on the press and isn't constantly blowing his own horn, he doesn't have anything up here." She tapped her forehead with her finger. "Paul is smarter than half the town put together," she said defensively. "For several years he's taken care of the national and state news, and I've handled the local stuff and the advertising. He's a better writer than I am, by far."

"Addie—hush," Paul said gently.

"I won't hush. If Kathleen is going to buy into this paper and be working here, she has the right to know that it's mostly due to you that we've kept our heads above water."

"*If* I'm going to buy into the paper? I was under the impression that you had accepted my offer. Don't tell me that you've changed your mind," Kathleen said.

"I've not changed my mind. I thought it only fair that you know what's been going on before we go into a partnership."

"Will my being here make a difference in how you run the paper?"

"Not if you don't object to Paul's being your partner as well."

"Why should I object?"

"We're lovers," Adelaide blurted.

"That's your business and . . . Paul's." Paul had turned his back to the two women and was looking out the window. "I told you in my letters that I wanted to invest my inheritance in something that would help to keep me out of the poorhouse in my old age. You agreed that for five hundred dollars I would own half the *Gazette,* the building it's in, and be a full partner in running it."

"None of that has changed."

"Well, then I don't see that we have a problem."

"You'll hear talk—"

"I probably won't be here a week until you'll be hearing talk about me. I'm not a woman who knuckles under. I stand up for myself, which rubs some the wrong way."

"There are other problems. Things are going on in this town that I mean to uncover if I can. It could be . . . dangerous, and you'd be involved."

"I'd like to hear more about it, but I doubt it would change my mind about my investment here."

"Oh, Kathleen, I knew that I was going to like you."

Kathleen laughed. "Tell me that a couple months from now when I've clashed with your biggest advertiser, written a story that offends the mayor, exposed the Baptist preacher's love affair with a high-school girl, and caused Mrs. Smothers to cancel her subscription."

"Are you really capable of all that? I'm going to love it. Paul, you were right. When you read her letters, you said that she was a woman with guts."

Paul turned and spoke to Kathleen. "There are people here who would want to tar and feather me if they thought I had as much as touched Addie's hand. I am nothing here but a linotype operator and a pressman. I want it to stay that way."

Kathleen shrugged. "Your choice."

"Before I came here four years ago, I spent time in Huntsville, Texas, penitentiary for—"

"—Oh, Paul . . . don't—"

"—For murder."

"Oh, Kathleen, please don't let that information leave this room!"

"I want all the cards on the table, Addie," Paul said, then looked directly at Kathleen. "I came through here on a freight train on Christmas Eve, hungry and cold. She let me in into the back room after I had been turned away all over town. She treated me like a human being instead of a dog to be kicked around. She brought down blankets and let me sleep there in the back room on a cot. I was warm for the first time in weeks. The next morning she invited me to come up for dinner." He paused, looked at Addie, his eyes soft and full of love, but there was nothing soft about his words when he spoke again. "Being with Addie is the nearest I'll ever be to heaven. I'll kill anyone who hurts her or tries to take her from me."

There was a long, deep silence. Kathleen glanced at Adelaide and saw that her eyes were shiny with tears as she gazed into the big man's homely face.

"Paul, dear. What would I do without you?"

"You don't have to do without me, Addie." He spoke

in a low voice, a quiet, intimate tone that struck a chord of longing inside Kathleen.

She felt a yearning for someone of her own, a feeling she'd not had for a long time. What would it be like to have a man love her so much that he would be willing to kill to keep her safe. Kathleen shook her head in order to rid her mind of the thought.

"Adelaide is very very lucky," she said, her voice shaky and barely about a whisper.

"Paul, doggone it, you're going to make me . . . cry."

"No, sweet girl, I don't want to do that. I just wanted Miss Dolan to know where I stand and that I don't have a life away from you . . . outside this building."

"But . . . it isn't enough for you. You're such a wonderful man. You should have a family . . . children—"

"Shhh— We've been over that before, and it isn't something we should discuss in front of Miss Dolan. Here's the bus. I'll take out the papers."

As soon as he was out the door, Adelaide spoke with a sad shake of her head.

"I didn't intend for all of this to come out before you even got to know us. Paul is an astute judge of character. He made a decision about you, or he'd never have said what he did about his past."

"I'll not betray his trust. I suspected yesterday, when he found you on the floor, that he was in love with you. He was beside himself with worry."

"His affection for me is largely due to the fact that he hasn't had much kindness in his life."

"Oh, I'm sure that's not the case. He adores you."

"He's a dear man, kind and gentle."

"You love him, don't you?"

"Yes, I love him. But . . . I'm ten years older than he is."

"So what? Martha was older than George Washington. I've not heard anyone complaining about that."

She removed her hat and stood for a moment under the cooling breeze of the ceiling fan as she waited for the man sitting at a desk to turn and acknowledge her. She waited a full minute or two, then rapped sharply on the counter with her knuckles. The man turned with a scowl that slowly disappeared from his face as he stood.

"Well . . . hello." He was a blocky man in his late thirties or early forties, with watery blue eyes and very noticeable false teeth. The uppers dropped slightly when he smiled.

"I'm Kathleen Dolan from the *Gazette*."

"Now this's a real treat. I heard that a pretty redhead was takin' over the *Gazette*."

"Correction. I'm *not* taking over the *Gazette*. Miss Vernon and I are partners."

"Partners? Now don't that jist frost ya? Adelaide finally got someone to come in and bail her out. Partners." He repeated the word in a tone of disbelief. "Is she goin' to share that mud-ugly bum she took in off the street? 'Pears to me three in a bed'll be a mite crowded. Huh?" He raised his brows several times causing wrinkles to form on his forehead.

Does he mean what his words implied?

In the silence that followed, she realized that he meant exactly what he had said after he raised his brows again in a gesture that irritated her. Her mouth drew down in a thin angry line and her eyes gleamed with temper.

"Are you the sheriff?" she snapped impatiently.

"Noooo— I'm Deputy Mitchell P. Thatcher, but my friends call me Ell." He lowered his voice and murmured

Chapter Four

During the week that followed, Kathleen learned very little more about Paul Leahy's background and a lot more about the merchants in Rawlings, the most important of which was that they were very tightfisted with their advertising dollar. The two grocery stores were competitive as the stores in Liberal had been. If one ran an ad, the other one did too. Each tried to worm out of Kathleen the specials the other store would be featuring the following week.

Legal notices were a sure source of revenue for the paper. Rawlings, being the seat of Tillison County, had a column of "Legals" each week. Adelaide explained that at times the county was a couple months behind in payment, but it was a sure source of income for the paper. Kathleen made a mental note to discuss the delay with the county treasurer.

The sheriff's office and county jail were in a low, flat building attached to the back of the courthouse. With a round-brimmed straw hat on her head to protect her sensitive skin from the hot Oklahoma sun, Kathleen opened the screen door and went into the sheriff's office.

the last in a confidential tone. He appeared to be totally oblivious to her sudden testiness.

Kathleen pulled in a hard, deep breath and tried to hang on to her temper. There was a nastiness and an arrogance about the man that rubbed her the wrong way. She had taken an instant dislike to the deputy and chided herself for letting it show.

"Is the sheriff in, Mr. Thatcher?"

"Name's Ell, honey. Ell to my friends." He leaned toward her with his elbow on the counter. The heavy smell of brilliantine came from his slicked-down bushy hair.

"I'm not your friend, Mr. Thatcher. I'm not even an acquaintance. I'm here to see the sheriff."

"He's not in. I take care of thin's 'round here when he's out. What can I do for you?" He wiggled his brows again in that irritating gesture.

Kathleen bit back a hundred answers to his question and looked at the coat of dust on the counter, the wads of paper on the floor, the overflowing ashtrays. Then her eyes met his head-on.

"From the looks of this place you haven't been overworking while the boss was away. Or does this place always look like a hog pen?"

The grin left the deputy's face. He leaned back and crossed his arms over his chest.

"Honey," he drawled, "you may've got by with that smart mouth up in Kansas, but it won't work down here in Oklahoma. We won't put up with it."

"Now that's just too damn bad, *Deputy do-nothing*." A pointed finger stabbed at him. "What are you going to do about it? Lynch me or just tar and feather me and run me out of town?" Her voice was razor-sharp, her face a rigid mask of indignation. She turned to leave, knowing she had made an enemy of the deputy, but too angry to care.

"Naw. Down here we got better uses for . . . a pretty woman." The deputy's words followed her out the door. "On . . . her backside."

Out on the sidewalk, Kathleen slapped her straw hat down on her head and walked swiftly to the corner, turned and headed for the heart of town, too angry to remember she had planned to stop at the office of the county treasurer. She fumed over the words of the stupid redneck deputy.

How did such a man keep his job? Except for the hijackers, only two of the people she had met during the past week had been less than friendly. Kathleen prided herself on breaking through people's reserve and making them like her. But the nurse and the deputy weren't worth the effort.

She had even won over the owner of the theater, who had wanted her to list the coming movies in a news story so that he wouldn't have to pay for an ad. By the time she left the theater he had agreed to take a two-inch ad each week, and she had promised to write a feature about a drawing for a ten-dollar bill he planned to have every Saturday night.

Her temper had dropped from a boil to a simmer and then petered out as she approached the shoe-repair shop and turned in.

"Howdy." The cobbler looked up as she entered.

"Hello. I need new leather on my heels. I've worn them almost to the wood." Kathleen removed first one high-heeled pump and then the other and handed them to him. She stood in her stockinged feet while he looked at them. "Can you do the job while I wait?"

"You bet. Have a seat. It'll take about fifteen minutes."

"I do a lot of walking. This is the second time I've had to have them fixed."

"It'll cost you thirty-five cents."

"Sounds reasonable to me."

Kathleen sat down on the bench next to the wall and put her hat and purse down beside her. There wasn't a fan in the small shop, but the front and back doors were open, allowing a slight breeze to pass through. She looked up and caught the cobbler glancing at her. He had a head of thick white hair, rounded shoulders and a bent back.

"I'm Kathleen Dolan. I'll be working with Miss Vernon at the *Gazette*."

"Figured you was her. There ain't many redheaded women 'round here."

"This red hair has gotten me into trouble more than once. I sure can't go around pretending to be someone else unless I put a sack over my head."

"Women can't even get hair like that outta a bottle. Seen some that tried. Some'll try anythin'."

"I don't know why they would want it. It isn't all that great to be different."

"Young folks nowadays is wantin' what they ain't got and figurin' on how they can get it without work. All they want to do is go to picture shows and honky-tonks and loll 'round on the grass in the shade."

"They're no different here than anywhere else. Hard

times have brought out the best in some and the worst in others."

"Workin' hard ain't never hurt nobody. Young folk don't want to put in a day's work. They want ever'thin' give to 'em."

"Most of them would work if they could find a job."

"In a few more years they'll be in charge of the country, then watch out. It'll go to the dogs fast. There'll be a saloon and a dance hall on ever' corner and a whorehouse between. Ya won't be able to tell the women from the men. Women is already wearin' men's pants, struttin' 'round smokin' cigarettes. Some even smokin' cigars. Old folks'll be kicked out into the street. It's the end of times, just like it says in the Bible."

If it wasn't for men who used the whore, there wouldn't be a need for whorehouses. Kathleen kept her thoughts to herself, hoping that he would get the hint and stop the tirade. But it didn't happen.

"Roosevelt's atryin' to give us all a number. Social Security, he calls it. Baa! It's the mark of the beast like it says in the last days. Folks won't have no names no more, just numbers. Mark my words, next they'll be putting that number on our foreheads."

"President Roosevelt only wants everyone to have a little income when they can no longer work." Kathleen tried to put some reason into the conversation, but she could have just as well saved her breath. The man was so full of what he wanted to say that he didn't hear a word she said, and continued his ranting as he worked.

"Women is like mares in heat these days. They get in the family way, go off, have a youngun and give it away like it was a sack a potatoes. I tell you, a old dog will fight to keep its young, but not some of these young fillies. They get hung up cause they're out flippin' up their skirts and showin' themselves. Can't blame a man for takin' what's offered."

Of course not. Poor weak men! Big strong women force them to get in bed with them.

It wasn't hard for Kathleen to realize that the cobbler disliked women. He blamed all the woes of the world on the females. She looked out the door and wished that he would finish putting the heels on her shoes so that she could leave. She dug into her purse for a quarter and a dime and held it in her hand so that the minute he finished she could get out of there.

"The Lord says that in the last days there would be for-nicatin' in the streets."

"I never heard *that* before." Kathleen was getting impatient.

"The good Lord didn't say it in just them words, but 'twas what he meant."

"Are you about finished? I've got lots to do this morning."

"Ya ort to get ya some sensible shoes. I got a pair hardly wore a'tall I'll sell ya for fifty cents. It's what I got in 'em for puttin' on half soles." He indicated a pair of black tie oxfords.

" 'Fraid they're not my size."

"Don't matter. Ya can stick a little cotton in the toes. Forty cents, and it's as low as I'll go."

Kathleen took one of her shoes from the counter, slipped it on, and waited for him to trim the leather around the heel of the other. As soon as he finished she put it on and placed her money on the counter.

"Thank you," she called as she passed through the door, thinking that she'd not had a very good morning.

Out on the brick sidewalk she paused to put on her hat. At that moment she saw Johnny Henry's old black truck pass with a small table resting on its top in the truck bed.

Kathleen waved, but there was no way he would have seen her unless he had been looking in the rearview mirror. She hurried down the street thinking that he would stop at the *Gazette,* but he passed it by and turned on the street where Mrs. Ramsey lived. He was delivering the table he had promised.

Adelaide was typing when Kathleen entered the office. She stood beneath the fan for a moment. Her dress was stuck to her back, and she could feel rivulets of perspiration running down the valley between her breasts. She fanned her face with the brim of her hat.

"You're getting a sunburn." Adelaide yanked a sheet of paper out of the typewriter.

"It's more windburn. It blows more here than in Kansas, and it's hotter. My freckles are having a coming-out party. I'm serving them a daily dose of buttermilk, but it doesn't seem to help much." Kathleen placed her hat on the counter and took papers from the folder she carried. "I got a couple of new ads. One from Ginny at CUT and Curl. She's got a special on permanent waves, a dollar and a half, down from a dollar ninety-eight."

"You don't need one of those, that's for sure."

"No, but I had to promise to come back for a cut." She

lifted the thick curls off her neck. "I may have her shave my head."

"That would be a sight."

"I do get tired of being referred to as that *redheaded woman*. What do you know about Mitchell Thatcher, the deputy?"

"He's a horse's patoot."

"That's an insult to the horse."

"Yeah, but he's the deputy supported by Sheriff Carroll."

Kathleen snorted. "You can put lipstick on a pig all day long, and he's still a pig."

"That bad?"

"We got into a little tiff, and he didn't like my smart mouth. I asked him if he was going to tar and feather me, and he said that they had better uses for women down here. Was that a threat?"

Adelaide didn't answer right away. Kathleen sat down at her desk and glanced over to see her partner staring off into space and tapping the rubber end of her pencil on the desk. Finally, when she spoke it was thoughtfully.

"Be careful of him, Kathleen."

"Why? Why should I have to take his insinuations without talking back?"

"What was he insinuating?"

"Oh, that he ran things when the sheriff was gone and . . . that women who had smart mouths didn't get along down here." *And that you were sleeping with Paul, and now that I'm a partner you'll share him.*

"He isn't a very nice man."

Kathleen rolled her eyes. "Say it again."

"I mean it, Kathleen. He and the sheriff may be involved in something here that isn't very pleasant."

Kathleen became very still. "Something that has to do with Louise Munday?"

"Why do you say that?"

"Because of something Paul said the day I arrived. He said Louise was afraid that you knew too much. Adelaide, what's going on?"

"Maybe something. Maybe nothing." Adelaide looked over her shoulder to be sure that they were alone. "Paul and I have wondered about the doctor's office. He calls it a clinic. But if someone gets really sick, he sends them to Altus or Lawton. About all he does is deliver babies. A lot of women come to Doc Herman."

"Is Louise the only nurse?"

"As far as I know. There are several other women who work there, and I've seen a couple of them in white uniforms, but without the cap. It just seems strange that someone from out of town would come here to have a baby."

"How do you know they *come here?*"

"Before I was cut off from seeing the records at the courthouse, I found registered birth certificates from couples giving their addresses as Colorado, Texas, and even as far away as Missouri. When I asked questions, I got a rebuke from Dr. Herman. He said that he had been recommended by family and friends. He acted as if I were questioning his qualifications. Shortly after that, Louise began to spread it around that I was a heavy drinker and had hallucinations. The story is all over town. When you came, it gave some legitimacy to her story that I'm not capable of running the paper."

"Good heavens! And I called her when you fell out of the chair."

"I didn't fall out of the chair, Kathleen. I was pushed, lost my balance, and fell."

Kathleen looked at her, her eyes full of questions. Finally, she voiced one of them.

"By the Indian woman who came out of the office as I drove up?"

"Yes. Her name is Hannah. She is a pitiful creature, drunk most of the time. I'm afraid that she's used by anyone who will buy her a bottle of rotgut whiskey. She's been pregnant twice during the past few years. Any man who takes advantage of her is not a man but a rutting animal, in my estimation."

"Who takes care of her children?"

"I never see them. They're probably being cared for. The Cherokee are very protective of their children, even the half-breed children of a woman who has been cast out."

"Why did she push you?"

"She wanted money. I've bought a few things for her at the grocery now and then. That day I asked her where her baby was because I could see that her breasts were leaking milk. She didn't say anything, so I asked again where it was. When she didn't answer, I asked her if she had *lost* it. She got mad and shoved me."

"You didn't want Louise to know Hannah had pushed you."

"Hannah is a drunk. A pitiful drunk." Adelaide rubbed the back of her neck.

"There's a social service woman in Oklahoma City. I think her name is Mable Bassett. She would know what to do about her."

"I've thought about calling her," Adelaide said, and reached for the telephone when it rang. "*Gazette*. Oh, hello, Johnny. Yes, she's here. Just a moment. For you, Kathleen."

Kathleen moved her chair back so she could reach the phone. "Hello."

"Miss Dolan, Johnny Henry. I took the table for your typewriter down to Mrs. Ramsey's."

"Thank you. I want to pay you—"

"Forget it. I wasn't using it."

"At least let me buy you a hamburger at Claude's."

"Yes, well, sometime. See you around. 'Bye."

"Good-bye."

Kathleen hung up the phone and turned back to face the window, feeling that she had been given the brush-off. She had been thinking that Johnny Henry was a man she would like to know. Evidently he didn't feel the same about her. She had thought about him often since the day she came to Rawlings and now was embarrassed to recall those thoughts. She had even thought about asking him to drive with her over to Red Rock to see her uncle, Tom Dolan, and Henry Ann Dolan. Lordy, she was glad the opportunity hadn't come up. She would have made a fool of herself.

"Got a date with Johnny?" Adelaide asked.

"Heavens, no! He called to say he had delivered a table he said he'd lend me."

"Oh, shoot! I was hoping you two could get together. Paul and I like Johnny Henry."

"Does he have a steady girl?" Kathleen hated herself for asking. She had given Adelaide a play-by-play description of what happened when she was hijacked.

"Not that I know of. He stays pretty much to himself. He goes away every so often for several weeks. When he does, he has someone look after his ranch. No one seems to know where he goes."

Kathleen knew where he went. Her uncle, Hod, had told her that Johnny Henry worked occasionally for the federal government. He and Hod had tracked the movements of Clyde Barrow and Bonnie Parker, and the information they passed on to Marshal Frank Hamer had resulted in their demise. Johnny evidently kept that part of his life from the people in this town. Kathleen was reluctant to reveal it even to Adelaide.

"We got acquainted with him a few years ago after the rodeo. Paul was having a little trouble with some toughs. He can be pushed just so far before he starts swinging. It was four against one. Johnny stepped in. Since that time he and Paul have been friends. Johnny is about the only friend Paul has, I might add."

"I was sure glad he came along when I was being hijacked. He said he turned the names in to the sheriff, but I've heard nothing about signing a complaint."

"And you won't."

"How often do they have a city council meeting here?" Kathleen asked.

"Whenever the mayor calls one. It's usually on short notice. Over and done with before I'm aware of it."

"Do they allow you to see the minutes?"

Adelaide snorted. "Sure. It's the law. They give me the bare bones. The meeting was opened, roll called, minutes read and approved. Usually they have a little discussion about a chuckhole in the street or a crack in the sidewalk, then adjourn. Nothing there you can report on. It's been that way for the past five years."

"Since the doctor became mayor?"

"Right."

"There isn't anyone who stands up against him?"

"He's an icon, a hero around here. If you criticize him, it's like criticizing Jesus Christ, motherhood, or baseball. The man and his cronies have a stranglehold on this town. Folks love him, and woe to the one who exposes the good guy as a bad guy. That kind of truth turns the people against the messenger every time."

"Has he tried to win you over to his side?"

"He asked me out to dinner a few times after his wife died. He was diplomatic about it; but he insinuated that, being an old maid, I think he said maiden lady, he, as my doctor, could teach me the pleasures of the flesh . . . my words, not his. I was so shocked I couldn't remember exactly what he said, but his meaning was clear. He was willing to give the old maid a treat." Adelaide shivered. "What little respect I had for him went right out the window."

"He's the only doctor in town isn't he? Do you go to him when you get sick?"

"Paul had been here only a few months when I got

really sick. He took me to Altus. Of course, Doc found out about it and sent the sheriff and the deputy in to question Paul. They didn't find out anything. Paul is very clever. He has managed to create a whole new identity for himself. I didn't know about Paul's past at that time. I'm glad I didn't. It wasn't until later that he told me."

"He's the best linotype operator I've ever seen. The operator in Liberal made ten times the mistakes Paul makes. Sometimes I don't find any in column after column, and I think that I've overlooked something."

Adelaide's eyes shone with pride. "He is good, isn't he?"

"He worked on a paper before he came here, didn't he?"

"Yes. A big paper. Paul is an honorable man. He thought it fair that you knew something about him when you put your money in the paper. He'll tell you more when he's ready. Do you have any objection to his writing the national news?"

"Absolutely not! He does a really great job; as good as the *Oklahoman and Times* or the *Wichita Eagle*. It's outstanding for a town of this size. I hope the readers realize what they're getting." Kathleen picked up her folder and headed for the door. "I'll get the ad from the grocery store, and we'll have the advertising in for this week except for the classifieds. I'll write the rodeo story when I get back so Paul can set it."

"I have two long obits. Both men were old-timers here. I wish I had time to send their pictures to Lawton for engraving. I may send them anyway and run the pictures next week."

"There was an engraver in Liberal, but he was expensive, and the publisher wouldn't let us put in a picture unless it was something important. We had an extensive file of engravings, pictures of all the prominent people for miles around, and local sites. By the way, I brought mine and put it in the file. You can use it in case I get run over by a truck."

"Oh, go on with you. You'd better not get hit by a truck. I'd be mad as a hornet. I hate doing ads," Adelaide called.

Kathleen laughed at her over her shoulder as she went out the door. The heat beaming up from the sidewalk hit her face. She hurried down the street to the store and failed to see the dilapidated old truck parked at the corner.

Chapter Five

Standing beside the grocery counter, Johnny saw Kathleen as she passed the window and again when she entered the store. He had caught a glimpse of her bright red hair earlier when he passed the shoe-repair shop and was relieved to see her there. She would not be at the Ramseys' when he delivered the table.

Hazel had opened the door for him and watched as he set the table against the wall and lifted Kathleen's type-writer from the floor. The room was neat as a pin; books and papers were stacked, the bed made without a single wrinkle in the cover. He was beset by a loneliness deeper than he'd ever felt before as he stood amid the little home spot she had made for herself. Embarrassed by his own feelings, he made a hasty retreat, even refusing the offer of a piece of sweet potato pie.

Later he had called Kathleen from the telephone office, where he had gone to pay for a call he had placed the week before.

Since their first meeting on the highway, he'd had plenty of time to think about her as he rounded up his horses down on Keith McCabe's range. He had bred his mares to Keith's stallion last April and would keep them closer to home during the winter months in case of a severe norther that could trap them for days without food. During that time he had convinced himself that any further contact with Miss Kathleen Dolan would be dangerous to his peace of mind. Therefore, the only thing to do would be to avoid her whenever possible.

Now, it appeared to be impossible. There was no escape.

He had just given a lengthy list of his needs to Mrs. Wilson when Kathleen came into the store, saw him, and smiled. He touched his fingers to his hat brim and set his dark eyes on her, letting nothing at all show beneath their impenetrable surface.

"Howdy, ma'am."

"Hello." Kathleen walked toward him as Mrs. Wilson moved away with his list in her hand. "Thank you for the table."

"You're more than welcome."

He turned away, scooped up coffee beans, poured them into the grinder, and began to turn the large wheel. He knew that she stood there, hesitant, before she walked past him. His thoughts had scattered when she came in the door, but now they were back in his possession. He was more convinced than ever that the two of them had absolutely nothing in common.

She was refined and educated.

He had barely finished the fifth grade.

She was smart enough to write for a newspaper.

It was a chore for him to write a grocery list.

She came from respectable people.

His mother had been Mud Creek trash.

The differences between them went on and on. It was better, he thought now, to have her think that he was uninterested in her as a woman than to have her know that the man who was on the verge of falling in love with her was the bastard son of a whore and a drunken Indian. It was a fact she would find out soon enough.

Johnny was not conceited enough to think that the welcome smile she had given him when she came into the store, was for him . . . personally. It was for the help he had given her the day she arrived and for the table he had just delivered.

Mrs. Wilson returned and bagged the coffee she took from the grinder.

"Our special next week will be soda crackers. You can have them for sale price if you want."

"I'll take a box. I was in a hurry when I scratched off the list. I'm surprised you could read it."

"I made out most of it. You'd better look it over in case I missed something. You've got quite an order."

"I sold one of my mares and decided to lay in a stock of grub."

"We appreciate your business, Johnny."

He could hear the click of heels on the wooden floor and knew that Kathleen was coming back to the front of the store. He busied himself checking over the list but was terribly aware when she stopped beside him. He folded the paper and put it in his shirt pocket.

"I forgot to put cornmeal on the list, Mrs. Wilson. Give me a five-pound bag." The grocer's wife nodded and went down the crowded aisle of the store.

"I hear that you'll be one of the contestants at the rodeo," Kathleen said. "I'll be cheering for you."

"Thanks. I enter every year just for the hell of it."

"Adelaide says that you usually win."

"Only the bronc-riding."

"You're being modest. She says you win the calf-roping and sometimes the steer-wrestling."

"Once in a while I get lucky." His tone was one of disinterest.

He hadn't looked directly at her except the one time when she first came into the store. Color tinged her face and neck as her irritation mounted. *Who the heck does he think he is? He has no right to snub me. I didn't ask for the darn table.*

"Have I stepped on your tail? Is that why you're giving me the cold shoulder?"

His head turned quickly, and he looked down at her. *Good. I got his attention at last.*

"Why do you say that?"

"I'm not so dumb that I don't know when I'm getting the brush-off. I thought that we could be friends as long as we're both connected to my Uncle Tom. Do you have something against being friends with a woman?"

"Of course not." Johnny felt his face tingle with embarrassment.

"Then perhaps I have body odor or bad breath. I'll keep my offensive body at a distance when I see you at the rodeo. Good-bye." She walked away from him with her head held high.

"Here ya are, Johnny." Mrs. Wilson returned with the bag of cornmeal. "Anything else?"

"I don't think so. Tally up the bill."

After he paid, she packed his order in boxes while he carried a five-gallon can of kerosene out to his truck.

"You should set your cap for Miss Dolan, Johnny," Mrs. Wilson teased when he came back for the boxes. "She's nice. Pretty, too. Every single man in town will be beating a path to her door."

"Ah . . . no," he stammered. "She'd not see me for dirt. I'm a poor rancher who's head over heels in debt."

"Who isn't? She works hard and isn't in the least snooty. By the way, I put a hunk of cheese in the box, our thanks for the big order."

"I'm obliged."

"Good luck at the rodeo, Johnny."

"Thanks."

When Kathleen left the store, she was angry at Johnny and angry at herself for having been glad to see him. Embarrassment mingled with her anger. She had been about to make a fool of herself and ask him if he'd like to go to Red Rock to see the Tom Dolans. She should be grateful that he made his feelings perfectly clear.

Damn him! If he thought she was chasing after him, he could just get that thought out of his block head. *But the idea that he could be thinking that cut her to the quick.*

She was so engrossed in her thoughts that she almost ran into the two men coming toward her. She looked up and recognized them immediately. The two toughs who had attempted to steal her car and her money stood there brazenly grinning at her. Temper that had been simmering since Johnny's snub, boiled up. With her hands on her hips, she stopped in front of them, barring their way.

"How come you're not in jail?" she almost yelled.

"Well, looky here. If it ain't that feisty redhead we helped get outta the ditch." The one called Webb grinned inanely, showing stained, broken teeth.

"Helped, my hind leg!" The tone of Kathleen's voice was keeping pace with her temper. "You . . . you piles of horse dung! You were hijacking my car."

"Hijackin' ya? Hear that, Webb? She ain't grateful a'tall fer what we done. You'd'a thought a uppity-up like her'd have manners and give us a little somethin' more than a jawin' out fer all the help we done a pushin' her car. Like a little kiss maybe."

"Listen to me, you mangy polecats,"—Her eyes glittered with the light of battle—"I don't know why you're not in jail where you belong, but you can bet your filthy hide I'm going to find out."

"Ya go on and do that, baby doll," Webb leered at her. "Say, sugar, how 'bout goin' honky-tonkin' tonight? Otis and his Ring-tail Tooters is playin' out at the Twilight Gardens. There's a gal there what's goin' to show us how to do the jitterbug dance. Ya've seen it done, ain't ya?"

"You're out of your mind if you think I'd be caught dead with warthogs like you." She wrinkled her nose in a contemptuous sneer.

"She ain't goin' to be friendly. It's a pure-dee shame. Guess we better be on our way."

"Not so fast . . . scum! Johnny Henry told the sheriff about you."

"Yeah. Fat lot a good it done him. Now get outta the

way. We ain't got no time to stand here jawin' with a . . . high-tone split-tail when we got things to do." He reached out and grasped her upper arms.

Rage gave Kathleen strength to jerk her arm loose and swing her fist. The blow caught Webb on the side of his face. He let out an angry yelp and raised his hand to slap her.

"Hit me, you yellow-bellied buzzard bait, and some dark night you'll get a belly full of lead!" she shouted as she was suddenly pushed aside. Johnny was between her and the two men.

"Touch her, and I'll bury you."

"She started it. She hit me."

"You grabbed her. I saw you."

"Yeah? Well go tell it to the sheriff. She ain't nothin' but a—"

"—Say it, and your nose will be smeared all over your ugly face."

"Why aren't they in jail?" Kathleen demanded.

"I don't know." Johnny glanced at her, then back, as the two men began to edge around him. "But I'll find out. Go on, get off the street. You've given the folks a show. I'll take them down to the sheriff."

"Won't do no good. We been there and told him how it was."

"You can tell him again why you threatened Miss Dolan. Come on," Johnny snarled, and prodded them ahead of him.

"She come on to us," Webb yelled. "She wild as a harelipped mule! Redheaded wildcat is what she is."

Kathleen watched as Johnny herded the two men off

down the street. He had rescued her again. She looked around and saw that several people had stopped along the street to watch the *show*. With tears of rage and frustration in her eyes, she hurried on down the street to the *Gazette*. Thank goodness Adelaide wasn't in the office when she reached it, and she had time to gather herself together before she had to face her.

This had not been her best day. Not by a long shot! First the randy deputy, then the ranting cobbler, and the embarrassment of being brushed off by Johnny Henry. Finally seeing the miserable jayhawkers who had tried to rob her walking the street as free as air. It was all too much. She desperately wanted to cry, but her pride forbade it.

She heard the linotype machine start up and knew that Adelaide would be coming back. She hastily put a sheet of paper in her typewriter, dug in the basket on her desk for the information about the rodeo, and began to write. She wrote three lines, Xed them out, then started again.

The fifth annual Rawlings rodeo will be held at the Tillison County fair grounds Saturday Sept. 23. Fifteen contestants have signed up to compete in nine different events.

Johnny Henry, local rancher, who took home the purse last year for "Best All-Around Cowboy" will enter seven events.

The stock for the event will come from the McCabe ranch just south of the river in Dallam County, Texas.

Again this year the local churches will be in charge of the concession stands, and a variety of food and drink will be available.

The screen door was jerked open, and a big man with a star on his chest came in. He looked around the office, then down at her.

"May I help you?"

"You can if you're Miss Dolan, and I think you are. There's not many women—"

"—in town with hair as red as mine." Kathleen finished for him and got to her feet. Looking up at him made her uncomfortable. "I've heard it a million times. You're the sheriff."

"How'd ya guess?" He hooked his thumbs in the pockets of his trousers and looked steadily at her.

Sheriff A. B. Carroll was a heavyset man with a big neck, broad shoulders, and short arms and legs. The hair beneath the brim of his Stetson was brown, the thick mustache on his upper lip brown sprinkled with gray. The bulge in his jaw, Kathleen suspected, was a plug of chewing tobacco. He wore his importance on his chest along with his badge. She decided then and there that she wasn't going to like him.

"It wasn't hard to figure it out. The star means that you're either the sheriff or from the Star Ice Company. We got ice yesterday."

"Smart-mouthed, just like Ell said."

"Speaking of your deputy, are all women treated with such lecherous behavior when they go to the county sheriff's office?"

"Those who ask for it."

"And who is to be the judge of that?"

"I am. When I'm not there, my deputy is."

"I'd like to remind you, Sheriff, that your salary and that of your ill-bred deputy, and the office you occupy are paid for by the taxpayers of this county, and they are entitled to be treated with civility."

"You've not paid taxes here. What are *you* yippin' about?"

"Hello, A. B., I thought I heard your voice out here." Adelaide had come quietly into the office.

"Hello, Adelaide. I think you've got yourself a little hot-tempered chili pepper here. She just got into a fight out on the street. You know that I can't have a woman, man either, brawlin' in public. Doc says it ain't a good image for the town."

"Wait a gosh-darn minute," Kathleen sputtered. "That man grabbed me. I had to defend myself."

"They disagree. It's two against one."

"The two you're referring to are the men who attempted to hijack me out on the highway the day I arrived here. They also took my money and would have gotten away with it if Johnny Henry hadn't come along when he did. I'll sign a complaint against them."

"Here we've got two sides again," the sheriff said patiently. He turned and addressed his remarks to Adelaide. "Webb and Krome, the men this woman is accusing, told me that they had stopped to help her get her car out of the ditch. She offered to pay them. They took the money, but when Henry came along she accused them of stealing it. Now, I know that Webb and Krome aren't good upstanding citizens; but I know them, and I don't know her from a bale of hay. Why should I put two men in jail on her say-so?"

Kathleen swallowed down the knot of anger in her throat and forced herself to speak calmly.

"This has nothing to do with Adelaide, Sheriff Carroll. I'm the one involved here. I'm the one accusing your friends, Webb and Krome. My name is Miss Dolan, not *her,* not *she,* and not *that woman.* I'll thank you to remember it and address your remarks to me."

The sheriff sighed. "I'm just trying to get along here. I've got to satisfy everyone in this county, not just one newcomer who more than likely won't be here this time next year."

"Oh, I'll be here, Sheriff. I'm not one to tuck tail and run when the going gets rough. I've been told that it's the red hair. I'm not sure about that, but I do know that I'm stubborn, I'm determined, and I know when right is right. I don't back down even when the law in town fails to do its job."

"All right," the sheriff said harshly. "This town is not paradise, miss. It's just like any other town. Folks here are like folks everywhere—some are pretty decent, others so rotten they stink to high heaven. We've got some saints and some snakes. We do what we have to do to put up with 'em. My advice to you is to do the same."

Johnny had opened the screen door and stepped inside while the sheriff was talking. Kathleen's eyes went to him and found him looking at her from the concealing shadow of his hat brim. His dark eyes bore down at her with an intensity entirely different from the only time their eyes had caught while at the store. With reluctance she turned her gaze back to the sheriff.

"You're not going to arrest them." It was a statement that needed no answer, but he gave one.

"No, ma'am, I'm not." His voice was stiletto-sharp.

The flat refusal drew a faint line of displeasure across her brow. It registered in the barest widening of her blue eyes; then, for an instant, her heavy lashes shuttered her gaze. Mentally, Kathleen had slumped. Physically, she stood with her shoulders back, her head up, and looked the man in the eye.

"I've learned a lot about this town today, Sheriff Carroll, but I'm reasonably sure that you're not interested in my assessment."

"You're right about that, miss. This matter is ended, and I'll be going." He turned at the door. "I'll speak to Ell about how you were treated in my office."

After he had gone, Kathleen shifted her gaze to Johnny and away. Color touched her face. She stared down at the papers on the desk. For a short while she was wholly still, fighting down her embarrassment. When her eyes came up, she was again in control of her emotions.

"Well, I guess that's that," she said.

"I told him how it was. I didn't know he was coming here until I saw his car," Johnny told her.

"Do you believe his version of what happened?"

"Lord, no!" Points of light flared in Johnny's dark eyes. "I was there, remember?"

"Not at first—"

"—I understand what's happening. The sheriff is between a rock and a hard place on this. Someone higher up is calling the shots."

"Doc Herman?" Adelaide asked, and turned her eyes to Paul, who had come from the back room with several pages to be proofed. More than likely he had waited until the sheriff left before coming in.

Kathleen spoke in answer to Adelaide's question.

"Why would the mayor of the town have anything to say about how the *county* sheriff's office is run?" She looked from one to the other, waiting for a reply. None was forthcoming until Adelaide sighed deeply and sank down in the chair behind her desk.

"It's long and complicated, Kathleen."

Johnny watched the emotions flick across Kathleen's face. She had an agile brain and a pair of eyes that missed nothing. She also had guts she hadn't used yet. A slow smile drew little wrinkles in the corner of his eyes. That redheaded temper of hers was going to get her in trouble. There was no doubt about it.

What surprised him was why he was here after he had gone to so much trouble to keep his distance. He had sprinted down the street when he saw one of the thugs she was talking to grab her. If the man had hit her, Johnny wasn't sure what he would have done. He might have torn the man apart.

A desire to protect her washed over him. *Christ, John Henry, if you have any sense, you'd say your good-byes and get the hell out of here.*

"Got a minute, Johnny?" Paul asked. "I've got to turn around one of the cylinders on the press and I've only got two hands."

"Sure. Glad to help."

Kathleen sat down at her desk, turned, and faced her partner.

"Did I embarrass you, Adelaide? I didn't mean to cause you more trouble." Her eyes were clouded with distress.

"You didn't embarrass me," Adelaide said staunchly. "It's hard for people in this town to accept strangers. They're used to folks *leaving* here, not *coming* here."

"Do you think it possible that those two men were sent out to hijack me, carry me off someplace, and frighten me so much that I'd be afraid to come back?"

"If they were, they met their match." A smile tilted the corners of Adelaide's mouth. "No, I don't think they'd go that far. I had let it be known that a very bright young woman was buying into the paper. Doc Herman had offered to buy in and so had several others in town. I knew that if I let that happen, it wouldn't be long before I lost control completely and Paul and I would be out on the street."

"I've been wondering about something. If Doc Herman runs the town, why doesn't he tell the merchants to stop advertising in the paper. Without advertising, you'd be out of business."

"He doesn't want us out of business. He uses us now and then when he wants to make his point about something."

"Like what?"

"Last year he wanted to get the Greyhound bus rerouted so that it would come through here. He used the paper to get up a petition and to persuade the bus com-

pany officials that a town this size with its own newspaper would help to provide a steady stream of passengers."

"Did it?"

"Oh, yes. It's a convenience for those who travel, and I think maybe it helped Doc Herman's clinic."

In the back room, Johnny washed his greasy hands.

"Thanks for the help." Paul handed him a towel. "I could have waited for Woody, but it would have made us late starting the run tomorrow."

"Anytime. I am fascinated with machinery. I've been looking for parts so I can fix up an old earth mover I bought for a song."

"What are you planning to use it for?"

"A storm cellar for one thing. I'm not anxious to dig it one spadeful at a time." Johnny waited for Paul to finish washing, then said, "I guess Miss Dolan being here has taken a load off Adelaide?"

"Yes. I was a little leery at first. I wanted Addie to meet the person she was going to bring into her business, but she said that she could tell from the letters and the recommendation from the Liberal paper that Miss Dolan was going to be just what the *Gazette* needed to put some life back into the paper. Addie is seldom wrong."

"Miss Dolan's got spunk all right. I hope it doesn't get her into more trouble."

"She pretty, and she isn't a dumbbell by a long shot." Paul's homely face broke into a grin. "Why don't you take her to the picture show or for a ride? The girl needs an outing."

"In my old truck? I'm sure she'd like that." Johnny

clapped Paul on the shoulder. "You're hog-tied, my friend, that's plain to see. I'm not, and I'm going to stay that way."

"You don't have to marry her. Just take her out a time or two."

"She'd laugh in my face if I asked her."

"Bet ya two bits. It'd pay for the movie."

"Naw. I'd best get on back to the ranch."

Chapter Six

Johnny left the *Gazette* and walked quickly down the street toward where he'd left his truck. As he passed the grocery store, Mrs. Wilson called to him.

"Johnny, can you come in a minute?"

"Sure." Inside the store he saw that Mrs. Wilson had an anxious look on her face.

"What's wrong?"

"I'm worried about Miss Dolan. The men who had a set-to with her came in a while ago. I was down behind the counter looking for a dime I'd dropped, and I heard one of them say that before they left town that redheaded bitch was going to get what was coming to her. They're downright mean, Johnny. They talked nasty about her."

"What else did they say?"

"They said some words I don't want to repeat."

"You don't have to. I can imagine what they were. Did they say anything about the sheriff or the deputy?"

"They said 'Ell' a time or two. It's wasn't 'hell,' Johnny, it was 'Ell,' referring to Deputy Thatcher. While they were here a couple of men came in and bought a box of shotgun shells. They were Cherokee. The one called

Webb made a remark about blanket-asses having money to buy shells because they could get work at the tannery and decent white men couldn't."

"Did they get a rise out of the Indians?"

"No. They ignored them."

"Mrs. Wilson, is it all right if I bring my supplies back in and leave them until morning? I've never had anything taken from the truck while it was parked on the street, but I don't trust those two yahoos. I think I'd better stick around, keep an eye on them, and make sure Miss Dolan gets home all right."

After Johnny left the office, Kathleen set her mind on the work at hand and refused to allow it to drift to other things. She finished the rodeo story that would be on the front page, then worked on the classified advertising section that took up three-quarters of a page.

"Adelaide, what do you think about starting a letter to the editor policy? We'll have space on the classified page."

"It's a good idea. Do you think we'd get any letters?"

"We won't know until we try. We can also fill that space with items from the paper files of ten or twenty-five years ago."

"That's a good idea, too. I've heard of doing that, but never had the time to do the research. We don't have time for it this week, but I could write up columns for several weeks ahead and Paul could set them. I think that we have some old engravings in the file we could use."

"After we get that going we could start a 'Cook of the Week' column featuring a lady from each of the church circles, then the clubs. In Liberal they crawled all over each other to get their names on the list. And we—"

She paused when Johnny came barreling into the *Gazette* as if he had only a minute to do something and he was determined to do it. He stopped directly in front of Kathleen's desk as if prepared to do battle.

"Go out to supper with me tonight, then I'll take you home." He blurted out the words as if he was in a hurry to get them out.

Kathleen stared at him with her mouth open. Then she snapped it shut, remembering that she had tried to be friendly with him at the store and that he had practically shunned her.

"Thanks, but Mrs. Ramsey is expecting me. I have to let her know ahead of time if I'll not be there for supper."

"I'll run down there and tell her. How long will it be before you're finished here?"

"I'm . . . not sure, and I don't think—"

"—You won't be finished before I get back. Don't leave. Wait here for me." Johnny spun on his heel and was out the door before Kathleen could open her mouth to protest.

"Well. What's got into him?" she sputtered. "He's got a lot of nerve. I suppose he thinks that he's doing me a great big favor."

"He wanted to take you out and was afraid you'd turn him down. Men are babies about rejection. That's why he got out of here in such a hurry."

"Oh? How about a woman who tries to be friendly with a man because he has done her a favor, and he gives her the cold shoulder? Is she supposed to jump a mile high when he asks her out?"

"When did that happen? I can't imagine Johnny Henry giving any woman the cold shoulder. He's one of the most polite men I've ever met."

"At the store—when I went for the ad. You'd have thought that I had the brand of a scarlet woman on my forehead."

"Are you sure?" Adelaide frowned. "That doesn't sound like Johnny. He's even nice to Clara Ramsey. Lord knows she chased him enough."

"Emily's mother? I wondered why he was so at home there. They welcomed him with open arms."

"They should. He's taken Clara home a few times when she couldn't make it on her own. She was pregnant again a few years ago and spread it around that the baby was Johnny's. He never mentioned it to us. He may have not even known she was spreading it around. Knowing Johnny, I think that if it had been his, he would have done the right thing."

"Where is the baby now?"

"It died right after birth. Clara left town after that. The last I heard she was down in Texas waiting tables in a beer joint."

"That's too bad. Emily is the one left to suffer the stigma of not having a father. She's such a sweet, cheerful little girl."

"That's Hazel's doing. She's had the care of the child since she was born. Sometimes we think that we've got troubles. Clara came home with that baby and left without her. Hazel has done everything she could to keep a roof over that child's head."

"I'm taking her with me to the rodeo. She was so excited about it last night she could hardly eat her supper."

The office door opened and two women scurried in. One was tall and thin. Her hair was scalloped around her face and held with bobby pins. The other one was about as wide as she was tall and wore a small hat with a tiny veil perched atop her henna-colored hair. They cast curious looks at Kathleen while they told Adelaide about the Methodist Church chili supper to be held after the rodeo.

Later a preacher in a black serge suit, sweat running down his ruddy face, arrived with a notice of a Pentecostal revival meeting that would begin on Sunday beneath a brush arbor a mile west of town. Every other phrase the man uttered was either "praise the Lord" or "hallelujah."

"I know there isn't a Lutheran church here, but is there one in one of the nearby towns?" Kathleen asked when the preacher left.

"None that I know of. Most are Pentecostal, Baptist, or Methodist. The churches here worked together creating the soup kitchen. They feed any hungry person who comes through. That's one pie Doc Herman doesn't have his fingers in."

"The churches did that in Liberal, too. There were so many to feed after the dust storms. The people in the area were so kind. Those that had, shared. Ranchers donated beef, hunters went to Colorado and brought back deer or elk. The whole community united to help those in need."

"We don't have as many as some towns do. We're too

far from anything. Most of the folks in our soup lines come in on the freight train."

"I thank God every day for my grandparents. If not for them, I don't know where I'd be. They paid for my business school and left me a little money. Without parents, brothers, or sisters, I have only myself to depend on. I could have easily been one of the unfortunate ones without a home or a job."

"You have your uncles."

"Yes, and an aunt in South Dakota that I've never met. I want to take a Saturday afternoon off in a few weeks and drive over to Red Rock to see Uncle Tom and his family. I'll come back on Sunday. I think it's too far to drive all in one day."

"Here comes Leroy Grandon. I think he's smitten with you. He's been in the office more often since you've been here than in the last couple of months."

"Maybe he's going to put in another ad," Kathleen murmured, then, "Hello, Mr. Grandon."

"Hello." He nodded to Adelaide, then turned back to Kathleen. "I was wondering—"

"—About your ad? Do you have a price change?"

"Ah . . . no. I was wondering if you'd—" He glanced again at Adelaide who was busy typing. "I wondered if . . . you'd like to go to dinner and the picture show tomorrow night."

"Well, ah . . ." Kathleen fumbled for words. "That's very nice of you, Mr. Grandon. I'd love to go."

"You . . . will?" His smile stretched his lips and showed missing teeth along his lower jaw. He wasn't a bad-looking man when he kept his mouth shut, even if he was older than Kathleen by a good fifteen years. "I'll stop in tomorrow and we can make plans. 'Bye." He lifted his hand and was out the door. He was smiling as he passed the window.

"Oh, dear. What have I done?"

"Leroy is a nice man," Adelaide said. "And he's president of the Chamber of Commerce, even if it is a token position. He doesn't have much say in running things.

"He's a careful businessman. His store is well stocked, and he keeps it clean and orderly.

"He's lonesome. His wife died about a year ago. They never had children and were devoted to each other. At first, the widows in town found any excuse to go to the men's store. It was too soon, though, for Leroy. I've not heard that he kept company with any of them."

"I couldn't think of a logical reason not to go," Kathleen confessed. "I saw how nervous he was and didn't want to hurt his feelings."

"You won't have to worry about Leroy. He'll be the perfect gentleman. Boring, but still a gentleman."

"Tomorrow is press day. More than likely, I'll fall asleep at the picture show."

A little later, Adelaide broke the silence. "Pssst, Kathleen, we're about to be honored by a visit from the big man himself."

Kathleen turned to look out the window to see a small man wearing baggy pants and a white shirt with sleeves rolled up to his elbows coming across the street toward the *Gazette*. The wind blew his sparse gray hair back from a high forehead above a small-featured face. He wore round, wire-rimmed glasses.

"You don't mean—?"

"I do mean."

The man came into the office and without a greeting went straight to Adelaide.

"Louise said you'd had a nasty fall."

"That was over a week ago, and it wasn't nasty."

"Have you suffered headaches, dizziness, nausea?"

"No. I'm fine."

"You should have come to see me right away. Blows to the head are not to be taken lightly."

"It wasn't that much of a blow."

"I should be the judge of that. You and this paper are important to this town, Adelaide. Your companion should take better care of you."

"If you mean Paul, he's the one who's important to this paper. I don't know what I'd do without him."

"Important in other areas as well . . . hum?"

"Of course," Adelaide said coolly, and Kathleen let out a silent whoop of laughter.

Dr. Herman looked long and hard at Adelaide. She looked back and, knowing that he was attempting to intimidate her, refused to look away. He finally pulled a handkerchief from his pocket and wiped the lenses of his glasses. He put them carefully back on and turned to Kathleen.

"Introduce me to your partner, Adelaide."

"Kathleen Dolan, Dr. Herman."

The doctor took the few necessary steps to reach Kathleen and held out his hand. His grip was firm.

"Glad to meet you."

"Thank you." *I'm not glad to meet you, you cold fish.*

"What do you think of our little town?"

"Very nice."

"And we want to keep it that way."

"I'm sure you do."

"Do I detect a Yankee accent?"

"It's possible. I was raised in Iowa by my Norwegian grandparents."

"It's been a long time since we've had a lady in jail for brawling on the street. Back in 1908 to be exact. Her name was Flora Eudora and she had flaming red hair."

"What a coincidence," Kathleen murmured drily.

"Yes, isn't it? Flora believed that her husband was fornicating with the town whore."

"Was he?"

"Of course. Flora met the woman on the street and attacked her. She knocked out a tooth and blackened her eyes. It was the wrong thing to do."

"I agree. She should have attacked her husband, blackened his eyes, and kicked him in a place that would have discouraged his wanderings for a while."

"Rawlings at that time was a mere speck on the prairie," the doctor continued as if Kathleen hadn't spoken. "The founder, a man by the name of Radisson Hoghorn Rawlings, was a man of law and order. Mistress Flora Eudora was hauled off to jail."

Kathleen whistled through her teeth. "Aren't you glad he didn't name the town Hoghorn? I can see it now—HOGHORN WEEKLY GAZETTE across the front of this building." She smiled sweetly at the man standing beside her desk. "What happened to the whore?"

"She went back to work."

"I'd have bet you'd say that. Are you the town historian, Doctor? We're looking for some stories from the past for a new column. Perhaps you can help us out."

"Young lady, this town has gone through some good times and some bad times. We're in better shape than any other town our size in Oklahoma. It's due to good planning, law, and order. During the early thirties a bank went under almost every day. Ours, here in Rawlings, remained solid."

"That's good news. Would you like for me to write an editorial on the economy in Rawlings? Of course, I'd need to have access to the city ledgers. By the way, I plan to attend the city council meetings. In Liberal, they were held the first and third Monday of each month. What is the schedule here?"

"We don't have scheduled meetings. No need for it. If something comes up that requires discussion, we have a meeting."

"You'll let me know?"

"You'll be given the minutes of the meeting."

"Not good enough. I want to attend and become acquainted with the members. I'd be able to write a much better report."

"The meetings are spontaneous. But we'll try to oblige you." Only the slight narrowing of the man's eye revealed his irritation.

"Thank you."

"Nice to have met you, Miss Dolan. Take care of yourself, Adelaide." He walked out the door, crossed the street, and went into the bank. Neither woman said a word until he had disappeared.

"So that's the man who runs things around here." The statement hung in the air for a few seconds before Adelaide answered.

"Can you believe it?"

"Not to look at him."

"He's tough as nails. He was warning you, Kathleen. Word had already got to him about the little set-to you had on the street. He knows everything that goes on in this town."

"He and the sherrif remind me of two dogs we had at home on the farm. One was a big, brown shaggy dog with a deep, loud bark. The other one was little, slick-haired, and quick. He looked like a gentle little pussycat. When strangers came, they would watch the big dog with the loud bark, and the little one would slip up and bite them."

Paul came from the back room with a worried frown on his face. His eyes sought Adelaide's. Kathleen had never seen him enter the office without first finding his Addie with his eyes. His devotion to her, and hers to him, was like a tangible thing. It reminded Kathleen of the love between her grandparents. When her grandmother died, the life had gone out of her grandpa, and he had died soon after.

Kathleen turned back to face the window and heard Paul speaking softly to Adelaide, asking her if she was tired. He would be behind her now, rubbing the spot between her shoulders, but with his eye on the door lest someone come in and observe him. Desolation washed over Kathleen. Seldom did she admit even to herself that it would be heavenly to have someone to lean on, to share her joys and her sorrows. Would she ever know the kind

of love that Adelaide knew? Right now that seemed to be as remote as the moon.

Johnny drove slowly along the dirt road trying to stir up as little dust as possible when he passed the lines full of freshly washed clothes. On the road ahead he saw a woman in high-heeled shoes struggling along, carrying a heavy suitcase.

Clara Ramsey. No doubt about it. How long had she been gone this time? Six months? A year? How long would she stay? Johnny hoped not for long. She reminded him of his half sister, Isabel. Tramps, both of them. Nothing or nobody would ever change them.

He slowed the truck when he came alongside Clara. The face she turned to him was pale with a bright slash of red lipstick. She had a bruise on one of her cheeks and a swelling on the bridge of her nose.

"Hello, Clara. Need a ride?"

"Oh, Johnny," she squealed, and let the bag drop to the ground.

Johnny got out of the truck and lifted the suitcase up onto the bed of the truck. Clara lifted her tight skirt up past her knees, stepped up on the running board, and slid onto the seat beside him.

"Jesus, you're a lifesaver. I wasn't sure I'd make it carryin' that damned old suitcase."

"Does Hazel know you're coming?" He knew the answer, but he asked anyway.

"No. I wanted to surprise her and Emily. I brought presents for Emily's birthday."

"Isn't Emily's birthday on the Fourth of July?"

"So they're a little late. A kid don't care. It's a hell of a lot more than I got on my birthday. I was lucky to get a piece of corn bread with syrup on it."

"It was worse for a lot of kids. Some were starving. Your folks did the best they could by you."

"Well, dog my cats! There it is. The old dump looks the same." Clara's quick dry laugh spoke of her contempt. She opened the door when the truck stopped, and slid out, her skirt slithering up to mid-thigh.

Johnny lifted the bag off the truck bed and followed her up the walk to the porch. Clara opened the screen door and went inside.

"Mama, I'm home. Put my suitcase in my room, Johnny." She winked at him. "You know where it is."

Johnny set the bag down beside the door just as Hazel came from the back of the house wiping her hands on her apron. When she saw Clara her face lit up like a full moon.

"Clara? Honey, is that you? I thought I heard you call, but I wasn't sure." Hazel folded her daughter in her arms. "Oh, honey, I'm so glad to see you. Here, let me look at you. My, but you're as pretty as ever. Emily will be beside herself. She been asking about you a lot lately." Hazel hugged Clara again. "I've been so worried. Why didn't you write?"

Clara twisted out of her mother's embrace and dropped down onto a chair.

"Don't start in on me, Mama. I just got here."

Hazel drew in a deep breath. Then, "Hello, Johnny. I didn't see you at first. I was so excited to see Clara."

"Hello, Mrs. Ramsey. I met her out on the road. Where do you want me to put the suitcase?"

"Put it in my room," Clara said. "Where else? I see you've got the door shut, Mama. I used to love havin' the door shut, but you'd come along and open it to see if I had a boy in my bed." She rolled her eyes toward the ceiling.

"Clara, honey, I rented out your room. You'll have to sleep on the couch here, or back on my bed with Emily. I'll take Emily's bed."

"You what?" Clara jumped to her feet and stormed across the room to throw open the door. She looked around the room with her hands on her hips. "Well, I swan. You really want me out of here, don't you? You rented out my room so I'd not have a place to come back to."

"It wasn't like that at all. I needed the money. I couldn't make enough by ironing to keep us going."

Clara picked up Kathleen's brush and flipped it over onto the bed. She pecked at the keys on the typewriter, pulled open the drawer in the table, and attempted to lift the lid on the trunk, but it was locked.

"What'd she lock the trunk for? She think you're goin' to steal somethin'?"

"You've no right to meddle with her things, Clara."

Clara ignored the rebuke. "You never kept it like this when I was here. Who is she? It is a *she*. I'd not be lucky enough for it to be a good-looking *he*."

"Her name is Miss Dolan, and she works for the newspaper."

"Now ain't that just a fine kettle of fish?" Clara brushed by her mother as she left the room.

Hazel closed the door and eased herself down onto a chair as if a sudden move might break her in two.

"What was I to do, Clara?"

"Oh, hell, I don't know. Whine, whine. It's all I ever get when I come back here."

"Then why don't you leave?" Johnny said quietly. "I'll take you to the highway."

"Oh, no, Johnny. Not before she sees Emily. It would break the child's heart."

"All you care about is that kid. Isn't that right, Mama?"

"That's not true. I—"

"—Mrs. Ramsey," Johnny interrupted. He had to get out of there before he shook the stuffings out of Clara. "Miss Dolan will not be here for supper. She asked me to tell you."

"You *feed* her, too," Clara spun around and glared at her mother who got to her feet and faced her angry daughter.

"I do what I have to do," she said firmly. "Miss Dolan pays for her meals if she eats here or not."

"She must pay pretty good. I saw a car out back when we drove up."

"It's Miss Dolan's car."

"She must be rollin' in dough."

"She's a nice lady, Clara. I won't allow you to be nasty to her."

"She took my room, for God's sake!"

"How long are you going to stay?"

"Is this my home or not? Should I write and ask if you have room for me before I come home?"

"I've got to be goin'," Johnny said. "But first I'd like a private word with Clara." He took her arm and propelled her out onto the porch and let the door slam behind them.

"Let go of me. You ain't got no right to be pushin' me around."

"I've always known, from the first time I saw you, that you are nothing but a worthless piece of shit. Until now I didn't know just how rotten you are. You go off and leave your mother to raise your child when that little girl is your responsibility. She's been workin' like a dog to keep food in that child's mouth. Then you have the guts to come back here and treat her like dirt."

"To hell with you." She jerked her arm from his grasp and tried to get back into the house, but his back was to the door. "You're not the boss of me. At least my kid ain't a half-breed. I didn't go out and screw some dirty Indian like your mama did."

"You're pitiful, Clara. You've got a mother who loves you and a little girl who thinks you get up every morning and hang out the sun. What do you do, but go whoring around and come back to them when you're broke. Has it ever occurred to you to come back here, get a job, and help your mother?"

"What kind of a job could I get around here? You think I'd go out to the tannery and work with the blanket-asses? Well, think again, Mr. Johnny Blanket-Ass Henry."

Johnny held his temper even though he ached to slap her.

"It's decent work. If not that, you could help your mother with the ironing."

"You may be surprised to know that I've been singing in a nightclub down in Fort Worth." Clara lifted her head and preened. "Ever'body thought I was really good. I just came home to get ready to go to Nashville and get on the Grand Ole Opry. When I'm a star, I'll come back here and ever'body in this shitty one horse town'll sit up and take notice of Miss Clara Ramsey."

Johnny shook his head. "You've got about as much chance of making it to the Grand Ole Opry as you have reaching up and touching the moon." He walked off the porch and headed for his truck. *Like Isabel, she wasn't going to listen to anything he said.*

"If you're so much, Johnny Henry," Clara called, "how come you're drivin' that old rattletrap of a truck?"

Johnny glanced over his shoulder at the girl with her skinny arms wrapped around the porch post. He tried to muster up some sympathy for her, but it just wouldn't jell. He thought of how his half sister, Henry Ann, had tried to reason with Isabel, and had offered her the opportunity to go to school and make something of herself. Isabel's mind, like Clara's, had been only on the pleasure of the moment.

Johnny started his truck and drove away wondering what was going to happen when Kathleen met Clara. One thing was sure. From now on, she'd better lock her valuables in her trunk when she left the house.

Chapter Seven

Johnny parked his truck behind the newspaper building and, with a bundle under his arm, went in through the back door. Paul was breaking down a page from last week's paper and throwing the lead into a bucket to be melted and reused.

"I'm going to leave my truck back here tonight, Paul. I took my groceries back to the store and will pick them up in the morning. The store will be closed by the time I'm ready to go home."

"You could've left them here."

"I never thought about it. I've never had anything taken from the truck, but I don't trust those two yahoos I took down to the sheriff."

"They're trouble all right." Paul dropped a handful of lead in the bucket. "There's a canvas cot over there in the corner if you want to sleep here. Pound on the door tonight, and I'll let you in."

"Thanks. Mind if I wash up here?"

"Go back to my room if you want. There's soap and water back there. There'll be no danger of your lady friend walking in on you while you wash that horse-hockey smell off."

"Thanks, *friend*. By the way, don't forget the two bits you owe me."

Paul's head swung slowly around. "That was for the picture show."

"You crawfishin' out of the bet?"

"The deal was to take her to a show." Paul's smile was smug. "Drag up enough courage to ask her out to a show, and the two bits is yours."

"To hell with you," Johnny snorted, and stomped off toward the partitioned room in the corner.

The room was nicely furnished with a neatly made bed, a bureau, and a long table on which sat a typewriter and two big radios with antenna wires running up along the ceiling and out the single window. Paul's clothes hung on a rod that spanned one corner of the room.

Johnny stripped off his shirt, poured water from a pitcher into a granite washbowl, and washed. He soaped his face and stared at his image in the oval mirror above the washbasin. Thank goodness he had shaved before he came to town this morning, although he hadn't expected to see Kathleen, much less take her out to supper. He borrowed Paul's comb and tried to tame his hair.

He pulled the new shirt out of the sack, shook it out, and put it on. He now regretted buying a white shirt. Kathleen would know that it was new. But, what the hell? Johnny slammed his hat down on his head and left the room. He paused just outside the door when he heard Kathleen's voice. She was showing Paul a two-page article she had written.

"Can we set the first four lines after the headline in ten point?"

"Sure. I'll set it tonight. If it isn't what you want, we can change it in the morning."

Kathleen hung the sheets of paper on the hook beside the linotype machine, turned, and saw Johnny.

"I didn't know you were here," she said, almost in an accusing tone.

"I came in the back door."

"I'll be ready to go as soon as I wash the ink off my hands, that is if you haven't changed your mind."

"I'm ready when you are."

Unaware that Paul was watching him, Johnny watched Kathleen. For days her image had stayed in his mind. Her fiery curly hair and her pretty face were enough to draw a man's eyes to her, but what riveted his attention to her now was her utter unawareness of just how striking she was. She accepted her good looks as being only a part of her, the other part being a woman completely at ease with herself and her abilities.

Johnny Henry, you don't have the brains of a loco steer or you'd get the hell out of here.

"Pretty, isn't she?" Paul murmured after Kathleen went back to the front office.

"You'd better not let Adelaide hear you say that!"

"She knows it. Sometimes beauty is more of a hindrance than an asset. Addie thinks you're just the man for Kathleen."

"Well, thanks for arranging my life. I don't agree. Now tend to your own business."

"She is my business, cowboy. What concerns Addie

concerns me. We're afraid that she'll be in deep trouble before she discovers how to get along in this town."

"She's already in trouble. Why do you think I'm sticking around? It was just luck that I found out that Webb and Krome bragged that she'd get what was coming to her before they left town. That could be tonight or tomorrow. I can take care of tonight."

"She's got a date with Leroy Grandon tomorrow night."

"Grandon? From the men's store? How do you know? She tell you?"

"Just because I'm back here doesn't mean I don't know what goes on up front."

"Shee . . . it. He's old enough to be her daddy." A chill held Johnny motionless for a long minute. "Webb or Krome'd chew him up and spit him out."

"Not if they got orders from higher up. They'd not want one of the merchants, the head of the Chamber of Commerce, to know. It might raise a stink."

"That's true." Johnny pushed himself away from the counter where he'd been leaning. "Guess we'll have to take one day at a time and see what happens."

Johnny had not concerned himself with the politics in Rawlings . . . up to now. He came to town a couple of times a month, and that was that. As far as he knew, it was a pretty peaceful town. The doctor ruled it with an iron hand in a soft glove. His friendship with Paul had opened his eyes to that. Adelaide, Paul, Claude, and the Wilsons were his only friends in town. He added Mrs. Ramsey as an afterthought. Other folks in town knew who he was because of the rodeo.

"Better get along, cowboy. It's six-thirty. Addie will shut the door and turn off the light soon."

"Yeah, I guess I better."

"A little advice, son. Don't pick your nose at the table," Paul murmured as Johnny passed him.

"You know what you can do with your advice, *Daddy*," Johnny growled, and Paul laughed.

Kathleen had been surprised to see Johnny in the back room. He had bought a new shirt. His dark skin against the white made him look incredibly handsome. She was still puzzled by the invitation. It was logical to assume that he intended to leave town as soon as he loaded his groceries. What had changed his mind?

Adelaide was busy typing when Johnny came from the back room. She looked up and nodded.

"Ready?" he asked Kathleen.

"I guess so." She got up from her desk. "See you in the morning, Adelaide."

"Have a good time."

Johnny opened the door, and Kathleen went out ahead of him. On the sidewalk, she paused, not knowing which way to go. He gripped her elbow and they started walking. It was almost dark. The time between sunset and nighttime was short this time of year.

"Let's try the Frontier Cafe? Have you been there?"

"I haven't been anywhere except to Claude's. We could go there for a hamburger. It's fast."

"Are you trying to get this *ordeal* over with?"

"I was just trying to be helpful," she said testily, thinking again of their encounter in the store. "I'm sure you're anxious to get home with your groceries."

"I left them at the store. I'll get them in the morning."

Johnny held tightly to her elbow as they stepped down off the curb and crossed the intersection. She had to admit that they walked well together, their steps matching. It was comforting to have him beside her. Her eyes darted back and forth; she half expected to see Webb and Krome lurking in the shadows.

They covered the three blocks to the café in almost complete silence. Its neon sign in the shape of a wagon wheel glowed in the twilight. Inside Johnny steered her to a high-backed booth, hung his hat on the hook on the end, and eased his long length onto the bench opposite her. Rather than look at him, Kathleen studied the box on the wall and read the selections available on the jukebox.

"See something you like?" Johnny placed a nickel on the table.

"Not really. It's all cowboy music."

"You're in cowboy country."

"Here's one that's quite appropriate—" she glanced at him to see him eyeing her intently—"Hoagy Carmichael's 'I Get Along Without You Very Well.'" She picked up the nickel, put it in the slot, and punched in her selection.

He ducked his head as if to avoid a blow. "Ouch! You're still mad."

"I'm not mad. It's not that important," she lied, unable to look at him.

"It is to me."

A young waitress with a perky red apron and headband

came to the booth with two glasses of water. She eyed Johnny with interest.

"We have hot beef with mashed potatoes or meat loaf with pork and beans."

They both ordered the hot beef. Kathleen asked for iced tea, Johnny for coffee.

The waitress gave Johnny a slant-eyed smile, then flounced away. In the backwash of silence that followed, Kathleen listened to the music. Johnny watched her. The hot Oklahoma sun had brought out a few more freckles. The rapid pulse at the base of her throat told him that she was nervous. That surprised him. To look at her, you'd think that she was as cool as a cucumber.

"I've a few things to tell you," he said softly.

Kathleen's eyes met his. "You had to bring me here to tell me? You could have said whatever you have to say at the office. You needn't have gone to all this trouble."

"It's no trouble."

"I should have said bother."

"It's not a bother either. You'd not understand if I tried to explain what happened at the store. I'll just say at the moment I thought it was the right thing to do."

Kathleen understood that that was the only apology she was going to get. She stared unblinkingly at him.

"I can take care of myself, you know. There's no need for you to feel obligated to look out for me because your sister is married to my uncle." She spoke quietly, but the very unexpectedness of her tone gave the words an abrupt, harsh quality.

"Get the chip off your shoulder, ma'am. You need

friends if you're going to stay in this town." Points of light flared in Johnny's dark eyes.

"Why, all of a sudden, are you interested in being my friend?"

"Let's just say that I changed my mind."

"Since I met Webb and Krome on the street? You didn't have to ride to my rescue. I could have handled them."

"Handle them my hind foot!" Air hissed from between his clenched teeth. "I want you to know that—"

He broke off speaking when the waitress came with their meal and placed a plate in front of each of them. The helping of mashed potatoes and the slab of beef on the white bread, both covered with steaming gravy, looked delicious. Kathleen stirred the small green lumps on the side of the plate with her fork.

"What's this?" she asked when the girl had left their booth.

"Fried okra."

"Never heard of it. Is it a vegetable?"

"Yeah. Grows on a bush like a green pepper. We grew a lot of it on the farm over at Red Rock. It's rolled in cornmeal and fried, or put in soup or cooked with tomatoes and onions. Try it."

"Humm—" Kathleen chewed and swallowed. "It's . . . ah . . . edible."

Johnny laughed. "You either like it or you don't. You don't have anything against potatoes, do you?"

"No. My Norwegian grandparents practically lived on potatoes. Have you ever had potato dumplings? Even though they are a Swedish dish, my grandmother made them as well as potato pancakes, potato bread, soup, salad, fritters, boiled potatoes, mashed potatoes, scalloped potatoes. She even made her yeast out of potatoes."

Johnny generously peppered his meal and Kathleen raised an eyebrow. He grinned at her.

"I don't suppose you used a lot of black pepper up there either."

"Not that much. This is good," she said after she had taken a bite, chewed, and swallowed. "I guess I didn't realize that I was so hungry. Up North we call this a hot beef sandwich."

"We call it that down here, too. Do you plan to go back to Iowa?"

"Nothing to go back to except a few acres of land. A neighbor rents it."

"I've heard that it gets pretty cold up there."

"It was thirty below for over a week in 1936. When it gets that cold, the ground freezes so hard and so deep that they have to use blasting powder to dig a grave. I was used to the cold and didn't mind it so much."

"I've not been any farther north than Kansas City. It was plenty cold there."

They ate in silence. Diners came in and occupied the booths on each side of them. Nickels were poured into the jukebox. "I'm an Old Cowhand from the Rio Grande" was a frequent choice. Kathleen gave Johnny a knowing look and smiled.

"I'm in cowboy country," she said.

Johnny found himself staring dumbly at the thick mass of curly red hair that brushed her shoulders. He had an almost irresistible impulse to reach out and bury his fingers in that glossy mane. He forced his gaze to wander away from her and out over the café. When she spoke, he turned to find her quizzically staring at him.

"You don't come to town very often, do you?"

"Only when I have to."

"Tell me about your ranch."

"It's just a little speck out there on the prairie," he said, and dismissed the subject. "Ready to go? I'll get the check."

"Are you sure we can't go Dutch. This isn't a date, so you're not obligated to pay for my supper."

A short dry laugh came from him. "I thought it was a date. I'm not so poor that I can't invite a *friend* out to supper."

"Now it's time for you to get off your high horse. I was just trying to make it easy for you in case you'd changed your mind . . . again."

"Let's get out of here. It won't do for me to shake you in front of all these people." He got up and waited for her to slide from the booth. "We can't talk in here."

Johnny paid the check, and they left the café. Night had fallen.

"I'll walk you home. I don't imagine you'd be too happy riding in that old truck of mine."

"So now you think I'm a snob."

"I didn't say that. I said . . . oh, forget it."

"I like to walk. It's a nice night, and I want to hear what you have to tell me."

Johnny threw caution to the wind, took her hand, and drew it up into the crook of his arm. He liked touching her, liked having her close to him as they walked. He liked being in the dark with her. He just wished his damn heart would stop beating so fast.

"I want to warn you about Webb and Krome. They were in Wilson's store bragging that they had a score to settle with you. I'd not put anything past them, so be careful. It's dark now when you leave the paper. Maybe you'd better drive your car up and park it in front of the office."

"Is that why you changed your mind and decided we could be friends?"

"No," he said abruptly. "Listen to what I'm telling you. Webb and Krome are out to get even with you. I think there's a connection between them and Deputy Thatcher. I don't know what it is, and I don't know if Sheriff Carroll is a part of it. But it's mighty fishy that he took the word of those two against ours and let them off the hook."

"Are they out to get even with you? You're the one who stopped them from hijacking my car. You're the one who marched them off to the sheriff's office."

Johnny snorted his disgust. "They're not sure how they'd come out in a fight with me. They might attempt to jump me. What they don't know is that . . . they'll get as good or better than they give."

"Webb had the nerve to ask me to go to a honky-tonk with them and learn the jitterbug dance."

"I suppose you told him you'd go," Johnny teased.

"Yeah. Sure. I've seen the jitterbug dance, and it isn't something I want to do. I like slow romantic tunes like 'Bury Me Not on the Lone Prairie' and 'Red River Valley.'"

"I thought you didn't like cowboy music."

"I was just being contrary. I get that way sometimes." Her soft laughter burst out unexpectedly.

Johnny chuckled. "Now, you tell me."

"I had to play 'I Get Along Without You Very Well.' That was too good to pass up. Considering—" She laughed again softly, teasingly.

"I'll remember that—about you being contrary."

They walked along in companionable silence. After a short while Johnny asked her what had happened at the sheriff's office. Kathleen told him about her encounter with the deputy.

"I couldn't believe the nastiness and arrogance of the man. He was insulting to me, to Adelaide, and to Paul."

Unconsciously Johnny pressed the hand in the crook of his arm tighter and tighter to his side as his anger at the deputy escalated.

"Did he threaten you?"

"Not directly. He said that they had better uses here in Rawlings for women like me than to tar and feather them and run them out of town."

"The son of a bitch!" Johnny tried to put a tight leash on his anger.

"After you and the sheriff left the office, we had a visit from Dr. Herman. He warned me about *brawling* on the street. Can you believe that? Brawling? He recited some of the town's history and told me about a woman with red hair like mine who was put in jail for attacking a woman on the street. She was . . . ah . . . well, she was a prosti-tute who had been with the woman's husband." Kathleen's giggle came out of the darkness and Johnny felt an unexpected surge of happiness within him.

"I told him she should have attacked her husband and kicked him in a place that would've stopped his whoring for a good long while. He didn't think it was funny. The doctor doesn't like me very much. He's not used to people talking back to him."

Johnny's hand came up to press the one tucked in the crook of his arm.

"Poor Adelaide,"—Kathleen continued—"he made some insinuating remarks about her and Paul."

"I don't know why they don't get married and be done with it."

"I think Paul is willing. He adores her. Adelaide worries that he is ten years younger than she is."

"What's the difference? It's their business."

"I'm glad you said that. It's what I think."

"Here's the school. Let's go sit in the swings. I've got more to tell you," he said, as if he needed a reason for prolonging their walk.

"Not more bad news, I hope."

It was a dark night. To Kathleen the stars seemed extra bright as she and the tall man beside her crossed the playground. She took her hand from his arm and sat down in a swing. She pushed with her feet, then lifted them.

"I haven't been in a swing since I left grade school." Moving behind her, Johnny pushed, his hands gentle in the middle of her back. After several minutes, her laugh floated to him on the night breeze. "Oh, Johnny, this is fun!"

She swung back and forth for several more minutes,

the only sound being the creaking of the swing. Holding tightly to the chains, she leaned back, and laughed up into his face. His hands went to her shoulders and he gave a gentle shove. Here with her on the playground, Johnny felt as though he was in another world. Aware that he must be vigilant, he tried to return to reality.

"The stars are so close and . . . so bright."

"Do you see the Big Dipper?"

"No. Where?"

Johnny caught her around the waist as she swung back, held her, and moved forward until her feet touched the ground. She stood, her face toward the star-studded sky.

"Where?" she said again.

He moved behind her, placed his hands on her shoulders, and turned her. Her hair brushed his chin. The sudden, delirious rush of joy was so acute his words came out in a breathless whisper.

"Look over the top of the school. See the chimney? Now straight up from there."

"I see it." She turned her head to look back at him. Their faces were inches apart. "Grandpa used to look at the stars. He showed me the Milky Way."

It came to Kathleen at that moment how glad she was that Johnny was with her; she felt so secure, protected, when she was with him. It gave her pleasure just to look at his tall erect body, shiny black hair, and quiet face.

They stood silently for a while, his hands still on her shoulders. It was a temptation not to close her eyes and lean back against him. The pressure of his hands turned her to face him. Her heart gave a choking, little thump, and she raised a tremulous gaze to his face.

"Are you tired walking? Would you rather sit in the swing while we talk?"

"I'm not tired. You said you had something else to tell me."

"Clara Ramsey came home. I saw her on the road when I went to tell her mother you'd not be there for supper." As they started walking, somehow his hand found hers and her fingers wiggled their way in between his.

"Emily's mother is back?"

"Clara's trouble, Kathleen. She had a fit because her mother had rented her room."

"Do you think I'll have to move?"

"Not if you like it there and can stick it out for a few weeks. Clara won't stay. Mrs. Ramsey needs the money you pay her."

"She's an old girlfriend of yours, isn't she?" The words spilled out as a keen disappointment that she didn't understand filled her.

Johnny stopped. The grip on her hand tightened. "What in the world gave you that idea?"

"Oh, little tidbits I picked up here and there." Kathleen would have walked on, but he held her back.

"I've seen that girl a total of a half dozen times. The first time was outside a honky-tonk. She was so drunk she could hardly walk. I put her in the truck and took her home. I think the next time was at a ball game, then at the rodeo. She reminded me of my half sister, Isabel, dumb as a clod of dirt and completely selfish. I felt sorry for her because she was so goddamn stupid."

"You don't have to explain anything to me."

"I think I do because you've probably heard that I was the father of her child. It's not true. I never touched that girl except to lift her into the truck when she was drunk, and another time when I came through town about midnight and found her sitting on the curb in front of the dry goods store. Someone had worked her over with his fists. I took her home. Later when she became pregnant, she told around that it was mine, but it was NOT." There was anger in his voice.

"I didn't mean to . . . pry into your affairs."

"You didn't pry. I realize that you don't know much about me."

"Or you about me. Tell me about your sister, Isabel. Where is she?"

"Oklahoma City, I guess. Be careful of Clara. She's only interested in what she wants and doesn't care who she hurts getting it. She's unreasonable and downright mean to her mother. You'd better put the things you don't want her rummaging through in your trunk and lock it when you leave the house. I don't trust her any farther than I could throw a bull by the tail. Poor Mrs. Ramsey has gone through hell with that girl."

Kathleen loosened her hand from his. He had held it so tightly it was numb. She put her hands on his upper arms.

"Rescuing damsels in distress seems to be a habit with you. I'm glad that I was one of them. I'll get along with Clara if . . . if she doesn't stay too long or push me too hard. That's as much as I can promise."

She looked up at him and smiled. Her eyes shone in the darkness. *Dear God, what has happened to me? A smile and a few soft words from this woman send my heart racing like a runaway train and my mind desperately groping to stay on the right track.*

From the first he had been attracted to her, much as he had been to other women from time to time. Suddenly it was amazingly clear to him that he was falling head over heels in love with this wonderful, magnificent, redheaded woman. Not that he would ever do anything about it. Still, he knew that she would be in his heart for as long as he lived. Some men lived all their lives and never met a woman who crept into their hearts. This one had come barreling into his, and he thanked God for the sweet memories this night would provide.

Chapter Eight

The music from the jukebox was loud, blasting into the heated shadows of the dimly lit room. It was not loud enough, however, to drown out the drunken laughter and crude shouts of encouragement to the two couples jitterbugging on the small dance floor. The air was thick with cigarette smoke, the odors of sweat and cheap perfume. The contortions of the two couples became wilder and wilder. Each time a man flipped his partner over his arm, showing her skimpy underpants, the crowd hooted and pounded beer bottles and glasses on the tables.

The dark eyes of the man standing in the doorway swept over the roomful of oil-field riggers and drillers and women with heavily made-up faces and tight dresses. This was a rough section of Oklahoma City. In polished boots, tailor-made fringed jacket and ten-dollar Stetson, the man stood out from the crowd, not only because of his dress, but because he was tall and broad. Well-dressed Indians were not uncommon in Oklahoma City. Oil had made some of them wealthy.

He waited for the dance to end and for the crowd to clear so he could approach the bar where the bartender was openly dispensing the 3.2 beer and filling beer bottles with whiskey under the counter. He had been told the girl worked here. He wouldn't know her if he saw her. He'd have to inquire.

He made his way along the side of the room, receiving plenty of glances from both the males and the females in the booths that lined the walls. As he stood at the end of the bar, the music came on again, and couples filled the small dance floor behind him, giving him a hemmed-in feeling.

"What'll ya have?" The bartender was thick-necked and meaty. He wore a dirty white apron and duck trousers. He had grizzled reddish hair and a thick red mustache. His eyes were small and suspicious as he looked at the tall man. "Got a little somethin' extra under the counter. Can get ya a case if yo're after that."

"I'll think about the case. Do you have a girl working here named Isabel Perry?"

"What's that little shit done now?" The bartender made a swift swipe at the scarred countertop. "Usually she's got one of the women after her for flirtin' with her man. She ain't interested in a man if he ain't tied to another woman. One of these days one of 'em'll split her throat."

"I'd like to talk to her if she's here."

"Oh, she's here. She was out there dancin' her head off. Now she's out back catchin' her breath so she can wait tables. What's she done? You the law?"

"I'm not the law. I'll pay for a half hour of her time if I can go back and talk to her."

"Okey-dokey, friend. Take the half hour, then tell her to get her skinny ass back in here."

The bartender's eyes bugged in surprise when he saw the five-dollar bill on the counter. He scooped it up, and the bill disappeared beneath his apron as he jerked his head toward the back door.

"What does she look like?"

"Blond and skinny."

"Thanks."

The back room was a jungle of beer and pop cases, discarded bar fixtures and litter. He edged his way through the maze to the back door, which stood open. The girl was sitting on the stoop smoking a cigarette. She looked up as he came out the door. In the light coming from the parking area, he recognized one of the dancers; a thin girl in a yellow dress. Her face was hard, her hair straw-colored.

"Are you Isabel Perry?" he asked, not waiting for her to speak.

"Who wants to know?"

"Barker Fleming." He waited to see if the name registered with her. When it didn't, he said, "Was your mother's name Dorene?"

"Yeah. Did someone die and leave her a million dollars? She's dead. Do I get it?"

"No one's left her anything that I know of. Do you have a brother?"

"Ya sure ask a lot of questions." She drew deeply on the cigarette and blew the smoke in his direction, then flipped the cigarette out into the night. She stood, peered up at him, then stepped behind him and turned on a light.

"Well, hello, Chief." She made a clicking sound with her tongue. "Are you the blanket-ass that knocked up Dorene a few years before the oil-field rigger screwed me into her, then took off like a scalded cat?"

Barker Fleming held on to his temper, pulled a silver cigarette case out of his pocket, opened it, and offered it to her. She took a cigarette and waited for him to flip the lighter on the end of the case. He lit cigarettes for both of them before he spoke.

"I'm not sure, Isabel. I was only with her a few times. A few months ago I ran into a fellow that told me she'd had a boy, part-Cherokee. Out of curiosity, I wondered if I'd dropped a colt somewhere."

The lie came easily to Barker Fleming. He had sensed immediately that telling this little floozy how long and how desperately he had searched to find his son would get him nowhere. Memories came flooding back. The little baggage before him was a copy of the woman who, almost old enough to be his mother, had flaunted herself before a naive eighteen-year-old Indian boy with a pocketful of money.

He didn't excuse himself. He had wanted what the woman had offered and had been too stupid to realize the consequences of his actions. Shortly after his wild fling with Dorene, his father had come for him and put him in a boarding school. At the time he had hated him for it.

"Henry's my legal name, but I never use it. Old Henry wasn't my pa. God only knows who was. I doubt if Dorene knew. She would've screwed the devil if he'd paid her." Isabel leaned up against the back of the tavern and drew heavily on the cigarette. "I'd probably better get back in, or Bud'll be havin' a cow fit."

"I asked the bartender for thirty minutes of your time."

"Bet ya had to pay him. He don't give nothin' for free. How 'bout payin' me? It's my time yo're takin' up. I could be in there makin' tips."

"I'll pay . . . if you tell me about the boy."

"Oh, I know about the holier-than-God son of a bitch. I could've got a third of Ed Henry's farm, but he sided with Henry Ann. She's Dorene's daughter by old Ed. The old man left the farm to her. The lawyer said that me'n Johnny was legal Henrys if Dorene was still married to Ed Henry when we was born. But Johnny wouldn't help me get what was ours. He honeyed up to Henry Ann. The two was thicker than hair on a dog's back."

Johnny Henry. His name is Johnny Henry.

"Is your brother still on the farm?"

"Naw. He's got a little piss-poor ranch over near Rawlings."

Barker could hardly contain his excitement. It had been difficult to trace a woman named Dorene who had lived in upstairs rooms on Reno Street and a disappointment to discover that she was dead. No one seemed to know what had happened to her son. Her daughter, too, had disappeared after she left an orphan's home at age eighteen.

The detective, who had been looking for her for almost a year, had notified him a week ago that he had found her working in a honky-tonk under the name Isabel Perry. Now in less than thirty minutes Barker had discovered his son's name and where he was.

"Do you ever see Johnny?" Barker asked casually.

"He came up here a couple of years ago and tried to correct my *wayward ways*." Isabel's laugh was dry and scornful. "He wanted me to come to his ranch and keep house for him. Can you beat that? I'd rather be dead than stuck out there on the prairie. I had enough of the sticks when Henry Ann dragged me back to the farm after Dorene died. 'Cause I demanded my rights, she sent me to the orphan's home. That damn Johnny let her! When I got out, I dropped the Henry name and took Dorene's maiden name."

And that's why it cost me five hundred dollars to find you.

"What'a ya want to find Johnny for? Good-lookin' as ya are, bet ya got by-blows all over Oklahoma. Looks like ya got money, too." Isabel plucked at the fringe on his leather coat. "Half the women out there"—she jerked her head toward the noisy tavern—"includin' me, would drop and spread for ya the minute ya took off yore hat."

Barker laughed, but he wanted to slap her face. "That's very flattering. My time's about up. I don't want to get you in trouble with . . . Bud." He took his wallet out of his inside pocket and gave her a bill.

"Wow! Twenty big ones. Thanks, Chief. That's the most money I ever made in half a hour. Anytime ya want'a talk again . . . or if ya get a itch that needs scratchin', look me up. I could show ya a trick or two that'd even cause old Dorene's eyes to bug out." She winked at him as she pulled down the neck of her dress and tucked the bill in her bra.

Barker Fleming waited until Isabel disappeared inside, then went quickly down the steps and around the building to his car. *Johnny Henry. Johnny Henry. Johnny Henry, Rawlings, Oklahoma.*

Kathleen and Johnny turned down the darkened street leading to Mrs. Ramsey's house. Kathleen wished that they still had miles to go. She had never spent a more pleasant evening. Her hand was snugly in his, their steps matched, as they walked in companionable silence. Johnny's voice broke the silence between them.

"You'll not forget what I told you about driving your car to work in the morning?"

"Do you think it's really necessary? It's only a few blocks."

"It'll be dark when you leave the office. You'll be safer in the car."

"The jugheads may have just been letting off steam."

"I don't think so. They didn't know Mrs. Wilson was listening."

"I'll have to start carrying a long hatpin." Kathleen laughed softly. "My grandma insisted that I carry one when I went to Des Moines to business school. She said that there was nothing that would get a masher's attention like a good poke with a hatpin."

"I think I'd like your grandma."

"She'd have loved you if you ate a lot. She liked to set what she called a *generous* table, and she liked to see a hearty eater. It's a wonder I wasn't as big as a moose by the time I grew up."

"I wouldn't have disappointed her when it came to eating. Henry Ann always said that she had to put plenty on the table, or I'd start in on the table legs."

A minute or two passed, then Kathleen said, "I don't like being afraid, Johnny."

"You'll be all right during the day. I'll worry about you at night." He drew her hand up into the crook of his arm and covered it with his. "If Webb and Krome had any brains, they'd get out of town and drop the matter."

"They'll not leave if they're getting paid to hang around."

"That's what I don't know . . . yet. I want you to be careful. Tomorrow I have to go down to the McCabe ranch and help drive the stock up for the rodeo. I can't be here tomorrow night."

"You don't have to feel responsible for me, Johnny. I've been taking care of myself for a long time."

"Maybe so. But you were not living in Rawlings, Oklahoma."

When they reached the house, it was completely dark. Johnny stopped near the porch steps.

"Thank you for dinner and for walking me home. I enjoyed it."

"Likewise. I'll be back in town in a—"

"Hi, Johnny." The voice came out of the darkness just as Clara stepped up onto the end of the porch. "Is this the *wonderful* Miss Dolan I've heard so much about? Well, kiss her good night. It's what she's waitin' for. Then we can go honky-tonkin'."

Johnny's throat clogged with anger, making it impossible to speak. Kathleen had no such problem.

"This must be the *wandering* Miss Ramsey. I've heard a lot about you, too, from a sweet little girl who wishes that her mother would stay at home and take care of her like other little girls' mothers do."

"Holy shit! The pussycat has claws."

"Believe it, sister. You scratch me, I'll scratch back."

"Clara?" Hazel Ramsey's quivery voice came from the doorway. "Please—"

"Don't worry, Mama. I'll not run her off. I've been waitin' for Johnny."

"It's all right, Mrs. Ramsey. I've had to deal with immature adults before. I'll not take anything she says seriously."

"Now ain't she just the cat's meow? She thinks that she's somethin'. Don't she?"

"Of course, I think that I'm *something*." Kathleen said. "I try to use common sense and good manners. I'll say good night. Thank you for the supper, Johnny, and for walking me home." She stepped upon the porch. "He's all yours, Clara."

Kathleen went into her room, paused just inside the door, and smiled when she heard Johnny's angry voice.

"Goddammit, Clara," he snarled. "Get in the house before I forget you're female and knock out a few teeth."

"Oh, goody. You're mad! I just love it when you're mad. That Indian face of yores—"

"—You're damn right I'm mad. Stay away from me, hear? I've done what I could for you, for your mother's and Emily's sake, not for yours. You're rotten, Clara. You don't deserve to have a mother like Hazel and a little girl like Emily. You're nothing but a millstone around their necks."

"John . . . ny." Clara sidled up to him and hugged his

arm. "Don't be mad. Let's go to town and have some fun."

"You stupid little twit! You didn't hear a word I said!"

"You can't like *her!* God, Johnny, she must be thirty years old. Sheesh! She's older'n you by a long shot."

"Shut up about her! And leave her alone, or you'll hear from me." He shook his arm free from her grasp and started down the walk toward the street.

"Clara, please," Mrs. Ramsey came out onto the porch. "Leave Johnny alone and come on in."

"You go in, Mama, and stop tellin' me what to do. John . . . ny—wait. John . . . ny—" Clara's voice became fainter as she ran down the street trying to catch up with the angry man.

Kathleen turned on the light, pulled down the window shades, and saw for the first time the table Johnny had lent her for her typewriter. It was perfect. Books and papers that had formerly been on the floor were now stacked neatly on the table beside the typewriter. She sat down on the edge of the bed and pulled off her shoes and stockings. Her feet hurt, and she had a big hole in the toe of her stocking.

In the doorway of the bathroom, she stopped and stared in anger and disbelief. Her bath salts were on the floor beside the tub along with her towel. The bar of scented bath soap she used so sparingly floated in the half-filled sink. A pair of lacy underpants, having evidently been washed with her scented soap, hung on the line Kathleen had strung to dry her hosiery.

"Miss Dolan." Emily's little voice came from the

doorway leading to the other bedroom. "I told her not to get in your things. Are ya mad?"

"Not at you, honey."

"I don't want ya to go." Emily had tears in her voice.

"I'm not going. Don't worry about it." Kathleen lifted the soap out of the water and placed it in the soapdish.

"I can't help it. Granny cried. Mama talked mean to her."

"We'll just have to make it up to your granny, won't we?"

"How?"

"We could take her with us to the rodeo."

"You're still goin' to take me?"

"'Course. I'm looking forward to it. We'll ask your granny to go with us."

"But not Mama?"

"I doubt that she'd want to go."

"She don't like it here. And . . . I don't care!" The little girl's lips trembled, but she held her head erect, determined not to cry. "She told me to get away and leave her stuff alone. I wasn't goin' to touch it."

The door banged and Kathleen heard Clara's angry voice in the other room.

"He ain't nothin' but a goddamn half-breed. He ain't no better'n them dog-eatin' redskins out on the reservation, but he thinks he is 'cause he's got that little old rinky-dink ranch and a beat-up truck. He must be hard up for a woman to take that . . . that freaky thing with the dyed hair."

"Don't talk about Miss Dolan like that. She's a nice woman. You ought to be ashamed, running after Johnny like you did. I'd think that you'd—" The radio suddenly came on so loud it almost shook the rafters. A few seconds passed, and it was switched off.

"Why'd ya do that for? I want to hear it."

"I want you to listen to me, Clara."

"It's all I've been doin' all my life. Listen to me, Clara. Do this, Clara. Do that, Clara," she mocked her mother's voice. "I wish to hell I'd never come back here."

"Why did you?" Mrs. Ramsey asked quietly.

"'Cause I need money, that's why."

"I don't have any money to give you. Emily and I just barely have enough to get along."

"I know where to get it without having to beg you for it."

"Where, Clara?"

"Wouldn't you like to know?"

"Yes, I would. You'll not bring any more disgrace down on Emily. She's suffered enough."

"What do you think I'm goin' to do, for God's sake? Open a whorehouse in the living room?" Clara let out a shout of laughter. "That'd jar the prissy Miss Dolan clear down to her dried-up old twat."

"I don't know what has happened to you. You were a sweet little girl and . . . pretty as a picture."

"I'm still pretty, Mama. Haven't you noticed? Men like me. Like me a lot. Rich or poor, they all like what I can do to them." Clara laughed at the shocked look on her mother's face. "I've got a rich one comin' up to see me in a few days. His folks has got a whole town named for them. Conroy, Texas. Ain't that somethin'? He don't know it yet, but he's goin' to take me to Nashville."

"You're never going to change, are you, Clara?"

"Why should I change, Mama? I have me a hell of a time when I'm away from this one-horse town."

"I'm going to bed. Keep the radio down. Miss Dolan gets up early."

"And if I don't?"

"I'll come out here and bust the tubes," Hazel said staunchly.

"Why, Mama," Clara said in surprise, then laughed shrilly. "Don't tell me you're gettin' some backbone?"

"You'll find out if you bring any more shame down on Emily."

"She's mine. I might take her with me."

"You won't. I'll not let you."

"Don't worry. You can have her. All she's done since I got here is whine. Where I'm goin' I don't need a kid hangin' around my neck. Did you hear me, Mama?" Clara shouted at her mother who had gone to the kitchen. "You can have her."

During the conversation between Clara and Hazel, Kathleen tried to keep Emily's attention on something else so the little girl wouldn't hear the hurtful words coming from her mother. She told her about Johnny swinging her in the swings at the school playground.

"It was such fun, Emily. You and I will have to go there some Sunday afternoon."

"Did you swing on the giant-strides? Marie Oden got hit in the head with one."

"Really? Hurt her bad?"

"Cut her head. But she's all right now."

"What's that big round tin thing on the side of the school?"

"The fire escape for the upstairs. We have fire practice and get to slide down it. It's dark and scary. We have a carnival and a spook house on Halloween. You can go down the fire escape if ya got a ticket."

"I'll have to think about it. I'm really a coward."

"Bet ya ain't."

"Bet I am." Kathleen heard Hazel in her bedroom and steered Emily toward the door. "I've got to take a bath, honey. See you in the morning."

"You ain't goin'?" Emily asked over her shoulder.

"Only to work in the morning."

Emily grinned a gap-toothed grin. "'Night, Miss Dolan."

"'Night, Miss Sugarpuss."

Chapter Nine

Before Kathleen left her room to go to breakfast, she locked her personal papers, her manuscripts and all her underwear and hosiery in her trunk, and her toilet articles, including her comb and brush, in her suitcase. All that was left in the room were her shoes, dresses, and coats.

Clara was asleep, sprawled on the couch, when Kathleen passed through the living room on her way to the kitchen. Hazel and Emily were at the table. Hazel jumped up.

"Sit down. I made your tea."

"Thank you. Good morning, Miss Sugarpuss. How would you like a ride to school this morning?"

"In the car?" Emily smiled, showing the big gap in her front teeth.

"In the car. I'm driving uptown this morning."

"Hear that, Granny?" The little girl had lowered her voice to a whisper. Without waiting for a response from her grandmother, Emily leaned toward Kathleen. "We whispered so we'd not wake Mama up."

"I wondered if there was something wrong with my

ears," Kathleen whispered back and stuck her finger in her ear.

Emily giggled. "I told Granny she could go to the rodeo with us."

"And I told you that I can't go." Hazel poured Kathleen's tea and set a plate of hot biscuits on the table.

"The *Gazette* has three tickets, Hazel."

"Won't Adelaide use one?"

"She said she'd just as soon skip it this year."

Kathleen drank her tea hurriedly and ate a biscuit with jam. She wanted to be gone before Clara got up. Emily was excited about riding in the car to school and was waiting at the back door when Kathleen came back after repairing her lipstick and putting on a light blue turban that matched her dress.

"You look pretty, Miss Dolan," Emily said.

"Thank you, and so do you."

Emily giggled and took Kathleen's hand. "'Bye, Granny."

"'Bye, honey. See you at noon."

Hazel stood on the back stoop and watched the car back out into the alleyway. She looked sad standing there. Kathleen had seen a tear on her cheek when they left, but Emily had been too excited about riding to school in the car to notice.

As soon as Kathleen entered the office, Adelaide wanted to know about her *date* with Johnny.

"It wasn't really a date," Kathleen said, taking off her turban and placing it on her desk.

"Looked like a date to me. He went out and bought a new shirt."

"He probably didn't want to go to supper in a shirt he'd worked in all day. You're making too much of it. He'd heard that the two men who tried to hijack me were going to get even because they had to go to the sheriff's office again. That's why he took me home."

"Does he think they might . . . attack you?"

"I don't know what he thinks they'll do, but he wanted me to drive the car up here so I'd have it to go home in."

"Good idea. Paul says he's got a crush on you."

"Paul's . . . crazy!" Kathleen felt heat on her cheeks.

"Why are you blushing?"

"I'm not," Kathleen protested, and rolled a sheet of paper into her typewriter. "I'm probably—Oh, never mind."

Good Lord, she had almost said that she was probably older than Johnny. Being conscious of the age difference between herself and Paul, Adelaide would have been terribly hurt. But Kathleen's age was what Clara had pointed out last night, and the taunt had stuck in her mind like a burr.

"How'd the big date go?"

Kathleen looked up to see Paul grinning at her.

"It wasn't a *big date!*"

"Johnny bought a new shirt."

"Paul, dear, I already mentioned that." Adelaide and Paul exchanged conspiratorial glances.

"All right, you two. Cut out the matchmaking."

Paul passed behind Adelaide and caressed the back of her neck.

He touches her every chance he gets, Kathleen thought as Adelaide smiled up at him. *Will anyone ever love me as much?*

"I told Johnny that you had a date with Leroy tonight. He didn't seem to be too pleased about it. It doesn't hurt to let a fellow know he's got a little competition." Paul winked at Adelaide and hurried into the back room.

"Oh, my gosh. I forgot all about Leroy Grandon. Sometime today I'll have to go home and tell Hazel that I'll not be there for supper."

For press day, the day went fairly well. Paul had two front page stories: one about Japan declaring that they would provide arms for Germany and Italy if it became necessary. The other story was about fifty-five thousand hungry people rioting in Pittsburgh. Kathleen was impressed, but she was not sure how many people in Rawlings were interested in what went on in Japan and in Pittsburgh. But it was good journalism, causing her to wonder once again about the man's life before he came to Rawlings.

"Paul thinks the war in Europe will spill over, and before long we'll be involved," Adelaide said after she had proofed the piece.

"Oh, I hope not. I don't know how the country could fight a war when we're having a hard time feeding our poor."

Hannah, the Indian woman Kathleen had seen the day she arrived, came into the office. She appeared dazed. Ignoring Kathleen, she went to Adelaide's desk.

"Hello, Hannah," Adelaide spoke gently.

"Baby."

"Is your baby with you?"

"Baby."

"Is it sick?"

"Baby."

"Where is your baby, Hannah?"

"Gone. Baby gone." She turned away and shuffled out the door.

Kathleen watched her as she passed the window. The skirt that came to her ankles was torn and dirty. The neck of her overblouse was torn and exposed one shoulder. The moccasins were so large that she had to shuffle in order to keep them on.

"The poor wretched thing." Adelaide shook her head sadly.

"Did her baby die?"

"I don't know. When she came in a month or two ago, she was as big as a barrel. The next time was the day you arrived. Her breasts were leaking and I asked about the baby. That was when she shoved me."

"Is she unbalanced?"

"She wasn't before she had the baby. She was a little strange but not like she is now. Grieving must be making her crazy."

The next person to come in was Earlene Smothers. She was huffing and sweating. The heavy coat of face powder had caked on her hairy upper lip.

"Adelaide," she wheezed, "I just saw that crazy Indian woman who roams around town. She was dirty, as usual, and muttering something. She should be put away. My goodness gracious! What's the world coming to when decent people can't walk the streets without running into trash like that."

"What can I do for you, Earlene? This is press day, and we're real busy."

"Not too busy, I hope," Earlene said, and sniffed peevishly. "I have something to add to the notice about the concession the First Baptist Church is going to have at the rodeo."

"What is it? I'll try to get it in."

"Add orange NeHi pop to the list of drinks. Ice cold, of course. Maude Ferman is in charge of the tubs of ice, and she says that we'll have room. I hope she's right after we've advertised."

"Oh, you want this in a paid ad?" Adelaide asked innocently.

"Heavens, no! Just add ice-cold NeHi pop to the notice. Surely you'll not charge us for that." The fat woman had a horrified look on her face.

"No. I'll see what I can get it in, but I'll have to hurry." Adelaide got up from the desk and headed for the back room. "Good-bye, Earlene."

"She'll *see* if she can get it in?" Mrs. Smothers echoed. "Who's boss around here? I thought she owned the place or is that . . . that person she took up with in charge now?"

Kathleen acted as if she were stone deaf and continued to type. As soon as the fat woman went out the door and passed the window, Adelaide came back into the office.

"She gets my hackles up," she explained as she sat back down at her desk.

"I know how you feel. Clara Ramsey got my hackles up last night."

"Is she back in town?"

"I'm afraid so. She is utterly self-centered and cares not a fig for anyone but herself. Poor Hazel. Clara had made herself at home with my soap, shampoo, bath salts, towels, and even my tooth powder. Little Emily apologized. This morning I locked everything in my trunk and my suitcase before I left."

"I wonder what she's doing back in town."

"She told Hazel she came back for money."

"I'm always afraid that Clara will talk Hazel into selling her house. Sam Ramsey worked like a dog to pay for that house so that Clara and Hazel would have a roof over their heads."

"I don't think that will happen. Hazel takes her responsibility for Emily seriously. She loves that child."

"Where will Clara get money in Rawlings? Everyone in town knows that she's a tramp."

At that moment, Clara Ramsey was leaving the house in a pout. Miss *Uppity-up* Dolan had stripped the bathroom, leaving only one ragged towel and a bar of Lava soap, and Mama had guarded the doors to the hussy's room as if it were a bank vault, giving her no chance to *borrow* a few things.

Clara picked her way carefully along the rutted road. The spike heels on her shoes were fragile. It wouldn't do to break one off before Marty got there. She would have worn her other shoes, but wanted the hicks in Rawlings to see her looking good. Her clinging pongee dress was blue with little black dots in it. She had used the curling iron on her hair, making high curls out of her bangs. Her lashes were heavy with mascara, her thin brows penciled, her lipstick bright red.

When Clara reached the street with a sidewalk, she tripped along making sure that her hips swayed so that the full skirt of her dress danced around her knees. She watched her reflection in the window as she passed the dry goods store. She looked damned good. No one would believe that she had a kid almost seven years old, but hell, she'd had her when she was sixteen. She'd make sure Emily stayed out of sight when Marty came. She had a surprise for him, and it wasn't Emily.

The Rawlings Medical Clinic was six blocks from the center of town. When Dr. Herman built it in 1919 right after the war, it was out in the country. Since then the town had expanded to reach it. Long and low and made of red brick, it sat slightly farther back from the walk than business buildings built later.

Clara was hot, and her feet hurt by the time she reached the clinic. She opened the door and stood for a minute beneath the cool breeze of the ceiling fan. Three of the four doors leading out of the small empty lobby were closed. The other was slightly ajar. Somewhere, far away, Clara heard the sound of a radio.

"May I help you?" A woman in a starched white uniform came silently into the lobby.

"I want to see Louise."

"Miss Munday is busy right now."

"Tell her to get unbusy. Clara Ramsey wants to see her."

"Have a seat. I'll tell her."

Like a shadow, the woman slipped back through the slightly open door. Clara sat down, reached down, and wiped the dust off her patent-leather pumps and picked up a week-old paper. She glanced at the headline, then looked to see what was playing at the Rialto Theatre.

"Wallace Beery in *The Champ*. Whoop-de-doo!" She tossed the paper aside, crossed her legs, and swung her foot back and forth impatiently.

"Come in here, Clara." The tone of Louise Munday's voice would have sent waves of apprehension through most young girls. Clara rose leisurely to her feet and followed the tall, stout figure into an inner office. Louise closed the door, turned, and said, "Sit down."

"Thanks," Clara said drily.

"What are you doing back in town? I thought you hated this place." Louise backed up to the desk, sat down on the edge, and folded her arms across her chest.

"I do hate this place. I came back because I need a hundred dollars."

"Who doesn't?"

"I doubt if ya do. Ya made plenty."

"What do you mean by that?"

"You know what I'm talking about. You told me never to mention it, and I haven't."

"You came to us, Clara."

"I was sick and pregnant."

"We helped you. Gave you money to get out of town. It's what you wanted."

"Well, I need a another hundred to get out of town again."

"You bitch! Six months from now you'd be back for another hundred. Is that the way it'll be from now on?"

"No. I'm goin' to Nashville and get on the Grand Ole Opry."

Louise rolled her eyes toward the ceiling. "I knew you'd be trouble. I told Doc as much."

"But I had somethin' ya wanted. Right?"

"And you had something you wanted to be rid of. It was a two-way street, Clara. You came to us. We didn't come to you. You'll get no more money than was agreed upon."

"I think I will. Do ya know who Mama's new roomer is?"

"Of course I do. Kathleen Dolan, the new partner at the *Gazette*."

"We . . . ll—"

"Are you threatening me?" Louise's breath quickened as she leaned forward and stared into Clara's face.

"No, but I can see headlines that'd shock folks outta their drawers." Clara reached up and fiddled with an earring. "I'm just tellin' ya that . . . I got things on my side."

"You rotten little slut. You're trying to blackmail me! I won't stand for it, and neither will Doc." Louise's heavy jowls turned red and quivered with anger. Her small red mouth was pressed into a thin line.

"So he knows what ya did? I didn't know *that*."

"Of course, he knows, you stupid little twit."

"He's got money. He owns half the town and wouldn't miss it if he gave me some."

"He's in Fort Worth and won't be back until Monday. In the meantime, keep your mouth shut."

"Monday? I can't wait 'round here till Monday." Clara jumped to her feet. "That's four days. I want to leave here tomorrow or the next day."

"That's just too damn bad." Louise went behind the desk. "Come back Monday, and I'll let you know what Doc has to say. Go on. Get out of here. I've got work to do."

A shrill scream came from another part of the building just as Clara opened the door.

"What's that?"

"What do you think you stupid little twit?"

"Someone's havin' a baby, and Doc ain't here. You're in charge."

The scream came again and was cut off abruptly.

"It's amazing how smart you can be . . . at times," Louise said sarcastically. "Get out of here and . . . if you breathe a word about anything, anything at all that happens around here, you'll wish you'd never heard of the town of Rawlings, Oklahoma."

"Ya ort to know, Louise, that I already wish I'd never heard of Rawlings, or you for that matter," Clara said sassily, and flounced out the door.

She walked out into the bright sunshine with the feelings that for once she had given Louise Munday something to think about. She and Doc would find out that Clara Ramsey wasn't a dumbbell like a few others she could name. Oh, well, if they didn't come through with the money, she had another card to play.

Marty, hurry up and get here.

Adelaide had finished stamping the papers to be mailed, and Woody loaded them in the coaster wagon to take them to the post office. The ancient press had cooperated, and they had not had a single clog-up to delay the run. Adelaide gave all the credit to Paul's knowledge of how to get along with the big, *dumb* machine.

"If Paul knew as much about the stock market as he does about that stupid press, we'd be rich." Adelaide placed a stop notice on the last stack of papers to be delivered in town and went to the back room to wash the fresh ink off her hands.

Kathleen sat at her desk, looked out the window and wished she hadn't made the date with Leroy. The paperboy came in, taking her mind off the evening for a moment. When she looked out the window again, a shiny black car pulled up and parked beside her Nash. A man wearing a light-colored Stetson was getting out. He was well dressed and carried himself like a man who knew where he was going.

Entering the office, he held open the door for the paperboy who was leaving with a bundle in his arms. Kathleen was surprised to see that he was an Indian, a very handsome Indian. She judged him to be in his middle or late forties. His dark hair was threaded with silver at the temples.

"Afternoon, ma'am. I'm looking for some information about the rodeo to be held here on Saturday. Do you have a list of participants in this issue?"

"The story is there on the front page."

He took a paper from the counter, placed a coin in the cup, and began to read. Kathleen noticed a large turquoise ring on his finger and, when his soft fringed jacket opened, a silver belt buckle. He was tall and broad-shouldered. While she was studying him, he finished reading, looked up, and smiled as if he were terribly pleased.

"Johnny Henry must be quite a cowboy," he said.

Kathleen had become used to the Oklahoma drawl. His accent told her that he had lived or had been educated in the East.

"I've been told that he's the best around here."

"You're not a rodeo fan?"

"I've not been here long enough."

He smiled. His teeth were white, his chiseled features perfect. In her other writings, Kathleen painted pictures of her characters with words. She hoped she could remember every detail of this man's face.

"You're from the upper Midwest. Let me guess. Minnesota."

"Close. I'm from Iowa."

"When I was young and foolish,"—he smiled—"I spent a couple of winters up on the Chippewa Reservation."

"I've not been that far north. Iowa was cold enough for me."

"I'm Barker Fleming."

"Kathleen Dolan." Kathleen held out her hand, and he clasped it politely.

"Pleased to meet you, Miss Dolan. It is *Miss*, isn't it?" She nodded, and he continued. "I'll be in town until after the rodeo. Perhaps I'll see you again. By the way, do you know Johnny Henry?"

"I know him, but not well because I've been in town only three weeks."

"Would you know where his ranch is?"

"It's west of here, I think. I can find out for you."

"That's all right. I was just curious." He folded the paper into a roll and clutched it in his hand. He smiled with his eyes, and little lines fanned out at the corners. "Would you be outraged at my audacity if I asked you to go to dinner with me. I'm harmless and not looking forward to an evening in a strange town."

Kathleen laughed. "I'm not in the least outraged. My Iowa grandma trained me to carry a hatpin should I have the need to defend myself. Thank you, but I've plans for dinner."

"I should have known. Lucky man." He put his fingers to the brim of his hat. "Nice talking to you, Miss Dolan."

"'Bye, Mr. Fleming."

Kathleen watched him get into his car. He was an interesting man, obviously well-off, and handsome enough to be a movie star. She was sure that she would've had a far more entertaining evening with him than with Leroy Grandon.

Adelaide came into the office. "Who was that? I was about to come in when I heard him ask you to dinner."

"His name is Barker Fleming. He was interested in the rodeo."

"He came in to buy a paper and ask you out to dinner. Fast worker. Did you say Fleming? That's a well-known name here in Oklahoma. If he's one of the Flemings from up near Elk City, he's not poor by a long shot."

"He was very nice as well as very good-looking."

Adelaide sniffed. "He was too old for you."

"He said something about spending a couple of winters on the Chippewa Reservation in Minnesota."

"If he belongs to the Oklahoma Flemings, he's a Cherokee. The story goes that Amos Fleming, a second-generation Scot, came out from Maine and married a Cherokee woman. They had a large family and he saw to it that all his children were well educated. A couple of them are doctors; some are teachers. They are very successful in business. I wonder if he's one of them?"

"He's staying for the rodeo. Maybe we'll find out. Oh, shoot! Here comes Leroy."

"He's dressed fit to kill. Maybe he's going to propose."

"Adelaide, I swear!" Kathleen put her turban on and pulled some of her hair around her face.

"Go right ahead, honey. If I had to spend an evening with him, I'd swear too. Hello, Leroy. My, you look nice. New suit?"

"No, no," he stammered, looking everywhere but at Kathleen. "Are you ready, Kathleen?"

"Sure, Leroy, and I'm hungry as a bear." Kathleen put her arm through his, smiled at Adelaide, and said gaily, "See you in the morning."

Walking down the street with Leroy was different from walking with Johnny. Because Leroy was no taller than she, she had none of the feeling of protection she'd had with Johnny. Realizing that the man was nervous, she chattered about this and that on their way to the only alternative to the Frontier and Claude's: the Golden Rule Restaurant.

They were directed to a table in the corner of the room.

It was covered with a white-linen cloth, and a vase held a single fresh rose. Leroy held her chair, and after he was seated, he pushed the vase across the table toward her.

"For you."

"For me? Why thank you." Kathleen leaned forward and sniffed the fragrant bloom.

Throughout the evening, Kathleen had to carry the burden of conversation. Leroy was a good listener, too good. She tried to talk about his duties as head of the Chamber of Commerce. He answered her questions and that was all. He perked up only when Barker Fleming came in. He spoke to Kathleen and was seated a few tables away.

"Who is that?"

"He was in the office today. His name is Barker Fleming."

"Fleming? What's he doing in Rawlings?"

"I don't know. He was interested in the rodeo. Do you know him?"

"I know who he is. Are you going?"

"To the rodeo? I'm covering it for the paper."

"Would you like to go out afterward?"

"I'm sorry, Leroy, but I've already made plans."

"Oh, well—"

After that he seemed to sink deeper and deeper into gloom and spoke only when she dragged a statement out of him. There were long stretches of silence. Kathleen was exhausted and wished fervently that the movie they were going to was short and so that she could go home to bed soon.

I'm sorry for you, Leroy. I know you're lonely, but please find someone else and don't ask me out again.

The offices in the front of the clinic on the edge of town were dark, but lights were on in the back and a car was parked beneath the portico. Louise Munday opened the door for a couple leaving the clinic and bade them good-bye. She waited until the taillights of the car disappeared around the corner of the building before she went back inside and locked the door.

A woman in a white nurse's uniform came from one of the rooms along the hall. She closed the door softly behind her.

"Everything all right?" Louise asked.

"She's sleeping."

"Good. You can go home."

Louise continued on down the hall to her office, went inside, and locked the door. After turning on the light and making sure the shades were drawn, she placed an envelope in the safe.

Later she sat at her desk and picked up the phone.

"Flossie, get me the Biltmore Hotel in Oklahoma City."

"Isn't that where Doc Herman is staying?"

"Get me the hotel, Flossie, and don't listen in."

"Forevermore, Louise! It makes me mad when you say that. It's against Bell policy to listen in and you know it."

"I know it, and don't you forget it. Get the number."

Louise had been in a state of agitation since Clara Ramsey's visit. How dare that little slut threaten them?

Their dealings with her had been a pain in the butt from the start. If she spilled her guts to that smart-mouthed redhead from the *Gazette* they could be in for some real trouble.

While she waited for the connection, Louise fumed about the lack of dial telephones in southwestern Oklahoma.

"Hello. Ring Dr. Herman's room." After three rings the doctor answered.

"It's Louise, Doc. When will you be back here?"

"Why are you calling? Is something wrong?"

"I have someone here who needs your attention, and I want to know when you plan to be back."

"Is it urgent?"

"It could be."

"And you can't take care of it?"

"I could, but I need your advice."

"If it's critical, I could come back tomorrow. You know that this meeting is important to me."

"I don't want you to cut your meeting short." Louise's tone softened. "You've looked forward to the conference."

"It's an important meeting, Louise. I told you that before I left."

"Don't worry about it, Doc. I can handle things here until Sunday."

"Are you sure?"

"I'm sure, Doc."

"I knew that I could depend on you. See you Sunday."

After Louise hung up the phone, she muttered, "Shit, shit, shit!"

If not for the possibility that Flossie was listening in, Louise could have explained the situation more clearly to Doc. One thing was certain—if she had to, she could take care of the little tramp herself.

"Is something wrong, Darrell baby?" The woman sat up in bed and leaned back against the headboard.

After Dr. Herman hung up the phone, he went to sit beside her. It gave him a warm intimate feeling when she called him by his first name. She was one of the few people who did. Almost everyone called him Doc, even his two sisters who lived in Ponca City. He pulled down the sheet and stroked the tops of her full breasts.

"Nothing that will take me away from you, Mommy." He spoke in a little boy voice and bent to her breast, took the nipple into his mouth, and suckled lustfully.

"Then come back to bed, baby." She held out her arms. "Mama will hold you."

With little whimpers, he settled across her lap and took her nipple into his mouth again. She wrapped him in her arms and, while she rocked him, he sank his nose into her soft flesh and closed his eyes contentedly.

"Sing to me, Mama."

The woman sang softly. *"A tiny turned-up nose. Two cheeks just like a rose. So sweet from head to toes—this little boy of mine."* She rocked back and forth, smoothing the hair back from his forehead. "Be a good boy," she whispered. "Be good or mama will spank."

"I be good, Mommy." He spoke around the nipple in his mouth.

After a while he reached for her hand and carried it into the opening of his pajamas.

"Want mamma to make you feel good, baby?"

"Uh-huh."

The woman held him, playing the part of his mama and his lover. He was the strangest of all her regular clients. They had been in this room since last night playing the game of mama and baby. Her nipples were sore. She hoped that he would reach completion soon and go to sleep.

Each time he came to the city, which was every month or so, he called her, and she was glad to play the part he required for the money he paid her.

Chapter Ten

Kathleen parked her car behind the house and went through the kitchen to her room. The radio was on in the living room. Clara sprawled in a chair filing her nails. Hazel sat in the rocking chair with Emily on her lap. The child looked as if she had been crying.

"Ya been workin' all this time?" Clara asked.

Kathleen ignored her and spoke to Hazel. "I think I'll take a bath and go to bed."

"Ya'll have to light the tank." After making that statement, Clara reached over and turned up the volume on the radio.

Smiling her understanding to Hazel, Kathleen went to her room, turned on the light, and closed the door. What a shame that such a sweet, gentle woman had a daughter like Clara! She would get latches to go on the inside of two of her doors of her room and a lock and key for the outside door. It would not surprise her in the least if while she was out, Clara prowled through her belongings.

Kathleen kicked off her shoes and, making sure the shades were drawn, pulled off her dress and went to the bathroom to light the burner beneath the water tank. It would be fifteen minutes before the chill was off the water.

While she waited, she took her manuscript and paper supplies out of the trunk. A letter to her publisher was long overdue. She rolled a sheet of paper into her typewriter and typed rapidly.

Dear Mr. Wilkinson,

STAGECOACH TO HELL, my story for the March edition of Western Story Magazine, will be in the mail the end of October. Since my move to Oklahoma, I have been unable to keep to my former schedule as getting settled into my new situation has taken time.

Let me assure you that GRINGOS DIE EASY, the story contracted for the June edition, will be in your office as scheduled.

Sincerely,

Kathleen Dolan
(K.K. Doyle)

After she signed the letter and addressed it, she took a quick bath, put on her night dress, and began to read the last few pages of her manuscript, despite the distraction of the loud radio in the next room.

"He jumped into the open, and dust spurted from his hat as a bullet slammed through it. His own gun spit fire. Durango yelled in sudden pain, and Frisco heard his body hit the ground. The Mex howled and swore as hot lead drilled a furrow along his ribs.

The blazing guns roared, throwing bullets in every direction.

Frisco aimed squarely at the crooked sheriff's breast and heard the hammer fall on an empty cartridge. He whirled around while he was still sheltered by—"

The volume of the radio in the next room was suddenly raised to a level that almost rattled the windows. Concentration was impossible. Kathleen put away her manuscript, turned out the light, and went to bed.

She would see Johnny on Saturday at the rodeo. Would he be cold toward her as he had been at the grocery store or as companionable as he had been on the walk home? At this time last night they were in the school yard and he was swinging her. She remembered how his arms had felt when they circled her waist to stop the swing. For an instant he had held her tightly against him. She would not have minded at all if he had kissed her. She had wanted him to.

Heavens! She was acting like a love-starved old maid. She'd had brief romances from time to time, but none of them had touched her deeply. The men had kissed her and held her close, but that was as much as she would allow. When the episodes were over, she'd not given them a second thought. She would have to be careful this time. A man like Johnny Henry could break her heart.

Long ago her grandma had said when her daughter and Kathleen's mother died, "If there were no heartaches, how would we know when we were happy?"

Kathleen lay for what seemed to be hours with her pillow over her head in an attempt to blot out the blare of the radio. Her mind refused to let her sleep.

Hazel was apologetic at breakfast.

"She won't stay long, Miss Dolan. She never does."

"Don't worry about it. Let's just wait and see what happens. By the way, I'll not be here for supper tonight. Where is Miss Sugarpuss this morning?"

"She's still sleeping. I'm going to let her skip school today."

"Is she sick?"

"Heartsick," Hazel said, and turned away.

Kathleen drove to work and left her car on the street in front of the *Gazette*. Today she planned to go to the courthouse and ask to see the delinquent tax records so that she could do a story on how many farms had been lost since the start of the Depression.

After she finished her "Yesteryear" column and hung it on the hook beside the linotype machine, she put on her hat and walked quickly up the street to the courthouse. She entered the building, and was surprised to see that every door was closed. Looking at her watch, she discovered it was noon and decided to go to Claude's for lunch while she waited for the offices to open.

Kathleen left the redbrick building, and as she passed through the arch of deer antlers that covered the walk, she came face to face with Deputy Thatcher. Standing beside him were Webb and Krome.

"Well, looky here, Ell. If it ain't the sassy redhead from the *Gazette*. Reckon she'll take our picture and put us in the paper?" Webb leered at her and moved to block her path when she attempted to go around the trio.

"Only if a buzzard flies down and scoops you up," Kathleen said scornfully.

"Ain't she a corker, Ell? Swear to goodness, she's more fun than a two-tailed monkey."

"Get out of my way, you dirty lout. I've nothing to say to you."

"Don't be in such a yank, Katydid. The law has stopped ya for a little chat. Least ya can do is be mindful of the law." Ell spit a mouthful of tobacco juice into the grass beside the walk.

Kathleen shuddered with revulsion. She had forgotten about his small eyes and receding chin.

"Law?" she said scornfully. "That's a joke. You're a joke."

"Watch yoreself, girl. Ya could find yoreself back there in my jail for a week eatin' bread and beans."

"Are you threatening to jail me? On what charge? Because I refuse to socialize with you? I'll tell you something, you two-bit yokel. Mess with me, and you'll find yourself in a jail cell."

"Well, golly-bill. Listen to that. What's all them big words she spoutin' mean?"

"We've had city people come down here crowin' before. It never got 'em nowhere."

"Have you ever heard of Alfalfa Bill Murray?"

"'Course I have, honey. Who in Oklahoma ain't? When he was governor he plowed up the ground 'round that big old mansion in the city and planted taters." The deputy grinned cockily and winked at his two friends.

"He did that and gave the crop to the poor. He's a good man, but he'll be hell on wheels when he finds out his only granddaughter has been threatened with jail by a two-bit deputy who doesn't have enough respect for his job to wear a clean shirt while on duty. If you annoy me again, my grandpa will be on you like a duck on a june bug."

The laughter went out of the deputy's eyes, and they turned mean.

"Ya think yore pretty smart."

"Smart enough to know a big blowhard when I meet one." Kathleen raised her chin in a superior manner, stepped around them, and proceeded down the walk. Her feeling of triumph faded when Krome and Webb caught up and flanked her.

"Ell wants to be sure ya get on down the street and ain't bothered by nobody."

Kathleen seethed as they crossed the street. When they stepped up onto the walk again she stopped and turned on them.

"Get away from me," she hissed. "Get away now, or I'll scream my head off. There's enough good men in this town to hang you if I say you're threatening to rape me."

"Why'd ya want to do that?" Krome held up his hands as if to ward off a blow. "We're bein' gentlemanly. Ell told us to look after ya, and it's what we're doin'."

"I'm game if'n it's what she wants to do," Webb smirked.

"You're disgusting," Kathleen said angrily and walked away. They followed. One of them touched her arm.

"Now wait, hon—"

Kathleen whirled around and balled her fist. "I'll hit you again if you don't get away from me!"

"Ya do, and ya'll go to jail fer brawlin' on the street." Webb giggled.

"Miss Dolan." Big and solid, Barker Fleming stepped out of a doorway and moved up beside Kathleen. "May I walk with you?"

"I would appreciate it."

"There's not room on the walk for all four of us." Barker faced the men. The difference between them was vast. The two men looked as though they had slept in their clothes for a week; they each needed a bath and a shave. Barker Fleming was well-groomed and confident. "You two run along. I don't want to hurt you."

"And if we don't?" Krome felt brave. He'd glanced down the walk to see the deputy watching.

Barker's hand came out of his jacket pocket. The knife in it suddenly produced a blade.

"If you don't want to be friendly, my friend here and I will have to do a little persuading. Get the picture? I'd mop up the street with your mangy hide, but I don't want to get dirty." Barker spoke as matter-of-factly as if he were talking about the weather.

Webb backed away. "She . . . it. He ain't nothin' but a breed," he said loudly when he was a safe distance from Barker.

"Come on, ya fool!" Krome hissed. They went back down the street where the deputy waited.

Barker looked down at Kathleen. "That takes care of that."

"Thank you."

"I'm on my way to get a bite to eat. Join me?"

"I'd love to."

"I like a woman who makes fast decisions."

At the Golden Rule Restaurant, they took a table at the end of the room. Barker placed his hat on the empty chair. His thick black hair, with gray threads at his temples, sprang back from his forehead and hung to the collar of his jacket. His Indian heritage was very evident.

"I had a good meal here last night," he said, and handed her the menu. She glanced at it and handed it back.

"A sandwich will do for me."

While waiting for their order, Kathleen smiled into the dark eyes observing her.

"I wish you could have seen the deputy's face when I told him I was the granddaughter of Governor Alfalfa Bill Murray. I was lucky the dumb cluck knew who I was talking about."

"Are you really related to Alfalfa Bill?"

"Heavens no! I was reading about him in the 1932 edition of our paper this morning as I prepared for my 'Yesteryear' column. As governors go, he must have been an unpredictable character. I just threw in about being his granddaughter to see if it would work. It did."

"I'll have to keep that in mind. I wonder whose grandson I could be."

"You'd have any number of good ones to pick from." They laughed together like old friends.

"Now tell me why the men were annoying you."

"It's a long story. I'm not sure we have the time."

"We can start it now and finish at dinner." He watched

her, concern pressing two little grooves between his eyebrows.

"I'd be glad for company for dinner. I was going to eat alone." She picked up her fork and made little dents in the tablecloth.

"Good. It's a rare woman who can make up her mind so quickly." They smiled at each other. "Six o'clock all right? I'll pick you up at the *Gazette*."

"Tell me about your family." It was amazing how comfortable they were with each other.

"My business keeps me away from home much of the time, I miss them."

"I'm sure that they miss you, too."

"I have four beautiful daughters and two sons. One daughter is at the university, one in high school, two in grade school, and my boy started school this year." There was pride on his face and in his voice when he talked about his children.

"You said you had two sons."

"My eldest is a rancher. Ah . . . here comes our meal. Are you sure that will hold you until dinner?" he said, looking at the small sandwich on her plate.

"It will be plenty." Kathleen noticed the interested glances the waitress had given Barker. He was an exceedingly attractive man who would radiate confidence if he stood barefoot and ragged. His eyes were as black as the bottom of a well. Deep crinkly grooves marked the corners, put there when the eyes had squinted at the sun. There were other lines, too, that experience had made.

"I was an only child," Kathleen said after the waitress

left them. "I think it would be lovely to belong to a big family."

"My mother was Cherokee. Cherokee take great pride in their children. I lost my wife five years ago, so I am both mother and father to my brood."

"Oh, I'm sorry."

"It's a fact we all have to deal with sooner or later."

"I understand that. I've lost my parents and the grand-parents who raised me. But I'm grateful that they instilled in me the ability to take care of myself."

"You were doing a fair job of it out there." He nodded toward the street. "Where was that hatpin your grand-mother gave you?"

"You remembered that?"

"Of course. Now tell me why the deputy and his cronies picked you out to pester, or do they pester all the pretty women in town."

"It started even before I got to Rawlings." She told him about working in Liberal and driving across country to Rawlings. "About five miles out of town a car was parked across the road. I knew they were hijackers. I tried to back up and ran into the ditch." Barker was an easy man to talk to. He gave her his full attention and nodded from time to time.

"I was too mad to be scared. They took my money, then had the nerve to want me to help push the car out of the ditch."

"They robbed you? Why aren't they in jail?"

"They told the sheriff they were helping me get my car out of the ditch and the twenty dollars they had was the money that I had paid them. He said it was their word against mine. I don't know what would have happened if Johnny Henry hadn't come along. He *persuaded* them to give my money back and sent them on their way. Johnny knew who they were and turned them in to the sheriff, but the sheriff let them go."

"Do you know Johnny Henry?"

"I've met him a few times." Kathleen felt the slight flush that covered her cheeks at the mention of the man who had occupied her thoughts of late, and she took a drink of iced tea before she continued. "He rescued me again the other day. Johnny said their names are Webb and Krome. I'd met them for the second time on the street. They were smart-alecky like they were today, and my temper got away from me. One of them took hold of me, and I hit him in the mouth with my fist." Kathleen laughed nervously. "I'd like to say that I've never done such a thing before, but I have. My grandma said I didn't get this red hair for nothing. I hurt my knuckles when I hit him, but it was worth it."

Barker had stopped eating and was watching her. She was a lovely girl. Her eyes were as blue as the sky. A spattering of freckles spread across her nose. Her face wasn't covered with a lot of powder and paint. She blushed so prettily, something women seldom did these days.

"Johnny took them to the sheriff," Kathleen continued, unaware of Barker's intense interest. "The sheriff let them go again and then had the nerve to come down to the *Gazette* and accuse me of brawling on the street because I hit the man."

"Strange action for a sheriff. Could be that someone is pulling his strings."

"Doc Herman, I imagine. He runs the town. Nothing happens around here that he doesn't know about. He came in on the heels of the sheriff and lectured me about *brawling*. Goodness gracious, how I have gone on. I shouldn't be laying out the town's dirty laundry to a visitor."

"Most towns have dirty laundry of some kind or the other."

"This one's got an extra share."

"I'm glad that you've got someone looking out for you."

"Johnny just feels responsible for me. His sister, Henry Ann, over in Red Rock, is married to my Uncle Tom. I don't think Johnny wants to bother with me, but feels obligated."

"Any man, if he's worth his salt, would jump at the chance to *bother* with you. You're a pretty girl. Is Johnny married?"

"No. Not that I know of. He made me promise to drive my car to work so that I'd not have to walk back to my room. It's usually dark by the time I leave the paper."

"Do you like him?"

The blunt question caught Kathleen by surprise, and her cheeks reddened. She found she wasn't offended by the personal question. Barker was different from any man she had ever met. She liked him, just as she knew she would when he first came into the office.

"Of course. I'd be foolish *not* to like him after he rescued me twice."

Barker glanced at her from beneath heavy eyebrows,

and genuine amusement quirked his mouth. His dark eyes warmed.

"He'd be foolish not to like *you*."

"He may like me as a friend, but that is all. I'm probably older than he is."

"I'd guess you to be about twenty-four or five."

"Twenty six as of a few weeks ago."

"A mere youngster. If Johnny doesn't set his cap for you, he isn't as smart as you think he is. Will you be at the rodeo?"

"I'll cover it for the paper."

"Maybe I'll get a chance to meet Johnny Henry."

"He'll be the star of the rodeo, so I'm told."

"Is there anything serious between you and Mr. Grandon? Oh, yes I found out who he was when I went into his store this morning to buy some handkerchiefs."

"Heavens no!"

"I didn't think so. You looked rather bored last night."

"Did it show? I wouldn't hurt Leroy's feelings for the world."

"I rather think that he realized that the two of you were not compatible."

Kathleen waited while he paid for the meal. "Thank you for the lunch," Kathleen said when they reached the sidewalk. "Tonight we go Dutch."

"Dutch? What's that?"

"We each pay for our own."

"How times have changed. I'm not sure my gentlemanly instincts will allow that."

"You have all afternoon to prepare for it. I'd better get back to work. I'm going to do a feature on the many farms in Tillison County that have been repossessed since the start of the Great Depression. I'll head on down to the courthouse to see the records."

"I'll walk with you. I have business there, too."

At the courthouse, Kathleen said good-bye to Barker and turned into the county recorder's office, but not before she heard a booming voice call out Barker's name.

"Barker Fleming, you son of a gun. What are you doing in Rawlings?"

"Hello, Judge Fimbres. Got a few minutes?"

"For you, Barker, I've got as much time as you want. Come in. Come in and tell me about the family."

Chapter Eleven

Johnny sat on the top rail of the corral with his friend Keith McCabe and looked over the tired stock feeding on the hay being pitched into the pen from the hay wagon.

"Good-looking bunch, Keith.

"A little weary from that long drive."

"Thirty miles is just a waltz around the block for that bunch. Some of them are wilder than a turpentined cat."

"Yeah." Keith grinned, threw his cigarette butt on the ground, stepped down from the rail, and ground it into the dirt with the toe of his boot. "You better hope ya don't draw that long-legged piebald over there; you'll have your work cut out for you. That sucker'll throw you from here to yonder."

"That'd tickle you plumb to death, wouldn't it?" Johnny moved down from the rail to stand beside him.

"Don't worry, sissy-boy, I'll be riding pickup." Keith, an inch taller than Johnny and quite a few pounds heavier, slapped him hard on the back. Johnny pretended to stagger.

"They're gettin' hard up for pickup riders, if ya ask me."

"What'er ya talkin' about, Johnny-boy? I'm the best pickup man in the state of Texas. Don't worry. I'll get to you before he stomps your pretty face into the ground."

"I'd be obliged," Johnny said drily.

Keith McCabe, a rancher from just over the line in Texas, was Johnny's best friend and one of the few who knew about his occasional activities with the federal marshals. Keith was also a good friend of Hod Dolan and his wife Molly. Molly and Ruth McCabe had been childhood friends in Kansas.

"When's Ruth coming up?"

"She and Davis will be here tomorrow. She'd not miss the rodeo especially if you're ridin'."

"How old is Davis now?"

"Two and a half years now. His baby sister should be here by Christmas."

"You certainly are a busy man. It's a wonder you've got time for ranchin'."

"Important things come first, boy. You'll find that out when you have your own woman. When are you going to find a pretty little gal and tie the knot?"

"When I get to be as old as you . . . say twenty, thirty years from now."

"Hey, I don't top you over ten years, if that much."

"If you're so young, why'd you quit rodeoin'?"

"I can give you a two-word answer to that question. *My wife.*" Keith was deeply in love with his wife, and his eyes always lit up when he talked about her and his son.

"Henpecked already, huh?"

"You bet! The year we married I entered the bull-riding contest over at Frederick. The crazy bastard I drew was meaner than a longhorn with his tail tied in a knot. After he threw me, he tried to stomp me to death. Ruth was mad at the steer but madder at me. It didn't matter that I was limping around on crutches; she ripped me up one side and down the other. She said that if I got myself killed, she'd be so mad she'd not go to my funeral and, what's more, when our boy was born, she'd name him Horsecock McCabe. That did it. I couldn't have my boy going through life named Horsecock."

Johnny whooped with laughter. "That sounds like Ruth."

"Yeah. She's a ring-tailed tooter when she's riled up," Keith said proudly. "I know which side of my bread is buttered. I quit rodeoing before she took off a patch of my hide."

"I saw your favorite relative on the way up here," Johnny said.

"Who's that?"

"Marty Conroy. Your cousin from Conroy, Texas. The little turd with the big head, the loud mouth, and shit for brains."

"Good Lord! Was he coming here? I haven't seen the little pipsqueak for a year. Every time I see him, he's trying to hang a big get-rich-quick scheme on me."

"We were on the road between the Kimrow and Dryden ranches when he pulled up behind us in his fancy car. He didn't have any more sense than to honk the horn and spook the herd. Old Potter, riding drag, had to go chase a half dozen head. He cussed a blue streak and threatened to horsewhip Marty if he blew that blasted horn again. I know it about killed the little blowhard to have to tag along behind, eating dust, until we made the turn."

"Marty likes to throw around the Conroy name. It doesn't mean squat except in Conroy, Texas. He thinks he's big-time, but lately he's come down a peg or two. The trustees of his granddaddy's estate are tightening the purse strings. It could be that the trust is about to dry up, and he'll have to go to work. Wouldn't it be a cryin' shame if old Marty had to do a day's work?" Keith grinned devilishly.

"Yeah, it would. I'd feel downright bad about it." Johnny beat the dust from his hat by hitting it against his thigh, then slapped it back down on his head. "I should get on out to the ranch and see about my own stock."

"Let's find a place to wash up, and I'll treat you to supper before we head out to your place for the night."

"Sounds good. I didn't want to cook for you anyway."

The instant he and Keith walked into the Golden Rule Restaurant, Johnny saw Kathleen seated at a table in the back of the room. The light above her head turned her hair fiery red. All that registered in his mind was that she was wearing something blue and laughing with the man she was with. He had thick black hair, was wearing a light doeskin jacket, and giving her all of his attention.

Wishing that he could turn around and go back out but knowing that if he did, he'd have to explain to Keith, Johnny led the way to the farside of the room. He unintentionally sat at a table against the wall that gave him a side view of Kathleen and her friend.

Trying not to let it show that his gut had knotted

painfully at the sight of her with another man, Johnny pretended to study the menu.

"What do you usually have here?" Keith asked.

"What? Well, I don't usually eat here. This is a little too fancy for me. I grab a hamburger at Claude's when I'm in town," he said gruffly.

"It'll not hurt you to get the manure off your boots once in a while." Keith turned to the waitress who was hovering at his elbow, smiled, and winked. "I want a big, thick steak, honey, some biscuits and gravy. Coffee, too."

"Give me the same." Johnny slapped the menu down on the table.

The overweight waitress glanced at Johnny then fixed her gaze on Keith, as she had been doing since they walked in the door. When Keith spoke to a woman, if she was sixteen or sixty, he gave her his full attention.

"What?" he said to Johnny when he saw him scowling after the departing waitress.

"I was just wondering if that woman was going to sit on your lap or go get our food." Johnny's gaze went again to the waitress, who was still watching them.

"She was nice and doing a good job. I made her feel good. What's wrong with that?"

"Nothing, if Ruth doesn't mind."

"Ruth knows I love her. She'd not mind me flirting a bit with a girl who needs to feel for a minute or two that a man thinks that she's pretty, even if she isn't."

"Who do you think you are? Dorothy Dix?"

"Dorothy Dix? Who's that?"

"The woman in the paper who gives advice."

"Never read it."

"I haven't either, but I've heard about her."

Keith leaned toward Johnny and slanted his eyes toward the corner where Kathleen was sitting.

"There's a pretty redhead over there that's giving you . . . or me the eye. Do you know her?"

"Yeah, I do. She's Hod Dolan's niece. She came down here about a month ago to buy into the newspaper."

"Hod's niece? Who's that big dude with her?"

"Never saw him before."

"Good-looking woman."

"Yeah."

The waitress came back to the table. "We got only two pieces of peach pie left. Want that I save them for ya?"

"Now aren't you just too sweet for words. Of course I do. I'll take them both."

She took her eyes off Keith long enough to ask Johnny, "What will you have?"

"I'm not much for sweets."

"Okey-doke. Be right back."

Minutes later she returned with the food. Johnny had just started to eat when he became aware that Kathleen and the man with her were leaving the restaurant. He kept his eyes on his plate until he was sure that they were out the door. His appetite left him, and every bite he took seemed to stick in his throat.

Kathleen was quiet as she walked beside Barker on the way to her car. She had seen Johnny when he came into the restaurant, and she knew that he had seen her, yet he hadn't as much as given her a nod of recognition. Not once had he looked her way after he and his friend were

seated. She would have liked for him to have met Barker. She was sure that he would have liked him.

Dammit! Why was she feeling so down in the dumps?

"You're quiet. You must be tired," Barker remarked when they reached the car.

"I am a little tired. I'm rather put out with you for not letting me pay for my dinner. This was a Dutch-date, you know."

"I'm not sure I understand this Dutch-date business. Me dumb Indian."

Kathleen burst out laughing. "Dumb like a fox!"

"That's better. I was afraid that you regretted wasting your evening with a lonesome old man."

"Absolutely not. I enjoyed it . . . and you're far from being an old man."

"I'm in the middle of my life. My son is twenty-five. Your age."

"I hope he realizes how lucky he is to have a youthful father. I never had a chance to know mine."

"Ah . . . you're an orphan. Maybe I should adopt you."

"I'm a little old for that. Thanks for dinner. Maybe I'll see you tomorrow at the rodeo."

"I'll make sure of it." He leaned down to speak after she got into the car. "Are you sure you'll be all right? I'd feel better if I knew those two shied-pokes weren't about."

"Shied-pokes? What kind of word is that?"

"An Oklahoma word for someone you had just as soon not know."

"Did you learn that word in college?" Kathleen teased.

"No, from my father, who sometimes used very colorful language." His smile crinkled the corners of his eyes. "I plan to be here for a few more days. If you have any trouble with that deputy or those other two, let me know."

"I may not have any more trouble. Not after the news gets around that I'm Alfalfa Bill's granddaughter." Unexpected laughter bubbled up. "Good night, Mr. Fleming."

"Good night, Miss Kathleen." He put his fingers to the brim of his hat.

Kathleen drove away leaving Barker standing at the curb. She liked him. He was easy to talk to, and he could converse on a variety of subjects. It was comforting to know that he was her friend.

She had enjoyed the evening until Johnny showed up. At times she thought that Johnny liked her; then at other times, like tonight, when he ignored her, she was sure that he had been looking out for her because of his obligation to her Uncle Tom. She wished that she could get him out of her mind. He was dark, quiet and completely controlled and, to her, utterly intriguing. There were unstirred depths in him that she longed to bring to the surface if they were reachable.

Damn you, Johnny Henry!

Clara snuggled close to Marty Conroy's side and waited for him to stop the car on the little-used road outside of town. As soon as he turned off the engine and the lights, his arms were around her, his hand beneath her skirt.

"Baby, baby—" His mouth devoured hers.

"Marty, honey, not so fast," she said as soon as her lips were free. "I was wantin' to go honky-tonkin'. There's a good nightclub right here in Rawlin's." She stroked the inside of his thigh, her hand teasing up higher and higher.

"I'm not sharin' ya, sweetie. I want ya all to myself. Let's get in back. More room." They got out of the car. He opened the back door, pushed her down on the seat, pulled her skirt up, and fell on top of her. "I been thinkin' of this all the way from Conroy." His fingers worked their way into her panties. "Take 'em off, honeypot," he whispered breathlessly. "I can't wait."

"You're randy as a billy goat, Marty. Have ya been down to Del Rio to have that old Doc Brinkley give ya a goat gland?" Clara giggled as she obeyed.

"I don't need help from a billy goat when I've got you." He grabbed her hand and pressed it to the hardness in his britches. "See how I get when I'm with you. Get me out, baby."

"After we do it, can we go honky-tonkin'?"

He plunged into her roughly before he said, "Sure, honey. Sure."

It was over quickly for Marty. He sat up, lit two cigarettes, and gave one to Clara. He stretched out and put his feet up on the back of the front seat. He was a small man, utterly selfish, with an ego the size of a blimp.

"Let me catch my breath, sweetie, and we'll do it again. I'd drive all the way to California to get that. You're the best piece of ass in Oklahoma. Texas, too."

"Ya think so? Do I get ya horny?"

"Ever'time, sweetie. Every damn time."

"We could go to the Twilight Gardens, dance a while, then come back here and do it again." Clara said hopefully. "You're somethin' special, Marty. I want to show ya off."

His hand traveled up her thigh to the junction of her legs. "I couldn't feel ya up at the Twilight Gardens. I want to get as much of you as I can while I'm here."

"You're goin' with me to Nashville, ain't ya?"

"I'm thinkin' about it, sweetie. You'll knock their socks off in Nashville."

"You said that maybe we could get married."

"I haven't forgot."

"When, Marty?"

"As soon as I get my business taken care of, baby doll. I got to make money so I can buy pretties for my sweetie."

"You got money?"

"Yeah. The town of Conroy was named for my grand-daddy. Conroys are big-moneyed people in Texas. I always have a few irons in the fire. Come sit astraddle my lap and whisper dirty words in my ear. That always gets me hornier than hell. You do it so good, baby."

Clara did as he asked and tried to act enthusiastic about it. When it was over, she was exhausted.

"Can we go now?"

"Why do you always want to go to cheap roadhouses?" he asked irritably.

"I like fun. Besides, they might want me to sing."

"Fat chance. The singer with the band out there knows you'd show her up. She'll see to it you don't get near the stage."

"We could just dance."

"Come here, honey-baby. This is what you're best at."

Clara held her temper with an effort. All the horny little jackass wanted to do was screw. She was beginning to think that the big promises he'd made her were dry holes and that he had no intention of taking her to Nashville or even to a honky-tonk. She'd just have to get there on her own; and if he thought she was doing all this for nothing, he had a big surprise coming.

"How long ya stayin', lover?"

"Until Saturday. Want to stay at the hotel with me tonight and tomorrow night after the rodeo?"

"Sure, honey. If you have a hotel room, why are we doin' this in the backseat of your car?"

"A relative of mine is in town, and I want to be sure he's not staying at the hotel. I'll know by the time we get back there."

"Anyone I know?"

"Naw, honey. Come here. I'm gettin' horny again."

"Are you sure you haven't been to Del Rio?" Clara asked irritably, but Marty didn't notice.

Chapter Twelve

By midmorning on Saturday the fairground outside of Rawlings was a scene of bustling activity. Concession stands were being set up beneath the grandstand; cowboys were driving stock into the holding pens; and the crowds coming to the rodeo were arriving by car, wagon, horseback, and on foot.

The day was bright and sunny and, for once, the Oklahoma wind had taken a rest. The hard-packed red dirt in the arena had been stirred, dampened, and stirred again to afford a softer landing for those unfortunates who would be thrown from their mounts.

By the time Kathleen drove onto the field near the fairground and parked alongside the other cars, Emily was jumping with excitement. Hazel was quiet, obviously worried. Clara had not come home last night nor sent a word to her mother. This was not unusual behavior for Clara; but Hazel was anxious, always hopeful that her daughter would settle down and accept her responsibilities.

Hazel and Kathleen walked down the road to the fairground, Emily between them. Kathleen gave the tickets to the man at the gate and, holding Emily's hand, went past the array of concession stands toward the bleachers.

"Do you want a soda pop now or later, Emily?" Kathleen asked.

The child looked at her grandmother, waiting until Hazel said, "You decide, honey."

"Now," the little girl whispered.

"All right. We'll get it at the school booth. The band is raising money to buy a new set of drums."

"Yoo-hoo, Miss Dolan," Mrs. Smothers called as they passed the church stand. "Are you taking pictures for the paper?"

"Only of the winners," Kathleen replied, and kept walking.

"Oh, well—" Mrs. Smothers words were lost as the school band began to play.

With the cold bottle of NeHi pop firmly clutched in Emily's hand, they went to the bleachers and found seats on the fourth row near an aisle so that Kathleen could go down to the fence and take pictures. Beneath the shade of her hat brim, Kathleen scanned the working area for a glimpse of Johnny. Finally she spotted him leaning against a pole corral talking to a tall dark-haired man who was holding a small child. A blond woman, obviously pregnant, stood beside him. The man had been with Johnny at the restaurant. As she watched, the woman grasped Johnny's arm and laughed up at him.

Kathleen tore her eyes away from Johnny and looked down at the Kodak in her lap. When she raised her eyes again, they landed on Barker Fleming standing at the end of the bleachers with the judge who had greeted him the day before at the courthouse. His eyes caught her looking at him. He raised his hand acknowledging her and continued his conversation. Her curiosity about him grew. He appeared to be as comfortable talking to a judge as he had been confronting Webb and Krome.

"There's Mama," Emily whispered loudly to her grandmother.

"Don't point, sugar." Hazel took the child's hand in hers.

Kathleen turned her eyes toward the entrance to see Clara, teetering on high heels and clinging to the arm of a dapper little man wearing a large Stetson and a blue shirt elaborately decorated with white braid. The legs of his twill britches were tucked into cowboy boots that had large white stars inlaid on the sides. The man strutted like a turkey gobbler in a henhouse. It was almost laughable.

"Now, ain't he a fine figure of a man?" Hazel said sarcastically.

"Who is he?" Kathleen leaned back away from Emily when she spoke.

"Mr. Conroy from Texas. He stopped in front of the house yesterday. Clara ran out and got in the car. I haven't seen her since." Hazel spoke in a loud whisper.

"Is he the one taking her to Nashville?"

Hazel snorted and rolled her eyes. An answer wasn't necessary.

"His car is big and has a loud horn," Emily said. "But he wouldn't be nice. Not like Johnny."

With raised brows, Kathleen glanced at Hazel over the child's head. The little girl was very observant. She made no attempt to call out to her mother.

The rodeo started with the contestants parading around the arena on horseback. Johnny, wearing a dark shirt and a red bandanna tied about his neck, was in the middle of the pack. His mount was a high-spirited dapple gray who danced sideways. Johnny kept him under control with a tight rein. As he passed the section where Kathleen was sitting, he looked straight ahead.

"Good luck, Johnny!" The shout came from the blond woman who had been talking to him earlier. She was seated on the first row. The child stood on the plank seat beside her and waved a red handkerchief.

"Who is she?" Kathleen asked.

Hazel shook her head. "I've not seen her before."

After the cowboys left the arena, Barker Fleming moved back from the fence and stood alone at the end of the bleachers.

The first event was the steer-riding contest. The first two contestants were unseated before the time whistle blew.

"These steers are mighty feisty today, folks. Give a hand to that boy who hit the dust." The announcer's voice came over the loud speaker. "The next rider is Johnny Henry, number twenty-two. He's drawn Brimstone, a three-year-old from the McCabe ranch. This sucker is mean, folks. You never know if he's goin' to turn right or left. Our Johnny has his work cut out for him if he plans to stay on for a full ride. You pickup men best keep a sharp eye. Old Brimstone has been known to turn and try to gore a fallen rider."

Kathleen drew in a sharp breath. Her eyes were fastened on Johnny mounted on the bull behind the stout wooden gate. He was winding the bull rope around his gloved hand. After anchoring his hat firmly down on his head, he signaled for the gate to open.

The steer with the man on its back shot out of the chute. Johnny held one hand high over his head, the other wrapped in the rope. The enraged animal leaped into the arena the instant the gate was opened, turned and came down on stiff legs. On the next leap the bull turned in midair and Johnny slipped to the side. He stayed astride for another leap, then he crashed into the pulverized dirt with a thud. In an instant he was on his feet scrambling for the fence, hoping to put distance and a solid object between himself and the charging bull.

"Get 'im, boys," the announcer shouted.

Kathleen's hands went to her cheeks when the maddened steer raced to gore Johnny with its long sharp horns. A rider shot between them throwing a blanket over the animal's head, giving it another target to attack. Johnny sprang up behind the rider and the crowd cheered.

"The pickup man is Keith McCabe." The excited voice of the announcer came over the loudspeaker. "He knows ol' Brimstone is meaner than sin. He owns him."

Kathleen's heart was thudding wildly. She was surprised to realize that she was angry at Johnny. Really angry. The idiot! He could have been killed or maimed for life, all for the sake of a few minutes of glory. She sat quietly, looking straight ahead but not seeing, until her heart settled to its regular beating. She became aware of Emily's tugging on her arm and looked down at the child.

"I was scared for Johnny."

"So was I."

"I wish Johnny liked Mama. If they got married, he'd be my daddy, wouldn't he?"

"Yes, honey." Kathleen's body tensed for a moment at the thought, then relaxed. *No. He'd not marry Clara . . . but does he have someone special? Will that account for the sudden changes in his attitude toward me?*

The afternoon wore on. Kathleen watched and waited for the events in which Johnny participated. He won the calf-roping contest easily, lost the barrel-racing event when his stirrup raked a barrel, and then it was time for the bronc-riding contest, the rodeo's main event.

Three of the first four contestants were thrown from their mounts. When it came time for Johnny to ride, Kathleen felt a tightening of dread in her stomach. She watched as two handlers held the head of a dirty gray, long-legged horse with a black mane and tail while Johnny settled himself firmly in the saddle. Johnny's lanky body was tense and ready. He tugged at his hat, wound the reins around his gloved fist, and dug his feet into the stirrups.

He leaned forward and said something to one of the handlers, then sat back into the saddle. The handlers sprang back, one ripping off the cloth that covered the eyes of the grulla, the other swinging open the gate. Both men dived for the fence out of the way of the slashing hooves. Out of the chute, the horse leaped into the air like a spring coming uncoiled. All four feet left the ground at once, and the animal twisted and came down on stiffened legs.

The gray remained still for a space of a few seconds as if surprised that the weight was still on its back. With awareness came a wild scream and an eruption of crazed fury. The grulla's eyes were wild and rolling with rage. He shot into the air again. Dust swirled as the enraged animal sought to rid himself of the hated man on his back who continued to rake his sides with his spurs.

The crowd whooped and shouted encouragement.

"Ride 'em, Johnny. Ride that cork-screwing cayuse!"

"Whoopee!"

"Watch it, Johnny, he's goin' to roll."

The longer Johnny stayed on the animal's back the more frenzied the grulla became. The man and the animal rose in midair, each time coming down with a crash that could snap Johnny's back. With its black tail and mane flying, its nostrils flaring, the horse charged the fence and would have crashed into it, but Johnny yanked the animal's head to the side. Sharp hooves churned the dirt, creating a cloud of dust.

Kathleen stood with the rest of the crowd. Her hand covered her mouth to stifle a shriek of fear as the horse reared. For an instant she thought it would go over backward and Johnny would be crushed.

"Time! Time! Get him off," the announcer shouted.

The crowd was jubilant. The drovers along the fence pounded each other on the back.

Johnny's hat was gone. His hair, black as the horse's mane, shone in the sun. His sinewy form was still anchored firmly in the saddle as riders flanked the bucking horse. Johnny slipped off and flung himself behind the pickup man.

Kathleen took a full breath for the first time since Johnny had mounted the horse.

"Ladies and gentlemen, settle down! Settle down! I wish to make an announcement. Johnny Henry has been named *All-Around Cowboy* of the Rawlings' 1938 rodeo. Let's hear a shout for Johnny!" The crowd yelled and clapped. When the noise died down, the voice came again. "Come on up here, boy, and collect your money."

Someone pushed Johnny up on the platform. He accepted an envelope, shook hands with the announcer and the judges, and made his retreat.

Kathleen looked down and saw the camera in her lap. Only now did she remember that she had come to take pictures.

"I've got to go take pictures, Hazel."

"You go right ahead. Emily and I will tag along behind. Don't worry about us. If we lose you, we'll go to the car."

As Kathleen made her way down the steps of the bleachers, she saw Barker Fleming waiting for her.

"Did you enjoy the rodeo?" she asked.

"I've not seen a better one. Not even at the stockyards in Oklahoma City."

"I'm on my way to take pictures of the *All-Around Cowboy*. Would you like to come along and meet him?"

"Thank you. I'd like that."

"Then let's go get the job done."

With Barker striding beside her, Kathleen made her way through the crowd to the stock pens, where they found Johnny surrounded by a group of people, including the couple that had been with him before the rodeo began. When he saw Kathleen, his dark eyes lit with pleasure.

"Congratulations, Mr. *All-Around Cowboy*. May I have a picture for the paper?"

"If you're sure you want one."

"I do. Stand back against the fence, face the sun, and tilt your hat brim so that it doesn't shade your face."

"You better take my picture, miss." This came from the smiling man holding the child. "This ugly old son of a gun will break your Kodak, sure as shootin'."

"I'll have to chance it 'cause he's the champ." Kathleen smiled at the man then let her gaze slide down to include the small blond woman at his side.

"Come on, let's get this over." Johnny shifted nervously from one foot to the other trying not to stare past Kathleen at the man who hovered at her side.

"Stand still and look at the camera." Kathleen backed away and looked down into the viewfinder of the Kodak. "I'd better take another one," she said after the first shot. "One might not turn out."

"You can always put one in the barn to keep the rats out."

"Keith, stop teasing. You're as proud of him as I am."

"Ruthy, darlin', I am proud. I'm damn proud he didn't break a leg. I need his help getting my stock back home."

"Don't swear in front of our son," she scolded. "He'll be swearing like a trooper by the time he starts to school."

"Miss Dolan, meet Mr. and Mrs. McCabe. They know your aunt and uncle in Kansas." Johnny seemed shy and uncertain about making the introductions, but Kathleen had never been accused of being shy.

"How do you do?" She held out her hand. "I've heard about you from Uncle Hod," she said to Keith. "And about you, Mrs. McCabe, from Aunt Molly. She said that you were best friends growing up. I was at their house in Pearl when Molly got the news about your son."

"We'll not hold it against you for being related to Hod, Miss Dolan." Keith said.

After they shook hands, Kathleen introduced Barker Fleming.

"Mr. Fleming, this is Johnny Henry, our *All-Around Cowboy*."

Barker stepped up to Johnny and held out his hand. The two tall men eyed one another as they shook hands.

"Hello, Johnny."

Johnny nodded, pulled his hand free, and fumbled in his pocket for the makings of a cigarette.

"Mr. and Mrs. McCabe." Kathleen finished the introductions.

Barker reluctantly looked away from Johnny and took Keith's hand.

"I understand that you own the stock used here today," Barker said.

"Not all, but a good part. Never thought Johnny'd be able to stay on that wild-haired mustang."

Barker glanced at Johnny. "That was some ride."

Johnny merely nodded. There was something about Barker that made him uneasy, not the least of it being that he was with Kathleen. Did she go for older, successful men? He was a breed, that was clear, and it didn't seem to bother her.

"I didn't like it," Kathleen said, tilting her chin to look up at Johnny. "That horse hated you and outweighed you by a thousand pounds. Getting on him was the dumbest thing I ever saw. Next time pick on something your own size."

Ruth chortled happily. "Here's a woman who thinks like I do. If Keith ever even thinks about getting on that horse, I'll take the horsewhip to him."

Johnny looked steadily at Kathleen after her outburst. There was a quizzical look on his face. Their eyes held until Kathleen felt the heat coming up from her neck to flood her face. *What in the world caused me to say such a thing?*

Barker sensed her discomfort and asked Keith the location of his ranch.

"Six miles across the river outside Vernon."

"I know about where that is. Good flat country."

"I've heard of the Flemings. Are you from around Duncan?"

"My brother is. I'm from Elk City."

"Now I remember. A Fleming from Elk City owns the tannery here."

"Only part of it. My sister and her husband own the controlling interest." Barker's eyes went to Johnny. "Where's your ranch, Johnny?"

"Eight miles south." Johnny threw his half-smoked cigarette on the ground and stepped on it.

Keith set his son on the ground beside Ruth. "Hold on to Davis, honey. I'm going to head off trouble."

Kathleen looked behind her to see the man who brought Clara coming their way. He had evidently instructed Clara to wait, because she stood with arms crossed, pouting, against the end of the corral.

"Keith, I heard this morning that this was your stock here at the rodeo."

"Are you offering to buy, Marty?"

"I don't deal in cattle. Hey, how is Ruth? She gets prettier all the time. Gonna kick out another kid, huh?" Marty hit Keith on the upper arm. "It must be handy having your own woman on the ranch. Anytime, anyplace. Huh, Keith?"

"Shut up, Marty." A dark scowl covered Keith's face. "What are you up to? What are you doing here?"

"Keeping an eye on my investment. Johnny Henry made me a little money today." He raised his brows. "Lost the bull ride, won the calf rope, lost the barrel race, and won the bronc-riding. Just the way I bet on him."

"What the hell are you saying, Marty?"

"Nothin'. Me 'n Johnny are shirttail relations, Keith. Just like you and me."

Keith snorted. "Your sister was married to the man who later married Johnny's sister. That's your only connection to Johnny unless you're saying that you and Johnny hatched up a scheme for him to throw some on the contests."

Marty smirked. "I've known the boy for a long time. Like him. Don't hold being a breed against him. Any little deal we cook up is strictly between us."

"In the first place, Johnny is NO boy. He's a twenty-five-year-old man. And if you want to keep your teeth, Marty, you'd better not be putting out the story that he threw any of the events so that you could cash in with the big gamblers."

"Trust me, Keith. I'll not give our secret away." Marty

looked unruffled and arrogant. "Listen, Keith. I'm willing to let you in on the ground floor of something big. I came up here just to look around, not knowing that you'd be here. But being that you're here and we're kin, I'll cut you in."

Keith folded his arms and rocked back on his heels. "What big things are you planning now? Are you going to dam up the Red River and flood my ranch?"

"Something bigger than that. I'm going to build a toll bridge across it like they did across the Canadian River up at Purcell."

"You go right ahead and do that, Marty."

"Don't you want in on it. All we'd have to do is sit back and collect the tolls."

"That'd be a good job for you, little man." Keith slapped Marty so hard on the back that he staggered. "Get yourself a rocking chair, sit on the bridge, and collect the tolls. I'm taking my family home."

Marty's face turned ugly. "One of these days I'll hit it big, and you'll be sittin' out there on that pig-turd ranch with nothin' but a handful of cows."

"Well, that's how I like it. Here comes your Kewpie doll, Marty. You'd better take her and get the hell out of here before I forget that I'm bigger than you are."

Marty looked over his shoulder and scowled.

"I got tired waitin', sugar." When Clara reached him she clasped his arm possessively, and smiled flirtatiously at Keith. "I'm Clara Ramsey, good-looking." She held out a hand.

"Howdy." Keith touched the hand briefly. "'Bye,

Marty. I hope you can find your way back to Texas."
Keith walked away.

"Oh, there's Johnny," Clara squealed, and began tugging Marty toward where Johnny stood with his back to the fence. "Come meet Johnny, Marty. We're old friends." She ran to Johnny and would have kissed him on the cheek, if he hadn't reared back and turned his head. "I'm so proud of you, Johnny. I was so . . . thrilled! Did ya hear me yellin' for you?"

Johnny's hands shot out to hold her away from him.

"This is Johnny, Marty. The *friend* I told you about." She giggled.

"I know who he is. Long time no see." Marty held out his hand. Johnny ignored it. The snub was obvious.

"All right, be a dumb Indian," Marty said angrily. "I was just trying to be friendly."

Johnny bristled. He was tired and sore. "This *dumb* Indian might shove your rear up between your shoulders if you don't get the hell away from me and take this bangtail with you."

"It's what I would expect from trash. Wasn't your mama a Mud Creek whore and your daddy a drunk Indian?"

Johnny yanked Marty's hat off his head and hit him across the face with it, then threw it at him.

"And yours was a buzzard. Get out of my sight, and if you come near me again, I'll break your stupid head wide open."

Kathleen glanced quickly at Barker. His dark, intense eyes were on Johnny. A thought in the back of her mind began to wiggle its way forward. Johnny would look something like Barker when he was older. His Indian features were not as prominent as Barker's, but he had the same quiet face. Both he and Keith were waiting to see what happened. Keith was tense, but smiling . . . broadly.

Clara, red-faced and angry, picked up Marty's hat and tugged on his arm.

"Let's go, sugar. He's mad 'cause I don't put out for him," she said in a confidential tone, then shrieked at Johnny. "You'll be sorry, Johnny Henry. You're jealous 'cause you'll never 'mount to any more than a rag-tail *breed* livin' in a shack out on the prairie. Marty and me are goin' to Nashville. We'll make it big and come back here and spit all over all of ya."

Kathleen's eyes went quickly to Johnny. He was clenching his teeth in an effort to hold his temper, and she was glad that Clara was able to pull Marty away.

Kathleen turned to the McCabes and began to talk to avert the attention from Johnny.

"I'll write Uncle Hod and Molly and tell them that I met you. Would you mind if I took a picture of the three of you to send to them?"

"I'd like that," Ruth said. "And maybe I could use the negative to make a copy for us."

"Of course. Turn now and face the sun."

Holding his son on one arm, Keith put the other around his wife and drew her close to his side.

Looking through the viewfinder, Kathleen said, "Now, smile." She took the picture and turned to Johnny. "Get in there, Johnny. Uncle Hod will want a picture of you, too." Johnny sauntered over and stood behind Ruth.

After she snapped the picture, Keith set his son on the ground and reached for Kathleen's Kodak.

"Hod and Molly would like a picture of you and Johnny."

"I don't know about that."

"I do. Now stand over there. Come on, cowboy."

Kathleen took off her hat and fluffed her hair with her fingers. She moved over to stand beside Johnny. He flung an arm across her shoulders and pulled her tightly against him. She looked up at him in surprise. He looked down at her. It was then that Keith snapped the picture.

"Try not to pay any attention to what Clara says. You know what she is," Kathleen whispered.

"Uh-huh," he murmured as his arm dropped from around her.

Kathleen put the straw hat back on her head and reached for her Kodak.

"I'd better get back to the paper and develop this film. Hazel and Emily are waiting for me at the car."

"I'll walk along with you." Barker said his good-byes to the McCabes, then held out his hand to Johnny. "You did a hell of a job out there today. I'll see you again."

"Thanks," Johnny murmured grudgingly.

It had been years since Johnny had felt anything like jealousy toward another man. He had that feeling now as he watched Kathleen walk away with a man who appeared to be well educated and was well-off if he owned half the tannery. Usually name-calling didn't bother him all that much, but today he had been embarrassed to be called a breed in front of the man, yet it was what *he* was, too.

Chapter Thirteen

After Kathleen took Hazel and Emily home, she went back to the *Gazette*. She let herself into the office with her key, then locked the door behind her. She could hear the radio and knew that Paul was in his room. After hesitating for a minute or two, she knocked on his door.

"I'm sorry to bother—"

"It's all right. Come in. Addy and I were going to listen to old Doc Brinkley down in Del Rio."

"How did the rodeo go?" Adelaide didn't seem to be the least bit embarrassed to be caught in Paul's room. She was wearing a lounge robe and sat on the bed with her back against the headboard. "Did Johnny win?"

"He won *All-Around Cowboy*. I took his picture. If we can get the print on the bus tonight, we'll have the engraving back in time for this week's paper."

"I'll develop the film." Paul glanced at the clock on his desk, then reached for the Kodak.

"I wish I knew how to do that," Kathleen said.

"I'll teach you how to develop and make prints, but not tonight. I'll have to speed up the process if I'm to have it ready by the time the bus comes through."

While he spoke he extracted the roll of film from the Kodak. He left them and went into the little closet he had made into a darkroom.

"Isn't he amazing?" Adelaide asked proudly. "He can do most everything. If he doesn't know how to do something, it drives him crazy until he learns. He set up the darkroom out of scraps of this and that. He takes beautiful pictures, too."

"Why not take pictures for the paper?"

"I wish he would, but he scarcely leaves the building. He insists on staying in the background. He is a dear, sweet man." Adelaide moved her feet and nodded for Kathleen to sit down.

"I think so, too. If he weren't head over heels in love with you, I might try to beat your time."

"I can't believe how lucky I am. Now, tell me about the rodeo. Was there a big crowd?"

"The bleachers were almost full. It seemed to be a good crowd, but I have nothing to compare it to. The concession stands were doing a good business. I managed to avoid Mrs. Smothers, thank goodness."

"I bet she wanted her picture taken."

"She did, but I avoided it. Mr. Fleming was there. Apparently he's on good terms with Judge Fimbres."

"If there's anyone in town Doc Herman is leery of, it's Judge Fimbres."

"I'm glad to know that there's someone who stands up to him. Sheriff Carroll and that lamebrained deputy were walking around." Kathleen slipped off her shoes and sat cross-legged on the bed. "Clara Ramsey showed up with an obnoxious little *jelly bean* who made Johnny really angry." Kathleen told Adelaide about the incident and finished up with, "The man was mean and vicious, calling Johnny's mother a whore, and then Clara called him a breed. I wanted to knock her teeth out."

"I'm surprised that you didn't." Adelaide laughed.

"I came to within an inch. I was embarrassed for Johnny in front of his friends and Mr. Fleming. Clara is nothing but trouble. She didn't come home last night, and Hazel was worried. Clara will come to a bad end. She's heading for it with breakneck speed."

"Who was the man with her? Was he from around here?"

"Hazel said his name was Marty Conroy, and he's from Texas."

"Conroy? Is he a little guy who wears flashy clothes, drives a fancy car, and struts around like a peacock?"

"I didn't see his car, but he wears flashy clothes and struts like a peacock," Kathleen said drily.

"The first year Paul was here, he and I were over to Red Rock to an air show. Conroy was there trying to sell oil leases. People we met there told us to steer clear of him, that he was a shyster."

"Clara thinks that he's going to take her to Nashville. I hope he does and gets her away from here. She's worrying her mother to death."

Kathleen slipped on her shoes. "I think I'll stop by Claude's for a hamburger. I'll come back and get the photo and wait for the bus."

"Go on home. Paul and I will see to it that the picture gets on the bus."

"I think I will, if you don't mind."

Kathleen let herself out of the office and locked the door. Someone was sitting on the curb beside her car. She approached cautiously and discovered that it was Hannah, the Indian woman who had come into the office several times since she had been here.

"Hello, Hannah." The woman looked at her with blurry, unfocused eyes. "Can I give you a ride home?" Kathleen asked.

"Want . . . beer—" she muttered. "Whish-key—"

"Let me take you home, Hannah." The woman was drunk. Kathleen wasn't sure if she could stand.

"Whish-key?"

"No. I'll help you up and take you home." She took hold of the woman's arm, but she wouldn't budge. "You'll have to help me. Come on, stand up."

"Whish-key—"

"No, whiskey," Kathleen said irritably.

While she was standing there wondering what to do, the sheriff's car pulled up beside them and stopped. He got out.

"Don't arrest her," Kathleen said quickly. "I'll take her home."

Sheriff Carroll ignored Kathleen, went to Hannah, and pulled her to her feet. He held on to her to steady her.

"You've had enough for today, Hannah."

"Whish-key."

"No more. I'll take you home. Come on. You can't stay here on the street." He handled her so gently that Kathleen could only watch with amazement.

"No." Hannah tried to pull away. "Whish-key."

"You can't have any more."

Sheriff Carroll got the front door of his car open and pushed her down onto the seat. He stooped and lifted her feet inside, then slammed the door. Without as much as a nod to Kathleen, he rounded the car, got under the wheel, made a U-turn in the middle of the street, and drove away.

Kathleen was puzzled by what she had just seen. The sheriff who had been so short and nasty with her for "brawling" on the street, had treated the drunken Indian woman far differently. He had been compassionate and gentle with her. Kathleen shook her head in wonderment.

People usually came to town on Saturday night, but there were far more than the usual number milling about because of the rodeo. Kathleen drove slowly down the street. All the stools were full at Claude's when she passed. She finally found a place to park in front of the bank. She walked the short distance to the Golden Rule Restaurant, went inside, and sat down at a booth near the door.

The waitress brought her a glass of water and a cardboard menu. She was trying to decide what she wanted to have when she became aware that someone was standing at the end of the booth. She looked up to see Johnny glowering down at her.

"What the hell are you doing roaming around this time of night by yourself?"

"It isn't night, and I drove the car."

"It'll be dark in fifteen minutes. Webb and Krome were sitting on a bench in front of the shoe repair not five minutes ago. They must have seen you park and come in here."

"So what if they did? I'll go to my car and go home. Do you think they'll chase me on foot?"

"Where's your boyfriend?"

"Boyfriend? What are you talking about?"

"The dude. The dressed-up city man."

"Mr. Fleming? He isn't my boyfriend. And my neck is getting tired looking up at you. Either sit down or go away."

"Come sit with me and the McCabes. After we eat I'll take you home."

"Oh, no. I'm not butting in on your—"

Johnny picked up the glass of water that had been left by the fuzzy-haired, overweight waitress. He turned his back to Kathleen and spoke to her as she came to the booth.

"She's moving over to our table."

"Okey-doke. Be right with you."

"Johnny, I don't want to intrude on you and your friends. I'll sit here; and if it'll make you feel better, I'll leave the restaurant when you do."

"Don't you like the McCabes? They're good decent people. Or is it me that you don't want to be seen with?"

"If we weren't in this restaurant," she muttered as she slid out of the booth, "I'd hit you right on that smart mouth."

"Don't let that stop you. I've been hit in the mouth in fancier places than this."

"Don't tempt me."

With his hand in the small of her back he pushed her toward the corner table where the McCabes were sitting.

Keith made an effort to get to his feet even though his son was asleep in his lap.

"Don't get up . . . please," Kathleen hastened to say.

"Sit down," Ruth invited. "I need another woman to help me hold down these two wild broncs. They're still all up in the air over the win at the rodeo."

"Thank you. Johnny insisted that I join you. I didn't want to intrude."

"It's a relief to be able to look at someone besides him," Keith said, and reached over and kissed his wife on the cheek. "I can't look at you all the time, sugarfoot. You've got to admit that Kathleen's prettier than Johnny."

"Don't revert back to your wild ways, Romeo. You're going home with me."

"See what a tight rope she keeps on me? I can't have any fun."

"Oh, poor you," Ruth said. Then she turned to Kathleen. "Molly's baby is due anytime, isn't it?"

"Around Halloween. Uncle Hod teases her about looking like she swallowed a pumpkin."

"Does George Andrews still come to the store everyday?"

"Not as often as he used to. Molly said that he's taken a liking to Catherine Wisniewski and her son Wally, and they to him. He spends a lot of time at the restaurant helping her now that Wally is away at college. Molly thinks that George had a lot to do with his going."

"Oh, wouldn't it be grand if they got married? George had a rough time taking care of his mother and then having her murdered and being blamed for it."

"I understand that it was you, Mr. McCabe, who figured out who killed her."

"Hod had a hand in it, too." The waitress came to the table to take their orders. "Choose the most expensive thing on the menu, Kathleen. We've got a rich man at the table."

"Oh, Keith, stop teasing," Ruth said, which seemed to be something she said often.

"I'll have a roast beef sandwich," Kathleen said. "And give me a separate ticket."

Ruth ordered a sandwich, then Keith and Johnny ordered steaks and fried potatoes.

"Put it all on one check," Johnny said in a tone that brooked no argument.

Kathleen grimaced at him and poked him on the leg with the toe of her shoe.

"You can pay our hotel bill if you want to, Johnny." Keith winked at his wife.

"That's generous of you," Johnny growled.

Kathleen liked the McCabes. They were in tune with each other. Keith looked at his wife as if she were the most precious thing in the world. She cut his steak for him because he was holding the sleeping child.

"Ruthy doesn't have much of a lap right now," Keith said to Kathleen by way of explanation.

"I'm sure she noticed," Ruth said, stabbed a piece of his steak with her fork, and put it in her mouth.

They were halfway through the meal when Barker Fleming came into the restaurant and directly to their table. He spoke politely to all, then directed his remarks to Kathleen.

"I saw your car parked down by the bank. It's got a flat tire. I was concerned."

"A flat tire. Oh, no. Uncle Hod put new tires on my car when I left Kansas. I must have picked up something out at the field where I parked today."

"Is your spare in good shape?" Johnny asked.

"It should be. Uncle Hod checked it and said it was."

Johnny got up from the table. "Stay here with Ruth and Keith. I'll change it. Give me your keys."

"I'll give you a hand," Barker said, and followed Johnny out.

Hod had made sure Kathleen had the equipment she needed for an emergency when she left Kansas. The spare tire as well as a jack, air pump, and tire iron were in the sloping trunk of the car. Johnny and Barker didn't speak until the car was jacked up and the tire removed.

"Son of a bitch," Barker said as he pulled the tube from the tire. "It's been slashed. She had trouble with a couple of roughnecks yesterday. I saw them hanging around on the street tonight. I'd not be surprised if they did this."

"What kind of trouble?" Johnny asked sharply.

"They had her hemmed in, giving her some sass. A little knife in my pocket persuaded them to back off."

Johnny cursed softly. "I'm goin' to have to break a couple of heads some dark night."

"Be glad to give you a hand," Barker said.

"I'll not need any help with those two," Johnny snorted. "She'll need a boot to go in that tire if she uses it again." He lifted out the spare tire and took a new tube out of a box. After he stuffed it in the tire, he attached the air pump.

Barker stood by, watching Johnny work. The scene today with the little twit and Conroy had cut him to the quick. Johnny had had to endure slurs like that all his life. He had a right to be bitter, for the circumstances of his birth were no fault of his own. Barker had hoped to get to know him before he approached him with what he had to tell him. Now was not the time.

Barker Fleming was not one bit disappointed in Johnny Henry.

When Johnny disconnected the pump, Barker knelt and lifted the tire. He bounced it to test the amount of air, then fitted it on the axle.

"That's dirty work," Johnny said, with a note of sarcasm he couldn't conceal.

"I've been dirty before," Barker replied evenly, working on the lug nuts. "Let it down."

Johnny worked the jack handle wondering about the man kneeling beside the wheel. Was he in love with Kathleen? Had he come to Rawlings just to see her? He appeared to be genuinely concerned about her.

After a little more air from the pump, Johnny kicked the tire and grunted his satisfaction. He put the tools away, slammed the trunk lid, and locked it. Without a word to Barker, he took off down the street toward the shoe-repair shop. Uninvited and ignored, Barker walked along beside him. Webb and Krome were lounging on a bench with their legs stretched out in front of them. Johnny kicked Webb's feet.

"Get up, you pile of horse dung, so I can knock you down."

Webb pulled in his feet, but remained seated. "What's the matter with ya?"

Krome snickered. "Did ya bring *Daddy* along to help ya?"

Johnny grabbed his shirtfront and hauled him to his feet. "Shut your mouth, polecat. I'm telling you both to stay away from Miss Dolan. If I find someone who saw you slash her tire, I'll come for you and stomp you into the ground." Johnny shoved Krome from him. The man hit the bench with a crash.

"What's goin' on here?" Sheriff Carroll walked rapidly toward them.

"We were just sittin' here, mindin' our own business, Sheriff—"

"—They jist come up and grabbed me," Krome finished.

"Johnny?"

"Nothing to do with you, Sheriff."

"It is something to do with me. I'm the law here."

"If you're the law, why haven't you stopped these two from harassing Miss Dolan?" Barker asked.

The sheriff turned on him. "Who'er you?"

"Barker Fleming."

"I've not seen you before. You passin' through?"

"No. I have business here."

"Pussy business if ya ask me," Krome said.

"I'll ignore that . . . this time." Barker looked down at the man with hard eyes. "Next time I'll put a fist in your mouth."

"Talks big fer a breed, don't he?" Webb snickered, feeling brave with the sheriff present.

"Keep your mouth shut," Sheriff Carroll snapped at Webb, then to Barker, "What kind of business?"

"I see no reason to explain myself to you. I've broken no law, but if you feel it necessary, Judge Fimbres will vouch for me."

"You might not have, but Johnny has. Brawling on the street is against the law."

"If you arrest me, arrest these two for slashing Miss Dolan's tire."

"You didn't see us do that," Krome said gleefully.

"I saw you do it." Johnny's intent gaze homed in on Webb.

"You were in the restaurant," Webb blurted, and Krome groaned.

"Jesus Christ," Sheriff Carroll said under his breath. "You two get out of town and don't come back for a month. If I see you around here, I'll throw your asses in jail."

"Hold on, Sheriff," Barker said. "They owe Miss Dolan for the tire."

"We ain't got no money," Webb wailed. "You think if we had money, we'd be sittin' here on the street?"

"You've got a pretty good pocket watch." Johnny reached over and jerked it out of Webb's pocket and handed it to the sheriff. "You could get enough out of this at the pawnshop to pay Miss Dolan for a tire."

"That's not the proper way a doin' thin's."

Barker said, "It'd save you feeding these two in jail for a couple of weeks, besides having a spread in the paper about two thugs slashing Miss Dolan's tire and the sheriff not arresting them."

The sheriff looked at Barker for a long while. "Do I know you from somewhere?"

Barker shrugged. "Maybe. I travel over the state some. If you're sure you can handle this, Johnny and I want to get back to our supper."

"I'll handle it."

Johnny and Barker walked back to the restaurant. At the door, Barker stopped.

"I've had supper. So you plan to see Miss Dolan home?"

"What's it to you?" Johnny asked bluntly.

"I like her. She's a lovely girl. I don't want those two catching her alone in the dark."

"She's a twenty-five year old *girl* . . . a little young for you, don't you think?"

"Maybe, but just right for you, is that it?"

"She might be age-wise, but that's all."

"That's something you'll have to figure out. Tell McCabe that if he's short a drover to driving the stock back to his ranch, I'll give a hand, if he's got a mount for me."

"Isn't riding drag a little out of your line?"

"I've done it."

"Christ! You're just an all-'round jack of all trades, aren't you!" Johnny declared rudely.

Barker slapped Johnny on the shoulder. "I'll be at the hotel." He walked away leaving a puzzled Johnny to go into the restaurant.

Johnny asked the waitress if they had a place where he could wash his greasy hands. She directed him to a back room, where he washed before he went to the table where Kathleen and the McCabes waited. He gave them a short rundown about what had happened, reporting the confrontation with Webb and Krome and noting that the sheriff was aware that they were the ones who slashed the tire.

"'Pears to me like we ought to limber up those old boys a mite some dark night," Keith said.

"Something's not quite right," Johnny said. "I'm not sure if it's the sheriff or the deputy. Hijacking is against the law. They should have put them in jail when I first turned them in."

"There's someone who doesn't want me here. Those two tried to keep me from coming into town. Adelaide said they seldom have hijackings around here. They were kind of dumb about it. I don't think they'd done it before." Kathleen's eyes clung to Johnny's face. He had avoided looking at her since he came back to the table.

"We should get our boy to bed." Keith moved his chair back and stood. "He's all tuckered out. You're tired too, aren't you, honey?" he said to Ruth. "You've carried that girl around all day."

"It could be a boy. Don't get your hopes up," Ruth said wearily.

"I've got to get home, too." Kathleen got to her feet. "Thank you for the supper," she said to Keith.

"Where's the ticket?" Johnny asked.

"It's all taken care of. Don't get in a fret, boy. We'll consider it even if you bring Kathleen down for a visit."

Kathleen's eyes went quickly to Johnny. His expression was unreadable.

"Thank you for fixing the tire, Johnny. I hope to see you again, Ruth."

"You will. I'd bet the ranch on it."

"Hold on." Johnny took Kathleen's arm as she made to leave. "I'll see you home."

"You don't have to bother."

"It's no bother."

On the walk in front of the restaurant, Keith and Ruth turned toward the hotel, Johnny and Kathleen to where her car was parked in front of the bank.

"Where is your truck?"

"Behind the *Gazette* office."

"I'll be all right now. Thanks again."

"I'll see you home."

"How will you get back?"

"I've got two legs, you know." He opened the passenger door of her car and waited for her to get in before he went to the driver's side. He tossed aside the pillow she usually sat on and got under the wheel.

"Is Clara giving you any trouble?" he asked as he turned onto the rutted street.

"I can put up with her . . . for a while. Hazel is worried. She didn't come home last night."

"She shacked up with Marty somewhere. Maybe he'll take her back to Texas. If he does, he'll dump her somewhere."

"Who is he? You and Keith seemed to know him."

"He's a distant cousin of Keith's. Keith isn't proud of it."

"Adelaide said that a few years ago she and Paul went

to Red Rock to an air show. He was there selling oil leases."

"I remember that show. I went up for an airplane ride."

"Were you scared?"

"For a few minutes. Then it was great." He looked at her and grinned.

They were silent until Johnny parked the car behind Hazel's house and turned off the lights.

"I hate thinking about you walking back to town. I've always heard that cowboys hate to walk." She liked sitting with him in the dark and wished it didn't have to end so soon.

"You could walk with me."

"Then you would insist on walking me back." She laughed nervously.

"I could bring you back in my truck."

"You'd better be careful. I might take you up on it."

"You mean it? You'll do it?"

"Why not? It's Saturday night."

Chapter Fourteen

"Marty, get off me. I got to tell ya somethin'."

"You want to go honky-tonkin'," he said with a deep sigh, rolled on to his side, and kicked the sheet down so he could see all of her naked body.

"Ya really want to go?" Clara asked hopefully.

"No. I wanna do this." He grabbed her bare buttocks and pulled her to him.

"We've already done it twice, Marty," she protested.

"We did it five times in one night in Wichita Falls. That's what I like about you, sweetie. You know how to get me up. We could break our record tonight."

"Be serious, honey." Clara propped herself on her elbow, leaned over him, and kissed him long and wetly. "When are we gettin' married, sugar?"

"How about Christmas?"

"While we're in Nashville?"

"Uh-huh." Marty tried to pull her over on top of him, but she resisted, and moved her finger down over his chest to burrow in his navel and then on down to his limp sex organ.

"Can't it be sooner?"

"What's the hurry?"

"We've got to get married, Marty. 'Cause—"

"This wouldn't be any better if we were married." He pressed her hand tightly to him.

"We'd be together all the time and do it when you wanted to."

"Why have you got this bug all of a sudden to get married?"

"Marty, I'm pregnant—" Her hand went to his cheek and turned his face toward her.

He laughed. "You can still screw, can't ya? Don't think I ever screwed a pregnant woman."

"You don't mind?"

"Hell, no."

"Oh, good. I was afraid you'd be mad."

"Why should I be mad? It ain't my kid."

"Yes, it is, Marty. It's yours, and we got to get married."

Marty's arm shot out, knocking her away from him as he sat straight up in the bed.

"My kid? Oh, no. You're not stickin' me with a kid."

"It's yours, Marty. What am I goin' to do?"

"Get rid of it. Shitfire! You've been around long enough to know what to do. Hell, you can get it done in Dallas or in Wichita Falls." Marty turned and sat on the side of the bed.

"It takes money for that. I don't know why you're so mad. You're hornier than a billy goat and had to know what would happen."

"I'm not going to be tied down with a brat. How the

damn hell do I know it's mine? You spread your legs for anyone who walks on two feet."

"I do not! I've only been with you since we met."

"Yeah. Tell that to the man in the moon."

"Come back to bed, sugar. Let's see if we can break that record. I really feel like I want to."

"I'm gettin' the hell out of here." He jumped up and started putting on his clothes.

Clara bounced up out of the bed and stood naked in front of the door.

"You're not running out on me, Marty Conroy."

"Oh, yes, I am. I never bargained for no kid."

"I didn't get pregnant all by myself! It happened, and it's as much yours as mine."

"You said you couldn't have any brats, so I never bothered with rubbers."

"The doctor said maybe I'd not get pregnant again."

"Then let the doctor pay for it." Marty was throwing clothes in a small straw bag.

"You never intended to marry me in the first place, did you?"

"You've got it right there. Mama would have a fit if I brought a cheap floozy like you home to Conroy."

"You miserable little rat! You ugly, dirt-cheap, little shithead! You never took me anywhere except to that dirty old rodeo. I'm surprised you didn't try to screw me there. I begged you to take me honky-tonkin', and you didn't take me, not even one time."

"I didn't want to be seen with you, you stupid bangtail. Didn't you catch on? You're as dumb as a pile of horseshit."

"Why did you tell me down in Wichita Falls that we'd get married and you'd take me to Nashville? I'd have screwed you without the lie."

"And I'd have had to pay you. It worked out better this way."

"You are cheap!"

"It's no big deal to let a woman think you'll marry her. I've told that to more women than I can count. When they hear that I'm the Conroy from Conroy, Texas they all want to be Mrs. Conroy."

"Godamighty," Clara shrieked. "Why else would they want a struttin' little pissant like you? Certainly not for that peanut-size thing you've got 'tween your legs."

"Shut up!"

"I won't shut up. I'll yell so loud that everybody in this hotel knows about . . . your peanut!"

"Stop yelling, or I'll slap you!"

"You just try it, you horny little turd, and I'll cut your head open with the heel of this shoe." She grabbed the shoe with the sharp spike heel and drew it back threateningly.

"Here, slut!" Marty threw some wadded-up bills on the floor at her feet. When she looked down at them, he swung his straw bag, knocking the shoe out of her hand. He quickly shoved her to the floor. "You're not that good a whore anyway."

"You . . . you shithead." Clara picked up three crumpled one-dollar bills. "You cheap dirt-eatin' son of a bitch," she yelled. "As soon as the courthouse opens Monday I'm goin' to Judge Fimbres and have you declared the father of my child. I'll tell him you raped me.

I'll make sure the hotel clerk sees me leave here lookin'
all beat-up! Then we'll see how much good it does you to
be *Mr. Conroy* from Conroy, Texas."

"You do that and I'll . . . I'll—"

"You'll what, big *little* man?"

"I'll kill you."

"Ha! Ha! You ain't got the guts."

Marty went out, closing the door softly behind him,
and hurried down the back hall to the stairs. Clara's anger
dissolved into misery, and she began to cry.

The evening was cool.

Before Kathleen and Johnny had walked a block, she
had goose bumps on her arms, but she was so happy
being with him that she wouldn't have mentioned icicles
hanging from her nose. Johnny had put his hand inside
her arm, slid it down to clasp her hand, and drawn her
close to his side. Their steps matched and they walked
across the school yard in companionable silence.

"Johnny—"

"Kath—" They had both spoken at the same time.
Johnny chuckled. "You go first."

"No, you, or you'll not tell me what you were going to
say."

"Will you?"

"I promise." Kathleen knew that she was acting like a
giddy schoolgirl, but she couldn't help herself. It was so
wonderful being with him. Unconsciously, she squeezed
his hand and hugged his arm closer to her side.

"I was going to ask you if you had used the typewriter
since you had the table."

"Almost every night. I am so grateful for it. It sure beats sitting on the floor."

"Every night? You've got that much news to write?"

"I'll tell you a secret if you promise not to tell."

"Cross my heart and hope to die."

"Poke a needle in your eye?" Kathleen laughed happily.

"It'll have to be a pretty good secret for me to go *that* far." He liked the light chatter between them. He liked to hear her laugh. *Does that mean that she is happy to be with me?*

"I'll accept the 'cross my heart.'"

They crossed the street and reached the sidewalk. Johnny moved to the outside and took her hand again.

"What's the big secret?" he asked, wondering how he could keep her from feeling the pounding of his heart.

"I write Western stories," she whispered.

"You what? Write stories?"

"For *Western Story Magazine*. I've had six stories published and contracts for four more. Do you ever read the pulp magazines?"

"No. I don't read much."

"I write under the name of K. K. Doyle. My publisher said it's mostly men who read the magazines, and they'd not want to read a story written by a woman."

"Humm. I wouldn't think that it would matter."

"I see his point. I've never read a love story written by a man. Oh, maybe I have. Shakespeare's *Romeo and Juliet* was a love story. *What light through yonder window breaks? It is the east, and Juliet is the sun!* That's all I know of it, but it's definitely a love story."

"Humm," Johnny said again.

"Doesn't make much sense, does it?"

"Not to me."

"Would you like to read one of my stories? I write about pounding hooves and blazing guns and hard-eyed strangers." She laughed softly. "Everything is exaggerated. It makes for more exciting reading."

"How can you tell if the stranger has hard eyes?"

"He stares, he squints, he scowls. His eyes are dull, flat and black . . . or blue . . . or gray. It's fun making up the stories. I can kill off the bad characters and save the good ones. I make sure that if a girl is in the story, she likes the good cowboy wearing the white hat. The bad cowboys wear black hats."

"Is that what you were going to tell me?" They had reached town and were about to cross the street when a car shot past them. "Marty's going somewhere in a hurry. I hope it's out of town."

"He isn't a very nice man. I wonder how Clara got mixed up with him."

"Birds of a feather," Johnny said drily. "If there's a rotten man in the country, Clara will find him."

"She didn't come home last night. Poor Hazel worried all night that something had happened to her. Today at the rodeo she didn't even come over and speak to her mother and Emily."

"Maybe she'll leave soon. Hazel and Emily are better off without her." He squeezed her hand tightly and looked down at her. "Now what was it that you were going to tell me. I'm not going to let you dillydally out of it."

"I'm not . . . dillydallying." This new freedom to talk

nonsense to him caused her eyes to shine when she smiled up at him. "I was going to tell you that next Sunday I plan to drive over to Red Rock to see Uncle Tom and Henry Ann and ask you if you'd like to go along."

She held her breath while waiting for him to speak. Had she been too bold? Johnny wasn't like any man she had ever known.

"You shouldn't drive over there by yourself."

"Does that mean that you'll go?"

"My truck isn't too . . . reliable."

"We can take my car if you'll promise to fix any flat tires. I don't have a spare now."

"You need a boot and a new tube."

"What's a boot?"

"It's a piece of leather that fits over the hole inside the tire. I'll get one and a tube and gas up the car."

"Are those your conditions for going?"

"I've something else in mind, but I'll not tell you now."

"Oh, you! I hate being in suspense!"

There were still quite a few people in town. Some were sitting in cars watching the people on the street. A few of them yelled at Johnny.

"Hiya, cowboy. Ya've lassoed a good-lookin' filly."

"Hey, Johnny. Ya better get on home. We're driving that stock out early in the mornin'."

Johnny lifted a hand to acknowledge the good-natured joshing and they walked on down the street and turned into the alley behind the *Gazette* building.

"Was there anywhere you wanted to go?" It was dark in the alley, and his voice came softly and intimately.

"There's not much of any place to go in Rawlings."

"There's the Twilight Gardens. But it would be crowded with drunks tonight."

"I'm not much for honky-tonks, but I like to dance."

"We'll go over to Frederick sometime. They've got a fairly nice dance hall over there. They've had Bob Wills playing there a couple of times."

Kathleen's heart leaped. Did he mean that he wanted to go out with her on a real date?

"Sounds like fun." She hoped that she didn't sound as eager as she felt.

"The light's on in Paul's room. Want to go in?"

"No," she said quickly. "I don't want to bother them . . . him."

"You . . . know about them?"

"They told me a day or two after I got here. They love each other. Adelaide worries because she's older than he is."

"It doesn't seem to bother Paul."

"Would it bother you?"

"It might if the woman was sixty. I'm twenty-five."

"I'm twenty-six."

"Really? You don't look over twenty-one."

"Thank you . . . I think."

Johnny chuckled, then drew in a shallow breath. His sore muscles were making themselves known. In the enjoyment of being with Kathleen he had almost forgotten about them.

"Will you drive home tonight and come back to the fairground in the morning?"

"I'm going to stay with Paul . . . rather, on a cot in the

back room of the *Gazette*. In the morning Ruth will take me and Keith out to the stockyards before she heads home."

"I like the McCabes. They seem to be well suited to each other."

"Keith met her when he went to Kansas on an investigation. He fell for her like a ton of bricks. She's just what he needed. They live with his grandmother on a ranch down near Vernon, Texas."

Johnny opened the door of his truck, pulled out an old blanket and shook it before spreading it on the seat.

"You might get your dress dirty," Johnny said, as she stepped up onto the running board.

"It's been dirty before." She settled herself on the seat as Johnny closed the door and went around to get under the wheel. Kathleen was sorry that the evening was almost over.

Johnny drove slowly out of the alley and down the street, dodging the potholes and the ruts, in an effort to make the ride easier.

"We didn't swing," Kathleen said regretfully as they passed the park. "I'm just a kid at heart," she added laughingly.

"Shall we stop?"

"Do you want to?"

Johnny slowed the truck to a stop beside a big old pecan tree, but made no effort to get out.

"I don't want the evening to end," he admitted suddenly.

Kathleen turned to look at him. He had pushed his hat

to the back of his head and was looking at her. He looked without speaking for so long that she became nervous.

"What?" she finally asked. "Is something wrong?"

After a full minute, he sighed. "There sure as hell is. One of those jolts today must have scrambled my brains. I don't know what I'm doing here with you."

"Oh, well—" Kathleen's heart suddenly felt like a rock in her breast. "I'm sorry to have inconvenienced you." She tried to find the door handle so that she could get out.

Johnny grabbed her arm. "Where are you goin'? What do you think I meant?"

"It . . . a . . . seems to me that . . . you meant that you wished you were anywhere but here with me. That if not for me, you could be doing something you really wanted to do." She finished with a rush.

"I didn't mean that!" The grip on her arm pulled her closer to him. "I meant . . . Oh, hell, I meant that this is the start of a hell of a lot of sleepless nights for me."

"I'm sorry—"

The arm he put around her drew her up close against his chest.

"Don't say you're sorry you're here with me," he said in an agonized whisper. A warmth ran over her skin, for he gave his words a sensual meaning.

"I wasn't going to say that. I don't understand—"

"You and I are not right for each other. Not like Keith and Ruth. They fit like a hand to a glove."

"Well . . . I'll understand if you don't want to get *romantically* involved with me. I'll never throw myself at any man." She almost choked on the words. "I had thought we could be . . . friends."

He groaned. "I'll never be just *friends* with *you*. It will be all or nothing. And if it's all, you'll live to regret it. For me it would be like being in heaven and suddenly plunged into hell."

Abruptly he moved and gathered her in his arms. His mouth found hers before she was aware he was going to kiss her. It was not a light kiss. He kissed her as if he were a starving man. She felt his lips, his teeth, his tongue. She opened her lips to his as the intimacy of the kiss increased, and she felt a strange helplessness in her limbs. When he lifted his head his eyes were staring down into hers. She was breathing fast, and so was he.

"I had to do that. I would have done it if I had known I would be killed for it."

"Don't apologize. It's all right."

"I'm not apologizing because I'm not sorry." His strangled voice sounded miles from her ears. He cupped a hand behind her head and pressed hard fingers under the disarray of her hair and drew her flushed face into his shoulder. "I've been alone all my life. I don't want to care for a woman, lose her, and be alone again."

"I've been alone, too, since I lost Grandma and Grandpa." Kathleen burrowed her face in the warmth of his neck.

"It's different for you." He stroked a strand of her hair behind her ear. "There isn't a single man in town, some married ones, too, who wouldn't give their eyeteeth to be here with you."

"I don't want to be with any of them."

"You'll meet someone."

"If you don't want me, don't shove me off on someone else." Impatience with him caused her to straighten up and try to move away from him. His arms tightened.

"I never said I didn't want you. Calm down."

"Why are we even talking about this? I'm not going to fling myself at you like Clara did."

"Whoa. You can sure get worked up fast."

"It isn't very flattering to know that you're with someone who doesn't want to be with you." She moved back from him.

"That isn't it, dammit. You've not been out of my mind since I met you out on the highway." His hands gripped her shoulders, and he shook her gently.

"Then why are you saying these things? Can't you just go along and let nature take its course?"

"I can see where that path is taking me. I've never known a girl like you."

"I'm no different than most other girls."

"Ha!" he snorted. "You're like a Thoroughbred running with a herd of wild mustangs."

In spite of herself she smiled. "That's the nicest thing you've said to me."

"Kathleen, you could take my heart and grind it into little pieces. I'm only trying to protect myself."

He pulled her to him again. With a swift look into her face he lifted her chin and fitted his lips to hers. He kissed her as openly and as intimately as a man could kiss a woman. Kathleen's arm moved up around his neck, her hand caressed his nape. She had never felt anything like the sensual enjoyment she was feeling now.

When he lifted his head, he looked down at the pale luminous oval of her face framed in the tumbled, gloriously red hair that was soft and shining in his fingers.

"You're eyes shine in the dark. Did you know that?" The gentle murmured words sent tremors of joy through her. *He isn't sorry that he kissed me. He enjoyed it as much as I did.*

"Like a cat's?"

"Prettier. Much prettier."

"Thank you," she whispered. "Yours are pretty, too. I think about you when I'm describing the hero in my stories." She cupped his cheek with her palm and reached for his lips. This moment was hers; nothing or no one could ever take it away from her.

"I never expected the evening to end like this." The note of awe in Johnny's voice echoed Kathleen's feelings.

The awe was still with her when Johnny started the truck, and moved on down the road to stop in front of Hazel's house. She sat close beside him, although he'd had to remove his arm from around her in order to shift the gears. After he had turned off the motor, he quickly put his arm around her again.

"Tell me something. What about this Fleming fellow? Is he one of your beaus?"

"Heavens no. He came into the office and bought a paper. He was interested in the rodeo. I saw him again after I left the courthouse the next day and ran into the deputy and the hijackers. The hijackers followed me down the street. Mr. Fleming came out of the bank and ran them off. We had supper together and he told me about his four daughters and two sons."

"And his wife?"

"His wife died."

"And he's looking for another one. He's too old for you, even if he does own half of the tannery and an interest in a packinghouse, a thousand-acre ranch, besides stock in the electric company."

"How did you find out all this?"

"Keith is a fountain of information. If he doesn't know, he finds out."

"Mr. Fleming is a nice man. He was lonely for his family. I enjoyed his company."

"I bet." Johnny removed his arm and got out of the truck. He came around and opened the door for her.

"Johnny? Why don't you like him?"

"I don't know. Maybe it's because he's a breed like me and has made something of himself."

"He had help from his family."

"No one can ever accuse me of that."

"Are you still going with me to Red Rock?" Kathleen asked on the way to the porch.

"Do you still want me to go?"

"Of course."

"Then we'll go. I'll come in next week and get your tire fixed."

They stepped up onto the porch. He pulled her close to him. She felt him trembling and wondered at the cause. She moved her hands up to his shoulders. He seemed to hesitate, then lowered his head and kissed her swiftly. His arms dropped and he stepped back.

"Be careful about being out after dark. The sheriff told Webb and Krome to get out of town, but they still may be here. I don't want them catching you alone."

"I'll be careful. Thank you for bringing me home."

"You're welcome." Still he stayed looking down at her.

"I wish you could get into a tub of water and ease your aching muscles."

"How do you know they're aching?"

"I've seen you wince from time to time and even groan a little."

"I didn't know I did that. Well, good night."

"Good night, Johnny."

Kathleen slipped into the house and leaned against the door until she heard Johnny start the truck and drive away. He was gone. She ran her tongue over her lips as his had done minutes before and her heart gave a joyous leap. Oh, Lord, how could it be that a few soft words, a smile, and a kiss from that cowboy could make her feel like this?

Chapter Fifteen

Riding behind the horse herd, Johnny grimaced as the bay he was on turned sharply. The animal had been trained as a cutting horse and knew without the slightest move from the man on his back that his job was to keep the herd bunched. Sore ribs and a crowded mind had kept Johnny awake most of the night.

The stock being driven back to the McCabe ranch was in two groups traveling about a mile apart. Johnny worked the horses and McCabe the steers. It was a warm, still October day. The dark sky in the west promised rain or a dust storm. Johnny hoped that it was rain lurking in the clouds.

Barker Fleming had been at the stockyard when Johnny and Keith arrived at daylight. Johnny had ignored him, but Keith had welcomed the help he offered.

"What's he butterin' you up for?" Johnny asked while saddling his horse.

"He thinks I'm pretty."

"Go to hell."

"Cheer up, son. You've got an extra man to help. You can sleep in the saddle all the way to Vernon."

After Barker had caught and saddled a skittish buck-skin, Keith had made the comment that he was a skilled horseman.

"Why wouldn't he be?" Johnny had remarked sarcastically. "He's an Indian, isn't he?"

By midmorning, after Johnny had been in the saddle for more than four hours, he felt as if he had been kicked in the back by a steer. It was not unusual for him to be sore for a week after a rodeo. His aches and pains had not, however, kept his mind off the evening he had spent with Kathleen. He had played over in his mind every word they had exchanged, every touch. That she had returned his kiss and one time had even initiated it, was still a wonder to him. He could close his eyes and smell the lemony scent of her hair as it swept across his face and feel her soft, seeking lips beneath his.

He groaned when he thought of his blundering words, and how she had reacted when she thought that he hadn't wanted to be with her. He had thought of himself as a man who had been around a bit after the work he had done for the Bureau with Hod Dolan, but, compared to her, he was pure backwoods. He felt like a clod when she talked about some feller named Shakespeare who made up silly verses.

Kathleen wrote stories for the newspaper and for a magazine. Hell, he'd never read a book in his life. How would she feel about him if she knew that? They had nothing in common. For all he knew she hated horses, and he loved them. She lived in town and mixed with people who talked stock market and shares and things like that. His bank was in a milk can in the barn. He and

Kathleen were as different as daylight and dark. He couldn't allow himself to fall in love with her. If he did, he could look forward to a lifetime of misery.

Is it too late? If a woman was constantly in your thoughts, he asked himself, if you saw her face while you lay in a sleepless bed, and if every word she said and every look she gave you were of utmost importance, did it mean you loved her?

Oh, Lord. It *was* too late!

Johnny watched Barker ride ahead and block off a road to keep the herd from turning off. The man had been on a drive or two and seemed to be enjoying the work. If he had to do it day after day, Johnny thought, it wouldn't be so much fun. *This was a little outing for a rich man who had some time to kill.*

The McCabe ranch was a sprawling compound. The main house, built before the turn of the century, was weathered, two-story, and had a wraparound porch. Ruth, who had left Rawlings ahead of the drive, stood on the porch and waved as the herds passed on their way to the lower pastures. By the time the stock was penned, it was noon. The drovers, including Johnny and Barker, washed at the bench on the back porch and went into the house for dinner.

Johnny had been to the McCabes' many times. Keith's grandmother greeted him with affection.

"You haven't been to see me for a while, John. Ya got another girl?" Mrs. McCabe was the only person who ever called him John.

"I've not seen a girl yet who could hold a candle to you, Granny," Johnny said, using the name every man on the place affectionately called her. He felt comfortable here. He knew the old lady genuinely liked him because he had seen her reaction to those she didn't like.

"Ruth said you did good at the rodeo, John. Wish I could a seen it."

"If you had been there, Granny, I'd have been so nervous, I'd not have stayed on long enough to get out of the chute."

"Ah, go on with ya. I knew ya was comin' and had Guadalupe make sweet potato pie," she added in a conspiratorial whisper.

"You're a woman to ride the trail with, Granny." He glanced at the smiling face of the Mexican woman who had been born on the ranch the year Granny McCabe, as a nineteen-year-old bride, came here to live.

With an arm across her shoulders, Keith proudly introduced Barker to his grandmother.

"Be careful. She rules the roost with an iron hand."

The frail little woman held out her hand. "Welcome to our home, Mr. Fleming."

"Thank you, ma'am. It's a pleasure to be here."

"You met my wife yesterday," Keith went on with the introductions. "And this is Guadalupe."

"Mrs. McCabe. Ma'am," Barker said smoothly. "Something smells mighty good."

The table took up one side of the large kitchen. Workers on the ranch had always taken their meals with the McCabe family. Guadalupe or Ruth got up to get more biscuits, pour coffee, or refill the platter of roast beef.

The talk around the table was mostly about the stock

drive and the rodeo. Then Keith asked Barker if he thought they would soon be in a war.

"I don't know how the United States can stay out of it if Hitler takes over Europe, and it seems that is what he has in mind."

"There's an ocean between us," Keith argued. "I can't see him attacking us."

"The only thing that would prevent it, if he's determined to rule the world, would be that he would be spreading his troops too thin." Barker's eyes caught Johnny's. "I'd rather we fight him over there than on our own territory."

"Unless we are attacked," Keith said. "I hate to see our boys dying on foreign shores."

Johnny had not heard enough about what was going on in Europe to make a comment. He lowered his head and finished his meal.

After the meal, Keith took Johnny, Barker, and another drover back to Rawlings. Barker sat in the front seat with Keith, and they continued their conversation about the possibility of war.

"I think Roosevelt is smart enough to keep us out of it," Keith said.

"Some of the big companies are already gearing up to furnish arms, tanks, and airplanes to the British. Hitler will hop over the channel as soon as he reaches Normandy."

"What about that *Maginot Line*? I thought that was supposed to stop him from taking France."

"It's my understanding that the *Maginot Line* was built to keep the Germans out during World War I. The French have strengthened it, but this is not going to be a war pri-

marily fought by foot soldiers like in the war against the
Kaiser. The Germans now have heavy tanks and airplanes. I'm afraid the *Maginot Line* is not going to be the
protection the French think it is."

Listening to the conversation, Johnny realized more
than ever just how little he knew about what was going
on in the world. What the hell was the *Maginot Line*?
Keith seemed to know.

"Those factories you're talking about are putting men
to work. Roosevelt likes that. He's done a fair job of
pulling the country out of the Depression, but there's a lot
to be done yet."

"What do you think, Johnny?" Barker half turned in
the seat to ask the question.

Johnny's hat was tilted down over his eyes. He feigned
sleep and didn't answer.

At the fairground, Keith stopped where Barker and the
other drover had left their cars.

"I'll give Johnny a lift into town to get his car and save
you the trip," Barker said. "I know you want to get back
home."

"That would save me time. Thanks. And thanks for the
help today."

"It was my pleasure and a real pleasure to be in your
home."

"Anytime you're down our way, drop in. The door is
always open and the coffeepot on."

Johnny got out of the car and lifted his saddle off the
carrier on top.

"You going into town?" he asked the drover who got
out on the other side.

"Naw." He grinned shyly. "I'm headed for Deval to see my lady friend."

"How about you and Kathleen coming down next Sunday, Johnny?" Keith leaned out the window.

"Can't make it, but thanks."

"Come down when you can. You're always welcome."

"Will do."

"Throw your saddle in the back of the car, Johnny," Barker said after Keith left. He regretted that Johnny was not pleased about being left here with him.

"Pretty fancy car for a dirty old saddle."

"It'll clean."

Instead of getting into the car, Barker went to the front of it and leaned against the fender. He pulled out a pack of cigarettes and offered them to Johnny. Johnny shook his head and built his own smoke from a sack of tobacco he took from his shirt pocket. Barker made no move to get into the car.

"I'm ready to go if you are," Johnny said.

"I'd like to talk to you." Barker's voice was not as calm and as sure as it had been. His dark eyes watched Johnny anxiously as he sought the right words to say.

"Yeah? You want to offer me a job? No, thanks. I've got one."

"Do you like ranching?"

"If I didn't, I wouldn't be doing it."

"I can understand that. You lived for a while with your sister on a farm near Red Rock. I thought you might prefer farming."

"How did you know that?" The coldness of Johnny's

tone reflected his emotions and alerted Barker that he might have started out on the wrong foot.

"I talked to Isabel Perry last week in Oklahoma City."

"You . . . talked to Isabel?" Johnny said it softly and menacingly.

"Yes. I wanted to know if her mother was Dorene Perry and if she had a brother."

Their eyes met in a long, silent war. Johnny's breath came fiercely.

"You knew Dorene?" Johnny's lips curved in a sneer. "That says a lot about you."

"Yes, it does. I knew her when I was a stupid, head-strong, resentful kid of eighteen. I went to the city to sow my wild oats and prove to my father that I was a man."

"Don't tell me the story of your life. I'm not interested in a hotheaded kid cuttin' his apron strings." Johnny spat out the words.

"I'm a half-breed. My mother was Cherokee, my father a white man. Back in those days, and even in some places now, you're looked down on as not worthy to associate with white people, even if you do have financial means. I resented that then . . . and I resent it now."

"You're ashamed of your people?"

"Not now. I was when I was a kid of eighteen. I didn't want my mother to be a Cherokee. I wanted her to be white like my father."

"At least you had a mother. Mine was a whore. She liked being a whore."

"You always knew that?"

"From the time I was old enough to know what a whore was. Before that I wondered why I had to sleep in the closet with the door shut while she slept in the bed with a strange man." Johnny dropped his cigarette and ground it in the dirt with his boot.

"I was with Dorene during the summer of 1912. She was young and fresh and pretty. I didn't know that she had a husband and daughter. I was fascinated with her."

"—And screwed her," Johnny said with disgust.

"Yes. At eighteen the sap runs high. I spent all the money I could get on her until Father came to the city and put a stop to it. He sent me back East to school. I hated him for it then. I love him for it now."

"Well now that you've told me your life story, I'd like to get to town and get my truck. I have things to do."

"I'm your father, Johnny." Barker's voice was quiet and anxious.

The words were dropped in the stillness of the afternoon. They were ordinary words, words that had no meaning to him, Johnny thought, until they seeped into his consciousness and he became aware that the man had said that he was *his* father.

Unreasonable anger flared.

"That's a fine thing to drop on a man."

"I didn't know any other way to do it."

"What do you want me to do? Get down on my knees and thank you for screwing a whore and bringin' a breed into the world who had to root-hog or die during his first fourteen years?"

"No . . ."

"You threw your seeds in the wind, mister. You think that one of them stuck in a whore named Dorene, and I'm the result?"

"I don't just think it. I'm sure of it. I've been looking for you for a long time." Barker knew that Johnny was confused and hurt.

"Yeah? I wasn't hiding anywhere." Johnny felt as if an iron band was squeezing his chest.

"I came through Oklahoma City six or seven years ago and wondered what had ever happened to the girl, Dorene. I knew, even at age eighteen, that she would have had a bad end. I think I felt a little responsible for it."

"Lookin' for more of the same?" Johnny said nastily. "I'm surprised if she didn't give you the clap."

"My wife was in the hospital at the time and being with a whore was the last thing on my mind. From the tavern where she had worked I learned that Dorene had a boy who was part-Indian. I couldn't do anything about finding you then. But after my wife died, I sent a detective to find the last man Dorene lived with. He told us that Dorene talked about her life when she knew that she was dying. She told him that the father of her son was an Indian kid. She wanted to see her boy, but knew that he was better off with her husband." This being so important to him caused Barker to speak hurriedly and in jerky sentences.

Johnny turned his back and looked off across the prairie. He wiped a hand across his face. This was something he didn't want to deal with. He had put the circumstances of his birth behind him, and he wanted to know nothing about the man who had sired him.

"Didn't you ever wonder about your father?"

Johnny turned. His eyes bored into those of the other man.

"I didn't have to wonder. I was told up until the time I

was big enough to fight that my mother was a whore and that my father was a drunk Indian, a blanket-ass, a dirty redskin, a dog eater, or anything else anyone could think of to make me feel dirty and worthless. No, I never wanted to lay eyes on the son of a bitch."

Barker winced at the raw hurt in his voice. "Was it so bad for you?"

Johnny ignored the question. "The best man I ever knew was Ed Henry, Dorene's husband. He gave me my name and a roof over my head. He taught me to love horses, how to fix a car, and how to be responsible for my actions. He suspected that I was Cherokee and even told me to be proud of my people. For the short time I was with him, he taught me a hell of a lot."

"I'd like to meet him."

"He's dead."

"Do you want to know about me, my family—?"

"Hell no! Why should I? You mean nothing to me. Nothing is changed. I've made my own path up to now and will make it alone from now on."

"I found your birth certificate in the courthouse in Oklahoma City. Dorene listed me as the father of a boy born April 15, 1913. I'll get a copy if you want to see it."

"I don't."

"I would like for you to come to Elk City and meet your half sisters, your brother, and your grandfather."

"Listen, mister, let's get something straight. I've gotten along without you for twenty-five years. As far as I'm concerned, you are like a bull that serviced a heifer. There is no more connection between you and me than between that bull and the calf."

"There is, but I'll not intrude in your life if I'm not welcome. I wanted you to know that you have a family, blood ties; and if you ever need us, we are there."

"What I need is to get to town and get my truck. I've got chores to do at home."

"All right. Get in."

They drove into town in silence. Not a word was exchanged until they neared the alley behind the *Gazette*, and Johnny said, "Stop here."

As soon as the car stopped, Johnny got out.

"This has been a shock to you, as it was to me when I first heard about it. I'm leaving for Elk City tomorrow, but I'll keep in touch." Barker spoke while Johnny was getting his saddle out of the backseat.

"Suit yourself." Johnny hoisted the saddle to his shoulder and walked down the alley toward his truck.

Kathleen began work on her story for the magazine after she had washed her hair. She needed to wash all of her underwear, but it wouldn't do to hang it outside on the line on Sunday. She washed a couple pairs of panties and her hose and hung them in the bathroom.

Clara had come home in the middle of the morning. She was in a foul mood. Kathleen could hear her arguing with her mother and tried not to let their voices distract her as she sat before her typewriter.

With effort she dragged her mind away from the time she had spent with Johnny. For her it had been wonderful. She would treasure the memory of his kisses forever. For just a small moment in time they had been the only people in the world. He had said that he had thought about her since he met her on the highway; yet, when he said it, it was as if she were a thorn in his hide. How would he act when she saw him again? He had promised to go with her to Red Rock. Surely he'd not back out on the promise.

Kathleen forced herself to go back to the story she was writing. After reading the last few pages of the manuscript, she began to type.

Durango wakened with a start. Someone was trying to get into his ranch house. He eased open the barn door and saw a shadowy figure. "Put your hands up, stranger. No funny business or you'll get both barrels." The stranger turned and the moonlight shone on her face. Durango gasped, "Oh, my God. Hallie, little sister. Is it you?" He shoved his gun into his holster. He—

Kathleen yanked the page from the typewriter, turned it over, and tried to start again. But the words wouldn't come. Johnny's face intruded into her mind's eye. She felt the roughness of his cheeks and the softness of his lips when he kissed her. Why had this man become so important to her?

Pressed by the magazine deadline, Kathleen determinedly brought her mind back to Durango and Hallie.

He ran to her and lifted her in his arms when she sagged against him. "Help me, brother. Hide me—"

It was no use. This wasn't the direction she wanted the story to go. Kathleen stood up and walked to the window. It was late afternoon and she had written only two pages.

To meet her deadline she had to write eight pages on Sunday and at least eight pages during the week. So far she was behind schedule.

Today Johnny was going to drive the horses and cattle back to Keith McCabe's ranch. Kathleen wondered how he was able to get back into the saddle after the beating his body had taken. He was hurting last night.

Johnny, Johnny, get out of my mind!

Kathleen started to turn from the window when she saw a car pull up in front of the house and stop. Why in the world was Mr. Fleming coming here? Kathleen opened the door and stepped out on the porch. He got out of the car, came up the walk to the porch, and removed his hat before he spoke.

"Miss Dolan, I hope you don't mind that I took the liberty to find out where you lived."

"Is something wrong, Mr. Fleming?"

"No emergency. I'm leaving in the morning, and I wanted to talk to you. Are you free to take a short ride with me? We could have dinner later."

"I'm not dressed to go out for dinner, but I can go for a short ride. I'll get a jacket."

Kathleen opened the door of her wardrobe and reached for a jacket. It was not there. She looked to see if it had dropped on the floor and checked to see if something had been hung over it. She didn't find it, so she put her coat around her shoulders and went back to the porch to find Clara talking to Barker.

"You from around here?"

"No."

"I saw you at the rodeo."

"I saw you, too."

"Ya did?"

"Yes, ma'am. You should be more careful of the company you keep."

"There's nothin' wrong with Marty." Clara said belligerently. "Bet he's got more money than you got, and he's got a town named after his granddaddy."

"Are you ready to go, Miss Dolan?" Barker said.

"I'm ready." Kathleen ignored Clara and stepped off the porch.

"You'll not have no fun with *her*," Clara called.

Barker opened the car door for Kathleen. When she was settled, he went to the driver's side and got under the wheel. Clara was still standing on the porch.

"I would move out of that house, but I don't think that she'll stay long. She comes and goes."

"She sure tore into Johnny yesterday."

"Yes, and he's tried to be a friend to her because he feels sorry for her mother and little girl. The only reason I stay there is because her mother needs the money from renting the room."

Barker turned south. He drove slowly along a dirt road.

"I helped drive McCabe's stock back to his ranch this morning. I got back a little while ago."

"Johnny told me last night they were driving the stock back. It's a long ride."

"Nice folks, the McCabes. I'm glad Johnny has such good friends."

Kathleen didn't know what to say to that, so she remained silent.

After a while Barker said, "I like to drive. I do my best thinking when I'm driving or riding a horse."

"That's funny," Kathleen turned to look at him. "So do I."

"See those buildings over there?" Barker pointed in the distance. "That's Johnny's ranch. Have you ever been there?"

"No. How did you know where it was?"

"I asked my friend, Judge Fimbres. He looked it up in the tax book."

"Why were you interested? Oh, I'm sorry. That was a rude question."

"I want to tell you." Barker pulled the car to the side of the road and stopped. He took off his hat and placed it on the seat between them. He looked at her until she met his eyes before he spoke. "I'm Johnny's father."

The silence was loaded with surprise and almost disbelief.

"Johnny doesn't know?" Kathleen asked when she was finally able to speak.

"He does now. I told him a little while ago."

"I don't know much about his background. His sister is married to my Uncle Tom. I knew that they had the same mother but different fathers."

"I met Johnny's mother, Dorene, in Oklahoma City. I was a stupid undisciplined kid of eighteen who thought he knew all that was worth knowing. I'm Johnny's father. My name is on his birth certificate."

"This is the first Johnny knew about you?"

"He didn't want to believe it. He's had a rough time and doesn't want me intruding in his life."

"He's shocked. After he thinks about it, he might change his mind."

"I'm afraid that he won't. The funny thing about it is that I understand how he feels. It's the way I would have felt."

"Johnny is a son you can be proud of. My Uncle Hod Dolan was in the Federal Bureau. He called on Johnny to help him trace the movements of Bonnie Parker and Clyde Barrow that resulted in the ambush that killed them. Uncle Hod thinks the world of Johnny."

"I'm glad to hear that." They didn't talk for a few minutes. Barker looked toward the distant buildings. "Do you care for Johnny?"

"I like him very much," Kathleen said, keeping her face turned away.

"I think he's on the verge of falling in love with you."

Kathleen's head swiveled around. "Why do you say that?"

"He's concerned for you, watches you when you're not looking. He was embarrassed yesterday that you were there when he had the set-to with that couple."

"It wasn't his fault."

"I'll be back down here in a week or two. In the meanwhile, if you should want to contact me, I'll be in Elk City."

"I don't think it will be necessary. I'll probably not see Johnny until next Sunday. We had planned to go over to Red Rock to see his sister and my Uncle Tom."

Barker started the car. "I wanted you to know about my being Johnny's father should there be something you could do to help him come to terms with it."

"He might never mention it to me. He's a very private person."

"It's his Cherokee blood." Barker looked at her and smiled for the first time.

"It's what makes him so handsome, too," Kathleen said, and smiled back.

Barker turned into a crossroad preparing to turn around and head back to town. A string of calves were crossing the road. Coming up out of the gully behind them was Johnny on horseback. He turned his head toward them, looked briefly, then put his heels to his mount. Johnny and the calves he was driving disappeared in a gully.

"Lordy. That put the hair on the cake," Barker explained. "He'll think I'm out here spying on him."

Kathleen couldn't have said anything if her life had depended on it. All she could think of was that at one time Johnny had thought that Barker was her boyfriend. What would he think now after seeing them together on a lonely road near his ranch?

"Let's go back to town." Kathleen's heart felt like a rock in her breast. "He'll think whatever he wants to think."

Barker heard the tears in her voice, and wished there were something he could say to ease her anxiety.

"Surely he won't think that there's . . . anything between you and me."

"I don't know what he thinks. He said that he and I were not right for each other. He doesn't want to get involved with me."

"Then he doesn't have as much sense as I thought he had."

*　　*　　*

When Johnny came up out of the gully and saw Barker Fleming's car blocking the road, he felt anger; but when he saw who was in it with him, he felt as if he had been kicked in the stomach by a mustang. His whole thought process had shut down. By the time he got the calves penned he was thinking again.

The son of a bitch was making a play for Kathleen!

The thought came to him on the way to the house. And Kathleen was falling for it. Why not? Fleming could give her a hell of a lot more than he'd ever be able to give her. It was a good thing to find out about them now before he made more a fool of himself than he had last night.

Johnny's mind churned while he got out a hunk of cheese and some crackers for his supper. He would have to give some thought as to how to let her know that he wouldn't be going to Red Rock next Sunday without having to go into the *Gazette* to tell her.

It would be hell to be cooped up in the car with her and have to put on an act in front of Henry Ann and Tom. He was not good in such complicated situations and he was not going to subject himself to handling them. From now on, if he wanted any peace of mind at all, he'd better put as much distance as possible between himself and Miss Kathleen Dolan.

And as for Barker Fleming, he was on the bottom of Johnny's list of concerns.

Chapter Sixteen

Dr. Herman was eating breakfast when Rita, his housekeeper, let Louise into the house.

"Mornin', Doc. Glad you're back."

"Mornin', pretty lady. Rita, get Louise a cup of coffee."

"How was the conference?"

"Informative, as usual."

Louise waited to speak until Rita had brought the coffee and she heard her in the room off the kitchen loading the washing machine.

"Clara Ramsey is back and demanding money."

"Is that what you called me about?"

"I was afraid to say too much. I never know when Flossie is listening in."

"Did she say how much she wanted, or was she after anything she could get?" Doc split a biscuit and spooned gravy over it.

"She wants a hundred dollars."

"Hummm—"

"She said that she was going to Nashville. The silly twit thinks she can get on the Grand Ole Opry."

"Hummm—"

"She threatened to talk to that Dolan woman at the *Gazette*. She rooms at Hazel's."

Doc's head came up. "She would get herself in a lot of trouble."

"She isn't smart enough to realize that."

"I don't want to give Miss Dolan any excuse to nose around. She has no loyalty to this town. She's a hard, brazen bitch!"

"I think so, too. She has a smart mouth and the guts to go with it." Louise was pleased to hear that he disliked the redheaded reporter.

"We'll fix that if she starts taking too much on herself."

"Clara is trouble, Doc. If she spills her story to the reporter, we could be in for a bad time."

"We've overcome bad times before. I trust you to keep a lid on things at the clinic, dear lady."

Doc knew what strings to pull with Louise. A flattering phrase here and there, and the woman would die for him. He enjoyed her devotion to him and the power he had over her, which he had cultivated carefully through the years. Most of all, he enjoyed the certainty that should the axe fall, he had a place for it to land.

"And I will, Doc. You know that. But Clara worried me. She came to us twice, and we helped her out. I thought the second time would be the end of it and we'd seen the last of her."

"We made a mistake with Clara."

"I know that, Doc. How are we going to fix it?"

"I'll have to think on it. As you well know, I don't make hasty decisions."

"I know that, Doc," she said again. "You're the smartest man I ever knew. I was anxious for you to get back because I knew that you'd know how to handle things."

"We've been a good team, Louise. I couldn't have done the work I have without you."

"You look tired, Doc. You wore yourself out at that conference."

"It was a lot of work, but made easier knowing that back here things were in capable hands. The last transfer go all right?"

"Slick as a whistle. Nothing to worry about. The papers are filled out. I'll take them to the courthouse this morning."

"I'll do it. I should go over and talk to Sheriff Carroll about Hannah. She was in town a couple of times this past week. That's far too often."

"I'd better get back to the clinic. Let me know what you want to do about Clara. I told her that you'd be back today and I'm expecting her to come in."

"Avoid her today. Tell her you haven't had a chance to talk to me. Give me a chance to figure something out."

"Maybe we should give her the money and get rid of her."

"Never give in to a blackmailer, Louise. Once we weaken, she would be back for money on a regular basis."

As Louise got up to leave, Doc reached out, took her hand, and brought it to his lips.

"I don't know what I'd do without you, dear girl."

Louise's face became warm beneath the thick layer of paint and powder. Her eyes shone with love as she looked down on the head bending over her hand. These were the tender moments she lived for. This exceptional man who held life and death in his hands needed *her*.

"Ah . . . Doc, you'd do all right. You'd do all right." She repeated herself because of the sudden lump in her throat, and it was something safe to say.

"Get along, my capable and beautiful assistant. I'll be over to the clinic later on this morning." He squeezed her hand tightly, kissed it again, and let it go.

Louise left the house feeling wonderfully light-headed, basking in the knowledge that she was important to the man she loved. They would stand together, depend on each other, and share the secret that was going to make it possible for them to be together.

No one was going to threaten him. She would see to it.

Kathleen arrived at the office half an hour before they opened for business. She told Adelaide and Paul about Krome or Webb slashing her tire while she was in the restaurant. She described the scene when Barker and Johnny confronted Krome and Webb and the sheriff's ordering them to get out of town. She was careful to avoid speaking about Johnny and Barker Fleming's relationship. If Johnny wanted it known that Barker was his father, it would be up to him to tell people.

"Law," Adelaide declared. "Things are going from bad to worse in this town."

"Something else happened when I left here last night

that I thought was unusual." Kathleen told them about finding Hannah sitting on the curb beside her car. "She was really drunk—could hardly stand. When the sheriff stopped, I thought that he was going to arrest her, but he was real gentle with her. He put her in his car and took her home."

"There's a story there. Hannah was a pretty girl about fifteen years ago before she started drinking. I saw her with Pete Carroll a few times. He lived with his mother and, knowing Ruby Carroll, she would never have stood still for her son's marrying an Indian. Maybe he still remembers that young pretty girl."

"His kindness to her raised him a few notches in my estimation."

"Carroll isn't so bad when you get right down to it," Adelaide said.

"Is he married?"

"He was at one time. His wife couldn't stand Ruby and left. I don't know if he got a divorce or not. Ruby died a few years ago."

Kathleen worked steadily all morning. News this week was plentiful. She wrote up the story about the rodeo and told Paul to save room on the front page for the picture of Johnny with the hope that the engraving would come in on the evening bus. When she had caught up on the news stories, she went out to pick up the ads.

"Miss Dolan," Mrs. Wilson said, after giving Kathleen a small grocery ad, "there's a young girl sitting back there by the stove and I don't know what to do about her. She was in the alley this morning when I came to open the store. She had slept in that old truck bed. I let her in and gave her something to eat."

"Is she from around here?"

"She said she came to Rawlings to find her mother."

"Do you know her mother?"

"There's no one that I know of named DeBerry in town, and she doesn't know her mother's maiden name."

"Maybe Adelaide knows."

"Come talk to her. She's a pitiful little thing."

Kathleen walked back to where the young girl sat huddled in a chair beside the stove. Her thin shoulders were hunched, her arms crossed, and her hands in the sleeves of a ragged gray jacket. She looked up at Kathleen with large, sad eyes. Dark hair and eyes, fine features, and golden skin spoke of Indian blood. She wore ankle socks and tie shoes much like those an older woman would wear.

"Hello. I work at the newspaper. Mrs. Wilson says that you came to town to find your mother."

"Yes, ma'am."

"I haven't been here long enough to know many people, but Miss Vernon down at the office may be able to help you."

"She would? Hope leaped in the girl's eyes, and her hands came out of the sleeves. "I come all the way from Fort Worth to find her."

"Oh, my. That's a long way. Did you come in on the bus?"

"No, ma'am. I got some rides and . . . walked a lot."

"That wouldn't be an easy trip for anyone."

"No, ma'am." One of the girl's hands fluttered to her

face as if to cover her mouth. Her eyes became misty, and her lips trembled in spite of an effort to keep them firm. She looked to be about twelve years old.

"My name is Kathleen."

"I'm Judith DeBerry. Most folks call me Judy."

"How old are you, Judy?"

"Sixteen."

"We can go down to the *Gazette* office and talk to Miss Vernon if you like. She's lived in Rawlings all her life."

The girl stood, leaned over, and picked up a canvas suitcase. She was short, thin, and reminded Kathleen of a little lost kitten. At the front counter, she stopped and thanked Mrs. Wilson for the food and for allowing her to sit by the stove.

"You're welcome, child. I hope you find your mother."

"Is that suitcase heavy?" Kathleen asked after they left the store and were out on the sidewalk.

"No, ma'am. It don't have much in it."

When they reached the office, Judy stood hesitantly beside the door while Kathleen put the ads in the ad box, then motioned for her to follow her to the back room. Paul and Adelaide were working at the proof table.

"I have two more ads to be made up, Paul. One grocery and one from the theater."

"Hello." Adelaide left the table when she saw the girl.

"Ma'am," Judy murmured.

"This is Judy DeBerry, Adelaide. She's looking for her mother, and I thought maybe you could help her."

"I will, if I can. What's her name?"

"I . . . don't know. But . . . I was born here. I think. It's what my birth certificate says."

"Well . . ." Adelaide's eyes turned to Kathleen. "Let's go into the office and sit down."

Kathleen placed Judy's suitcase behind the ad counter, then pulled out a chair for the girl.

"Your father's name was DeBerry?"

"Yes, but he ain't my father." Judy kept her eyes on her hands in her lap.

"Do you know your mother's maiden name?"

"No, ma'am. You see, she wasn't my mother." When she looked up she had big quiet tears creeping down her cheeks.

"Judy, you're going to have to explain a little more if we're going to help you." Kathleen exchanged a look with Adelaide and pressed a handkerchief into the girl's hand.

"I have always known that Mama and Daddy didn't like me very much." Judy told her story haltingly. "I heard Mama say to Daddy that it was his fault they had me; and he said it was her fault, and she should have known what she was getting. I didn't understand any of it, then one day Mama got mad at me and told me how they had always wanted a pretty little girl and how disappointed they were in me . . . that . . . I looked like an Indian or a . . . a . . . darky."

Pride kept the girl's head up. "I asked her what she meant. She said . . . that she wasn't my mother . . . that I was . . . ugly and dark. She said for me to keep my mouth shut about what she said, or something bad would happen to me."

Kathleen groaned inwardly, almost feeling the hurt of the young girl who'd had to hear that she wasn't wanted.

"Mama and Daddy fussed all the time. Daddy slapped her one night, and I heard him say that he was going back to Rawlings and get his money back. Mama said he'd go to jail. After that, they hardly ever looked at me."

Judy wiped her eyes with the back of her hand. Kathleen exchanged a glance with Adelaide.

"Daddy was gone when I came home from school one day. Mama said it was my fault and told me to get out. She gave me five dollars and said she never wanted to see my . . . face again. I didn't know what to do, so I came here thinking that if she wasn't my mother, my mother would be here."

"Judy, did you ever ask your mother why they were in Rawlings?" Adelaide asked.

"She said they were passing through Rawlings and . . . and they found me on a dung pile."

Kathleen and Adelaide both shook their heads at the unspeakable cruelty.

The door opened, and Mrs. Smothers came into the office.

"Oh . . . Adelaide, I'm all out of breath. I was afraid I'd be too late to get my story in."

"The deadline is ten o'clock in the morning, Mrs. Smothers." *As you well know, you old busybody.*

"We . . . ll— Who do we have here?" She turned her beady eyes on Judy. "I've not met you before."

"Of course, you haven't met her. She's my cousin from Constantinople." Kathleen stood and moved between the woman and Judy.

"From where? Is that in Oklahoma?"

"Give me the facts about your sale, Mrs. Smothers, and I'll add it to the front-page story."

"You will? That would be sooooo . . . nice of you."

While Kathleen took notes, Adelaide motioned to Judy and they went quietly into the back room. Mrs. Smothers was so excited that the success of her booth at the rodeo would be prominently displayed on the front page of the paper that she didn't even notice when they left.

After Kathleen got rid of the woman, she went to the door and said, "All clear."

Adelaide was laughing when she came back into the office.

"How did you come up with Constantinople?"

"It was the first outlandish place that came to mind. By the time she left she had already forgotten. She asked me if my cousin from *Cincin—mople* would be staying long. I explained that she would be going on to visit another cousin in Winnebago."

Adelaide laughed. "Where is that?"

"It's a river in Iowa."

"Kathleen, you're the limit."

"That nosy old woman irritates me."

"I want to talk to Paul about what Judy told us. We've had a suspicion for a couple of years that something was going on at the clinic that they didn't want anyone to know about."

"What can we do with Judy? We can't turn her out on the street. I shudder to think of her meeting up with Webb or Krome, or a dozen other undesirables in this town, including that lecherous deputy."

"We can't turn her out to fend for herself."

"I'd take her home with me and let her share my room for a night or two if it weren't for Clara. It would give her a reason to rant and rave—not that she needs one."

"I'll talk to Paul and see what he thinks about her staying upstairs with me for a day or two. I know what he'll say—that we know nothing about her and that she could have escaped from the asylum. He's very suspicious."

"Suspicious? I'd say he's very protective of you." Kathleen pulled a sheet of paper out of her typewriter. "As soon as I have time I'm going down to the courthouse and look up her birth record. But our job at the moment is to get the paper out. After it's wrapped up tomorrow, I'll nose around and see what I can find out."

Judy slept the entire afternoon on the cot that Johnny used when he stayed overnight with Paul. She was so tired that the clanking noise of the linotype machine didn't seem to bother her at all.

At the end of the day it was decided that Judy would spend the night in Adelaide's apartment upstairs. Nothing was said directly, but Kathleen assumed that Adelaide would spend the night in Paul's room.

The days were getting shorter, and it was dark by the time Kathleen left the office to go home. She parked her car behind Hazel's house and went in through the kitchen door.

"Miss Dolan's home," Emily called to her grandmother.

Kathleen noticed that only three places were set at the table, meaning that Clara was not at home.

"Hi, Sugarpuss."

"Supper is ready, but Mama won't be here. She went somewhere."

"After I hang up my coat and wash the ink off my hands, I'll be right back."

"Miss Dolan," Emily whispered, and pulled on Kathleen's hand. "Mama wore your jacket and . . . and Granny's cryin'." The little girl's eyes were anxious.

"Did they quarrel?"

"Hu-huh."

"Well, don't worry about it, honey," Kathleen whispered back. "I'll tell your grandma that it's all right."

"I don't want Granny to cry." Emily's lips trembled.

"I don't either. I'll be right back."

As she washed her hands in the bathroom, Kathleen wished she had Clara's neck between them so she could throttle her. The selfish girl had taken her jacket, not caring a whit about the embarrassment it would cause her mother or the anguish it caused her child.

When she returned to the kitchen, Hazel was putting the supper on the table. Her eyes were swollen from crying, and Emily hovered close to her anxiously.

"Something smells good, Hazel."

"It's brown beans, tomatoes, and onions."

"Granny made corn bread," Emily said.

"I'm so glad. I'm hungry enough to eat you, Sugarpuss."

Before Hazel sat down, she gripped the back of the chair and looked straight across the table at Kathleen.

"I've got to tell you something." Tears clouded her eyes. "Clara wore your jacket. I feel so bad about it. I'm sorry, really sorry. I told her to leave your things alone.

I'd not blame you if you want to find another place to stay."

"It isn't your fault, Hazel. When she comes back, I'll take it and lock it in my trunk. Don't worry about me moving. I like it here. I like you and I *love* this little sugarpuss." She reached out an arm and hugged Emily.

"She'll leave soon. She always does. I always wonder when she goes if I'll ever see her again."

"Maybe she *will* make it in Nashville."

"She won't. I don't know where she ever got it in her head that she can sing."

While they were eating, Hazel seemed to calm a little. "She went somewhere this afternoon, and when she came back she was madder than a wet hen. Someone owes her money and won't pay. I can't imagine who it could be. She swore to get even with them."

"Where is she now?"

"I don't know." Tears filled Hazel's eyes again. "She took the three dollars I had hidden in the baking-powder can. I guess she remembered that I hid things there when she was a little girl."

After the meal Kathleen stayed in the kitchen to dry the dishes as Hazel washed them and dropped them in the hot rinse water. Emily sat at the table drawing pictures on scraps of newsprint that Kathleen had given to her.

"Hazel, do you remember a family named DeBerry being here in Rawlings about sixteen or seventeen years ago?"

"I don't think I ever heard that name. A lot of people have left Oklahoma since the start of the Depression."

"Someone was in the office inquiring about the family. I thought you might know.

"If they had school-age kids, a record would be at the school."

"That's true." A roll of thunder prompted Kathleen to say, "We may be in for a rain."

"I wish Clara hadn't gone out. I told her that cloud bank in the southwest looked like rain."

"She'll be all right. She probably went to the picture show."

"No," Hazel said slowly and sadly. "She went to a honky-tonk. She loves honky-tonks."

Later, in her room, Kathleen stood by the window and looked out at the star-studded sky before she turned on the light. In the back of her mind all day had been the vision of Johnny looking at her as she sat in the car with Barker Fleming, then, without acknowledging either one of them, turning and riding away.

What had he thought? *He had just learned that the man she was with was his father.*

Kathleen wanted to cry.

Chapter Seventeen

It rained during the night, a typical Oklahoma rainstorm; wind, lightning and a downpour which lasted for only a short time. It was still overcast when morning came. The moment Kathleen entered the kitchen she could tell by the worried look on Hazel's face that Clara had not come home.

"Good morning." Kathleen removed the saucer from the top of the blue crockery pitcher where the tea had been steeping and poured a cup. "How are you this morning, Sugarpuss?" she said to Emily.

"All right."

"I'll give you a ride to school, if you want."

"All right. Mama didn't come home."

"She probably didn't want to get caught in the rain and stayed with a friend." Kathleen glanced at Hazel who kept her face turned away. "I'll have to leave as soon as you finish your breakfast. The paper goes out today."

"I'll be ready."

It wasn't fair that a child Emily's age had to carry the burden of an irresponsible mother. Kathleen fumed all the way to town after she had let Emily off at the school.

The child had not said a word after she got into the car and only "'Bye, Miss Dolan" when she got out.

Kathleen went by the bus stop, picked up the engravings for the paper, then parked her car in front of the office. Paul had already set the front page, leaving a two-column-by-three-inch space for the picture of Johnny above the story Kathleen had written about the rodeo.

In order to be ready for the press by noon, Kathleen and Adelaide worked steadily after only a brief mention of Judy.

"She was still asleep when Paul and I had breakfast. I left a note telling her to help herself to bread, butter, and preserves that I left on the table."

Shortly before noon the phone rang, three short rings and two long ones.

"I wonder what's happened. That's the emergency call," Adelaide said and reached for the phone. "*Gazette*."

"That you, Adelaide?"

"It's me, Flossie. What's going on?"

"Oh, Adelaide . . . oh, Adelaide—a call came to the sheriff that . . . a woman's body is in the ditch out south of town."

"Where, Flossie? Exactly where?" Adelaide motioned frantically to Kathleen.

"Just before you get to the corner that goes to the Kilburn ranch."

"Thanks, Flossie. I owe you, and I'll not forget it." Adelaide hung up. "Kathleen, a woman's body was found in the ditch out south of town. Go straight out Main Street, turn when the pavement ends and go straight south. The sheriff will be there. We'll hold the front page until you get back."

Kathleen was already checking the camera for film while Adelaide spoke. She grabbed her purse and went out to her car. Following Adelaide's instructions, she turned onto the dirt road made soft by last night's rain. She stayed in the ruts made by the other cars, and after a mile, she saw the sheriff's car and another car ahead of it. She stopped behind them and got out.

A growing sense of dread filled her as she walked toward the group standing alongside the road. The sheriff came toward her as she approached.

"This isn't something a lady should see," he said gruffly.

"I'm a reporter, Sheriff. Who is it?"

"Clara Ramsey."

"Oh my goodness! Poor Hazel." Somehow Kathleen had known who the girl was before he spoke. "What happened?"

"She didn't kill herself, that's sure."

"How long ago did it happen?"

"After the rain."

"I'd like to take some pictures . . . not of the body, but of the scene. Would you stand over there by the sheriff's car?"

"Sure." The sheriff made an attempt to pull in his stomach and puff out his chest as he posed beside the car.

Kathleen took pictures from several angles and one quick shot of the body still clothed in the jacket Clara had taken from Kathleen's room. The pitiful heap sprawled in the ditch looked like a rag doll.

"What do you think happened, Sheriff?" Kathleen took out her pad and pencil. "I'd like to quote you to be sure it will be right." She had learned that the best way to get information was flattery.

"It looks like she was hit by a car and thrown over in the ditch." Sheriff Carroll took off his hat and scratched his head. "Someone beat hell out of her first. Being hit by the car wouldn't have cut up her mouth and blackened her eyes. Her legs are broken . . . but that was from being hit by the car."

"Could it have been an accident?"

"What would she be doing out here by herself at three o'clock in the morning? Why didn't the driver stop and help her? Off the top of my head I say she was beat up, thrown out of the car, run over to be sure she was dead, and then tossed in the ditch."

Kathleen wrote quickly. "Who found her?"

"Mr. Kilburn on his way to town."

"What are you waiting for, Sheriff?"

"Doc Herman. I think that's him coming now. He's the coroner."

"The . . . king . . . the mayor . . . the *savior*—" The sarcastic words came out before Kathleen could hold them back. The sheriff didn't seem to notice as he watched a car come slowly toward them.

"I sure hate to have to tell Hazel," he said. "She's had a peck of trouble with Clara since she was twelve or thirteen years old."

"Would you like for me to go with you to tell Hazel, Sheriff?"

"You'd do that?"

"Hazel is a friend. Shouldn't you ask her minister to be there?"

"Good idey. I've not had to do this but a time or two. It ain't something that's easy. Here's Doc."

The car stopped behind Kathleen's, and the doctor got out. As he came toward them, his shiny shoes became coated with mud. Kathleen looked down at her own shoes and wondered if they would ever be the same again.

"What are you doing here?" Dr. Herman barked at her. His eyes behind the round-rimmed glasses were not friendly.

"Why do reporters go anywhere? To get news," she shot back sharply.

"Did you call her?" Doc asked Sheriff Carroll, jerking his head toward Kathleen.

"No. I only called you after Mr. Kilburn called me."

"Then it was Flossie."

"If it's important for you to know, a man stuck his head in the office door and yelled that he'd heard a body was found out here in the ditch." She hoped that the lie was convincing and would take the blame from Flossie.

"Bullfoot! What happened here?" He turned his back on Kathleen to shut her out of the conversation.

"See for yourself. She's over there in the ditch."

"Drunk?"

"I don't think so."

"Let's take a look."

"I'll be at the office, Sheriff, when you're ready to go to Hazel's," Kathleen said.

Sheriff Carroll nodded, and the two men went down

into the ditch. The sheriff knelt beside the body and lifted the cloth he had used to cover Clara's face.

Kathleen went back to her car, drove down to the crossroads, turned around, and headed back to town. As she passed back by the scene, Dr. Herman had come back up onto the road. Later, she remembered that he had not asked *who* was in the ditch.

At the office she gave Paul and Adelaide the news. Adelaide was shocked and saddened that the dead girl was Clara Ramsey.

"Has Hazel been told?"

"I offered to go with the sheriff to tell her."

"I don't envy you."

Paul had already made room on the front page for a headline and short story. Kathleen typed up the story, after getting some background information about Clara from Adelaide, and took it back to be set on the linotype. The headline, in big black letters, was in place.

LOCAL WOMAN FOUND DEAD.

"I wonder if we have an engraving of Clara in a group picture."

"I looked," Paul said. "Nothing in the file."

"We could use one of the sheriff above his quote. I have a feeling we need to butter him up. We may want him to help us find Judy's mother."

"That would push Johnny's picture down under the fold."

"Then let's skip it. We'll butter the sheriff up in another way."

Paul grinned. "You've got newspaper ink in your veins."

On her way back to her desk, she stopped in the office doorway. Her heart began a crazy dance in her chest. Johnny was standing beside the counter talking to Adelaide. From the shocked look on his face, she knew that Adelaide had told him about Clara. Kathleen went on to her desk and sat down.

"You've been out there?" Johnny asked without a greeting.

"Just got back."

"What does Carroll think happened?"

"She was hit by a car after she'd been beaten up."

"It wasn't an accident?"

"He didn't seem to think so." She rolled a sheet of paper into the typewriter just to be doing something.

"I came in to fix your tire." Johnny stood in front of her desk on spread legs, his hands in the back pockets of his jeans.

"Don't bother. I'll get it fixed." Without looking up at him she knew he was gazing down at her. For some reason, unknown even to herself, she was angry with him.

"I said I would fix it, and I will," he said stubbornly. "First I want to go out to where they found Clara."

"Why? The sheriff won't welcome your help."

"I don't give a damn if he does or not. I know a hell of a lot more about tracks than he does."

"You'd better get going then. People by the dozens will be swarming out there out of curiosity."

"I'm going, but I'll be back to fix that tire."

Kathleen wanted to put her head down on the desk and

cry. The combination of troubles set her nerves on edge: worry about Johnny and his thoughts about seeing her with Barker, worry about having to tell Hazel that her daughter was dead, and worry about the poor little waif who had come to Rawlings to find her mother.

An hour passed, and Kathleen was beginning to fear Hazel would hear the news before she and the sheriff got there. Then he drove up in front of the office. A gray-haired man was with him. Kathleen went out to the car.

"Sheriff, I've been thinking about Emily, Clara's little girl. Why don't I go to the school, get Emily, and take her home? In the meanwhile you and the Reverend can tell Hazel. I'll . . . try to tell Emily. It will take some of the burden off Hazel."

"I'd forgotten Clara had a girl."

"A few of the ladies from the church are going out to be with Mrs. Ramsey," the preacher said.

"Where did they take Clara, Sheriff?"

"To the funeral parlor. Doc said it was accident." When he spoke he looked away from Kathleen.

"An accident? She was beaten up, Sheriff. You said so. Doc is full of hot air," Kathleen said angrily.

"It's what he said, and that's final. He's the coroner."

"For Christ's sake! Doesn't anyone in this town have enough backbone to stand up to that little dictator."

"Watch your mouth, girl!"

"I'll pick up Emily."

Back in the office, Kathleen faced Adelaide and gave vent to her frustration.

"Doc Herman had pronounced Clara's death an accident. She had been beaten around the head, has black eyes, and a cut mouth. I know enough to know that if she had been killed instantly when she was hit by a car, she'd not be bruised like that, especially when the ground is soft. What's going on here? Sheriff Carroll didn't want me to question Doc's decision.

"Another thing was strange, Adelaide. He wanted to know how I knew to go out to the scene. He blamed Flossie. I tried to cover for her by telling him a man came to the door and told us."

"We'll stick to that. He could have Flossie fired."

"I'm disliking that man more and more."

Kathleen's heart was beating with dread when she stopped at the schoolhouse and went to Emily's classroom. She motioned to the teacher to come to the hall and then waited for Emily to come out.

"Hello, Sugarpuss."

"Miss Ryan said I could go home."

"How would you like to go for a little ride first?"

"Did Mama come home?"

The question caused Kathleen to pause. "No, sweetheart, she didn't."

"Then I better go home and see about Granny."

"All right." Kathleen took the child's hand, and they went out to the car.

She told the child about her mother as they sat in the car beneath the pecan tree at the edge of the playground. Emily cried, Kathleen cried. It was one of the hardest things Kathleen had ever had to do. Although Emily was not attached to Clara as a child is normally attached to her mother, she had feelings for her.

"Granny's goin' to feel awful bad," Emily said after she had stopped crying.

"Yes. Your mother was her little girl."

"I'd better go home and see about her."

Kathleen wiped her eyes and started the car.

Kathleen's eyes were red when she returned to the office and heard the sound of the press printing the paper.

"You didn't have to come right back," Adelaide said, "Judy has been helping stuff the papers."

"Three of Hazel's friends are with her and Emily. That child is old for her years. Her concern was for her grandmother."

"The only good thing Clara ever did for Hazel was to give her Emily. She adores the child. Was anything said about services?"

"Not to me. I think Hazel feared that something like this would happen to Clara but didn't expect it here in Rawlings."

Adelaide tilted her head to look out the window. "Johnny's back. I wonder what he found out."

Johnny's dark eyes swept the office when he entered, then moved over to the desks where Kathleen and Adelaide sat and came right to the point.

"I'd bet my life it was no accident."

"At first Sheriff Carroll said it was not an accident. He's changed his mind now that Doc Herman says it was," Kathleen replied.

"Yeah. That's what I was told down at the funeral parlor."

"You've been there?"

"Eldon is sort of a friend of mine."

"He's the undertaker," Adelaide explained to Kathleen.

"Would you be squeamish about taking pictures of the body?" Johnny addressed his words to Kathleen.

"I've never done anything like it, but I can if it's necessary."

"Then get your Kodak. Eldon agrees with me that it wasn't an accident. Pictures may be the only way that we can prove it. I owe it to Hazel to find out the truth if I can."

"You mean there's one man in this town that isn't in Doc Herman's pocket?"

"I know several . . . Paul, Claude, Eldon, and probably more if it came right down to it."

Kathleen checked the Kodak. "There are eight pictures left on this roll. Is that enough?"

"I'd think so. Let's go out the back and walk down the alley. No need to advertise where we're going."

"Johnny, be careful," Adelaide cautioned. "Be careful about going against Doc Herman."

"I'll be careful; but if Clara was murdered, it's only right that her murderer be found."

Kathleen and Johnny walked behind the stores to the funeral parlor in back of the furniture store.

"You must have good cause to do this." Kathleen had to walk fast to keep up with Johnny's long steps.

"After looking at the body and talking to Eldon, I came to the conclusion she was beaten up; and while she lay in the road, the car ran over her, backed up and ran over her again. Then, not sure that she was dead, the murderer put his foot on her throat."

"How do you know he ran over her while she was lying in the road?"

"Tire tracks. When I was a boy in Red Rock, Tom taught me to read tire marks because we were trying to catch rustlers coming into the fields and killing beef. He showed me the marks made by different tires. I used what he taught me once before when I worked with Hod."

"Oh, gosh! I just remembered Hazel said that Clara had gone somewhere yesterday afternoon and when she came home, she was very angry. She told Hazel that someone owed her money and that she would get it or get even."

"Maybe we can find out where she went." At the door of the funeral parlor, he stopped. "Are you sure you're up to this? It's not a pretty sight. I'd not ask you to do it, but I'm a lousy picture taker, and these need to be as good as we can make them."

"I'll be all right. We'll need plenty of light."

"I'll ask Eldon about that. The body is on a cart that can be moved to the window, and if that isn't light enough, we may be able to open the double doors on the back. The danger would be that someone would see us."

"We'll need as much light as we can get in order to get good close-up pictures."

"Come on. We'll give it our best shot."

To Kathleen's surprise, Johnny put an arm protectively around her as they approached the building.

The instant Johnny rapped on the door it was opened. Eldon Radner was a small, thin man with wiry faded brown hair. He never just walked anywhere but scurried or sprinted. Owner of the furniture store and the funeral parlor, he took the business of laying out the dead very seriously.

"Come in, come in. I've rigged up some lights. Hello, Miss Dolan. We haven't met, but I know about you from Johnny. This is a terrible thing for Rawlings. We must hurry, Johnny. I've work to do on the body before Mrs. Ramsey comes down, and you can never tell who else. Folks are curious, especially in a case like this. There hasn't been a woman murdered in Tillison County in a long time. Doc Herman will want it hushed up. Oh, yes, I discovered her jaw is broken and some of her teeth are missing."

Most of this was said without Eldon taking a breath. Kathleen was to learn that was his natural way of speaking. He threw out a hand beckoning them to follow and bustled through another set of doors, a long white duster flapping about his legs.

Clara's body lay on a waist-high cart just as it had come from the ditch where she died. A string of hooded lights hung above the body and when Eldon turned them all on, Kathleen had to blink. To keep from looking directly at the pitiful heap on the cart, Kathleen fiddled with the adjustments on the camera.

"What do you think, Kathleen? Is it light enough?"

"Do you want overall, or just up-close areas?"

"Mostly close-up."

"Can one of the lights be lowered to the area you want?"

"You betcha," Eldon said, and scurried to the other

side of the cart. "Show her the tire marks, Johnny. I'll hold the light where you want it, Miss Dolan. This is sorry business, I tell you. I've not had a corpse this tore up in a long time. I don't know if I can make her presentable for the laying away. Oh, poor Mrs. Ramsey. It'll be hard for her, that's sure."

Kathleen tried to tune out the voice of the undertaker. Johnny folded Clara's skirt up over her thighs. Oklahoma red clay was clearly imprinted on the white flesh.

"Take the thighs, Kathleen. These are tire tracks." He pointed to the mud streaks.

Eldon held the hooded light, and Kathleen lowered the camera until only the area of the marks was visible in the viewfinder and snapped the picture. The prints on the lower, broken legs were not as distinct, but she took a photo of them anyway. Johnny folded back the gray jacket to reveal prints from the muddy tire on Clara's white blouse where the wheel of the car had run over her chest. After the picture was taken, Johnny pointed to the flicks of mud on her side.

"This will be rough, Kathleen," Johnny said as he removed the cloth covering Clara's face.

Kathleen steeled herself to think that what she was seeing and photographing was a broken doll. Clara's face was a sight that would long haunt Kathleen's dreams. When the light was lowered, she snapped the picture. Eldon tilted Clara's chin so a picture would be taken of the neck area. Her windpipe had been crushed. By the time Johnny covered the face, Kathleen was swallowing rapidly.

"How many exposures left?" Johnny asked the question in a sharp business like tone.

"Two."

"Let's turn her over, Eldon." After the body was turned, Eldon lifted Clara's dress up over her bare buttocks. "Are you all right, honey?" Johnny asked gently. Kathleen nodded. "See this bruise? It was made before she died because you don't bruise after your heart stops pumping. It's a bootprint. You can see the heel. He stomped on her before he killed her. Take the last two pictures of it."

Eldon was careful to get the light just right, and Kathleen took the two pictures, each from a different angle. When she finished, she stepped back, turned away, and headed for the door. Johnny caught up and put his arm around her.

"Are you all right?" After she nodded, he said, "I'm proud of you, Kathleen. I've seen men faint after seeing such a sight."

"It wasn't . . . easy—"

"Let me know how the prints turn out, Johnny." Eldon unlocked the back door. "I've got work to do. Poor girl. Poor, poor girl. She was worked over all right. Didn't deserve it even if she was ah . . . loose. Hazel and Sam Ramsey were fine folks. I knew Sam back in the twenties. He was in the war and fought in France. Hazel will be here soon. I don't know how she's goin' to pay for a funeral. I'll do the best I can, but I've got expenses, too."

"I'll check back with you, Eldon."

"He would wear me out," Kathleen said after the door closed.

"It took me a while to get used to him. But he's a man of his word, and he doesn't knuckle under to Doc Herman." Johnny held her arm as they walked back up the alley to the *Gazette* building.

"I hope the pictures are plain enough to do some good. Paul will develop the film and enlarge the pictures."

"I want to show the prints to Keith. He worked on a tracking case once with me, and he's pretty good."

"Can you tell what kind of car ran over her by looking at the tracks?"

"Maybe not the kind of car, but we may be able to match the prints to tires on a car. This was a big heavy car, I know that."

"Who would have done such a terrible thing to Clara? She was just a stupid, terribly irritating girl."

"She was a girl that started her loose ways young. She must have had Emily when she was fourteen or fifteen."

"Does Hazel know who Emily's father is?"

"I doubt if Clara knew."

"What will a funeral cost?"

"There may be room to bury her beside her daddy. If not, I'd say between fifty to a hundred dollars."

"Hazel doesn't have that kind of money."

"I don't imagine she does," Johnny said sadly.

Chapter Eighteen

"I don't want to ever have to do that again." Kathleen was in the office with Adelaide. "It was just awful. Poor, poor girl. She looked like a broken doll."

"Johnny seems sure that Clara was murdered. Doc Herman won't stand for there being a murder in his simon-pure town."

"Is that why Sheriff Carroll now calls it an accident?"

"He must have his reasons."

"I wonder if the doctor is afraid of the attention it would bring to the town if it becomes known that a woman was murdered here?"

"I can't think of any other reason." Adelaide leaned back in her chair wearily and stretched her arms over her head. Press day was always hard, but this one had been especially difficult.

"You're worn-out. You had to do my share of the work today."

"Judy was a big help. She and Woody stuffed all the papers. Paul helped me get them ready for the post office."

"With all that's happened, I had almost forgotten about Judy."

"She a quiet girl. She hasn't asked me one time about finding her mother. She has thanked me a hundred times for letting her stay. When I went upstairs this morning, the bed was made; and you couldn't tell that she'd been in the kitchen."

"Her sorry excuse for a mother must have taught her something."

"I was glad that she was here today. She pitched right in, and I didn't have to explain things to her but one time."

"Tomorrow I'll go to the courthouse and look at the birth records."

"You'll not be greeted with open arms, I'll tell you that. When I insisted on seeing them a year ago, the clerk watched me like I was about to raid the U.S. Mint."

"They have to let me see public records."

"I was surprised at how many babies were born here. Doc must advertise in Dallas, Fort Worth, Waco, and even as far away as Denver. When I came back and told Paul what I had discovered, we both decided that something wasn't quite right about so many out-of-town women coming here to have babies."

"Did you ever mention it to Sheriff Carroll?"

"Heavens no! Pete is a good man . . . or he used to be. But he's cowed where Doc is concerned. He'd tell me to tend to my own business . . . or something like that."

"I've a niggling suspicion in the back of my mind about all this. I'm going to wait until I see the birth records and get it sorted out before I tell you because you're going to think that I've lost my mind."

"I doubt that. I think you've got a pretty good hold on that mind of yours."

Lately Adelaide appeared to be more lighthearted than when Kathleen had first arrived. It was as if a burden had been lifted from her shoulders. An astute student of human nature, Kathleen was sure that Adelaide's change of mood was because she now shared the secret of her love for Paul with someone who didn't disapprove.

"I should go back to Hazel's, but I'm not eager to be in a crowd of women and make small talk. There were six or more ladies there when I left."

"Stay here then. Come upstairs and I'll fix us some sandwiches. Paul mentioned going to Claude's and bringing back hamburgers."

Kathleen and Adelaide went to the back room where Paul and Johnny were looking at the photos spread out on the ad table.

"It was a big tire. It went over her thighs, came back over her legs, and broke them. It then went over her chest. Damn, but I hope that she wasn't conscious at that time." Johnny swore softly under his breath. "That's about all I can tell from these prints. I'd like for Keith McCabe to see them. I'll give him a call, but not from Rawlings. Too many ears on the line."

"You'll be making a couple of powerful enemies if you stick your nose in this," Paul said. "Doc Herman has declared it an accident and so has the sheriff."

"I can't just stand by and do nothing when I think that girl was murdered."

"If they could figure out a way to do it and make it appear to be legal, they could blame it on you."

"Let them try. I don't see how anyone could pass this off as an accident. Clara's ribs and her legs were broken when the car ran over her, but it sure as hell didn't run over her neck and head. Hellfire, Paul, her jaw was broken, her teeth knocked out! I wish I had gotten there before the place was trampled over. I might have found the track he made when he dragged her into the ditch and got a decent footprint."

"Can you tell anything from the one on her back?"

"It was a boot, and not a very big one according to the space between the heel and the sole."

Paul snorted. "Doc Herman will never admit that it's even a bootprint."

"The best track man in the country is Frank Hamer, the former Texas Ranger, now a U.S. Marshal. I'd like for him to see these prints. Doc Herman would sit up and take notice if he came to town."

"Do you know Frank Hamer?"

"I know him, but not as well as Keith McCabe does."

When Kathleen came up beside him, Johnny moved the picture of Clara's tortured face out of sight.

"Where is Judy?" Adelaide asked.

"She's sleeping there on the cot. It's like she hasn't slept in a week," Paul replied.

"If she walked and hitched rides all the way from Fort Worth, she probably hasn't slept much in a week. Johnny, did Paul tell you about Judy?"

"He said she was here looking for her real mother." Johnny's eyes shifted from Adelaide to Kathleen. "Are you going back to Hazel's?"

"Not right away. There's a houseful of people there, or was when I left this afternoon."

"I'm going to call on her after I fix your tire."

"You're determined to fix that blasted tire, aren't you?"

"I said I'd fix it, and I will."

"Then let's get it over with so I can go home," she said irritably.

Johnny followed Kathleen through the office and out onto the street where her car was parked.

"Why are you mad?"

"I'm not mad! Well, I guess I am . . . but I'm not sure why." She got the keys out of her purse and dangled them in front of him. "It's in the trunk, but I'm sure you know that."

He swept the keys from her hand. "Get in."

Later she waited in the car while Johnny carried the slashed tire into the back of the filling station. He was a puzzle to her, always leaving her with a thousand conflicting emotions. It made her angry that her heart fairly jumped out of her chest at the sight of him. How dare he come into her life and make her so miserable?

She watched him come back to the car with the tire. What was it about this man, this cowboy, that, with a look or a word, could bring her so stupidly close to tears.

"How much did it cost?" She began digging into her purse as soon as he got in the car.

"Forget it. It's taken care of."

"I'll not forget it. I'll not have you paying to fix my tires," she said crossly.

"I'm not rich like *your* Mr. Fleming, but I can afford to fix a tire."

"He's not *my* Mr. Fleming."

"No? Then why are you always hangin' around his neck?"

"Hanging around his *neck!* You make me so damn mad! Where are we going?"

"To Hazel's. I've got to pay my respects."

Not another word was said until they stopped in front of the well-lighted house. A number of people were milling about.

"Stay here. I'll be right back." Johnny took the keys from the car and held them up for her to see before he put them in his pocket. "So that you'll not be tempted."

Kathleen immediately dug into her purse and brought out the extra set of keys her Uncle Hod had insisted that she have made. She was very tempted to drive off and leave him, but she didn't. She waited and when he returned he found the extra set of keys in the ignition.

"You've got to have the last word, haven't you?" It was dark, she couldn't see his face but she knew that he was grinning.

He drove back uptown, turned into the alley behind the *Gazette*, and parked beside his truck. He turned off the lights and reached for her arm to prevent her from getting out of the car. She said the first safe thing that came to mind.

"How are Hazel and Emily?"

"They're hurtin'. The reality of it hasn't soaked in yet. There are plenty of people there, and the table is piled with food." He paused, then said, "Hazel hasn't been to the funeral home yet. Eldon sent word for her not to come until morning."

"It will be a difficult time for her. I was very young when my father was killed, and about Emily's age when I lost my mother. My grandparents, though, lived to be in their sixties. It was terribly hard when I lost first Grandma, and then Papa."

"It's funny, but when you lose someone you care about, you can think of things you wish that you had said to that person, but never did."

"Who have you lost that you cared about?"

"Ed Henry. He was the nearest thing to a father I had. He said things, quietly, that at the time I didn't pay much attention to. Later, after he was gone, I thought about them. I'd not been to a funeral before I went to Ed's. Aunt Dozie ironed one of Ed's white shirts for me to wear. Henry Ann needed me. I'd never been needed before either. Being needed kind of makes a fellow take heed of his responsibilities." Johnny's voice was low as he reminisced about the past. Kathleen hesitated to interrupt him by asking a question, but finally she did.

"I didn't have an aunt when I was growing up. My mother was my grandparents' only surviving child."

"Aunt Dozie is a colored woman who lived with us on the farm. She still lives there with Tom and Henry Ann. She's getting old. I should get over there more often to see her." He turned and looked at Kathleen. "I love that old woman and Henry Ann. They're my family. They cared about me when not another soul in the world cared if I lived or died."

Kathleen was quiet for a long while before she said, "Are you telling me something, Johnny?"

He looked out the window and fiddled with the steering wheel. Long minutes passed before he said anything. When he spoke, it was as if the words were pulled out of him.

"He told you that he thinks he's my father, didn't he?"

"Yes."

"He can think it all he wants. It makes no difference to me. It could have been him or a dozen others who, for two bits, paid for a half hour in her bed. The woman that had me was a whore not because she had to be one, but because she *wanted* to be one."

"Why do you think that you have to tell me this?"

He grabbed her, giving her no chance to resist, and pulled her tightly against him.

"So that you'll know that the son of a whore and a drunk Indian is going to kiss you."

His face came to hers and he kissed her long and hard. At first her lips were compressed with surprise, but then they softened and yielded. Her palms rested on his chest before they moved around to his back and she hugged him to her. He raised his head. They looked into each other's eyes; his had little lights. He kissed her again, softly, sweetly. She was happy, even though she knew it wouldn't last.

"Don't talk like that about yourself to me again." She had not meant to say that at all, and especially not angrily.

"I'm trying to be fair to you."

"I don't care about your mother or your father. She could have been Lizzie Borden, and he could have been Attila the Hun for all I care. You are not responsible for what they did. Why can't you understand that? Are you afraid I'll interfere in your life? I'm not going to *ask* you for anything."

"That, right there, says it all. You'll never *ask* a man for anything, will you? You'll never *need* a man. Fiery, independent, little Miss Dolan can take care of herself, fight her own battles, fix her own tires."

"You've got it right, mister. I've had to take care of myself for the past eight years because there wasn't anyone there to help me. If what you need is some clinging vine who can't wipe her own nose, you've got the wrong woman."

"I've got the *right* woman," he gritted angrily. Even before the words were out, his arms were crushing her to him. She uttered a little grunt of surprise. "Be quiet!" he snarled, but he didn't kiss her. He held her, his lips against her ear. "You smell so good . . . and feel better."

His voice was husky, tender, his lips nuzzled her ear. He knew that he shouldn't be doing this, but damned if he could stop. The feel of her soft body against his and the scent of her filled his head. He swallowed hard, because he wanted her so much. His hand moved up and down her back and over her rounded hips. He moved his head and found her hungry lips. The kiss was long and passionate, his mouth parting, her lips seeking fulfillment. She clung to him, melting into his hard embrace. The kiss seemed to last forever, both reluctant to end it.

"You are an irritating woman. Why can't I stay away from you?" He kissed her quick and hard and moved away from her.

"You're a moody, unpredictable, complicated man. I never know where I stand with you," she retorted. "On rare occasions you can be very nice and then, like now, a complete horse's patoot! There are times when I don't like you at all!"

"You use all kinds of big words. I don't have the slightest idea what they mean."

"Irritating is a big word. You evidently know what that means." She pushed her hair back with shaky fingers.

"Do you like Fleming?" he asked bluntly.

"Of course, I do. He's a nice man."

Johnny let out an angry snort. "Nice? Bullfoot! How the hell do you know? If he's so damn nice, how come he goes around knocking up whores?"

"He did that when he was very young. He's a well-mannered gentleman. You'd know it, too, if you weren't too damn stubborn to let yourself get to know him."

"I'm not sharing a woman with a damn Cherokee half-breed!"

Kathleen opened her mouth, closed it, and gritted her teeth in frustration.

"Look who's talking? That was a rotten thing to say, Johnny Henry."

"Rotten or not, it's what he is, and it's what I am!"

"Does your Indian blood bother you? It certainly doesn't bother me."

"It would . . . after a while, but forget it. I've got to get the photos and get on home."

"Forget it. That's your favorite thing to say when you don't want to face the facts. Now listen to me, you mule-headed dimwit!" She held his arm to keep him from getting out of the car. "Mr. Fleming told me that he'd been looking for his son for a long time. He's had detectives out looking for you. They finally found your sister in Oklahoma City. He was so proud of you at the rodeo. It seems to me the least you could have done was to be decent to him."

"So he came crying to you, did he?"

"He did not! Johnny Henry, I don't know why I even bother with you."

"If he got anything out of Isabel, it was while she was on her back."

"Get out of my car so I can go home."

"Gladly. I'll be back day after tomorrow to go to the funeral. Sunday we'll go to Red Rock."

"I've changed my mind. I'm *not* going. I'll not torture myself by spending a day with a stubborn, addleheaded, idiot with . . . feathers for brains!"

"*We* made plans to go to Red Rock on Sunday, Kathleen. *We* are going. I'll be in for the funeral on Thursday." He got out of the car and waited until she moved over under the wheel before he closed the door. "Go straight home. I've not seen Webb and Krome, but that doesn't mean they're not around." He closed the door, but stood there looking at her for a minute before he moved away.

Kathleen was furious as she drove out of the alley, but by the time she turned onto the street, a warm glow of happiness had replaced her anger.

Why can't I stay away from you?

I'll not share a woman—

Johnny liked her in spite of himself! He might even be a little in love with her.

Kathleen's grin blossomed into a full smile.

Chapter Nineteen

As soon as Kathleen arrived at the office the next morning, she pinned the pictures she had taken at the site where Clara was killed on a bulletin board. Beneath the photo of the crumpled heap in the ditch, she wrote:

A few hours before this picture was taken, Clara Ramsey was a living, breathing human being.

Beneath the picture of the sheriff:

A. B. (Pete) Carroll, Sheriff of Tillison County. At the time this photo was taken he stated: "This untimely death is not an accident." Later he said that it WAS an accident. After viewing the crushed windpipe and the broken jaw it appears to this reporter that Clara Ramsey was beaten, then run over and tossed in the ditch.

Kathleen placed the bulletin board in the office window and soon everyone who passed by the office stopped to view the display. Word spread and at times three or four people at a time were gawking at the pictures.

The display had not been in the window an hour until the sheriff's car stopped out front and he came into the office.

"I never gave you permission to put my picture in the window, and I didn't say that."

"I didn't have to get your permission. You're a public official. You posed willingly for the picture, and you did say that. I wrote it down word for word."

"Hello, Pete." Adelaide came into the office. "That's a good picture of you. You look real official. Haven't you lost a little weight?"

"Ah . . . maybe a little."

"Are you sticking to your story that Clara's death was an accident?" Kathleen asked.

"I've heard nothing to change my mind."

"Did you examine the body?"

"That's not my job, missy."

"Did the car run over her head? Is that the reason her jaw was broken and her windpipe crushed?"

"Now look here. You have no right to question my decision."

"Was it your decision or Doc Herman's to put out the story that Clara's death was an accident?"

"I was mistaken. I suggest, for your own good, that you drop the matter and tend to your own business."

"Reporting the news is my business."

"Then stick to it."

"If I don't, will you have me knocked off?" Kathleen made a clicking sound with her tongue, imitating a rapidly fired machine gun, shaped her hand like a gun, and pointed it at the sheriff. He never cracked a smile. "Not funny, huh?"

"Not a damn bit."

"Sheriff, what does Dr. Herman have on people in this town that makes some of them forget morals, honor, and basic decency? They allow him to rule this town as if he were a king?"

Sheriff Carroll's face turned a fiery red as he choked down his anger. "You're walking on dangerous ground, miss. Adelaide, you'd better put a rein on her. She doesn't know the lay of the land here."

"I'll speak to her, Pete," Adelaide said calmly. Then, "By the way, Pete, have you ever heard of a family here in Rawlings named DeBerry?"

He took off his hat and turned it around and around in his hands. Kathleen noticed that he had a full head of iron gray hair that was neatly cut.

"Why do you ask?"

"I had an inquiry. It's not important."

The sheriff turned his back, and for several minutes he watched a couple of men as they studied the pictures in the window.

"You've got quite a little sideshow going on out there." When he turned his face seemed to have aged. His shoulders had slumped. He looked directly at Kathleen. "You'd best be careful, Miss Dolan, that it doesn't backfire on you."

"I've taken precautions, Sheriff. I left a letter with my lawyer that if anything happens to me to look in my lock box and to arrest you and Dr. Herman." She grinned at him.

He slapped his hat down on his head. "If there's anythin' I can't stand it's a smart-aleck woman." He left and got into his car without ever taking a close look at the display in the window.

"Did I embarrass you, Adelaide?"

"Absolutely not. You can go after anyone in this town you want to. I just don't want you to put yourself in jeopardy."

"If I wasn't so angry with him, I'd feel sorry for Sheriff Carroll."

"When we were kids the sheriff was called Pete, I think because his father's name was Pete. After he died, Mrs. Carroll insisted that her son be called A. B. Basically, he's a good, decent man, who loves his job as sheriff. When he was growing up, his mother was constantly telling him that he was fat and dumb. For the first time in his life he's looked up to. He goes along with Doc Herman because he needs that little bit of respect."

"That's a heck of a reason for not doing his duty. There's no excuse for refusing to give a murdered girl justice, even if she was what some of the people here considered a tramp. She was a human being."

"I know, and I'm shocked and disappointed in Pete."

Wearing a light coat because it was a chilly, cloudy day, Kathleen walked down the street toward the courthouse. She reached under the lapel of her coat and felt for her grandma's long wicked hatpin she had put there this morning. From now on she was going to have something handy with which to defend herself.

She entered a high-ceilinged courthouse. It was so quiet that she wondered if she were the only person in the building. The heels of her shoes made tapping sounds as she walked down the long corridor to the records department. Three desks occupied the middle of the office, filing cabinets lined the walls. A man wearing a visor sat at one of the desks. He made no attempt to get up.

"Hello," Kathleen said pleasantly. "I'm Kathleen Dolan from the *Gazette* and—"

"I know who ya are."

"Well, then, I'll get directly to the point. I want to look at the birth records."

"What for?" He pushed back his chair and stood. It was probably as much exercise as he'd had all day. The saying, wide as he is tall, came to Kathleen's mind.

"Are they public records or not?"

"Yes, but—"

"Are they public records or not?" Kathleen repeated.

"Yes, but we can't have just anybody coming in off the street prowling through the records." The man's eyes shifted between Kathleen and the door as if he expected someone to come in.

"I understand that." Kathleen was still trying to be pleasant. "But if you know who I am, you know that I'm from the *Gazette*."

"It don't make any difference where you're *from*."

"Oh, I thought it did. If you're telling me that I can't see the birth records, I'll just run along, see Judge Fimbres, and get a court order."

"What year do you want?" he asked grudgingly.

"All of them," she said with a pleasant smile.

"There's the files." He jerked his head toward three tall files next to the window.

"Are they cross-referenced?"

He walked to a cabinet and flung open a door. Ledgers were stacked on the shelves in alphabetical order.

"Thank you. On which shelf are the birth records?"

"Third."

"Thank you again. You can go on with your work; you've been very helpful."

Kathleen took off her coat and draped it over the back of a chair. After the records clerk moved away, she took out the ledger marked "D" and quickly found DeBerry. Judith DeBerry was born September 30, 1923, to Martha and Donald DeBerry, Fort Worth, Texas. Attending physician, Darrell Herman, M.D. Kathleen jotted the information down on her notepad, closed the ledger, and placed it back on the shelf.

Without looking at the clerk, who was watching her every move, she went to the file cabinets where she found the birth certificates filed by the year. In the 1923 file, she found the DeBerry birth certificate. She quickly thumbed through the documents and discovered that Dr. Herman had delivered twenty-two babies that year, ten of them to out-of-town parents.

More curious than ever now, she quickly wrote down the date of birth, parents' last name, and the place they were from. After she finished with the 1923 file, she went to the 1938 file. So far this year he had delivered thirty babies, sixteen of them had out-of-town parents. The latest birth was last week. The parents were from Tulsa.

An hour later, fingers cramping, feet hurting, Kathleen closed the file. She had listed the last ten years of births in Tillison County. After putting her notebook in her purse, she slipped on her coat.

"Thank you," she said to the man at the desk, and received only a grunt in reply.

As she was going out the door she saw the deputy hurrying down the hallway. She had heard the low murmur of the record clerk's voice, and now it occurred to her that he had called the sheriff's office.

"Well, hello, pretty little lady. Imagine seeing you here." The deputy had a nervous grin on his face. He stood in front of her.

"I'm sure you're surprised."

Kathleen stepped around him and walked down the corridor toward the door. He kept pace with her and when they reached the door, he put his arm out as if to open it. Instead he held it closed.

"What's the hurry?"

"All right, buster. Let's just stop waltzing around. The clerk called you. Why? I was looking at public records. What are you going to do about it? Put me in jail?"

"Maybe. It's against the law to steal public records."

"Are you saying that's what I did?"

"Melvin saw you put them in your purse."

"He couldn't have because I didn't."

"I'll have a look for myself."

"No, you won't!"

"Are you resisting arrest?"

"Damn right." She lifted her hand as if to adjust her coat and pulled the hatpin out of the lapel.

"This can be settled right quick. Give me the handbag." When he reached for it, she viciously jabbed the hatpin in the back of his hand.

"Yeow!" he yelled, and drew his fist back to hit her.

"Hit me, and I'll shove this hatpin all the way to your gizzard."

"What's going on here?" Judge Fimbres had come out of his office and was walking rapidly toward them.

"Look what she did to me, Judge." The deputy held out his hand. Blood was welling from the wound made by the pin. "I was just opening the door for her."

"Judge, he's accusing me of taking public records. I'll be glad to show you what's in my handbag, but not in front of him!"

"Did you see her take something, Thatcher?"

"Melvin called. He said she put some records in that bag."

"Come into my office, Miss Dolan." The deputy followed them back down the hall. "Stay outside, Thatcher."

"You know my name," Kathleen said when the door was closed.

"Barker Fleming spoke of you. Now let's see what you have in the handbag and get this mess straightened out."

Kathleen put the hatpin back in the lapel of her coat, opened her purse, and dumped the notebook, pencils, compact, lipstick, comb, and several bobby pins onto the desk. From a compartment on the side of the purse, she brought out her coin purse, car keys, and a small folder with the pictures of her grandparents. She extended the empty handbag to the judge. He shook his head. She turned the pockets in her coat inside out.

"Why did Deputy Thatcher think you had taken something?"

"The record clerk called him." Kathleen began putting things back in her bag. "I came to look at the birth records. We had an inquiry from a girl looking for her mother, and I wanted to see if the mother's maiden name was on the girl's birth certificate."

"Was it?"

"Yes." She looked steadily at him. "I wrote it down on a pad and put it in my purse. I poked the deputy with the hatpin when he attempted to grab it."

The judge chuckled and shook his head. When he opened the door, the deputy was standing close to it.

"Did we talk loud enough, Thatcher?" Judge Fimbres asked drily.

"Huh? Look at my hand. I ought to arrest her for attacking an officer." Blood showed through the handkerchief he had wrapped around his hand.

"It's what you get for grabbing a young lady's breast, Thatcher. You should know better."

Kathleen's eyes shot to the judge, then to the gaping deputy.

"Her . . . brr . . . brr—" the startled man couldn't get the word out. "She's a liar."

"You can file charges, but I warn you when the case comes to my court you will be the one to pay the court cost."

"You believe her over me?"

"You have a reputation of being less than respectful to

ladies, Thatcher. We both know that." The judge held open the door for Kathleen. "I'm sorry, my dear, that you received such despicable treatment in our courthouse. I'll speak to Sheriff Carroll. Deputy Thatcher should be relieved from duty if such conduct continues."

"Thank you, Judge Fimbres."

Kathleen managed to keep the smile off her face until she reached the sidewalk.

"I like that Judge Fimbres."

Kathleen had just finished telling Adelaide what had occurred at the courthouse.

"Forevermore! That beats all. That jackass was going to take your notebook." Adelaide's eyes brightened in response to her anger.

"Well, he didn't get it." Kathleen flopped the shorthand book down on her desk. "I can't believe how many babies have been born right here in Tillison County, and since 1925. Doc Herman delivered most all of them."

"Of course he delivered them. He's the only doctor in the county. A few babies are delivered by midwives."

"I found a few of those. There is something else interesting here. Hazel told me that a little over a year ago, Clara came home pregnant. Her baby was stillborn, which is no surprise considering how she lives. There wasn't a birth certificate in the file with Clara Ramsey's name on it. Even if the child was stillborn, it was born."

"I remember when that happened. She left town right after that."

"My grandmother used to say, 'There's something rotten in Denmark.' She meant cheese. I'm referring to that clinic."

In the middle of the afternoon Kathleen looked up from the chart on her desk to see Doc Herman standing in front of the window looking at the pictures she had put on the bulletin board. He was wearing a gray overcoat. A gray felt hat sat on his head at a jaunty angle. When he came into the office, she kept her head bent over her desk and continued to write dates on the chart until he spoke.

"Do you like stirring up folks, Miss Dolan?"

Kathleen looked up and smiled. "Why, hello, Dr. Herman." She pointedly slid a sheet of paper over the chart on her desk to cover the figures she was working on. "What do you mean by stirring up folks?"

"I think you know what I mean. You don't appear to be thickheaded."

Kathleen laughed. "Thank you."

She began to feel good about this encounter. Her cheerfulness irritated him. A frown covered his foxlike features. He stared at her, thinking that his silence would intimidate her. She stared back, not allowing her gaze to waver.

"Is there something you wanted? Have you reconsidered writing a column for us on the history of Rawlings? In Liberal we had an older man who wrote a column for the *Press*. His column was full of little anecdotes of long-ago Liberal. A column about the olden days in Rawlings by you, Doctor, would be very popular."

It was evident that the doctor was having a hard time

hiding his anger. His lips were a tight line; his eyes narrowed, and his nostrils flared.

"Young lady, I suggest you get in touch with the paper in Liberal and see if you can get your job back."

"Why would I want to do that? This town is jumping with news. It's a reporter's heaven. Saturday was the rodeo. A big success, by the way. That night my tire was slashed right on Main Street. Can you imagine that? Yesterday a murdered girl was found in a ditch along a rural road. There is more news in this town in a week than in six months in Liberal."

"Where is Adelaide?"

"I think that she and Paul are in the rooms above. The day after paper day is usually slow. It gives them some time to be together," she added in a conspiratorial tone.

The doctor looked at her for a long moment, then turned and walked out the door. Kathleen knew that she had made an enemy, a powerful enemy. But if what she suspected was true, the man was an unscrupulous, money-grabber who took advantage of desperate people. The thing that troubled her was how was she going to prove it.

"Kathleen!" Adelaide exclaimed after being told about the doctor's visit. "He must be madder than a wet hen."

"I don't care how mad he is. There is something here in these records that stinks to high heaven. I need someone with know-how to help me ferret this out." Kathleen tapped her pencil on the desk, then suddenly got to her feet. "I think we should keep Judy here, out of sight, until we find out what's going on. She could be part of this. If she's out on the street asking questions, something could happen to her."

"Paul agrees with you, and so do I."

"Are you and Paul thinking the same thing I am?"

"We think that he's selling babies. But where is he getting them?"

"It has to be from unwed mothers."

"This is dangerous, Kathleen. I'm worried about you."

"They wouldn't dare hurt me if I can get someone with influence on our side. The only one I know that may be able to pull strings is Mr. Fleming, and he's in Elk City."

"Do you know him that well?"

"I know him well enough. He said if I ever needed him, to call Elk City, but with Flossie's loose mouth—" Kathleen paced to the door and back to her desk. "What the heck. I'm going to call anyway. I'll think of something."

"He might not want to come back down here."

"I won't know until I ask him." Kathleen sat down at her desk and pulled the phone toward her. She lifted the receiver from the cradle and waited for Flossie to answer.

"That you, Adelaide?"

"No, it's Kathleen Dolan. I want to place a call to Mr. Barker Fleming in Elk City. I don't know the number, but I'm sure the operator can find him."

"Is this person-to-person?"

"Of course."

"Person-to-person costs more than station-to-station."

"I know that. I want to speak with Mr. Fleming." Kathleen rolled her eyes toward the ceiling, and Adelaide smiled.

Three or four minutes passed before Flossie came back on the line.

"The operator rang Old Mr. Fleming. He said he was at his ranch. She's ringing now. It'll be a minute . . . oh, here he is. Mr. Barker, you have a person-to-person call from Kathleen Dolan in Rawlings."

"Put her on, operator. Kathleen, is everything all right?"

"Yes, yes, I'm sorry if I alarmed you. I left the picnic basket in your car, and I was wondering when you would be coming back down here. The basket belongs to Mrs. Ramsey and she'll be needing it soon."

"I see." During the small silence Kathleen held her breath. "Have you spoken to anyone about that matter we discussed?"

"Not really, but I have seen the party you were interested in. I don't think the situation is hopeless."

"That's encouraging."

"Mr. Fleming, I really do need the picnic basket. Of course, if you're busy, I'll understand."

"As a matter of fact, I'm coming down to the tannery day after tomorrow. Will you need the basket before then?"

"No. Day after tomorrow will be fine. If you'd drop the basket off at the *Gazette* office, I'd appreciate it."

"I'll be glad to. See you on Friday."

"Good-bye and thank you."

Kathleen hung up the receiver. "He's coming down on Friday and will come to the office."

"Kathleen Dolan, that was quick thinking. He caught on right away, didn't he?"

"There was a short silence . . . at first. I feel better already just knowing that we can lay all this out; and if there is something here, which I certainly think there is, he may be able to help us with it."

"You've opened a can of worms, Kathleen."

"I'd appreciate it if you didn't say anything to Johnny about my calling Mr. Fleming. He doesn't like him very much."

"He's jealous. Johnny is falling in love with you. If you have no feelings for him, let him think you like Mr. Fleming. It will be easier for him in the long run."

"Mr. Fleming is a friend, nothing more, and never will be," Kathleen said firmly. Then her tone softened, and she murmured sadly, "Johnny could very well break my heart."

Chapter Twenty

Johnny stopped by the office shortly before time for the funeral. He wore a dark suit, white shirt, and string tie. He was absolutely handsome. Kathleen couldn't move her eyes away from him.

"I know enough to dress up for a funeral," he said defensively.

"I was just thinking that you clean up pretty well."

"Hazel asked me to be a pallbearer."

"She told me this morning. She's worried there'll not be very many at the funeral."

"Clara's reputation was not the best."

"Adelaide and I will be there . . . for Hazel and Emily."

"I'll go with Eldon." He stopped at the door and looked back. "You clean up good, too." He winked at her.

Kathleen's heart hammered, and a fluttering sensation settled in the pit of her stomach. She had wanted to look nice today because she knew she would see him. She wore a navy blue dress of soft material, its full skirt gathered onto the bodice. A wide sash with small, light blue flowers circled her waist and tied on the side. Her hair, bright from a rainwater washing, curled softly about her face and shoulders. Around her neck was a silver chain and hanging from it a small locket.

The church was half-filled when Kathleen and Adelaide arrived. It was a testimony to Hazel's standing in the community. The service was an opportunity for the preacher to preach a "hellfire and brimstone" sermon, and he took full advantage of it.

When it was finally over, the congregation stood while the casket was wheeled out followed by Hazel and Emily. The mourners quickly left the church to follow the hearse to the cemetery. It was then that Kathleen saw Dr. Herman helping Hazel and Emily into the backseat of a big black car. Louise Munday was with him.

"Look at that . . . that hypocrite," Kathleen exclaimed.

"He plays every angle. That's how he keeps his popularity up."

"He knows damn well that girl was murdered."

"Like I said . . . this is his town, and he'll not have it soiled by a murder."

"It's more likely that he's afraid he'll get a Federal Marshal in here."

At the gravesite Sheriff Carroll and another man stepped forward to help Johnny and the undertaker carry the casket to its final resting place. Kathleen seethed to see Dr. Herman and Louise flanking Hazel and Emily as they stood beside the gaping hole to watch Clara's body being lowered into the ground.

Poor little Emily. Kathleen remembered her own anguish as she stood with her grandparents at her mother's burial. It was a consolation to know that Emily's life would not be as disrupted as hers had been. The child had not been attached to Clara as a child is normally attached to her mother. In time she would forget the bad things about her mother and remember only the times when Clara came home bringing presents.

Dr. Herman and Louise stood by as if they were family while the mourners came to express their sympathy to Hazel then shake hands with the doctor. After hugging Hazel, Kathleen stooped down to whisper to Emily.

"Your grandma is so lucky to have you, Sugarpuss. You'll take care of her, and she'll take care of you. After a while it will not hurt so much. I'll see you tonight."

Kathleen straightened, looked directly into Dr. Herman's eyes, but didn't offer her hand as the others had done. She met the eyes of the smirking woman who stood beside him. Louise was a half head taller than the doctor even with his hat on. She wore a black coat with a huge silver fox collar. Attached to her small black hat was a black-dotted veil that came down to her penciled brows. On her face was the usual heavy coat of makeup.

Kathleen looked at the woman, and needing to do something to show her contempt, rolled her eyes in a derisive gesture. Louise's cheeks became suffused with color, her balled gloved fists evidence of her surprised anger.

Johnny was waiting beside the car when they reached it.

"Are you going to the house?"

"No. I told Hazel this morning that we'd not come."

Johnny held open the passenger-side door, plainly indicating that he was going to drive. Kathleen dug into her purse for the keys. He stilled her hand and, dangling her extra set between his thumb and forefinger, smirked at her.

"The extra set wouldn't do much good if you can't keep track of them."

"You're . . . sneaky!" She slid onto the seat, moved to the middle to make room for Adelaide, removed her hat, and looped her hair behind her ear with trembling fingers. *Lord! Why do I get the trembles when I'm with him?*

Johnny's hand brushed her knee when he grasped the round ball handle on the gearshift. Her shoulder was behind his, her hip tight against him. It was such a wonderful feeling to be sitting close to him that Kathleen had to caution herself not to be giddy.

"Dr. Herman and Louise were acting like family," Kathleen said in order to occupy her mind with something other than the man beside her. "He's got a lot of nerve. I've never heard Hazel even mention him."

"He wasn't there for Hazel. He was there to show the public how much he *cared*." Adelaide's tone was heavily sarcastic.

"I took the pictures down to Vernon yesterday to show Keith. He agrees that Clara was not hit by a car. A car going forty miles an hour would have tossed her into the ditch, but wouldn't have crushed her windpipe and knocked her teeth out."

"The next question," Adelaide said, "is why. She wasn't raped, or was she?"

"Eldon said there was no evidence that she was." Johnny parked the car in front of the *Gazette*, turned, and put his arm across the back of the seat. "Whoever killed her was in a rage. She wasn't just run over. She was beaten up in a car because there was very little blood at the scene. Afterward he pushed her out of the car, then ran over her as she lay in the road. To be sure that she was dead, he stopped the car and got out. She was still alive, probably trying to get up. He pushed her over and stomped on her back. She may have yelled. That's when he stomped on her neck and crushed her windpipe. After that he dragged her into the ditch."

"That makes sense," Kathleen said proudly. "You'd make a good detective, Johnny."

"Yeah? I thought about it, but I don't like living in the city."

"Oh, dear, there's Hannah, and she's drunk again." Adelaide opened the car door.

Johnny's hand slipped from the back of the seat and squeezed Kathleen's shoulder. His arm tightened for just an instant before he withdrew it and got out of the car.

"I'll take her home, Adelaide. Keep her here while I get my truck."

"No need for that, Johnny," Kathleen said quickly. "Take my car."

Johnny went to where Hannah was leaning against the building.

"Come on, Hannah. I'll take you home."

"Baby—" She looked up at Johnny with big sad eyes. "Baby, baby," she babbled.

She had once been a pretty girl. Now her face was ravaged and gray streaked her raven black hair. Her dress was well worn, but clean.

"Where is your baby, Hannah?" Kathleen asked.

"Baby . . . gone . . . gone—" Tears rolled down her cheeks.

"Did your baby die?" Kathleen asked insistently. Then repeated the question. "Did your baby die?"

Hannah continued to babble and tried to pull away from Johnny, who was holding her up.

"Johnny will take you home," Adelaide said soothingly. "He's a nice man, Hannah. He won't hurt you."

"Whis . . . key—"

"I think you've had enough," Johnny said kindly as he tried to steer her toward the car.

"Leave her alone!"

Kathleen jerked her head around at the belligerent tone and saw the sheriff hurrying toward them.

"Don't you dare arrest her and put her in your rotten jail so that . . . that pervert of a deputy can molest her. Don't you dare!"

"Shut her up!" Sheriff Carroll said to Johnny.

"She can say what she wants, and I'll back her up."

"Hannah's drunk, Pete," Adelaide said. "Johnny's going to take her home."

"Hannah, you . . . promised."

Kathleen's sharp ears heard the murmured remark.

"I'll take her home." Pete elbowed Johnny out of the way and put his arm around Hannah to hold her up.

"Where is she getting the whiskey?" Adelaide asked.

"I don't know, but when I find out, somebody's head's goin' to roll." The sheriff guided Hannah across the sidewalk to the car and opened the door.

"No, Pete—"

"Get in, Hannah." Pete eased her down on the seat,

lifted her feet to the floor of the car, and closed the door. Without a word, he got under the wheel and drove away.

Paul got up from Adelaide's desk when they entered the office and helped her off with her coat.

"Where's Judy?" Adelaide asked, when she heard a familiar sound coming from the back room.

"At the linotype machine," Paul grinned. "I've been showing her how to use it. She's a smart kid."

"Forevermore! She'll hurt herself with that hot lead."

"No, she won't, mother hen," Paul said affectionately. "She'll be careful."

"I hope so. Landsakes, whatever caused you to let her touch your precious machine?"

"She's at the age to learn things, honey. Her mind is like a sponge. That girl needs to know that someone has confidence in her."

"Paul darlin', you're right as usual."

"Of course, I am. Remember that the next time we get into an argument." He hung her coat on the hall tree. "Were there very many at the funeral?"

"Hazel's friends turned out. Doc and Louise were there being very solicitous of Hazel and Emily. Kathleen, did you see the spray of fresh gladiolas? They must have come in on the bus from a greenhouse and must have cost four or five dollars. Who around here has that kind of money to spend on flowers?"

"Doc Herman."

"But why would he send flowers to Clara Ramsey's funeral?"

"It looked to me like he was trying to throw up a smoke screen. It was overdone. He probably sent the big ham I saw this morning on Hazel's kitchen table. The show-off!"

"Smoke screen? You think he could have killed her? What reason would he have?"

"Maybe they were . . . ah maybe he was . . . you know—"

"I doubt that it was Doc's car that ran over Clara, if that's what you're thinking," Johnny said. "His car was the only big one at the cemetery beside the hearse. The tread on his tires is a different shape. Does Louise Munday have a car?"

Adelaide answered. "An Oldsmobile."

"If I get a chance, I'll take a look at the tires."

"Louise was dressed to kill," Adelaide said.

"She looked like a moose in that big fur collar." Kathleen broke into laughter. "It was really catty of me to say that." Her eyes flashed to Johnny and found him watching her with a sweet and tender smile on his quiet face. She couldn't look away and became lost in depths of his dark eyes. Only Paul's voice talking about Hannah brought her back to the present.

"Hannah came to the door, but she was too drunk to open it. I didn't help her because I was afraid it might cause problems if someone came in and found her in here alone with me.

Adelaide explained that just as Johnny was getting ready to take her home, the sheriff arrived.

"Did you notice how gentle he was with her?" Kathleen asked. "He was that way the other night. She called him Pete. Isn't that what he was called when he was young?"

"They knew each other quite well at one time, but Pete's mother was dead set against him having anything to do with an Indian, even a half-breed Cherokee whose daddy had a large spread and a good herd of cattle at one time. Heck Lawson was well respected in the town, even if he did have an Indian wife. He lost most of his land during the twenties and died shortly after."

"Where does Hannah live?"

"Out on the edge of town with her mother and a brother who works at the tannery."

"She isn't married?"

"Never has been as far as I know."

"Who was the father of the baby she had just before I got here?"

Adelaide lifted her shoulders. "Who knows."

"Last night I asked Hazel about the baby Clara had a year ago. She said Doc Herman told Clara that it was dead when he took it from her and that it was badly deformed. He put it in a box and had it buried on the lot beside Hazel's husband. Hazel felt bad that it didn't get a proper burial."

"A plank with the word *baby* and the date is there. I saw it while I was helping Eldon," Johnny said.

"And shortly after Clara had that baby she had enough money to leave town."

"I'd like to know what's in the box buried out there by Sam Ramsey," Adelaide said.

"Watch it, Johnny," Paul warned. "These two have something devious on their minds."

"Why are you interested in what's buried on the Ramsey lot?" Johnny asked.

"We've got another mystery on our hands, Johnny. I haven't had a chance to tell you about it."

"You can't tell him now," Adelaide said quickly. "Here comes Leroy."

"Don't make a date for tonight," Johnny said to Kathleen as he and Paul hurried to the back room.

"Afternoon, Leroy," Adelaide said as he came into the office. Kathleen echoed the greeting. She didn't have time to completely digest Johnny's words, but she felt wonderful.

"Hello, Adelaide, Miss Dolan."

"If you're thinking about an ad, Leroy, we've got a new ad book."

"No. I . . . ah . . . well—" Looking only at Adelaide, he stood on first one foot and then the other as he struggled for words.

"What is it?"

"We had a Chamber meeting this morning."

"I didn't know or I'd have been there."

"It was a special meeting, Adelaide. About you . . . the paper."

"For goodness sake. What about me . . . the paper?"

"Some feel that you're taking too much on yourself to question the sheriff's decision about . . . the accident."

"That's what papers do all the time, Leroy. It's our job to question."

"We . . . ah want you to stop it and take that board out of the window."

For a minute or two silence throbbed between them. Leroy rocked back and forth on his heels, Adelaide looking steadily at him. Finally she spoke.

"If I don't do as you wish, what will you do?"

"Stop advertising."

"That's the word that came down from Doc Herman?"

"We all think that it's bad for the town."

"You weak-kneed, spineless jackass!" The words burst from Kathleen as she shot to her feet. "A girl has been brutally murdered in this town. Her reputation was not the best, but she was a living, breathing human being. Would you feel the same if it had been . . . an upstanding citizen like . . . Louise Munday?"

"Sheriff Carroll says that it was an accident. It was night, the driver may not have even known he hit her. She was drunk and staggering down the road."

"The sheriff is so tied in with Doc Herman that he'll say anything Doc tells him to say. I'm disappointed in you, Mr. Grandon. I thought you were one man in this town with a mind of his own."

"I've got a business here. I've got to get along."

"At the price of losing your integrity?"

"You're new here. You don't understand."

"I'm not new, Leroy, and I don't understand how a group of grown men can knuckle under to one-man rule," Adelaide said.

"I'm just carrying the message, Adelaide."

"Here's one you can carry back. You tell that dim-witted bunch, who have no more backbone than jellyfish, that I'll not take that poster out of the window; and if they withhold their advertising, so be it. I carried every one of them, including you, Leroy, until I almost went broke. I'll not let you or them or Doc Herman tell me what to do."

"Hurrah!" Kathleen shouted and clapped her hands. The red-faced man glanced at her and then away.

"I'm sorry you feel that way, Adelaide. We've been friends for a long time."

"Not friends, Leroy, or you'd have stood up with me for what is right."

"I've told you. It's all I can do."

"No, it isn't," Kathleen said. "You can get those merchants together and tell them it's time to take their town back from the tyrant who's had control for so long."

"The town has prospered under his control," Leroy replied bellicosely.

"You're mistaken," Adelaide said quietly. "The prosperity here is due to the tannery, and you know it. Who comes to buy at your store, Leroy? Could you make it without the tannery people?"

"They help," he admitted, "but Doc Herman sees to it that we have law and order. He talks to our congressman to get WPA projects for our city. His clinic brings people to town, and they buy gasoline, food, and lodging."

"The congressman is obligated to spread the projects over the counties in his district. Rawlings is the only town in the county any larger than a wide spot in the road. There are not enough votes in Tillison County for anyone in Washington to pay any attention to a pipsqueak like Doc Herman. He has you all buffaloed." Disgusted, Kathleen flopped back down on her chair.

"I've told you what the Chamber members think, Adelaide. The rest is up to you." Leroy turned quickly and left the office.

"Adelaide, I'm sorry. This wouldn't have happened if I hadn't come here."

"No, I would've rocked along and lost the paper anyway. I hate to think that you may lose your investment."

"If we lose it, we'll go down fighting, and I intend to do everything I can to take Doc Herman and Louise down with me. If I have to do it all by myself, I'm going out to the cemetery and dig up that box he buried on the Ramsey lot. I'll bet my entire interest in this paper that it will be empty."

"I swear, Kathleen. Doesn't anything get you down?"

"Some things get me lower than a snake's belly, but not him. He just gets me mad." Her blue eyes were hard and shone with rage.

"I'm proud of you, love." Paul's voice came from the doorway before he came on into the office and went to stand behind Adelaide's chair. His hands massaged her shoulders.

"We may lose the paper, Paul."

"It wouldn't be the end of the world, would it? I know it means a lot to you; but if we have to leave, we'll still be together."

Adelaide's hand went up to cover his.

Kathleen felt an ache in her heart. Not at the thought of losing her investment, but with a longing to have the kind of love Adelaide and Paul shared.

"Did Johnny leave?"

"He went home to do chores. He said to tell you to be ready to go honky-tonking and that he'd come to Hazel's to get you."

"Honky-tonking? For crying out loud. That's the last place I'd've thought he'd want to go."

"Tell Johnny about the birth records and how the deputy tried to get your notebook."

"I also have to tell him that Barker Fleming is coming tomorrow. I kind of dread telling him that."

Chapter Twenty-one

Dr. Herman walked Hazel and Emily to the porch.

"Do you have time to come in, Doctor?"

"No, thank you, Mrs. Ramsey. I've a patient waiting at the clinic. I must get back. I wanted to make sure that you and the child were all right. It was a terrible accident, just terrible. If there's anything I can do, anything at all, send word. If I'm unable to come myself, I'll send someone."

"Thank you, Doctor. Is there a chance they'll find out who . . . who ran over Clara?"

"Not much, dear lady. The driver could be deep in Texas by now. He may have hit her and been too frightened to stop. It happens in and around the cities. It's something new for us here in Tillison County."

"Thank you for the ham."

"You're welcome." He glanced at the street. People were coming by car and on foot. "You're going to have plenty of friends to share the rest of the day with you. I'll run along."

"'Bye, Doctor, and thanks again."

Dr. Herman made his escape back to his car without

having to stop and chat with the mourners. They were well away from the house before he spoke to Louise.

"That little problem is solved."

"It cost you a ham and flowers."

"Cheap compared to what she was going to stick us for."

"Do you think the sheriff will stay in line?"

"He will. He likes the prestige of being sheriff."

"You understand that we have a problem bigger than Clara was."

"I'm not deaf or blind, Louise."

"I didn't mean that you are," she said hastily. "Mitchell said that Dolan woman from the paper was fooling around in the records department at the court-house."

"And he would have stopped her if not for that old fool Judge Fimbres. You told me that," he added impatiently.

"The excuse she gave for looking at the records is as thin as water."

"It could be that she was doing just what she said she was. It certainly would be the place to go to look up the maiden name of someone's mother."

"The records clerk told Mitchell that she wrote some things down in a notebook."

"Where else would she write down the information, for God's sake? Use your head, Louise."

Louise was becoming irritated at his logical reasoning where that redheaded bitch was concerned. She had de-voted her life to Darrell Herman. The least he could do would be to agree with her once in a while. After all the years they had worked together, he was still a mystery to her. She was sure that he was capable of doing whatever needed to be done to rid them of Clara's threat. That was all right with her; it made him even more fascinating. The little man had a steel trap for a mind and the guts to go with it.

"I wonder what really happened to Clara," she said as they neared the clinic.

"Don't play games with me, Louise." Doc's eyes were as cold as a stone. "We both know what happened to Clara. Don't speak of it again."

It was already dark when Kathleen left the office at six. She, Adelaide, and Paul had had a talk with Judy. They explained their suspicions about the number of births at Doc Herman's clinic and why they wanted to keep her reason for being here quiet for a while. Adelaide had spoken to Mrs. Wilson, and she had agreed to *forget* about Judy being in her store.

After a couple of days' rest and good food, Judy was a different girl. She was bright, personable, and had become attached to Paul, drinking in every word he said. Adelaide explained that the girl probably had never had attention from her father other than in a derisive way and was fascinated with Paul because he treated her like a young person with a mind. It confirmed Adelaide's belief that Paul would make a wonderful father.

Kathleen left the car behind the house and went in through the kitchen. Hazel and one of her friends were putting away the leftovers of the food that had been brought in to serve after the funeral.

"Hello, Mrs. Ashley, Hazel." Kathleen put her arm around Hazel. "You doing all right?"

"I guess so. I'm still in shock."

"It was a nice funeral." Kathleen didn't know how any funeral could be *nice*, but it was something people seemed to say at a time like this.

"Even Dr. Herman came," Mrs. Ashley said. "Wasn't it good of him, being so busy and all?"

"Very good," Kathleen dropped a kiss on the top of Emily's head. "Hi, Sugarpuss."

"Grandma saved you some supper."

"Good. I'm starved. Let me get out of this dress, and I'll be right back."

Kathleen hadn't even been aware that she was hungry. Her mind was forging ahead to the date with Johnny and what she would wear. She changed into a soft blue blouse and a black jersey skirt gathered on a wide band. She exchanged the spike heels she had been wearing all day for a pair of pumps with medium heels.

After cleaning her face and applying fresh makeup, she went back to the kitchen.

"My, you look nice." Hazel placed a clean plate at the end of the table so that Kathleen could help herself from the platters and bowls of food.

"You smell good," Emily whispered.

"Thank you," Kathleen whispered back, and helped herself to a slice of smoked ham. She felt guilty being so happy when she looked at Emily's sad little face.

Johnny followed Hazel into the kitchen after she had answered his knock on the door. Kathleen's heart jumped alarmingly when his dark eyes caught and held hers. He was back in his twill pants, white shirt, and boots. She was glad that she hadn't dressed up.

"I was going to take you to Claude's for a hamburger."

"I like Claude's hamburgers, but this ham and potato salad is delicious."

"Sit down, Johnny, and help yourself. There's plenty here, and I don't want any of it to spoil." Hazel placed a plate in front of him.

"Do you have ice in your box?" he asked.

"It's chuck full. Dr. Herman sent the iceman down."

When Kathleen went to her room to get her purse, Emily went with her. Kathleen placed a little dab of *Coty* perfume behind Emily's ears and powdered her nose with the puff from her compact.

"Are ya comin' back?"

"Of course, honey. I'm just going out with Johnny for a while."

"Don't go to one of them old . . . honky-tonks. Mama did, and she didn't come back."

"Don't worry, Sugarpuss. I'll be back. I promise."

Johnny had spread a clean blanket over the seat in the truck. After he started the motor, he reached for her arm and pulled until she moved over into the middle of the seat.

"This is a date. You're not supposed to sit way over there."

"Do all your dates sit this close to you?"

"Only the pretty redheaded ones."

Kathleen's breath suspended. "Where are we going?" She really didn't care. This was all so new, so wonderful.

"To the Twilight Gardens."

"The honky-tonk?"

"You got something against honky-tonks?" He grinned down at her. "You said you liked to dance."

"I do. Emily asked me not to go to one because her mama did, and she didn't come back."

"That's why we're going. If Clara was there, we may be able to find out who she was with."

"Didn't Sheriff Carroll try to find out where she had been that night?"

"No, he closed the case. That's why we're going to nose around."

"And you need me to do that?"

"Of course."

Kathleen wrinkled her nose. "So you're just using me as a prop for your sleuthing?"

"Pretty smart of me, huh?" His lighthearted words and his smile set her heart dancing.

"It'll depend on how successful you are."

Cars were parked in front and alongside the Twilight Gardens when they pulled in and stopped. Traveling neon lights, in a zigzag pattern, ran across the front of the building. A beer sign flashed in one of the windows.

"Here we are," Johnny said, but made no attempt to get out. "This isn't a very fancy place."

"I didn't expect it to be."

"I heard what Grandon said today. Will you lose the paper if the merchants stop advertising?"

"Maybe. But we won't go down without a fight. I'll write a story about the reason for their boycott and spread it all over the front page. Our subscribers buy the paper for news as well as the advertisements. The merchants' boycott could backfire on them."

Johnny reached out to touch her hair. "Come on, my feisty little redhead. Let's see what we can find out."

Even coming in from the outside, Kathleen's eyes took a minute or two to adjust to the dim lights. A row of booths surrounded a small dance floor where couples were swaying to a slow waltz. A big nickelodeon, with a rainbow of lights, stood at one end of the room and a bar at the other.

"Howdy, cowboy. That's Johnny Henry, the *All-Around Cowboy*." The voice came from one of the booths.

"Howdy."

"Hey, Johnny. Good ridin'."

"Thanks."

Johnny steered her along the edge of the dance floor to an empty booth at the end. Kathleen scooted in, and he slid in beside her. They had a clear view of the entire room.

"You've got friends here."

"Not friends. They saw me at the rodeo."

"Do you come here very often?"

"A couple times a month when I want to get a cold glass of 3.2. Oklahoma only sells beer with 3.2 percent of alcohol. Some people go across the river to get stronger Texas beer. What will you have? Coke or beer?"

"Coke."

Kathleen watched him as he went along the row of booths to the bar. He stopped a couple of times along the way to speak to people who hailed him. He spoke with the man behind the counter for a minute or two then returned with two bottles.

"Like I said, it isn't fancy. No glasses."

"That's all right. I've drunk out of a bottle before." Kathleen placed his hat on the seat beside her to move it away from the water left by the wet bottles. She wiped the neck of the Coke bottle with her handkerchief and took a deep swallow. "Whee . . . the fizz goes up my nose!"

As they watched the couples on the dance floor, Johnny reached for her hand. She folded her fingers over his, pressing her soft palm tightly to his rough one. Kathleen was as certain as she was breathing that this man would forever occupy a place in her heart. She shoved from her mind the knowledge that before the evening was over she must tell him that Barker Fleming would be in Rawlings the next day. He was going to be angry, and she dreaded that.

"Do you want to dance?" The soft inquiry brought her eyes to his. He was watching her with a half smile on his face. "Let your Coke sit a while and it'll not be so fizzy."

"Your beer will get warm."

"You've not been paying attention, Miss Dolan. I finished my beer."

"Oh, my goodness. I must have been daydreaming."

"Come dance with me. 'Springtime in the Rockies' is a good slow one. Just right for an old cowboy like me."

"You really are old, you know," Kathleen teased as she slid out of the booth.

Johnny took her hand, put his arm around her, and drew her close. She allowed him to mold her body to his and gave herself up to his tight embrace. When he moved it was impossible not to move with him. Her hand on his shoulder slipped up until she could feel the hair at the nape of his neck. He pressed his cheek tightly to the side of her head. Her heart throbbed in her throat.

"You're very soft and sweet tonight, Miss Dolan." He tipped his head and his lips tickled her ear when he spoke.

"You're full of blarney, fer sure, me boy," she answered in a breathless whisper.

Kathleen's eyes were half-closed, and for a short while she forgot that anyone else existed except the two of them. Johnny was a wonderful dancer. Their steps fit perfectly. Kathleen floated in a golden haze. He moved his head, and she tilted hers to look at him. His dark eyes were warm and his mouth slightly tilted at the corners. Emotion was there on his face. Was it love? Whatever it was, it had the power to stop her breath. His arms tightened convulsively when her lashes fluttered down. He pressed his cheek to her hair again, and they glided around the small dance floor to the strains of the slow waltz.

Johnny brought them to a halt when the music stopped. He took a step back, then lifted a hand to finger-comb the hair back from her temple.

"I like your hair. It reminds me of a sunset." A slow smile lit his face. "Shall we try it again? You're good at keeping my big old boots from stomping on your feet."

"They didn't even come close. You're a great, I might even say magnificent, dancer."

His arms closed around her and they began to move to

the music coming from the jukebox. Bing Crosby was singing: *When the blue of the night meets the gold of the day, someone waits for you*—Johnny didn't understand what he was feeling. He didn't have words to describe it. There might not even be words. All he knew was that holding this woman in his arms was wonderful, different from anything he ever felt before.

The sheen of her fiery red hair, the delicacy of her profile, and the strength of her personality were enough to intimidate any man. To a dumb cowboy like him she was . . . unreachable. Yet here she was, in his arms and enjoying it. He wasn't so dumb, he told himself, that he didn't know that.

The music ended. They stepped back and looked at each other.

"Shall we go see if your Coke has lost some of its fizz?" Johnny's lips felt stiff as he spoke. His hand rested at her waist as they walked back to their booth. He leaned over to speak to her after she was seated. "Will you be all right for a few minutes? Someone just came in that I'd like to speak to."

"About Clara? Go ahead, I'll be fine."

Johnny crossed the room to where two young cowboys leaned against the wall. They worked on a ranch just outside of town, and both had participated in the events at the rodeo.

"Howdy, Buddy. Hi, Mack."

"I've not seen you out here before, Johnny."

"Showing my girlfriend the sights. Twilight Gardens is one of them."

"She's a looker, Johnny. But I guess the *All-Around*

Cowboy has the pick of the litter, huh?" Buddy gave Johnny a good-natured slap on the shoulder.

"It helped," Johnny said confidentially out of the side of his mouth. "Listen, fellows, I'm kind of in a pickle. Were you all here Monday night?"

"Yeah, we came by. It was kind of late."

"Was Clara Ramsey here?"

The young men looked at each other. Finally one of them said, "Yeah."

"Was she with someone?"

"If she was, you'd never know it. She was booth-hoppin' all over the place. Even me'n Buddy could've taken her out for a while if we'd a had the price."

"Here's my problem, boys, and I don't want my lady friend to know it. Clara got hold of my *All-Around Cowboy* belt buckle. I won't tell you how."

Buddy snickered. "You don't have to. We've got a idey."

"When they found her in the ditch, it wasn't on her. I've got to think that she gave it to someone she was with, or sold it. I want to find that man and get it back."

"Wish we could help you, Johnny. We met a couple of girls and you know—"

"Did you see her talking to anyone you know?"

"She was talking to everyone."

"She sat in the corner for a while with Gus Webb," Mack said.

"Gus Webb. Someone said the sheriff had run him outta town."

"He might of, but he come back. He was here Monday night and again last night."

"If he's got my buckle, I'll work him over till I get it back. Thanks, fellows. Keep this under your hats will you. I don't want folks to think I was dumb enough to let some woman take it from me."

"Sure, Johnny."

Johnny went back to Kathleen. She moved to make room for him to sit beside her.

"Clara was here Monday night. I guess she was making a show of herself."

"Was she with anyone?"

"Everyone, I guess. The boys said she was in a back booth for a while with Gus Webb."

"Well, for goodness sake! Do you think he killed her?"

"Not with that old car of his. Are you ready to leave? I've talked to the bartender. He won't admit that she was even here. He's afraid it'll hurt business."

Kathleen handed Johnny his hat, then took the hand he offered as she slid out of the booth. They walked along the side of the dance floor toward the door. As they passed the two young cowboys, Johnny winked. One of them snickered.

Gene Autry was singing "Be Nobody's Darling But Mine," as they left the smoke-filled tavern. Kathleen appreciated the clean, cool air. She held tightly to Johnny's arm as they walked across the uneven ground to his truck. Once they were inside, she shivered.

"Are you cold?" Johnny asked.

"I should have worn my coat."

"Come here." She moved close to him. He put his arm around her and pulled her closer. "I'd like for us to sit out here for a while to see if Webb shows up, but I don't want you freezing while we do it."

Kathleen cuddled against his warm body. "You're warm," she whispered, snuggling her cold nose against his neck.

"You're . . . sweet—" His voice was husky. "I may have to kiss you."

"I couldn't stop you. You're bigger than I am."

"In that case—" His fingers tilted her chin. His mouth was warm and gentle. Every bone in her body turned to jelly. His hands moved across her back and hips, tucked her closer to the granite strength of his body and moved his fingers over the soft mound of her breast. He continued to press sweet kisses to her moist parted lips before his mouth trailed to her ear.

Kathleen's mind felt like it was floating. Primitive desire grew inside her, and she became helpless to stop it. She clung to him weakly, giving back kiss for kiss. He lifted his head, his breath warm on her wet lips.

"I've got to stop this while I can." His voice was a shivering whisper that reached all the way to her heart.

They sat quietly. Johnny didn't speak again until after his breathing had returned to normal.

"This is a good place to watch for Webb. We'll see him before he gets to the door . . . that is, if we're paying attention."

Kathleen glanced up to see him smiling down at her. Without hesitation, she reached up and kissed him gently on the lips.

"That'll have to do for a while."

"You're some woman. Why is it that you never married?"

"I never met a man I wanted to spend the rest of my life with—" *Until I met you, Johnny, my love.* "How about you? Have you ever been in love?"

"Not even close to it."

"You're a good dancer."

"So are you."

"Did you ever know an Irish lass that couldn't dance?" she said sassily.

"Even if my ancesters did do a rain dance around a campfire, I had two left feet until Henry Ann took me in hand. Then after I came back from Kansas, I spent time at the McCabe ranch. Down there you can go to a dance once a week if you want to. The neighbors get together, clear the furniture out of one room, and wind up the Victrola. Ruth, Keith's wife, danced with me and, after a while, I got to where I liked it."

"And the girls lined up, I bet."

"Woop! There's our friend Webb!" Johnny removed his arm and opened the truck door at the same time. "Stay here," he said urgently.

Three men had come around from the back of the building and stopped to pass around a bottle. They didn't see Johnny until the last one had put a cap on it and shoved it in his pocket.

"Wait right here, Webb," Johnny said sharply. "You fellows go on in. I want a word with Webb."

"I ain't got nothin' to say to you. The sheriff knows I'm here." Webb attempted to follow his friends into the tavern. Johnny grabbed his arm and threw him up against the side of the building. "Hey, ya got no call to do that."

"Go on in, boys," Johnny said again. "My beef is with Webb."

"Don't go," Webb whined. "He's gonna beat me up."

The men shrugged and disappeared inside the tavern.

"Gimme my belt buckle," Johnny demanded. "Give it to me or I'll beat the hell out of you."

"What the shit ya talkin' about? I ain't got yore goddamn belt buckle."

"Clara Ramsey had it. It wasn't on her when she was found, so I figure the last man with her has it. I mean to get it back." Johnny held Webb up against the wall and drew back his fist.

"Hell, man. 'Twasn't me. I come outside with her. She was only chargin' four bits."

"You screwed her out here?"

"Didn't even get 'er to the car. We was 'bout to get in when she spied a big fancy car and let out a squeal. I had my whacker out, ready to do business, when she run off and got in the fancy car. Damn bitch took my four bits and I got nothin'."

"Tell me about the car, Webb. So far you're my best bet. If you've sold that buckle, I'm going to choke the life out of you." Johnny fastened a hand around Webb's neck and bounced his head against the wall of the tavern.

"I told ya. I ain't got yore buckle."

"The car? What kind was it?"

"I ain't knowin' what kind. It was big and black . . . had lots . . . of shiny on it. Stop it! Yo're hurtin'—"

"What else . . . out with it. I don't think there was a car," Johnny said angrily.

"I swear it, Johnny. It kind of sloped down in the back. I saw it when it . . . went by and it had a big old thingamabob for a radiator cap."

"Had you seen it before?"

"I . . . don't think so. I swear to God, Johnny. I don't have your buckle. If that twister tail had it, she sure didn't give it to me."

"Why didn't you go to the sheriff and tell him Clara was with a man in a big car the night she was killed?"

"I ain't tellin' that sheriff nothin'. The deputy told me 'n Krome to lay low. It's what we been doin'."

Johnny let up on Webb's throat. "Don't tell a soul what you told me, or I'll be back, and there'll not be enough of you left to tell a tale about."

"What'a ya gonna do now?"

"Find that guy in the big car and get my buckle back. Go on in and keep your trap shut."

Johnny waited until Webb was inside the tavern before he went back to the truck.

Chapter Twenty-two

Johnny hurried back to the truck. He reached for Kathleen as soon as he closed the door and hugged her tightly.

"You brought me luck, sweet Kathleen," he murmured against her cheek. "You're my lucky charm! I know who Clara was with. I'm almost sure I know who killed her, but I don't know how we're going to prove it." He was clearly elated.

"Oh, Johnny. How in the world did you find that out?" She was being held tightly against him, happy to be sharing this moment with him. "Who was it?"

"Webb told me that she got into a big black car. I'm sure it was Marty Conroy's, the little jelly bean who was with her at the rodeo. She must have really made him mad, or else she was threatening him with something, and he had to get rid of her. He's usually a spineless blowhard."

"Did Webb see him?"

"No, just the car. He told me about coming outside with Clara. They were going to his car when she saw the car sitting back down the road. She ran to it and got in.

Webb was—" Johnny began to laugh. "I can't tell you the rest."

"Why not? I'm a big girl."

"He paid for something he didn't get."

"Uh-oh. Say no more."

Johnny then told her the story that he had spun about Clara taking the belt buckle he had won along with the prize money at the rodeo and about him looking for someone she might have given it to.

Kathleen reared back to look at him. "Johnny Henry! You are devious! But . . . that was a brilliant idea. Wait a minute. How did you tell them she got it in the first place?" She framed his face with the palms of her hands.

"I didn't tell them; I let them use their imaginations."

"You didn't! The story will be all over town."

"Webb will be too scared to tell. The cowboys will think that they know something no one else knows and will keep it to themselves."

"Where do we go from here?"

"I'm not sure. I've got to talk to Keith. He knows Marty better than anyone. We're not going to have real proof. We'll have to get him to admit that he did it."

"Does that mean you'll make another trip down to the McCabe ranch?"

"I'll go down tomorrow. I want to stay on this while it's hot. Want to come along?"

"I can't go tomorrow." She sat back and looked at him. *Oh, Lord! How is he going to take this?*

"Okay. I just thought you might want to go."

"I do want to go, but . . . Johnny there is something

else going on in this town. Something very wrong. Adelaide and I are trying to get someone to look into it."

"You don't have to give me an excuse."

"I'm not giving you an excuse. It's a matter of conscience. I'm obligated to do this other thing. I haven't told you what Adelaide and I suspect because we had nothing really to go on until Judy DeBerry, a young girl from Fort Worth, came to town looking for her real mother. I went to the courthouse and looked at the birth records. And, Johnny, you won't believe how many babies are born in this town."

Please, darling, don't be mad and ruin this special time I've had with you.

Kathleen talked steadily for five or more minutes, telling about meeting Judy, her reception at the courthouse, the deputy trying to take her notebook, and Judge Fimbres's interference. The more words tumbled from her, the faster they came, and the more she feared that she would never be able to find the right ones to tell him that she had asked the man that he'd turned his back on to help them. She closed her eyes briefly before she told him.

"We decided that we needed someone who had some credibility with not only Judge Fimbres, but with the district attorney's office in Oklahoma City. We decided to ask Barker Fleming to help us. He will be here tomorrow." She finished the last few words in a rush.

Her last words cut into Johnny like a knife. *The son of a bitch is going through Kathleen to get to me. A hell of a lot of good it will do him.* With his eyes on her face, Johnny retreated to the safety of silence. Tension was alive between them.

"Johnny, Paul, and Adelaide agreed that we must do something. Please come and help us." Her lovely blue eyes were clouded with worry. "We think that over the years there could be as many as two hundred babies sold out of that clinic."

He realized that he didn't dare linger in silence for too long or he might lose the will to break it at all. He'd start the truck and take her home without a word. Should that happen, it would be the end of his ever being with her again.

"Did you call him?"

"Yes. We needed someone who is not under Doc Herman's thumb to investigate him." Her hand shook when she pushed hair back from her face.

"Why bring *him* in?"

"Because he owns the tannery. He has an interest in the town. You don't have to like him or have anything to do with him, Johnny. Just tolerate him for the sake of the girls like Judy, who was sold to people who hated her when she began to show her Indian blood and threw her out on the street to fend for herself."

"I thought I made it plain to you that I don't want anything to do with him."

"I need . . . you to . . . be with me on this. Help me. Please, Johnny. I can't do it without you." Her voice came through quivering lips. Her eyes were bright with tears; her hands clutched at his shirt as if she was drowning.

"Don't cry," he said harshly.

"I can't help it. This is terribly important to me."

"Who? Fleming or Dr. Herman?" he asked harshly.

"You! You, idiot!" she said tersely. "I'm twenty-six years old. I'm not a silly girl with a crush, for Christ sake! It's stupid of me to tell you this, but where you're concerned I seem to have lost my pride. You've become very important to me. I . . . might be . . . in love with you."

He was silent. She was beginning to regret her words when he gritted out angrily.

"Don't play with me, Kathleen."

"Don't play with you? Sheesh! Are you so blind that you can't see what's right under your nose? Are you afraid that I'll chase after you like Clara did? I have pride, too. If you don't want me, all you have to do is start up this truck and take me home."

"I *am* afraid . . . but not that you'll chase me."

"You couldn't possibly be afraid of me," she said tiredly.

"If you want to know the God's truth, I'm scared to death of you."

"I don't understand you at all. Why are you warm and wonderful some of the time and at other times as cold as ice?"

He grabbed her forearms and jerked her to him. Tears had run down her cheeks and stopped at the corners of her mouth. The zigzagging neon lights on the front of the tavern were reflected in her eyes.

"I know I can't have you, and it's tearing me up," he snarled. "I'm only trying to protect myself, dammit to hell!"

"From me?"

"And from myself. Oh, Lord! Don't cry."

"I'm trying not to. Are you married? Is that why you—?"

"—Hell, no, I'm not married."

"Are you . . . in love with someone?" Her voice was a mere whisper.

"I *think* I am." He pulled her tight against him. With his face buried in the curve of her neck, he said, "I *know* I am, and it's hell. I wish you were a waitress at the Frontier Cafe, a ticket-seller at the theater, or a girl from one of the ranches around."

Kathleen pulled back from him. She was trembling and wildly flushed. A corner of her mind believed that he was saying he loved her. Then—

"Why do you say that? What's wrong with me?" She put her hand on his chest and held herself away from him.

"Nothing is wrong with you. You're the smartest, prettiest, spunkiest, most wonderful woman I've ever met. There's plenty wrong with me."

"What's wrong with you? You're a man with principles. You're kind and compassionate, proud and independent. You cared about a girl like Clara and tried to help her. Johnny"—she put her hands on his shoulders and spoke earnestly—"you've got all the qualities I ever hoped to find in the man I'd share my life with."

"Aunt Dozie used to say that 'birds of a feather flock together.' You're a beautiful redbird, Kathleen. I'm just a crow."

"I heard what that Marty person said that day about your mother. Mr. Fleming also told me. He made no excuses for himself for what he did. He only wants to make it right now. Do you think that I'm such a shallow person that I'd care who your parents were?"

"It's not only that. I only went to the fifth grade in school," he said, and the words almost choked him. "When I went to live with Henry Ann and Ed, I was ashamed to go to school because I was so far behind. That's one of the reasons why I'm not with the Federal Bureau. I'd never pass a test. Hell, I've never even read a book, and you *write* them."

"—Thomas Edison only had three months of formal schooling."

"I have a rag-tail ranch with a big mortgage," he continued, determined to say it all. "I could lose it lock, stock, and barrel by next year. I've nothing to offer a woman, especially a woman like you."

"You've got yourself, Johnny. We could be a team. What I lack, you make up. What you lack, I make up." In desperation, Kathleen wrapped her arms about his neck and held him tightly. "If you care for me at all, give us a chance. Don't throw it away before we give it a try. We may regret it for the rest of our lives."

He kissed her softly, sweetly, to close her mouth. His lips then roamed over her tear-wet face, and returned to hers again and again, hard, demanding. His fingers forked through her hair to cradle her head, while other fingers grasped her hips, pulled her closer, then moved up to caress her soft, round breasts.

"Please don't break my heart, Johnny," she gasped when his mouth left hers.

"Ah, sweet woman. You'll likely break mine when you realize what an ignorant, rough man I am. But you're a fever in my blood, and I can't stay away from you."

"Oh, I'm glad! Then you do care for me?"

"Care? I'm crazy about you!"

"I love you, too. Love you so much."

"You do? Really—?"

"Yes, yes, yes. You're every hero I've ever written about all rolled up in one."

He laughed joyously against her face.

"Are you as happy as I am?" she asked, and leaned back to look into his face.

"I don't know. How happy are you?"

"Let's see . . . happy as a dog with a tub full of bones. Happy as a fox in a henhouse. Happy as a boy with a new slingshot—"

"Happy as a cowboy kissin' a pretty, sweet little redbird?"

"As happy as that! Johnny? I need to hear you say it."

"Sweet girl, I'm not good with soft words. I've never said those words in my life. I'm crazy about you—"

"Say you love me, but only if you mean it."

"I love you," he said with a touch of desperation. "But I'm scared! So many things could go wrong. What if, after a while, you change your mind . . . and see me as nothing but an ignorant breed with manure on my boots? Christ, that's why I'm so damned afraid to take that step over the line."

"I love you." She drew back to cradle his face in her hands. "You're afraid since we have the power to hurt each other simply because we love each other. I understand what you mean," she said, and kissed him gently on the lips. "I'm afraid, too, you know."

"I don't want you to ever be afraid of anything."

"But I am . . . at times." She rested her cheek on his shoulder. "I'm afraid of being old and having no one to love me. Now I'll be afraid of losing you."

"The same goes here," Johnny gently reminded her.

It didn't matter that they were sitting in front of a honky-tonk. They could have been sitting on a busy street in the city. The cab of Johnny's old truck was their world. Johnny told her of his dream to have a large cattle and horse ranch. She told him how lonely she had been growing up and that she would like to have lots of children. He hugged her, kissed her, and said that he would do his part to help her get them.

They laughed, hugged, kissed, and talked nonsense. It was past midnight when Johnny stopped the truck in front of Hazel's and walked Kathleen up to the porch.

"I'll not go down to Vernon tomorrow if you'll go with me on Saturday."

"Does that mean that you'll come in tomorrow and sit in on the meeting?"

"Kathleen, sweet girl, don't expect me to accept that . . . man. I simply can't. He means nothing to me."

"He told me that he understands how you feel because he would feel the same. He just wants to know you."

"Kathleen, I don't want him hanging around waitin' for me to call him *Daddy!*"

"Just come help us. If what we suspect is true, it will turn this town upside down."

"Do you still want to go to Red Rock on Sunday to see

Tom and Henry Ann? It's about fifty miles over there. We'll have to leave early."

"I wasn't going to let you wiggle out of that." Kathleen wrapped her arms around his waist. "I don't want to go in. I'll not sleep a wink."

"I've got to get home. I've got stock to tend to."

"Tonight?"

"At daylight." He kissed her quick, then with a groan, long and hard. His hand moved down to her hips and for a moment held her tightly against his aching maleness. "Go in while I'm still able to let you go," he whispered.

"You'll not get much sleep."

"More than if you were sleeping with me. 'Night, sweetheart. See you tomorrow."

Kathleen did sleep, so well that she had a bounce in her step and a sparkle in her eyes when she came into the office and went through to the back room.

"Morning," she called out to Adelaide and Paul, who were standing close together beside the table where Paul was tearing down a page and throwing the type in a bucket.

"My, you look bright-eyed this morning." Adelaide's hand lingered on Paul's arm when she turned to speak to Kathleen.

"Must be the date she had last night with that cowboy, huh?" Paul said with a wink.

"We did some great detective work last night. But I'll wait and let that *cowboy* tell you about it when he gets here."

"He's coming back in today? He spends more time here than at the ranch. We ought to charge him rent," Paul said in a complaining tone.

"All right, you two. I am happy this morning. Happy as a dog with two tails to wag."

"Are we invited to the wedding?" Adelaide asked with wide-eyed innocence.

"It hasn't gone that far, but if it does, you'll be at the head of the list." Unable to keep the smile off her face, Kathleen went back to her desk determined to get as much work done as possible.

She worked steadily to catch up on the items for the next week's paper. She wrote the church and school news first, then a story about the local baseball team, who would play their last game of the season next weekend. She had begun to work on an editorial she had started about the need for a benefit for the local Volunteer Fire-fighters' Association when a husky gray-haired man came into the office.

"I was lookin' at the pictures ya got out there of that girl. I was the one who found her. Name's Kilburn."

"Hello, Mr. Kilburn. I'm Kathleen Dolan. I took the pictures."

"It warn't no accident, miss. I said that when I brung the sheriff out there. That girl was beat up bad and throwed out."

"The car did run over her—"

"Pete Carroll's brains is scrambled," he continued as if she hadn't spoken. "When he looked at her, he said that she couldn't a got all that done to her gettin' hit by a car. Now he's changed his tune."

"Perhaps someone changed it for him, Mr. Kilburn."

"Why'd anyone go and do that? It's plain as yore nose on yore face. I hit Pete up about it this mornin'. He said Doc Herman looked at her and said she was hit by a car. That's what he said. 'Course, if Doc said black was white, Pete'd take it for gospel."

"I wonder why that is. Do you know?"

"I ain't knowin', miss. I ain't wantin' nothin' to do with that Doc Herman."

"Why is that, Mr. Kilburn?"

"He's got too uppity to lance boils, sew up cuts, or come out to see sick folks. He's got that nurse to do it all, and she ain't no doc."

"He delivers babies," Kathleen said, and watched his face.

"Harrumpt! I heared tell that he'll take in a girl what got ruint and not charge her folks a dime. Folks come from all over bringin' him girls that ain't wed."

"Do you know that for a fact?"

"No, missy, I don't know it fer a fact, but it's been talked about 'round here for years."

"A lot of *married* women come here to have their babies," Kathleen said softly.

"I ain't knowin' 'bout that. When any a my folks get sick, we go down to Vernon."

"Do you mind if I quote you saying that you think Clara Ramsey's death was no accident?"

"In the paper?"

"Yes, I'm writing a story about it for next week's paper."

"Ya can say so if ya want. I'm sayin' what I think."

"I'll see that you get a copy of the paper."

"I ain't sayin' this just to get my name in the paper."

"I know that. You seem to be a man of conscience."

"I ain't been able to think of nothin' but that poor girl since I found her." He anchored his battered hat down on his head. "Got to get back home to Mama. She's all tore up, too, thinkin' what happened out there on the road."

"Thank you for coming in, Mr. Kilburn."

As soon as the man left, Kathleen ripped the paper out of her typewriter, inserted a fresh sheet and began to type rapidly.

The death of Clara Ramsey was not an accident according to the rancher who found her body in a ditch alongside the road last Tuesday morning. Mr. Dale Kilburn, whose ranch is a mile south—

By midmorning she had finished the last page of her story, read it and edited it, and was ready to put it on the hook beside the linotype machine. She looked up. Johnny was lounging in the doorway leading to the back room, watching her. Her heart fluttered with a joyous surge of pleasure, then took off like a runaway horse.

"I didn't know you were here." She stood, her eyes bright with happiness at the sight of him.

"You were writing. I didn't want to bother you."

"I've got a story from Mr. Kilburn, who found Clara's body. Do you want to read it?"

"Tell me about it."

Unable to keep her feet from going to him, she crossed to the doorway. His eyes feasted on her face.

"Tell me I didn't dream last night," she whispered, her hand on his chest.

"What did you dream?" he teased.

"That you and I . . . that we—"

"That we what?"

"Johnny Henry!" she scolded. Both hands were against his chest, now, pushing him back out of sight of the front window. She tilted her face, her eyes smiling as her hands and her arms encircled his waist. "Don't . . . tease me, you nitwit!"

Johnny's face was creased with smiles. *Oh, Lord, he is beautiful, and sweet and dear and thank you, God, for bringing me here!*

He lowered his head and kissed her, softly, gently, and quickly.

"Hey, there, cut that out!" Paul's voice was stern. "We can't be having such as that going on in our pressroom."

"It's been going on in this pressroom for three or four years when you thought I wasn't looking," Johnny retorted. "You kiss Adelaide every chance you get."

"Yeah, but . . . Addie and I are adults."

"I'm not forgettin' that you owe me the price of two tickets to a picture show. And where's that two bits you owe me?"

"What are you two talking about?" Kathleen kept her hand on Johnny's arm as if she was afraid he'd disappear if she wasn't touching him.

"A while back he offered to pay if I'd take you to a picture show. Now he's trying to chicken out."

"Well of all things! You had to be bribed to take me out?"

"I was going to take you anyway; but if he was dumb enough to offer to pay, I wasn't going to turn it down."

The smile in his eyes and on his lips was real.

Chapter Twenty-three

At noon Kathleen and Johnny walked down to Claude's and ordered hamburgers. Seated at the end of the counter they watched Claude at the grill and listened to Gene Autry singing "Red River Valley." Johnny put a nickel in the jukebox and soon Bing Crosby was crooning, *"I don't know why I love you like I do, I don't know why, I just do."* His hand beneath the counter searched and found hers.

"Well, well—" Claude brought the hamburgers and lifted his brows up and down several times. "What's going on here?"

"None of your business, you nosy old goat," Johnny retorted angrily, but he was smiling.

"Knowed it the minute ya brought her here. Ya was lookin' all cow-eyed then." He wiped his hands on his apron and glanced at the other diners before leaning close to say in a confidential tone, "You owe me, son. My burgers draw pretty girls like flies."

"What do you want, Claude? My arm or my leg?"

Claude's face had lost its grin when he spoke to Kathleen. "You've stirred up a hornets' nest, miss, with those pictures in the window. Some of the merchants are wanting to boycott the paper. The sheriff says she was hit by a car."

"Dr. Herman says it was an accident. We think she was murdered—beaten, thrown out of the car, and run over."

"Doc says folks won't come here and buy goods if they think a murderer is running loose."

"If they withhold advertising because we're trying to get to the truth about a poor girl's death, then we'll fight back with a story that will shake up this entire county; and the merchants might find themselves being boycotted by their customers."

Claude's laugh was as dry as corn shucks. "Ya got ya a little fighter here, boy. Hold on to her."

"Pressure was put on the *Gazette* to accept *his* decision that what happened to Clara was an accident. Why? Don't you want to know why he was so anxious to do that? It isn't because people won't come to town. That story won't wash."

"Town's got a clean record compared to some."

"They had a hijacking, but I guess they didn't want it on the *record*," Kathleen said drily. "Johnny will find out what happened to Clara. He worked with my uncle to track Bonnie Parker and Clyde Barrow and the result was—"

"Kath! Hush!" Johnny hissed.

"What's this?" Claude said.

"Nothing. She's been listening to her uncle's tall tales."

"I thought for a minute we had us a hero here."

Kathleen was almost giddy with embarrassment. Her

eyes glittered with both anger and despair. A customer came in, and Claude moved away. She couldn't look at Johnny. With fingers that trembled, she picked up a slice of pickle Claude had placed on her plate.

"People around here don't know anything about that part of my life."

"Why? Are you ashamed of it?" Kathleen pressed her lips tightly together and half turned so that he couldn't see her face.

"I just don't want my business spread around."

"Do Adelaide and Paul know that you've worked with the Federal Bureau from time to time?"

"They know that I go away sometimes for a while."

"I'm proud of what you did. I didn't think that I would offend you by telling Claude. Evidently I was mistaken."

"Let's drop it."

"There is a lot we have to learn about each other."

"Yes," he said dejectedly.

They finished the meal in silence. Kathleen decided that this man she loved was far more complicated than she had imagined. It wasn't until they were walking back toward the *Gazette* that Kathleen spoke.

"I don't understand why it's so important to Doc Herman to hush up what happened to Clara. Could he have had anything to do with it?"

"Stranger things have happened."

"I keep thinking about the baby buried out on the Ramsey plot. It was buried before Hazel knew anything about it."

"I see the wheels turning in your head right now."

When he grinned down at her with that unfettered look

of love in his eyes, happiness flowed over her. They would have their ups and downs, but if they loved—

"Do you think we should—?"

"Look in the box? I thought about it."

"Oh, my. It gives me goose bumps to think of it."

"I'm thinking Clara came home pregnant and had her baby at the clinic. Doc paid her for it and she left town again. Didn't Hazel say that someone owed her money?"

"She did. Do you think Clara went back to the clinic to hit them up for more?"

"She could have."

They were so absorbed in their conversation that they didn't notice the man who got out of a car parked in front of the *Gazette* and stood waiting for them. With her hand tucked into the crook of Johnny's arm she felt his steps slow, looked up, and saw Barker Fleming.

"Hello, Mr. Fleming."

Barker tipped his Stetson. "Hello, Miss Dolan. Johnny."

Kathleen wasn't sure, but she thought Johnny grunted a reply.

Barker stepped over to the car and opened the door. A small dark-haired boy slid off the seat and got out. Two girls several years older than Emily got out of the backseat. One girl wore a pink-checked gingham dress, the other blue-checked. The boy was dressed in duck pants and scuffed shoes. All had the dark hair and eyes of their Cherokee ancestors.

"These are my three youngest," Barker said proudly. The flickering of his eyes from the children to Johnny betrayed his nervousness. "They're having a holiday from school. This is Lucas." He touched the boy on the head. "The girls are Marie and Janna. This lady," he said to the children, "is Miss Dolan, who works for the newspaper. And this is Johnny Henry, the *All-'Round Cowboy*, I told you about. I saw him ride at the rodeo."

"Gol . . . ly!" Lucas took a couple of steps forward and looked up at Johnny with hero worship in his eyes. "Gol . . . ly!" he said again. "Can I see your spurs? Do you have a lasso? Gol . . . ly!"

"Daddy, can't he say anything but Gol . . . ly?" the older girl complained. "He's so . . . dumb."

"Yeah, he's dumb," the younger girl echoed.

"He gets carried away once in a while," Barker explained patiently to the girls, "But he is *not* dumb."

Lucas didn't seem to care if his sisters thought he was dumb. He was still looking expectantly up at Johnny.

"Yeah, I got a lasso," Johnny finally mumbled. He reached out and tousled the boy's hair.

"Can I see it . . . sometime?"

"Sure."

"Daddy! I can see his lasso . . . and his spurs." Lucas grabbed Barker's hand.

"He didn't say anything about spurs," Marie said irritably, and rolled her eyes.

"The girls are tired from the trip. Lucas slept part of the way." Barker opened the car door. "Hop in," he commanded. "I'm taking them out to stay with Mrs. Howland—"

"Daddy, it stinks out there," Marie whined.

Barker ignored his daughter's complaint. "Howland is

manager at the tannery. They live about a quarter mile south of the plant. I'll be back in say . . . an hour?"

"Daddy—"

"Girls, we had this settled before we left home. Hush your complaining and get in the car. We'll eat dinner at the restaurant and spend the night at the hotel."

"Oh . . . goody." Janna clapped her hands.

"I want to stay with Mr. Henry," Lucas said.

"Some other time," Barker said patiently.

Kathleen moved away from Johnny and went to the car. She leaned down to speak to the girls.

" 'Bye. Nice to have met you."

"I wanted to see your typewriter," Marie said sulkily.

"You can see it when your daddy brings you back."

" 'Bye, Mr. Henry," Lucas called. "Ya won't forget?"

"No." Johnny shook his head as he spoke. He stood as if his feet were stuck to the sidewalk.

After the car moved away, Kathleen put her arm through Johnny's.

"You can say one thing for Barker Fleming, he has beautiful children." Her eyes laughed up at him. "Let's go tell Adelaide and Paul about our idea."

"What idea?"

"About what's *not* in that box out at the cemetery, my dear and beautiful man."

"Now I know your brains are scrambled." His voice was stern, but his lips were smiling.

If Adelaide and Paul noticed that Johnny didn't address any of his remarks to Barker Fleming during the afternoon session in the pressroom, they attributed it to the fact that he was jealous of the man.

After being introduced to Barker, Judy had gone upstairs to Adelaide's apartment to bake a cake.

"She took homemaking in school and is a good cook," Adelaide explained, and sat down where she could see if anyone came into the office.

Kathleen started from the beginning and told Barker about being hijacked before she reached town and about the sheriff refusing to arrest the men despite the fact that she and Johnny could identify them. She related every encounter she'd had with the sheriff, the doctor, and the records clerk at the courthouse.

"Birth, death, and arrest records have not been made available to the paper," Paul explained. "Time and again Adelaide has tried to get these records only to be told they are not yet recorded. They haven't been sent over, and at times the records office door has been locked. I think Kathleen took them by surprise when she got in the other morning."

Kathleen's chart showing the names and dates she had copied from the public birth records was placed on the table. The discussion then centered on the unusual number of women who came to Rawlings to have their babies.

"Tulsa, Oklahoma City, Dallas, Fort Worth; Denver, Colorado? All these women came to Rawlings to have their babies? Unbelievable," Barker exclaimed.

"Almost two hundred over a fifteen-year period," Kathleen said. "Mr. Dale Kilburn was in this morning. He's sure that Clara didn't die from being hit by a car.

During the conversation he told me that it had been ru-
mored for years that unwed girls came to the clinic to
have their babies."

"We need to have more than rumors," Barker said. "It
seems to me Dr. Herman has a stranglehold on the whole
county. Do you have an extra copy of the names and dates
of birth you got from the records department?"

"Judy made a copy for you. Her parents, or rather the
people who now say they are not her parents, Mr. and
Mrs. DeBerry, live in Fort Worth. They were disappointed in Judy when it became apparent that she had Indian blood. Judy said she heard Mr. DeBerry say
something about getting his money back."

"She's a sweet girl. Paul and I have become quite attached to her," Adelaide added.

"They told her that they'd gotten her here?" Johnny
asked.

"She had seen her birth certificate and heard Mr. and
Mrs. DeBerry discussing the fact.

"Her name is there on the list." Kathleen said, point-
ing to it. "Baby girl born to Mr. and Mrs. Donald De-
Berry, Fort Worth, Texas. Attending physician, Dr.
Darrell Herman."

"Darrell Herman and Louise Munday are selling babies out of that clinic," Adelaide said staunchly. "I think
that's why he wants Clara's murder declared an accident.
He's afraid that the state or Federal Marshals will get
wind of it, come here to investigate, and maybe turn up
something about what they are doing."

"Doc Herman goes to Oklahoma City quite often for

medical meetings. There may be a connection there," Paul said.

"That's right." Adelaide said as she suddenly remembered. "Flossie said he was there last week."

Barker made a few notations in a small pad.

"We'll not get any help from the sheriff, Mr. Fleming." Kathleen folded her notebook. "He's in the doctor's pocket."

"Grant Gifford would be interested in this. He was elected attorney general a year ago. He'll know what to do." Johnny dropped this bit of information into the conversation.

"I heard that he was a crackerjack lawyer and straight as a string," Barker said.

"He is."

"I'll get in touch with him when I go to the city. I know a good man up there who will investigate the doctor's background and look up the parents of some of these babies born here. We could find a few more cases like the DeBerrys."

Kathleen was burning with the urge to ask Johnny if he knew the attorney general and was relieved when Adelaide did it for her.

"Do you know Mr. Gifford, Johnny?"

"Yeah. He taught me how to pick out a tune on a guitar. He's good, too, at lancing boils, milking, and chopping cotton among other things." Johnny was trying not to smile.

"The state attorney general lances boils?" Kathleen asked.

"Among other things." Johnny's lips quirked with a

supressed grin. "Don't get in a snit. I knew him when I was a snot-nosed kid who didn't know straight up. He's as good a man as I ever met."

Barker refrained from asking Johnny any questions. The relationship was fragile, and he didn't want to put a strain on it.

Paul went to the front office, where Adelaide was collecting for a subscription.

"My father wants me to take over the running of the tannery here," Barker said when the three of them were alone. He folded the papers Kathleen gave him and put them in his pocket.

"Will you be moving to Rawlings?" Kathleen asked.

"Not until after the first of the year. The children are in school in Elk City, and I don't want to disrupt them."

"They are beautiful children, Mr. Fleming. You must be very proud of them."

"I am. They are usually well behaved. I feel that I should apologize for Marie's and Janna's behavior. They're at the age where everything that Lucas does is dumb and stupid. But Elena, their sister in high school, thinks everything *they* do is dumb and stupid. The one in college thinks they all are dumb and stupid. So it evens out." Barker's eyes smiled as he talked of his children.

"I never had a brother or a sister. They don't know how lucky they are."

Barker threw up his hands. "Try and tell them that." He stood and reached for his hat. "I'd like to take the two of you to dinner if you think the bickering between the girls and Lucas wouldn't ruin your appetite." He looked directly at Johnny.

"I've got chores out at the ranch."

"And I'm going with him," Kathleen said quickly. "But thanks anyway."

"I'll leave early in the morning and get the kids back to Elk City. I'll be back when I have some news. I take it you don't trust the telephone operator not to listen in."

"You take it right."

"I'll figure out another way to get in touch. Good-bye, Johnny." Barker held out his hand.

Kathleen held her breath until Johnny accepted it.

"Good-bye, Mr. Fleming." She took his hand when he offered it. "Thank you for coming and for any help you can give us."

"There's something not quite right here. It deserves an investigation."

They heard Barker talking to Adelaide and Paul in the office before he went out the door. Alone, Kathleen tugged on Johnny's hand and pulled him behind the press. She put her arms around his waist and laid her head on his shoulder.

"I'm tired. I just want to be with you."

He lowered his head and rested his cheek against hers. He held her gently, but firmly.

"I must go home and do chores," he whispered after a short while. "Come with me and we'll go on down to Vernon tonight and see Keith."

"Will we stay all night?"

"Not unless you want to."

"We can take my car."

"You don't like riding in my truck?"

"I have a special place in my heart for your truck . . . when it's parked at the Twilight Gardens."

He laughed against her forehead. "Come on. Let's gas up the car and go tell Hazel you won't be home."

It was dusk when Kathleen and Johnny drove into the yard at the McCabe ranch.

"Just can't stay away, can you?" Keith shouted the good-natured greeting as soon as they stepped out of the car. He had come out onto the porch. Ruth stood in the doorway.

"I'm thinking about moving in," Johnny said as they approached.

"Not during my lifetime, boy."

"Come in, Kathleen," Ruth called. "Pay no attention to these two. The feud goes on all the time."

"He's always trying to get my woman," Keith complained. "But now that he's got one of his own—"

"We just finished supper, but there's plenty left."

"We had something at Johnny's."

"It was only pork and beans," Johnny grumbled.

"Poor Johnny. Come sit down. I'll find you some biscuits and beef gravy. But first you'd better say hello to Granny and introduce her to Kathleen."

"See there?" Keith said in a confidential tone to Kathleen. "My women fall all over him 'cause he's little and cute."

Kathleen liked the McCabes immediately and longed for her and Johnny to be like them, easy and relaxed in the company of their guests. They were being themselves, very happy and secure in their love for each other.

She also saw a side of Johnny she had not seen before. With genuine affection he had carefully hugged the fragile old lady and played with Davis, and he was obviously fond of Ruth.

While Kathleen helped Ruth finish the cleaning in the kitchen, Keith and Johnny went to a front room lit by several big glass lamps.

"How's Gertie getting along?" Johnny asked when the women joined them. Kathleen went to sit beside Johnny on the sofa. Keith sat in a big leather chair.

"Getting more rambunctious every day."

"She kicked me last night 'cause I was gettin' too close to Mama." Keith pulled Ruth down and cuddled her on his lap.

"Johnny has called this poor little baby Gertie so often that even I'm getting to where I think of her as that." Ruth rolled her eyes. Keith rubbed her protruding stomach. They were completely at ease talking about their unborn child.

This, too, was new to Kathleen. Pregnant women she had known had not talked about their pregnancy in mixed company. Keith McCabe adored his wife. Would Johnny be that loving when she was round and clumsy with their child?

Johnny told Keith and Ruth that he suspected Marty Conroy had killed Clara, or if he hadn't, he knew something about what had happened to her out on that lonely road.

"I talked to someone who saw her get in a big fancy black car. The car was sitting off down the road from the Twilight Gardens as if the driver was waiting for someone and didn't want to be seen. There was a fancy doo-dad on the radiator cap."

"Sounds like our Marty. He loves big doodads."

"I'll be surprised if Marty did that," Ruth said. "He's obnoxious, but I never thought he was the type to kill a girl."

"You can't tell what a little bugger like Marty will do, honey, if he's backed into a corner. Especially if he thinks somebody's goin' to take away his doodads."

"We've got two problems," Johnny said seriously. "We'll not be able to prove he killed Clara with the pic-tures of the tire tracks. There are too many big cars with big tires. We have to get him across the line into Okla-homa, and we have to get him to confess."

"Uh-oh," Kathleen said. "I hadn't thought of that."

"I'll get him across the river, Johnny; you get him to confess." Keith's big hand was massaging Ruth's back.

"How are you going to get him to cross the river?" With her fingers on his chin, Ruth turned her husband's face toward her.

"Sweetheart, have you no faith in your husband?" Keith chided gently and punctuated each word with a kiss. "Remember when I told you his latest hare-brained scheme was to build a toll bridge across the river? He said we could just sit back and collect tolls. I'll call and tell him that I changed my mind and that I want to look over the spot where he wants to put the bridge. He'll come running with a grin on his face like the wave on a slop bucket."

"I'd like to figure out a way to give Sheriff Carroll the credit for the arrest, that is if there is an arrest," Johnny said seriously. "I think he's a decent sort, but under Doc Herman's thumb for some reason."

"He owes him for his job," Kathleen murmured.

"Yeah, but if we can get him to go over Doc's head and do something on his own, it might give him the confidence to help us on another matter that's cookin' up in Tillison County."

"That's a perfectly brilliant idea," Kathleen explained. "Johnny, I'm so glad you thought of it."

"She's in love," Keith whispered loudly to his wife. "I think it's a dumb idea. Old Marty will be a hard nut to crack."

"Maybe not. If he beat her up in the car, there was blood. Blood is hard to clean up. Chances are he waited until he got back over the line, and it would have been dried by then. If he's our man, there will be bloodstains in that car."

"All right, cowboy, deal me in. Where do you want him and when?"

"How about Wednesday at noon? Be sure you get him on the Oklahoma side."

"Leave it to Cousin Keith, son. He's been after me for years to go in on some deal or the other. He'll be there."

Chapter Twenty-four

The headlights of the Nash forged a path into the darkness. Johnny maneuvered the car with his left hand on the wheel, his right arm around Kathleen. Snuggled close to his side, Kathleen glanced at his sharply etched profile. Not only was Johnny Henry handsome, but he was a moral, decent man and, she suspected, an utterly ruthless one if the occasion demanded it.

"How long have you known the McCabes?"

"A few years. I met them when I went up to Pearl to help Hod, when he was working on the Pascoe and Norton case."

"They were the Kansas City gangsters who killed Molly's parents. I remember."

Kathleen was extremely happy. She looked out onto the dark Oklahoma plains. The car lights were the only ones she could see in any direction. She felt comfortable and safe here in this small spot on earth with Johnny. A few short months ago she had not known the man behind the name Johnny Henry. It was strange, she thought, that she hadn't realized she had been lonely. Would she ever be satisfied again to spend long evenings alone with only the creaking of the house and the sound of her typewriter to break the stillness?

"Johnny," she snuggled closer against him pressing her lips to the side of his neck, "I love you."

"Hummm, what brought that on?"

"I was thinking how lonely I'd be without you."

"We've not been together all that much."

"I may sound silly, but since I met you, you seem to be a part of me." Her hand slid across his chest to hug him closer.

"Better stop that, or I'll have to stop and kiss you."

"Right here in the middle of the road? You wouldn't dare!" Her lips moved over his neck, while her hand caressed his lean midsection.

The car came to a sudden stop in the middle of the road. He wrapped her in his arms and kissed her soundly. He lifted his head to look at her, then settled his mouth against hers again. The lips that touched hers were warm and sweet as they tingled across her mouth. A longing to love and be loved washed over her. The kiss became more possessive, deepened, her lips parted, his tongue touched hers, and his hand slid beneath her jacket to cup her breast. She unbuttoned her blouse and his fingers moved inside to stroke soft flesh.

"I want to hold you, love you." His voice was choked with the harsh sound of desire.

Johnny's arms were the only arms in the world, his lips the only lips. His tongue circled her mouth, coaxing it to open. Her skin tingled; the tiny hairs on her body seemed to be standing on end.

"You . . . taste so good—" He took his lips away and buried his face in her throat.

"Are we very far from your house?"

"Not far."

"Let's go there."

For a moment he was still. Then, "Are you sure?" he asked in a hoarse whisper.

"I was never more sure in my life." Her fingers inside his shirt moved lightly over his chest. His body answered the movement of her hand with a violent trembling.

The car moved down the road. They didn't talk. She wanted to tell him what she was feeling, but she felt certain he knew. A minute or two later he turned the car off the main road, and after another minute he stopped in front of his house. He turned off the motor and the lights and looked down at her.

"This is a big step. Once I get you in there, I'll not be able to let you leave."

"I won't want to go." She cupped his cheek with her hand. "I've waited all my life for a man like you and for a moment like this."

He kissed her. His mouth tender on hers, reverent. They got out of the car and, with his arm around her, they went to the house.

Kathleen stood inside the door while Johnny lit a lamp in the kitchen. Only a faint ribbon of light came through the doorway. He came to her and to her surprise lifted her in his arms, carried her to the bed, and sank down on it with her still in his arms.

"I'd love you on a feather bed in a fancy room . . . if I could." He laid her down and leaned over her.

"I don't need a feather bed or a fancy room. I need you." Her arms encircled his neck and drew his face down to hers.

It was all so sweet, so right, so natural. He was unhurried and tender when he undressed her. She was terribly conscious of the part of him that throbbed so aggressively against her. His lips and his hands sent waves of weakening pleasure up and down her spine.

His callused palm lightly stroked the curve of her hip, then slid up to her breasts. His fingers squeezed her nipple and she hurt deep, deep inside of her. So many sensations crashed through her body and mind that she was unable to distinguish one from another. It was all too pleasurable, too wonderful.

If this is the coupling men and women do together, dear God, how beautiful!

Her body arched, seeking, wanting. She became aware of a hard pressure against her, a slow, gradual filling of that aching emptiness. A sudden movement brought a pain-pleasure so intense that she cried out.

"Sweetheart . . . I had to!" he whispered in her ear and lay still for a long moment.

"It's all right . . . all right!" She kissed his face with quick, passionate kisses and clutched at him to keep the throbbing warmth inside her.

Later she heard him cry out, as if from a distance, "Kath . . . Kath, sweetheart—"

She couldn't speak, aware of only that thrusting, pulsating rhythm that was pushing her toward a bursting, shivering height.

When she came back into reality, Johnny's weight was

pressing her into the bed. She moved her mouth against his shoulder. He lowered his head to kiss her lips. She wrapped her arms around him in a wave of protective love. He buried his face in the curve of her breast like a child seeking comfort, and she held him there.

He rolled away, taking her with him. They lay side by side. His mouth teased her lips, her lashes.

"It was wonderful," she breathed.

"I didn't use anything. You could be . . . pregnant."

"I hope so. Oh, Johnny, I hope so."

They loved each other deep into the night, until sheer exhaustion sent them into a deep sleep where she lay molded to his naked body, her cheek nestled in the warm hollow of his shoulder.

It was the middle of the morning when they drove into Red Rock, Oklahoma. At daylight, Johnny had heated water on the kerosene stove for Kathleen to wash while he did chores. Then, as they passed through town they had stopped at Hazel's so that Kathleen could change clothes. Since Hazel and Emily were not awake, Kathleen left a note saying that she and Johnny were going to Red Rock and would not be back until late.

Red Rock was not nearly as large a town as Rawlings. Only the main street was paved. They passed through, and a mile out of town, Johnny turned into the yard of a neat farmhouse surrounded by huge pecan trees.

"Johnny!" As soon as Johnny got out of the car, a young boy came running from the house. "Mama, Daddy, Johnny's here."

"Is that you, Jay? Lordy! I thought your daddy had a new hired man. You've grown a foot."

"You haven't. You're gettin' shorter, Johnny."

The two clasped hands, then wrestled a bit. It was clear that they were happy to see each other. By the time Kathleen had slid out of the car a slim woman and a man who looked amazingly like Hod had come out onto the porch.

Henry Ann Dolan, her face laced with smiles of welcome, hurried across the yard. Johnny went to meet her, put his arms around her, and hugged her tightly.

"Johnny! It's so good to see you."

"Hello, sis. I've brought someone to meet you."

"I see you have, and I'm guessing it's Kathleen Dolan."

"You guessed right. Kath, come meet my sister, Henry Ann."

"Hello." Kathleen held out her hand. "I've heard a lot about you from Johnny."

"Johnny and I had to grow up suddenly and fast when we had this farm to run. Meet your Uncle Tom, Kathleen. He's been champing at the bit to get over to Rawlings to see you."

Kathleen was suddenly enveloped in strong arms. "Welcome, Kathleen."

"I'm glad to meet you, Uncle Tom. Oh, my, you look so much like Uncle Hod."

Tom laughed. "I've heard that a lot. That red hair of yours reminds me of Aunt Biddy, our mother's sister."

"My mother had red hair. I always thought that was where I got it."

"Your daddy's hair wasn't black like mine and Hod's. It was a sandy color."

"I don't remember him at all. I was about two years old when Mama and I went back to Iowa to live with her parents."

"Git yo'self on up here, boy, if'n yo ain't wantin' me ta tan yo hide." A large colored woman, a blue handkerchief tied about her head, stood on the porch. Johnny strode quickly to the porch and put his arms around her.

"Hello, Aunt Dozie. You're gettin' prettier every day."

"Hee, hee, hee! Yo is still jist a runnin' off at the mouth, ain't ya?"

"Kathleen, come meet the first girl I ever had a crush on."

"Lawsy, ain't ya jist as pretty as a redbird." Dozie's round face was split with a big smile.

"Thank you." Kathleen held out her hand.

"I ain't a handshakin' woman. I a huggin' woman, if it be a gal my boy here brung to see me," Aunt Dozie said.

"In that case—" Kathleen's laugh rang out. She put her arms around Dozie's ample waist and hugged her.

"Ya like my Johnny, gal?" Dozie asked bluntly.

"He's all right," Kathleen's twinkling eyes sought Johnny's.

"Hee, hee, hee. Lawdy mercy. I gots ta show ya how to make tater pie. It keep him happy an' like dough in yo hands."

A little girl came out onto the porch and threw herself at Johnny, who caught her up in his arms. His hat fell to the floor of the porch as he nuzzled her neck.

"You tickle," she yelled. Her fingers searched his shirt pocket and found a stick of chewing gum.

"Did you think I'd forget, punkin?" Johnny's eyes caught Kathleen's over the child's head.

"Let's go in," Henry Ann urged. "Aunt Dozie is getting cold."

Kathleen would remember this as one of the most enjoyable days of her life. At noon they gathered around the big kitchen table. Kathleen couldn't keep her eyes off Johnny. He smiled continually. This was his family. He adored the children; nine-year-old Jay, six-year-old Rose and baby Eddie. It was apparent that they adored him.

Later in the afternoon, while the older children were out playing and Aunt Dozie sat in the rocking chair with baby Eddie in her lap, Johnny told Henry Ann and Tom about Clara's death and about it being ruled an accident when he was sure it was murder.

"I want to prepare you, Tom. I think it was Marty Conroy who killed the girl, and I'm going to do my best to see that he pays for it."

"We haven't seen him in years. He steers clear of here."

Henry Ann looked at Tom before broaching a new subject. "I had a letter from Isabel."

"I suppose she wanted money."

"She didn't ask for money this time. She said a man who claimed to be your father came to see her at the honky-tonk where she worked. He was part-Indian and according to Isabel well-off. Of course, she would think that anyone with two dollars to rub together was well-off." Henry Ann waited for Johnny to say something, and when he didn't, she said, "Isabel wanted to know if I had heard from you and if I knew the man's name. I'm sure she wants to get in touch with him."

"Sheesh!" Johnny snorted. "Why?"

"Only one reason that I know of. Money."

"He came to see me. Told me he was my father. I want nothing to do with him and told him so. Ed was the only man I'll ever think of as being anywhere near a father to me." Johnny got up and stood looking out the back door, his hands in his back pockets. When he turned around, he had the saddest look on his face Kathleen had ever seen. "How did you escape the Perry curse, Henry Ann? All that inbreeding down on Mud Creek made Dorene what she is and Isabel what she is."

"Being from Mud Creek had nothing to do with it, Johnny. Look at yourself. I couldn't be prouder of my brother. Our mother was what she was because it was what she wanted to be. It's the same with Isabel. Blood has nothing to do with it."

Johnny's eyes caught and held Kathleen's. She knew what he was thinking and longed to reach out and hold him and reassure him. He came to stand behind her chair. She felt his fingers brush through her hair before they settled on her shoulders.

"We'd better get on down the road. It'll be dark by the time we get back to Rawlings."

Tom arose, gathered the sleeping child out of Aunt Dozie's lap, and carried him into a bedroom. Henry Ann took the old lady's arm and helped her up out of the chair.

"I sits ta long, I gets stiff," Dozie explained.

After saying good-bye to Aunt Dozie, Kathleen and Henry Ann walked out to the car. Johnny and Tom had disappeared into the barn.

"Did you meet the man who says he's Johnny's father?" Henry Ann asked as soon as they were away from the house.

"Yes, and he is very nice. He had been looking for Johnny for a long time. He was just eighteen when he . . . had his fling with Dorene. Five years ago he learned she'd had a son who was part-Cherokee. He looked up the birth certificate and, sure enough, she had listed him as Johnny's father."

"Johnny seemed bitter."

"He is. We don't talk about Mr. Fleming. He came to Rawlings the other day and brought three of his children to meet Johnny. He wants to claim him as his son, but he'll keep his distance as long as Johnny feels the way he does."

"I used to get so mad when Isabel would throw it up to Johnny that his daddy was a dirty, drunken Indian."

"Mr. Fleming came to see Johnny ride in the rodeo. He was so proud when Johnny won *All-Around Cowboy*."

"I saw him ride one time. The bull tried to gore him. It scared me to death." Tom and Johnny came from the barn and stood by the well. "Thank you for telling me about Mr. Fleming. I'll not tell Isabel, but don't be surprised if she shows up in Rawlings someday."

"Johnny has me now. I love him, Henry Ann."

"I'm glad. I love him, too. Johnny came to us an angry boy of fourteen. He hadn't had a happy childhood. But after Daddy died, I couldn't have made it without him.

He worked like a beaver. Half of this farm belongs to him because without him I'd never have been able to keep it."

Later, after they had said their good-byes and were on the road to Rawlings, Kathleen snuggled close to Johnny's side.

"This has been a wonderful day. Thank you for bringing me."

"You liked Henry Ann?"

"Oh, yes. She loves you. They all love you. You're lucky to have such a family."

"She and Ed took me in. I probably wouldn't have amounted to a hill of beans without them."

Kathleen tucked her shoulder behind his and hugged his arm. He took his hand from the wheel and held hers. She wished they could ride on like this forever through the dark vast prairie land. She had enjoyed the day, but . . . last night. There would never be another night compared to it. The only cloud on her horizon was the fact that Johnny hadn't said anything about their getting married.

Johnny had a lot on his mind. Monday morning, he was up at daylight, did his daily chores and went to the shed where he worked on the stock tank that had sprung a leak. After he tarred the hole in the tank, he turned on the windmill to fill it and went to the house to fix a bite of breakfast.

His eyes were drawn to the sagging bed with the dingy covers as soon as he entered the door. Here he had made love to the only woman he would ever love. Thank God, the lamplight had been dim. And they had left before daylight. In the unforgiving glare of the sun the place looked like what it was . . . a shack.

Lord, she is sweet, loving, giving. How can I ever ask a woman like her to share my home?

At midmorning Johnny headed to town to talk to Sheriff Carroll. He parked his truck on the street beside the courthouse and went into the sheriff's office. Deputy Thatcher looked up when he entered.

"Whatta *you* want?"

"I want to see Sheriff Carroll."

"What for?"

"None of your goddamn business."

"Now see here. Ya better keep a civil tongue in yore head when talkin' to the law."

"Bullshit! Is the sheriff here or not?" Johnny raised his voice and slapped his palm down on the counter with a sharp crack to emphasize his words.

"Ya don't have to get all shitty about it."

The door of the inner office was flung open. Sheriff Carroll stood there with his hands on his hips, a scowl on his face.

"Who'n hell's makin' all that racket out here?"

"Wasn't me." Thatcher jerked his thumb in Johnny's direction. "Was him."

"Got a few minutes, Sheriff? I'd like to talk to you."

"Go ahead."

"Not in front of him." Johnny imitated Thatcher's gesture and jerked his thumb toward the deputy.

"Come in." The sheriff went back through the door of his office. Johnny's voice stopped him.

"Not here. Outside." He glared at the deputy.

"Jesus Christ!" Sheriff Carroll stomped to the door. "This goddamn job is killin' me."

"Ya can always quit," Thatcher said to the sheriff's back, as he and Johnny went out and down the sidewalk.

"Why do you put up with him?" Johnny asked when they reached the curb where his truck was parked.

" 'Cause I ain't boss, that's why," Sheriff Carroll snarled.

"That's what I want to talk to you about and why I didn't want to say it where Doc's stool pigeon could eavesdrop." Johnny watched the sheriff closely before he continued. "I'd be obliged if what I tell you goes no farther."

"I ain't no blabbermouth."

"I'll take your word because Adelaide says that you're a decent man who got his tail in a crack. That's why I'm trusting you." Johnny leaned against the side of his truck and folded his arms over his chest. "For the last four years I've worked on and off with the Federal Bureau on special cases. I've worked with Hod Dolan, Frank Hamer, and others."

"Hamer, the Texas Ranger, who caught Bonnie and Clyde Barrow?"

"Hod Dolan and I tracked the Barrow gang's movements. Hod and I found the farmhouse where Charles Urschel, the oil man, was kept when he was kidnapped by Machine Gun Kelly and his gang."

Sheriff Carroll looked at Johnny with new interest. Johnny was silent for a minute or two, letting what he'd said soak in before he spoke again.

"Something's going to happen here soon that'll break Doc Herman's hold on this town. Adelaide hates to see you go down with him."

"That's a pile of horseshit. He's in here tighter than a miser's purse."

"I want to know if you're with us or if you're ears and a mouth for Doc."

"If I cross him, I'll lose my job. It's plain as that."

"At times a man has to do what's right regardless. You'll lose it for sure unless he's in jail."

"Jail? Shit! I was afraid it would come to this. It's the clinic, ain't it?"

"I'm not saying. Why did he want Clara Ramsey's death declared an accident?"

"I swear I don't know. He insisted and threatened my job if I didn't go along."

"Clara Ramsey was murdered. I think I know who did it, and it had nothing to do with Doc Herman. He's scared about something, and I'd like to know what it is."

"I don't know, and that's the God's truth."

"Are you willing to stick your neck out and arrest the man who killed Clara if I can get him to confess?"

"Hell, yes. Somebody beat the shit out of that girl before he threw her out and ran over her."

"Doc may think he knows who killed her and is protecting that person. The man I think did it is from Texas and has no connection with Doc Herman."

Johnny spent the next ten minutes telling Sheriff Carroll about Marty Conroy and the meeting he and Keith had set up for Wednesday morning.

"Keith McCabe will get him across the river into Tillison County. Will you come with me and arrest him if I can get him to confess?"

"Damn right. Hell, Johnny, I hated seeing that girl go to her grave with folks thinking she's just wandered out there on the road and got hit by a car."

"All right. Come down to my place Wednesday morning, and we'll go down to the border." Johnny turned his back and leaned on the truck. "Thatcher is watching us from the doorway."

"Bastard! He's probably already called Doc." Carroll let out a stream of obscenities. "Tell you one thing, Johnny. Doc is all het up about Miss Dolan being in the records office. Tell her to watch her step."

"If Doc or one of his thugs lays a hand on her, he'll answer to me." Johnny's face had never looked more Indian than it did when he turned to the sheriff.

"I knew that things would come to a head around here sooner or later. Doc thought they could go on forever."

"You mean the selling of babies born to unwed mothers at the clinic?" Johnny spoke matter-of-factly as if it were common news. It caught the sheriff by surprise.

"Hell and damnation! You . . . you know about that?"

"A girl came to town a week or two ago. She was looking for her *real* mother. Adelaide is keeping her out of sight down at the *Gazette*. She's not much more than a kid. You should go talk to her. Her folks, the DeBerrys, got her here sixteen years ago. They don't want her now and threw her out. She says DeBerry wants his money back because he wasn't told she had Indian blood."

Johnny was taken aback by the stunned look on the sheriff's face. He went as still as a stone. Seconds passed before he swallowed, coughed, and muttered something under his breath before he spoke.

"Doc . . . know about this?"

"No. Miss Dolan went to the records office to check Judy's birth certificate. What she found surprised the hell out of her."

"For God's sake, don't let Doc find out about the girl!" Carroll blurted.

"We're doing our best. We'd appreciate your help."

"You got it." He wiped his brow with a handkerchief he pulled from his back pocket.

"Sheriff," Thatcher called from the door of the office. "Phone."

"See you Wednesday." He turned away as if he had the weight of the world on his shoulders.

When the Sheriff Carroll walked into the office, Thatcher handed him the telephone receiver.

"Carroll, what's going on down there?"

"Whatta you mean, Doc?" Sheriff Carroll glared at his deputy, who grinned brazenly back at him.

"What business does Johnny Henry have with the sheriff that he doesn't want your deputy to know about? Thatcher seemed to think you're hatching up something behind his back."

"Horsecock! Johnny Henry wouldn't talk to Thatcher if he was the last man on earth. He hates his guts. As for what we're *hatching up*, somebody rustled a couple of Johnny's steers, and he's mad as hell about it."

"Explain that to Thatcher. He's a good man and we need good men, Carroll." The call was abruptly cut off.

At the door of his office, Sheriff Carroll turned his head to stare at Deputy Thatcher.

"You son of a bitch," he said, and slammed the door.

Chapter Twenty-five

Sheriff Carroll sat at the scarred table that served as his desk, adjusting his weight to take pressure off the broken spring in the seat of the chair. It was an unconscious action. He had been sitting in this chair for twelve years . . . a lifetime. Each year the weight of the guilt he carried became heavier. In a small corner of his mind he was glad it was coming to an end.

The door was pushed open, and Thatcher leaned against the doorjamb.

"Want me to go out ta where the steers were rustled and take a look around?"

"No! And shut the goddamn door!"

"Johnny musta really twisted yore tail." His grin showing his tobacco-stained teeth, the deputy stepped from the room and gently closed the door.

"Son of a bitchin' bastard sneak!" Sheriff Carroll muttered. A few minutes later he reached for his hat and slammed it down on his head. Thatcher was leaning on the counter, a cigarette hanging from his lips when he opened the door. "Clean this place up!"

"You're gettin' mighty bossy, Sheriff. Somethin' eatin' on ya?"

"Yeah. You're eatin' on my nerves. I'm going out to where those steers were rustled. Be gone a couple of hours."

"A half dozen bums built a fire in the gulley back down the tracks. Want me to run 'em off?"

"Hell, no. Leave 'em alone."

"You're the boss," Thatcher said with a snicker as Sheriff Carroll went out the door.

Goddamn him. He's been a millstone around my neck long enough.

The sheriff drove south out of town toward Johnny's ranch but turned off at the first crossroad he came to, slowed the speed of the car until it was crawling along, then stopped. *No use burning up gas even if the county does pay for it.*

He placed his hat on the seat beside him, mopped his face with the palms of his hands, and let his mind wander back to when he was a nineteen-year-old kid and had just graduated from high school. The previous year had been the happiest of his life. He'd found a girl who loved him, a girl who didn't laugh at his blunders and didn't make fun of him because he was overweight. A girl he didn't dare let his mother know about.

Hannah had been so pretty, so sweet. She had been a happy, smiling girl then. It broke his heart to see her now. She was what she was because he'd not had the guts to face down his mother and take her for his wife. Dr. Herman had made their problem so easy to fix, and Hannah had loved him enough to let him make the decision; but afterward, grief for the loss of her child had broken her spirit and driven her to whiskey for forgetfulness.

She'd had two more babies since she had given birth sixteen years ago. He doubted that Hannah even knew who had fathered them while she was in a drunken stupor. The disgrace of her pregnancies had caused her family to take her to the clinic where her first child was delivered. Both babies had been declared stillborn by Dr. Herman, but Pete knew better than that.

Doc had arranged for him to get the job as deputy and later helped him get elected sheriff. From that day on, he'd been firmly under Herman's thumb, paying the price to keep the doctor from talking about his affair with Hannah, the town whore. After his mother died, he would have been free to marry Hannah, but it was too late.

He enjoyed the respect he received as sheriff. For the first time in his life he was an official and not merely Pete and Ruby Carroll's fat kid. Through the years he had thought of the baby he and Hannah had had. He'd even made it his business to find a birth certificate that had listed the date and time Hannah had given birth. Someday, he had told himself, he would go to Fort Worth, look up the DeBerrys, and see his and Hannah's child, if only from a distance.

He tilted the rearview mirror and looked at himself. The years had not been kind. He was thirty-six years old and looked ten years older. His hair was gray; his jowls sagged. He had bags beneath his eyes. It was time to face up. Maybe he could make up . . . a little, for the damage he'd done to the only person who had ever loved him.

*   *   *

The sheriff parked behind the *Gazette* and went in the back door. The first thing he saw was a small, dark-haired girl picking type from a rack with a long pair of tweezers. Without conscious thought, he took off his hat.

"Hello, Sheriff." Paul positioned himself protectively between the sheriff and the girl. "Adelaide is up front. Go on through."

Pete Carroll felt a heavy lump in his chest. On stiff legs he went through to the front office. Both Adelaide and the redheaded reporter were busy at their typewriters. Alarm showed on Adelaide's face when she looked up and saw him. Her eyes darted to the door leading to the back room.

"Hello, Pete. I didn't know you were here."

"I need to talk to you, Adelaide. Can we go somewhere . . . private?"

"Well . . . ah, yes, but wait here until I talk to Paul."

"I've seen her. You don't need to tell him to hide her."

"For gosh sake, Pete—"

"I'm not here to cause trouble. I just had a long talk with Johnny Henry."

"Go on, Adelaide," Kathleen said. "I see Mrs. Smothers and a couple of her cronies across the street. They may be headed this way."

Paul looked askance when Adelaide came into the back room with the sheriff. Under Carroll's intense scrutiny, the young girl moved closer to Paul as if seeking protection. Her dark eyes went from the man with the star on his chest to Adelaide. She put her hand on Paul's arm.

"It's all right, Judy. The sheriff isn't here to arrest you. Pete, this is Judy DeBerry. She's been helping us here for the past couple of weeks."

"How do you do, sir?" Judy's voice was barely above a whisper.

"Hello." Pete's throat was so clogged he could barely speak.

Oh, Jesus. This is my little girl. Hannah and I made this pretty child out of our love for each other. She could almost be Hannah sixteen years ago. What did I give away . . . so long ago?

"Pete," Adelaide said, then repeated it when he didn't seem to hear. "Pete, we can go into Paul's room, but I want him to hear whatever you have to say. I have no secrets from Paul."

"Honey," Paul said to Judy, "use the type out of this number six tray for the headline and out of number four for the subheading."

"All right." Judy looked anxiously at the sheriff. He was still staring at her with a strange look on his face. Then he turned and followed Adelaide. Paul gave her shoulder a squeeze before he left her.

As soon as the door closed behind them, Sheriff Carroll turned and faced them.

"She's my . . . mine," he blurted. "She's my little girl." Sobs came up out of his throat and threatened to choke him. "Mine and . . . Hannah's."

Tears flooded his eyes and rolled down his cheeks. For a minute he tried to hold back the flow, then in a defiant action threw his hat on the floor. He stood like a swaying oak before sinking down on the edge of the bed. He leaned over, his forearms on his knees, and his thick shoulders shaking with sobs.

Adelaide and Paul looked at each other helplessly. Paul opened a drawer, took out a handkerchief, and pressed it into the sheriff's hands. Paul was the only grown man Adelaide had ever seen cry. He had cried almost silently when he had told her about his life until the time he came to Rawlings. Pete Carroll was not so reserved; he sobbed as if his heart were broken. Adelaide sat down on the bed beside him and put her arm around him.

"Do you want to tell us about it, Pete?" she asked when he had quieted a bit.

He dried his eyes and blew his nose on the handerchief Paul had given him.

"I'll wash . . . this and give it back."

"Pete, how do you know that Judy is yours and Hannah's?" Adelaide asked.

"Hannah had a baby sixteen years ago. It was mine. Doc said the thing to do would be to find it a good home. We let him have it. I found out he gave her to people named DeBerry."

"We know what Dr. Herman and Louise are doing. They don't care if the baby has a *good* home. They are selling the babies to whoever has the price," Paul declared angrily. "We're trying to get proof so they can be stopped."

"Doc's a dangerous man. Louise Munday is just as bad. I've known it for a while, but didn't know how to get out from under it." Pete Carroll's eyes were still wet, but he held up his head and looked each of them in the eye.

"May God forgive me for what I've done to that girl and to Hannah."

"There nothing I can say that will bring peace to your mind, Pete. I know what pressure you had from your mother. It still is no excuse. But that's in the past. What you do in the future is what is important."

"He'd not think twice about getting Judy out of town if he finds out who she is. He didn't want Miss Dolan to come here; he was afraid an outsider would dig up something."

"He hired Krome and Webb to hijack her?"

"Yeah, they were to take her to Texas and scare hell out of her so she'd not come back. They were not to hurt her. I'd not stand for that."

"Are you willing to help us, Pete?" Adelaide asked.

"I'll do what I can. I'm turning in my badge."

"Don't do that," Paul said hastily. "You've got to carry on as usual until we hear from a fellow who is doing some investigating. We don't want Doc or Louise to get wind that anyone suspects anything."

"Pete, do you think Dr. Herman had anything to do with Clara Ramsey's death?"

"I don't know. Clara gave him that last baby she had. I know he paid her off and she left town. She might have come back and wanted more money. She was out at the clinic while Doc was away in the city." The sheriff stood and ran his fingers through his hair.

"There's a baby buried out on the Ramsey lot. Do you know about that?"

"Harrumph!" Pete snorted, but said nothing.

"Pete? Do you know anything about it?" Adelaide persisted.

"Nothing for sure. Doc uses men passing through to do his dirty work. He might have buried something out there to satisfy Hazel." Pete stooped and picked up his hat and looked at Paul. "Can I talk to the girl, Judy, for a minute?"

"She's a sweet kid, and she's had a hell of a time. Don't put the burden of who you are on her now," Paul said sternly.

"I just want to look at her and hear her talk. I'd not hurt her for the world."

The sheriff stood back from the counter where Judy was setting type while Paul inspected her work.

"You did good, kid, but we've got some white space in that top headline. Instead of saying: *Skating Rink Coming to Town,* why don't we lengthen it to say: *Skating Rink Coming to Rawlings*? Town is five spaces and Rawlings takes up eight."

"Yeah." Judy laughed, forgetting for a minute the sheriff was there and looking at her.

"Have you ever skated?" Paul asked.

"Not on a skating rink. I skated on the sidewalk."

"Same thing. How about you, sheriff. You ever been on a rink?"

"Once or twice when I was young."

"You don't need to worry about the sheriff knowing you're here, Judy," Paul said when he saw anxiety return to her face. "We explained to him why you had run away from home."

Judy looked across the counter at the sheriff. Her eyes

were large and deep brown. Her hair, too, was deep brown and not Indian straight like her mother's, but with a bit of natural curl. *She is so pretty.*

"Don't worry," he managed to say. "You'll not have to go back there. No one will make you do anything you don't want to do."

"I'm glad of that. I'm never going back *there*." She smiled at him, and it encouraged him to say,

"You like being here with Adelaide and Paul?"

"Oh, yes! I'm going to hate to leave. But I . . . know I can't stay here forever."

"I don't know about that," Paul said with genuine affection. "You're the best printer's devil I've ever had."

"The printer's devil," Judy said, her eyes twinkling at the sheriff, "is the one who does the dirty work of tearing down the pages. Paul let me think that's a very important job."

"It is, you little twerp." Paul jerked on a strand of her hair.

Pete choked down his jealousy of the friendly affection that was evident between Paul and his daughter. Maybe someday she would feel that way toward him.

After he left the building and got into his car, he could still see in his mind's eye the face of a pretty young girl with soft brown eyes and dark fluffy hair.

We have a daughter and she is beautiful. I wish you could see her, Hannah. You'd be so proud.

A message awaited Sheriff Carroll when he arrived at the office on Wednesday morning.

"Doc wants you down at the city office."

Thatcher had ceased taking orders from the sheriff and made no bones about it. He had not cleaned the office. He went out without saying where he was going and made no pretense of being civil.

"What for?"

"You'll find out when you get there."

Instead of walking the half block to the city office, the sheriff got in his car and headed south out of town. By defying the doctor's orders, he faced losing his job; but, what the hell, he was getting his self-respect back. He had enough money stuffed in the mattress to last a little while, even with a daughter to support.

Judy had been constantly in his mind since he found out about her. Judy Carroll. He wondered how he could go about getting her name changed. Would she be angry when she learned that he had fathered her and given her away? He hoped that he could get Hannah sobered and cleaned up before Judy met her. When that was all over, he would sell his house, take his money and his daughter, and go someplace where they were not known.

Yesterday he had gone to the *Gazette* on the pretense of paying his subscription. Adelaide and Paul seemed to understand that he just wanted to see Judy. Even the fiery redhead had been friendly. Judy had greeted him when he came in the back door.

"Morning, Sheriff. Paul is showing me how to load the press."

"Foolish move on my part," Paul had growled. "She'll be taking my job."

Sheriff Carroll thought about Paul Leahy. When he had first come to town Doc had insisted that they find out everything they could about the man. They learned that he had been a reporter for a paper in Houston, Texas, and worked his way up to the position of editorial editor. From a family of means himself, he had married into a prominent Houston family.

After an explosion and fire that killed his wife and mother-in-law, his father-in-law had insisted that he be arrested for murder even though he had been badly burned in an attempt to save the two women. Paul had served ten years in Huntsville prison before a man, who had been having a love affair with Paul's wife, confessed to the crime on his deathbed. He had intended to destroy the house, not knowing the women were inside.

Paul Leahy had been given a full pardon by the Texas governor and money from the rather large insurance policy he'd had on his wife, and his home had been restored. He had promptly given it to a hospital that specialized in treating burn victims, then disappeared.

Doc tried hard to find out something to discredit the man. He didn't dare use the fact that Paul had been in prison for murder lest he alienate the Texas governor who had pardoned him. Doc finally had backed off, hoping that Paul would move on. But he had stayed and provided the strength Adelaide needed to keep the paper out of Herman's hands.

Johnny had not been sure the sheriff would show up to go with him to the river to meet Marty and Keith, and was relieved when Carroll drove into the ranch yard. He went out to meet the sheriff when he got out of the car. The man looked as if he hadn't slept in a week.

"Morning, Sheriff."

"Morning. I wasn't sure what time you wanted me to be here. I may be a mite early."

"No, just right. We've got to keep you out of sight down there until I whistle for you. We can go on down and find a place. Things go all right, Sheriff?"

"I talked to Adelaide and saw the girl. It was like a blow in the gut, Johnny. She's mine and . . . Hannah's."

"I figured there was a connection. You looked like a poleaxed steer when I told you about her."

"There's no turning back the clock to make good a mistake."

"No, but you can help us to put a stop to the baby-selling. I might as well tell you, I plan to dig up that box on the Ramsey lot and see what's inside."

"Let me know, and I'll stand watch."

"Thanks, Sheriff."

"I'm turning in this badge as soon as this is over. 'Course, if you don't pin Doc down, I'll be fired and won't get a chance to resign." His laugh was a dry cackle. "I hope they don't give the job to Thatcher."

"You might have to stay sheriff just to keep him from having the job. We'd better get going. I'll fire up the truck, and you can follow me down to the river."

Marty Conroy's cord britches were tucked into the tops of spit-polished boots with white stars on the sides. His Stetson was light tan with a brown band around the crown that matched his string tie. He was all business when he arrived at the McCabe ranch. Keith went out onto the porch to meet him.

"Mornin', Marty. You're right on time."

"Well, I try to be when I'm doing business."

Keith stepped off the porch. "You got a map and all the figures on the deal?"

"I've got the map. I'm still working on the figures." Marty spread the map out on the hood of his car and pointed to a little-used county road that ran east of the McCabe property. "The bridge here is a one-laner."

"How about the bridge over the main road? It would get more traffic. The relic that's there was built in the 1880s."

"Cost a little more money."

"I think we'd better go whole hog or nothing."

"Okey-dokey." Marty folded the map.

"Let's go take a look at it."

Keith opened the door on the passenger side. His eyes swept the light gray upholstery and saw the splotches of stain on the seat and on the back of the seat. *Just as Johnny had suspected; the little shithead had killed that girl!*

Marty was clearly elated to be talking to Keith about the toll bridge. He was surprised that of all the schemes he had proposed to his distant cousin this was the one that he was interested in.

"Ever since I crossed that bridge up at Lexington I've thought of putting a toll bridge across the Red River. There's a lot of traffic between Oklahoma and Texas in this area."

"How much are you going to invest, Marty?"

"I haven't decided. We can get backing; I'm not worried about that. Your name carries weight, Keith." Marty grinned.

"Hummm . . ." Was Keith's noncommittal answer.

"I was thinking of a name for our company. How does Conroy and McCabe sound to you? The sign would hang on the bridge just over the toll booth. Twenty-five cents would be a fair price for a car and fifty cents for a truck. Some might want to cross on the riverbed if the river is low. They do that up in Lexington because the Canadian has a good sandy bottom. Highway number 77 crosses there; that makes a difference. No one will cross free under our bridge. If we own the land on the riverbank, they'll have to pay to get to the riverbed. That'll put a stop to that."

Marty talked continuously until they reached the rickety bridge that crossed Red River. He stopped the car on the Texas side. Both men got out.

"We would want to put our bridge just a little east of here so that the old bridge can be used while the new one is being built." Marty walked along the riverbank.

"It's all right on this side of the river, but the other side is overgrown with trees and brush. You can't see what kind of a bank is over there. Let's go take a look."

"Shall we walk?" Marty asked, and stepped out onto the bridge.

"Take the car," Keith said nonchalantly. "We may want to drive down that lane that runs alongside the river."

"Okey-dokey."

"Turn right," Keith said after they had crossed the bridge.

"Looks like a car down there."

"Somebody fishing. There's catfish in the Red a yard long."

Keith got out of the car and walked to the bank. Marty hurried around the car to join him.

"What do you think, Keith? This is—" Marty cut off his words when Johnny came out of the bushes that grew along the bank.

"Hello, Johnny, catchin' any fish?" Keith stepped back behind Marty and nodded as he spoke.

"Not biting today. How are you doin', Marty?" Johnny sneered. "Still blowin' and goin'?"

"No need to be sarcastic," Keith said evenly. "Marty and I are discussing a business deal."

"Why didn't you come to your girlfriend's funeral, Marty? You did know that she was killed."

"Who . . . was killed?"

"Clara Ramsey, a week ago."

"How would Marty know the girl was killed? He was down at Conroy. Isn't that right, Marty?"

"That's right. How would I know?"

"You were outside the Twilight Gardens the night she was killed."

"That's a lie. I was in Conroy."

"Now see here, Johnny, don't be accusing my cousin of something if you don't have proof."

Johnny stepped over and opened the car door. "Explain these bloodstains, Marty?"

"Stay out of my car. You've no right—" He started around the car to the driver's side. Keith moved in place and leaned against the door.

"Tell him, Marty, so we can go."

"I spilled soda pop."

"Liar," Johnny said. "Those are bloodstains. It's almost impossible to get them out once they've dried." Johnny bent over the seat and started looking on the carpeted floorboard and around the seat.

"What're you doing? Stay out of my car!" Marty tugged on Johnny's arm.

"Keep your hands off me, or I'll use you for catfish bait," Johnny snarled and brushed him off. He continued to search, lifting the mat running his hand along the floor beneath the seat.

"Uh-oh!" He straightened and turned to face Marty. Keith was watching over the top of the car. Johnny opened his hand, and lying on his palm was a small white tooth. "Here's my proof, Keith. Eldon Radner, the undertaker told me that Clara had two teeth knocked out. Here's one of them. Explain that, Marty." Johnny closed his fist over the tooth.

"It's . . . it's not hers."

"We can dig her up and find out. Or did you beat up another girl in your car?"

"No, I didn't. Keith . . . ?"

"Tell him, Marty. We'll all stand by you. Johnny, go easy on him. He is my cousin."

"Keith, I . . ."

"The only thing that'll keep him out of the electric chair is a confession, and he's too stupid to realize that. Hell, I'll drag him in and turn him over to the Feds. They got ways of making a man confess he killed his grandma even if she's still alive."

"Do you have to go that far?" Keith asked.

"I'll go as far as I have to. Clara's mother is a friend of mine."

"Keith, I didn't mean . . ."

"Didn't mean what, Marty? Johnny, stay out of this. Marty is my cousin."

"She was going to— Keith, I didn't mean to."

"What was she going to do? Tell me so that I can help you."

"She was going to tell . . . Mother she was pregnant. Jesus, Keith, Mother wouldn't have let me marry a whore like Clara even if she was pregnant."

"She told you she was pregnant? Hell, Marty, that was no reason to kill her."

"She called Mother. She told her we were engaged and that she was coming down to see her. Mother got all worked up and—I had to stop her."

"How'd it happen?" Keith asked gently.

Chapter Twenty-six

"I waited at the honky-tonk 'cause I knew she'd go there," Marty said, his voice squeaky. "She came out and got in the car. We drove out and parked on the road. She just wouldn't listen to reason. Then she hit me. I wasn't going to let a whore get away with hitting me. I hit her back. She bit me on my . . . you know where."

"You had your tally-whacker out?"

"Well . . . she wanted to do it. Begged me to. After I hit her she said she was sorry and then she just leaned down and before I knew what she was going to do, she bit me. Hard. It hurt like hell. I lost my temper."

"So you beat her, threw her out, and ran over her with the car. You're a big man, Marty," Johnny sneered. "What did you hit her with?"

Marty ignored Johnny's question so Keith asked it. "What did you hit her with?"

"A soda pop bottle."

"The deed is done," Keith said. "We've got to decide what to do about it."

"Can't we just . . . forget it?"

"Not with Johnny knowing about it. Use your head."

"Well . . . we could . . . could—"

"Kill him? I don't think so. We'd have to kill the sheriff, too."

"What? Where?"

"Right behind you."

"Oh, Jesus! Oh, God, Keith. What'll I do?"

"Let me think. What's the best thing to do?" Keith took a notebook from his pocket. He placed it on the top of the car and began to write. "I'll put this down, Marty. You read it and sign it and go along with the sheriff. I'll hightail over to Mineral Wells and get the best lawyer I can find. He'll be up there to see you pronto."

"But . . . I don't want to go to jail."

"Clara didn't want to get killed either, you shithead!" Johnny growled the words.

" 'Course you don't want to go to jail," Keith assured Marty, "but this is the best way to get out of this fix. There's too much evidence. The bloodstains, the tooth, and they've got pictures of the tire tracks that ran over the girl. You can explain it all to your lawyer."

Keith finished writing. "This is what I've written. I, Marty Conroy, do freely confess to killing Clara Ramsey in Tillison County on the night of October 20, 1938. Read it and sign it, Marty."

"You didn't say anything about her biting me," Marty whined.

"You'll have to tell the lawyer and the judge about that."

"Do you think this is the best thing to do?"

"Absolutely. You said that you killed her."

"But I didn't mean to." Marty signed the confession and gave it back to Keith.

"She's still dead."

"You didn't mean to run over her three times after she was down and lying in the road?" Johnny taunted.

"You just stay out of this. You always wanted to get something on me." Marty turned on Johnny. "You're nothing but a dirt farmer and the by-blow of a drunk Indian and whore. Your own sister said so."

Johnny hit him squarely in the mouth. Blood spurted from his split lip. Marty took several staggering steps backward, then stretched out on the ground.

"That wasn't for what you said to me. It was for Clara's little girl and her mother. Get up, you son of a bitchin' bastard. Sheriff, put the handcuffs on him and haul his ass off to jail. I hope I'm there when they fry you in the chair."

The sheriff put Marty in the back of his car and handcuffed him to a bar that had been installed along the back of the front seat. By the time they left, Marty was blubbering like a baby.

"I don't feel one bit sorry for him," Johnny said. "You should have seen that girl. Her jaw was broken, her mouth split, and she had bruises all over her face and arms. The bastard stomped her when she was down. Then he ran over her, backed up, and ran over her again."

"You were lucky to find that tooth," Keith said with a grin.

"Yeah, wasn't I? I found it out in the barn where old Becky had her pups. Pups are getting old enough to shed teeth. I was thinking I'd have to pull one."

"Even surprised me when you came up with it. That was a pretty good act we put on. Maybe we ought to go out to Hollywood and get in the movies."

"Hod and I did that a time or two, but Hod was the mean one. He could be meaner than a cornered polecat."

"I'll take Marty's car back to the ranch until they decide what they want to do with it." Keith slapped Johnny on the back. "You done good, son."

"You're no slouch yourself. I'm going on into town. I don't think Carroll will have any trouble with Marty, but he might with Doc Herman. I told him to put that confession in a safe place."

"Marty's arrest will tear up Conroy, Texas."

"It just might tear up Rawlings, Oklahoma, too."

Marty Conroy had not been locked up in the Tillison County jail ten minutes when word reached Doc Herman at the clinic. He hurried down the hall to where Louise was supervising two aides and told her to come to the office.

"Thatcher called and said Carroll has arrested a man for killing Clara Ramsey."

Louise sat down heavily in the chair. "I thought . . . I thought—"

"That I had killed her. That's rich. I thought you had. That's the reason I insisted that what happened to her was an accident."

Louise began to laugh. "You were protecting me?"

"Of course. I reward loyalty. Speaking of loyalty, I'm going to have to do something about Carroll. He's assuming too much authority. I sent word for him to come in this morning. He didn't. He never said a word to me or to Thatcher about a suspect. I think it's got something to do with Johnny Henry."

"You might have to bring out your ace in the hole, Doc. Threaten to tell that he sold his and Hannah's kid. He'll knuckle under. He loves that job as sheriff."

"I don't want the state marshals coming in here. Carroll knows that."

"You think the state marshals are interested in the murder of a whore down here in Tillison County."

"They might be. I think we should shut down here for a while."

"The girl from Shawnee will give birth any day now."

"Maybe we should send her packing."

"We can't do that. We've got a couple coming in from Waco for that baby. I told them five hundred dollars."

Doc paced up and down the room. "All right. This will be the last for a while." He placed his hat carefully on his head and tilted it to just the right angle. "I'll go down to the jail and see what's going on."

Louise watched through the window as Doc left the clinic. Her heart was soaring. Doc, her love, had been protecting her at the risk of his own credibility when he believed that she had killed Clara to keep the little bitch from demanding more money.

He loved her. It was clear to her now that he might never tell her, but it was all right. She knew in her heart that he did.

Johnny came into the back door of the *Gazette*, went to the door of the office and beckoned to Kathleen and Adelaide. He had a large grin on his face. After swooping down and kissing Kathleen soundly, he told his news.

"We got a confession out of Marty Conroy. He killed Clara."

"Johnny! That's wonderful!" Kathleen hugged his arm.

Paul turned to Judy. "Start taking out the skating rink headline, Sweet Pea."

"Keith managed to get him across the river. The sheriff and I were waiting for him. We didn't call the sheriff in until after Marty had confessed. We got a signed confession. He said he had to stop Clara from telling his mother that she was pregnant."

"She couldn't have been pregnant. Hazel told me that when she had that last baby, Doc Herman fixed her so that she wouldn't have more children."

"He killed her for that?" Adelaide asked.

"What really set him off was that she bit him after he hit her." Johnny realized he was getting onto a subject unfit for Judy's ears and quickly changed it. He told about the stains in the car and *finding* the tooth.

"I'll write up the story. I'll need quotes from Sheriff Carroll. I don't know if Rawlings can stand this much excitement."

"Honey, this is just a drop in the bucket," Johnny said. Then, "Have you heard anything about the other?"

"Nothing, but it's only been a week. We've got Sheriff Carroll on our side, thanks to you." Kathleen slid her hand down his arm to capture his.

"Adelaide's instincts about him were right. He's a good man who got in over his head and didn't know how to get out." Johnny loosened his hand from hers and put his arm around her. "I wonder what's going on down at the jail. Doc isn't going to like having his decision proven wrong."

Sheriff Carroll looked up when Doc Herman opened the door.

"It didn't take Thatcher long to call you."

"I understand you arrested a man for Clara Ramsey's murder."

"That's right. He's back in the jail."

"Just how did this come about?"

"I have feelers out all the time, Doc. I heard that a Texas Ranger knew that he was the killer and was bringing him across the river. I went down, talked to him, got him to confess, and brought him in. It's that simple." The sheriff glanced at Thatcher and saw the smirk on his face.

"Who is he?"

"Marty Conroy from Conroy, Texas."

"I've heard of him. His family has influence."

"He's still a killer."

"Let me see the confession."

"I don't have it."

"Who has?"

"The ranger."

"You mean to tell me that you put a man in jail and you don't have your hands on his confession?"

"I'm saying it's not in my hands at the moment, but it'll be here in time for the hearing."

"Let him out."

"No. He stays where he is at least until Judge Fimbres gets here."

"I say let him out. We'll be the laughingstock of the state if we try to convict a man on a confession you got out of him after you worked him over."

"I suppose Thatcher told you Conroy had a busted mouth." Sheriff Carroll sneered. "He don't miss much."

"We have the reputation of the town to consider. What's got into you, Carroll? You've been acting strange lately."

"I'm doing my job, the job the people elected me to do."

"Give Thatcher the keys so that he can let that man out. He'll be on his way. Once he's in Texas, he's out of our hands."

"I won't do that. He killed that girl, and he'll stand trial."

"You're going to be sorry for this when this town is overrun with state lawmen. Your skirts are not entirely clean. Mark my word, Carroll. You'll be very sorry."

"I'm already sorry, Doc. I'm sorry that I never had the guts to stand up to you a long time ago. Better late than never. I'm doing it now."

"Speak to you for a minute, Sheriff." Johnny opened the door, but didn't enter the office.

"What are you doin' back here?" Thatcher said. "You might as well move in."

"Move in with a stinkin', lowdown skunk like you?" Johnny said. "I'm not that crazy."

Doc Herman brushed past Johnny without speaking. His face was red, and he was breathing hard in an attempt to control his anger. He jerked his head, and Thatcher followed him out.

"Doc givin' you trouble?" Johnny asked when they were alone.

"He wants me to let Marty out and forget about this thing."

"What's his reason?"

"He's heard of his family. Says they've got influence. He's afraid state marshals will come in."

"What are you going to do?"

"I'll not turn that son of a bitch loose. They'll have to kill me first. Judge Fimbres is a straight shooter. I don't think he approves of all that Doc does. He might help if I can get word to him. I don't dare leave the jail."

"Want me to get the judge?"

"I'd appreciate it. Give him a rundown about what's going on. I'll not be able to talk freely because of Thatcher. I want the judge to hold the confession. If I turn my back, Thatcher will tear this place apart looking for it."

Later when Johnny was in the back room of the *Gazette,* Kathleen came back with the story she had written about the murder and the arrest for the next day's paper.

"I'll read it to you. I've edited it so many times it's hard to read." She sat down beside him on the cot he used sometimes when he stayed overnight and read her story. When she finished she asked, "What do you think?"

"You could mention that Keith is a member of the Texas Rangers. A former member, but you can forget that.

You're giving me too much credit. Give the credit to Carroll. He needs it, and I don't."

"I could couple his name with yours when I write about the pictures and the stains in the car. I didn't think I'd better mention the tooth trick." She laughed and wrinkled her nose at him.

Kathleen scribbled on the paper. "I'll have to retype this. Paul will be totally confused when he tries to set it on the linotype. Are you coming in tonight?"

"Kathleen, phone," Adelaide called.

"Oh, shoot," Kathleen said and stood. "You won't run off, will you?"

"Not right away. Go on, take your call."

She hesitated, then leaned down and whispered in his ear. "I'm so proud of you." She kissed his ear, hurried to the front office, and picked up the receiver. "Hello."

"Miss Dolan, Barker Fleming."

"Hello," she said again, motioning for Adelaide to stop typing.

"I have a picnic basket for you to replace the one I lost."

"You needn't have gone to the trouble." Kathleen heard a click on the line, then another.

"I took the liberty of filling it, Miss Dolan. I think you'll be pleased."

"I'm sure I will. When will you be coming this way?"

"Would Friday afternoon be convenient? I'll be bringing a friend. Gifford is interested in seeing a fellow he used to work with. And, Miss Dolan, could I impose on you to deliver a message to Judge Fimbres that I would like to see him sometime Friday afternoon."

"I would be glad to. Shall I tell him that you will come to the courthouse?"

"If you will, please. How are things in Rawlings?"

"Fine, Mr. Fleming. I'll be looking for you on Friday."

Kathleen was smiling when she hung up the receiver.

When the phone rang at the clinic, Louise hurried to answer it. Doc could be calling from the city office.

"Hello."

"This is Flossie. A long-distance call came to the *Gazette* from Oklahoma City, but it was nothing important."

"Who called? You don't have to give me your valuable opinion."

"Barker Fleming talked to Miss Dolan. You know, he's that good-looking Indian with the big car. I think he's got a crush on her. He lost her picnic basket and is bringing her another one. I heard someone talking from the tannery last week. He's going to be running it. His family owns it, you know."

"What else did he say to Miss Dolan?"

"He's bringing a picnic basket and he's filling it for her. Isn't that romantic? I can't help it if they didn't say anything important. You told me to let you know of any out-of-the-area calls." Flossie sounded peeved.

"I know I did. Thanks, Flossie. Let me know if there are any calls between the paper and the sheriff's office."

"Sheriff's office? Why—"

"Just let me know," Louise said impatiently, and hung up the phone.

Chapter Twenty-seven

Kathleen and Johnny sat in the truck parked behind the *Gazette*.

"Such beautiful hair." Johnny stroked her curls, then tipped her chin with a finger and kissed her.

"Not everyone likes red hair. I'm stuck with it."

"And stuck with me."

"I'm happy to be stuck with you, Johnny Henry. How come you changed your mind about digging up the box at the cemetery?" Kathleen asked and snuggled her hand into the open collar of his shirt.

"I began to think of it as evidence. If I go out there and dig it up, find nothing in it and put it back, it could be said I removed what was in it. If we wait and dig it up with witnesses, maybe Grant and Judge Fimbres, and find it empty, it'll be credible evidence."

"That makes sense. I hadn't thought of it that way although one of the dates I got at the courthouse corresponds with the date Clara's baby was born. Hazel remembered it because it was her mother's birthday."

"You got the ball rolling, honey."

"Are you eager to see your friend, Mr. Gifford?"

"Yeah, I haven't seen him for a couple of years." He drew her head to his shoulder. "The paper goes to press tomorrow. Tonight we'd better tell Hazel about Marty being arrested. We don't want her to hear it from someone else."

"You'll go with me?"

"Sure."

She curled her arm around his neck. "I like you a lot, Mr. Henry."

"That's a relief. I was thinkin' you kissed men you didn't like."

His lips touched hers, lightly at first, then with longer and more intense kisses, concentrating his attention on doing this while his palm wandered from one of her breasts to the other.

"Did I tell you that the other night was the most wonderful night of my life?" she murmured.

"Only about a dozen times. It *was* great, wasn't it? I might have to marry you so that we can do it again." He kissed her again and again; his mouth wandering over her nose, her eyes, her cheeks. When he lifted his head, his breath was warm on her wet lips. "I've got to get crackin'. I'll take you around to your car and follow you home."

The first paper to come off the press was displayed in the window of the *Gazette*. Paul had done an excellent job making up the front page. TEXAN ARRESTED FOR MURDER blazed across the top. A picture of Clara Ramsey lying in the ditch and a picture of Sheriff Carroll beside his car were stacked along one side. The subtitle read: SHERIFF CARROLL BRINGS IN CONFESSED KILLER OF LOCAL WOMAN.

In the story, Kathleen had given as much credit as she could to Sheriff Carroll, reported that at first he thought the death was an accident, but after viewing the body in the funeral parlor, he realized that Clara Ramsey had been murdered. Assisting in the arrest, Kathleen wrote, had been Johnny Henry, a local rancher, and Keith Mc-Cabe, a Texas Ranger. A paragraph detailed Marty Conroy's background, stating that he was from a prominent Texas family and had been seen with the victim at the rodeo and again at the Twilight Gardens on the night she was killed. The hearing would be held November 3, allowing time for Conroy's Texas lawyer to find representation for him in Oklahoma.

The usual number of papers reserved for sale in the office were gone within an hour. Paul had wisely increased the print run, and more papers were brought from the back room. Adelaide said she couldn't remember when there had been such a demand for the paper.

Johnny came to the office just as Woody was taking the bundles to the post office. He held the door until the wagon cleared, then came in, his eyes on Kathleen and hers on him.

"I've been down to the sheriff's office. He spent the night at the jail since he didn't know how much he could trust Allen Lamb, his extra man."

"So he's hanging in there?"

"You bet. He was afraid Thatcher and Doc Herman would find a way to let Marty out and get him back over the line into Texas."

"Doc is in a panic, or he wouldn't even think of doing anything so foolish," Paul said.

"He came back last night and told Carroll that he was fired and to give his keys to Thatcher. The sheriff is more of a man than I thought he was. He told Doc that he had been elected by the people of the county and, as mayor of Rawlings, Doc had no authority to fire him. Judge Fimbres backed him up."

"Oh, my. If you think Doc is mad now, wait until he finds out he's being investigated." Adelaide's eyes sought Paul as they always did when she was worried.

"He won't find out unless they come up with something that'll stand up in court."

"They've found something, or Grant Gifford wouldn't be coming down. Judge Fimbres has called in a state marshal from Elk City. He'll be here tonight. I told Carroll to keep his gun handy until then. Desperate men do desperate things." Johnny took a paper off the counter and dropped a nickel in the cup.

"You don't have to pay for a paper," Adelaide protested.

"I'm taking this down to Carroll."

"Paul and I are going to talk to Judy tonight. We think we should tell her everything. She took a big risk coming here and has the right to know."

"Even about the sheriff?" Kathleen asked.

"Even that."

Paul rolled his eyes when Kathleen took Johnny's hand and led him to the back room.

"I remember when *you* got *me* in the back room every chance you got." Adelaide cocked a brow.

"I don't have many chances nowadays with so many people around." Paul complained, then came to her, and whispered. "I'd rather get you in *my* bed."

Out of sight of the front office, Johnny put his arms around Kathleen and kissed her.

"I'm going to stay with Carroll until the state marshal gets here. Then I'll go home and get some things done."

"You'll be here tomorrow?"

"I don't figure the others can get to town before noon. I'll be here before then."

At the clinic, Doc Herman paced his office. Louise sat in a chair beside his desk, her rabbitlike front teeth worrying her lower lip. She had chewed the thick coat of lipstick, and it was smeared on her teeth.

"I've got a feeling there's things going on here that I don't know about. Carroll has got his back up. He's getting encouragement from somewhere."

"Johnny Henry. And he's being egged on by that redheaded bitch at the newspaper."

"What could she have found out from the birth records except that there are more births here than in most towns? For obvious reasons, none of the people who send their girls here would talk."

"Maybe we don't have anything to worry about. If the marshals come in, it will be only to work on the Conroy case. They've no proof of anything."

"Call the people in Waco and tell them not to come. Tell them the baby died."

"What'll we do with the baby when it's delivered?"

"Keep it for a while and see what happens. Destroy the

file of places we've advertised the clinic as a home for unwed mothers. That will be a start."

"Let's shut down and go away, Doc. You said we would when we got enough money."

"The money wouldn't last any time at all, Louise. I want to show you the world."

Louise hoisted herself up out of the chair. Her dyed hair was stuck to her forehead with sweat, and perspiration stained her uniform beneath her armpits. Revulsion made Doctor Herman close his eyes for a long moment, preparing himself for the ordeal of kissing her. He went to her and kissed her gently on the mouth, forcing himself to take his time.

"Now run along, my dear. I need to think about what's best for us to do."

"You're the best man in the whole world, Doc. Just tell me what to do. I'll stick my head in the fire if it'll help you."

"Thank you, dear, sweet lady. No man has ever had a more faithful lady friend." He patted her cheek.

Christ, but I'll be glad to see the last of you and your rabbitlike teeth, your painted face, and your cowlike devotion.

By Friday morning Kathleen's nerves were standing on end. At breakfast Hazel had been quiet. To lose her daughter by accident had been bad enough, but to know that someone had deliberately killed her was devastating. Kathleen hoped that Marty Conroy's conviction would help ease her pain.

As soon as she reached the office, Kathleen asked

Adelaide how Judy had taken the news that Sheriff Carroll was more than likely her father and that her mother was a Cherokee girl who, unable to cope with the loss of her baby, had turned to alcohol.

"She is so mature for her age," Adelaide said. "Her response to that was, 'She must have loved me very much.'"

"What did she say about Sheriff Carroll?"

"Not much. She said he was nice."

"It was a lot for a young girl to swallow all at once."

"Paul explained to her how important she was to the building of a case against Doctor Herman and Louise Munday. He asked her to write down every word she could remember that either of the DeBerrys said to her about when they came here to get her. She was never adopted by them, because their names are on her birth certificate."

"I wish you would marry Paul. He's such a wonderful man."

"I'm thinking about it. He loves children. His wife wouldn't give him any, and I'm too old."

"Adopt one. You and Paul would make wonderful parents."

"We could have *bought* one from Doc," Adelaide said bitterly.

Kathleen cocked her ear toward the back room. "Johnny's here."

"When are you two going to get married?"

"He hasn't asked me, Adelaide."

"He will." Adelaide said confidently, then, "Mr. Fleming is here."

With Barker Fleming was a man dressed in a light tan suit with a Stetson to match and wearing round wire-rimmed glasses. Another car pulled up alongside Barker Fleming's and two men got out. All four came into the office.

After greeting Kathleen and Adelaide, Barker introduced Grant Gifford and two marshals.

"Miss Dolan and Miss Vernon, meet Grant Gifford, Oklahoma State Attorney General, and Marshals Whitney and Putman."

After shaking hands with the two women, Grant Gifford looked past them to where Johnny lounged in the doorway leading into the pressroom. A smile lit his face.

"Johnny Henry, I've a notion to give you a damn good licking for not coming up to see us." Grant threw his hat on the desk, dropped into a crouch, and put up his fists. Johnny did the same.

"You've got so soft you couldn't whip Aunt Dozie," Johnny retorted.

"Think not? Want to take me on, boy?"

The two met, clasped hands, and pounded on each other. "Good to see you, Grant."

"Good to see you, too, Johnny. It's been two years. We're not going to let that much time go by again."

"How's Karen?"

"Sassy. Our Mary Ann is going to be just like her. Margie is more like me, calm and sweet!"

"Has Karen heard you say that?"

"Lord, I hope not! We got down to Red Rock a few months ago. Karen's dad is getting on."

"Aunt Dozie told me you were there."

"Don't yawl be trackin' dat cow-doo on my clean 'noleum. I wearin' de flowers off scrubbin' after yawl." Grant imitated the old woman, and both men laughed. "She was a crackerjack."

"She still is and she's getting on, too," Johnny said.

Barker introduced the two marshals to Johnny and Paul, then stood back and proudly admired the way Johnny presented himself to the marshals. He had not mentioned to Grant Gifford that Johnny was his son, leaving it to Johnny to tell his friend if he wanted him to know.

They went into the pressroom and, after Paul was introduced, Johnny told Grant that Marty Conroy was locked up in the jail.

"Marty Conroy? What's the little jelly bean done now?"

Johnny explained about Clara's death and Dr. Herman's part in wanting the death to be declared an accident. He told how he and Keith had worked together to get a confession.

Grant chuckled. "It's nothing to laugh about, but I can just hear Marty telling the judge that he is the Conroy from Conroy, Texas."

"The doctor ordered the sheriff to let him out, but the sheriff refused. Then he tried to fire the sheriff, but Judge Fimbres interfered."

"What connection would Conroy have with Dr. Herman?" Grant asked, looking from Johnny to Paul.

"We don't think he has a connection," Paul said. "We believe he feared the state marshals coming in and uncovering some of his activities."

"Fleming laid out a good case against the doctor," Grant said. "We went to work right away investigating every aspect of the doctor's life. We contacted Mr. and Mrs. DeBerry in Fort Worth. Mr. DeBerry is bitter and will testify against him. I understand the DeBerry girl is here."

"She is," Paul said. "She doesn't want to go back to the DeBerrys. We are quite sure we know who her father is. She was born to an unwed mother. We don't want her going to the orphans' home. Adelaide and I will take care of her."

"If she's safe and content here. We can decide what to do about her later."

"Clara Ramsey, the girl Marty is charged with killing, had a baby a year ago," Johnny said. "It is supposed to have been stillborn and buried out on the family lot. Kathleen discovered in the records at the courthouse a birth certificate made out to a couple from Weatherford, Texas, just one day later. Kathleen and I believe the box Doc had buried to satisfy Clara's mother is empty."

Kathleen was glad to leave the telling of the details up to Johnny. There was genuine affection between him and Grant Gifford. She wished he would direct some of his remarks to Barker Fleming, but that would have to come when he was ready to acknowledge the relationship.

Grant glanced at the pretty redhead who sat beside Johnny listening with rapt attention to every word he said, and realized that they were more than friends.

"We should find out what's in that box. I'll take Marshal Putnam and go see Judge Fimbres." Grant stood. "Meanwhile, Fleming, why don't you and Johnny go with Marshal Whitney to the cemetery. There should be two witnesses to what's in it, or not in it. Then come down to the courthouse. If it's empty as you suspect, you'll need to sign an affidavit."

In the middle of the afternoon two cars drove up to the clinic. Barker Fleming and Grant were in one car, the two marshals in the other. Johnny had been invited to come along, but had declined.

The woman at the desk looked up with large frightened eyes when four men came into the reception area. Grant and Barker held back and the marshals took the lead.

"May I help you?" the woman asked timidly.

"Dr. Herman," Putnam said. "Where is his office?"

"I'll get him."

"Is he with a patient?"

"No. I don't think so." She stood and moved toward the door behind her.

Marshal Putman stepped quickly around the desk. "Don't bother. Sit back down, ma'am, and stay here. We'll find him."

Marshal Whitney flung open the door. Dr. Herman was standing in the middle of the room.

"I thought I heard voices out there. Who are you?" Doc's eyes went beyond Marshal Whitney to the other three men. "What do you mean coming into my office without knocking?" The four men said nothing, but looked at the doctor, letting their silence work on his nerves. "Is this a holdup?" Doc's voice was hoarse when it broke the silence. "I don't keep money here."

Marshal Putman opened his coat, showing a holstered revolver, then reached into his inside coat pocket and flipped out a badge.

"Federal Marshal James Putman. This is Marshal Whitney, Mr. Gifford, Oklahoma State Attorney General, and Mr. Barker Fleming."

"What can I do for you?" Dr. Herman's face was flushed, and his voice trembled slightly.

Grant stepped forward. "Sit down, Doctor, and tell us why you buried an empty box out on the Ramsey plot."

"What are you talking about?" The doctor moved behind the desk but didn't sit down.

"I think you know, but I'll tell you anyway. Clara Ramsey had a baby a year ago. She told her mother it was stillborn. She sold you a live baby, took the money, and left town. You sold that baby to Mr. and Mrs. Carl Sheldon of Weatherford, Texas. You fixed the records to show that Mrs. Sheldon had come here and had had the baby."

"Why . . . why . . . that's the most ridiculous thing I ever heard of! The Sheldons were on their way home when she went into labor. They stopped here, and I delivered their baby."

"Sit down, Doctor." After the doctor was seated, he asked, "Why did you bury an empty box?"

"It had the body of a stillborn child in it when I hired a man to bury it."

"Mr. Fleming and Marshal Whitney just dug up the box and all that was in it was medical waste, bandages, gauze, and several empty bottles. The trash in that box came from this clinic."

"That's a lie!" Doc jumped to his feet. His face was beet red and cords stood out on the sides of his neck.

"Well, never mind that. Sit down, Doctor." Grant said patiently. "Sixteen years ago you sold a baby to a couple named DeBerry for two hundred dollars. You told the father of the baby that you knew a couple who were well-off and would give the baby a good home, something he couldn't do. The DeBerrys threw her out and want their money back. You told them that the girl's mother was blond and blue-eyed. The truth is that the baby's mother was a Cherokee. The girl is here in town looking for her real mother."

"That redheaded hussy at the paper has dug up all this nonsense."

"We have talked to a number of women who supposedly had babies here. Some of them have admitted you furnished them a baby for a fee. We'll have a number of these people at the trial."

"Trial? You can't prove anything. It's their word against mine. I'm a respected doctor. I've looked after this town and kept it going when other towns this size dried up."

"The First National Bank in Oklahoma City released your bank records. It seems that for eighteen years you have sent checks in the amounts of one hundred, two hundred, then three or four hundred dollars. You increased the price to fit the demand."

"My assistant must . . . have . . . could have. I never—" Doc stammered.

"Do you know a woman by the name of Ardith Moore? She visited you each time you stayed at the Biltmore in Oklahoma City. You like the kinky stuff, huh, Doctor?" Grant lifted his brows. "What you do in bed won't have much bearing on the trial, but it'll be good juicy stuff for the newspaper."

"You're out to ruin my good name."

"It's already ruined."

"I've worked for years to help unfortunate girls." Spit ran down the side of Dr. Herman's mouth, and a vein throbbed in his temple.

"Did you ever stop to think that selling a human being is a federal offense? This is big-time stuff, Doc. So big that you'll not have to share a jail cell with Marty Conroy. You'll get a cell all to yourself in the federal prison."

"I've done nothing wrong! My assistant will tell you—"

"We plan to talk to her. She'll turn on you if it means saving her own hide."

On the other side of the door leading into the examination room, Louise Munday listened, and her world fell apart.

They're arresting Doc! My beloved Doc is going to jail. My darling Doc, who kissed me so sweetly just this morning. We'll never be able to leave this dreadful town and go away together.

This can't be happening! They'll use me to send Doc to prison! She looked frantically around. *They'll not use me, if they can't find me.*

Louise grabbed her purse and headed for the door, then went back to her desk, took out a small pistol, and shoved it in the pocket of her uniform. She tore the starched cap from her head, grabbed the blue nurse's cape, and flung it around her shoulders. She ran down the hall past the kitchen and the laundry room to the back door. Just as she reached it, a loud pop came from the front of the clinic. Without giving a thought to what it was, she hurried to her car and drove away.

Chapter Twenty-eight

Sheriff Carroll was relieved when the state marshal arrived from Elk City. Judge Fimbres had told him that he had the authority to fire Deputy Thatcher; but he knew that there would be trouble, so he waited for the marshal. When he told Thatcher to turn in his badge and leave, the man refused to go quietly. Johnny arrived during the confrontation and when the deputy stated his intention of going to Dr. Herman, Johnny suggested that he be put in a jail cell for a few hours.

"Only until Grant and the Federal Marshals get back," Johnny told the state marshal. "We don't want Thatcher going over to the clinic and gumming up the works."

Down the street at the *Gazette*, Kathleen had tried to write some routine stories while she waited for Johnny to return to tell them what had happened at the cemetery. Finally she gave up and stared out the window.

Judy had come down from the floor above and was helping Paul tear down the pages from this week's paper. The only sound in the office was the *clunk* as lead that was to be melted and reused hit the bucket.

When Johnny returned to the *Gazette* from the courthouse, Sheriff Carroll was with him. They went to the back room so that Paul and Adelaide could hear what Johnny had to tell them.

"The box at the cemetery was full of trash. Fleming and I signed affidavits, and Judge Fimbres issued an arrest order for Dr. Herman. Grant and the marshals are out there now."

Sheriff Carroll looked as if he hadn't slept for a week. His eyes kept darting to Judy. Her head was down, and she didn't look at him. Finally, he spoke to her.

"Ah . . . Judy?" When she didn't answer or look up, he tried again. "Judy, can't you look at me? I know Adelaide told you that I'm . . . I'm—who I am."

When she didn't answer, Paul said, "Honey, this is hard, but it's best if you and Sheriff Carroll talk a bit. We'll go leave you alone—"

"Don't go." She grabbed Paul's arm, her big dark eyes pleading. "Please stay."

Kathleen and Johnny moved away and went into the office.

"Judy, I was a nineteen-year-old scared kid when I gave you away," Pete Carroll began, his voice scratchy. "I had no way of making a living for myself, much less for a wife and child. My mother was the ruling force in my life. I did what I thought was best at the time."

"It's all right."

"No, it isn't. I ruined your mother's life by being so gutless. Thank God, you got away from those folks before yours was ruined."

"I'm all right now."

"That damn doctor told me that he knew people who

would give you a good home, treat you like a princess, and provide you with things I'd never be able to afford. I'm sorry. I can't tell you how sorry I am."

"It's all right."

"I talked to Judge Fimbres. You don't have to worry about going back to Fort Worth or anywhere you don't want to go. I've saved up a little money. It's all yours. Every last cent of it."

"I don't want it. I want to see my . . . mother."

"She's ah . . . not well right now."

"Adelaide told me. I don't care if she's a drunk. I want to see her, help her. You should have helped her. It was hard for a mother to give up her baby."

Tears came into Pete Carroll's eyes. He turned away for a moment. When he turned back the tears ran down his face.

"You're right. I should have tried harder to help her. I was a weak-kneed fool."

"Well, you can't put spilt milk back in the bucket. You just have to go on from here." Judy said with maturity far beyond her years.

"I have a house—"

"I don't know you. I'll stay here for a while, if it's all right with Adelaide and Paul."

"Let me know if you need anything. I think I still have a job."

"I don't need anything. Not now. Paul was right. I'm glad I talked to you."

"I'd better get on back down to the jail. Things are happening fast now." Sheriff Carroll addressed his words to Paul. "Thank you for . . . looking out for her."

"It's been no trouble. I've got a lot of free work out of the little twerp. She's learning so fast that I'm afraid I'm going to have to start paying her a wage."

"I'm planning to start my own newspaper. Didn't I tell you?" Judy said with a sassy grin.

"What do you think is happening at the clinic?" Kathleen asked, when she and Johnny were in the office.

"I think they'll arrest him and get him out of town. Marshal Whitney filled the gas tank on the car before they went out there."

"Will Mr. Gifford go with them?"

"I would think so."

"This town is going to be turned upside down."

"It'll recover. There are good people here. They just found themselves under the thumb of Doc Herman and didn't know how to get out. A good talker can make folks think black is white. Look what that fellow Hitler is doing over in Germany."

"You're so calm and reasonable."

"Not all the time." He pulled her back from the window and kissed her.

"I'm glad you're not reasonable all the time."

They were still standing close together when the door opened. Kathleen looked around Johnny's broad shoulders to see that Barker Fleming had come in. He stood just inside the door, his hands buried in his pockets, his face grim.

"What happened?" Kathleen asked.

"He's dead." Barker placed his hat on the counter. "It happened so fast!"

"Doc Herman is . . . dead?" The back of Kathleen's hand went to her mouth, and her eyes went wide with disbelief. She recovered and headed for the back room, calling, "Adelaide and Paul—"

The four of them stood in shocked silence while Barker told them what had happened at the clinic.

"Gifford had been talking to him, telling him that he was charged with a Federal offense. When he told him it was time to go, Herman said he wanted to find his address book so that he could contact another doctor to take over the clinic. He opened a drawer, came up with a pistol in his hand, put it under his chin, and pulled the trigger."

"Oh my goodness!"

"It was a powerful slug. In a fraction of a second, his head seemed to explode. He knew what that gun would do."

"What are they doing now?" Johnny asked.

"The undertaker is there. The only staff out there are a laundress, a cook, and a nurse. The woman in the office is hysterical. They have only four patients, not very many for such a large, well-equipped clinic."

"Louise Munday will be able to take over." Adelaide held tightly to Paul's arm. "They say she's almost as good a doctor as Dr. Herman."

"She's not there. The cook said she left. I don't know if it was before we got there or while we were there. According to the staff, she runs the place."

"She was crazy in love with him and had been for years," Adelaide said. "She'll be out of her mind when she finds out."

"She's as guilty as Dr. Herman. He had to have had help in running that baby-selling business." Johnny voiced his opinion solemnly.

"I agree." Kathleen squeezed Johnny's hand. She looked up at him. He was her anchor in this tilting world of events.

"All right, ladies. Get crackin'," Paul said. "The *Gazette* is about to put out it's first *extra* edition."

"Do you think we should?" Adelaide asked.

"Absolutely. You're a newspaper woman, aren't you? The people of this town are entitled to know what's happened. If we get cracking on it, we can have it on the street by midnight."

"We . . . can't."

"We can. Judy will run the linotype, I'll get the press ready. Kathleen write your story. Adelaide set the headlines."

Excitement put a shine in Kathleen's eyes. "Johnny, while I'm taking down Mr. Fleming's account of what happened, will you go out to the clinic and ask Mr. Gifford if he'll come in when he's finished out there and give a statement?"

"Sure. Sheriff Carroll just left here. Has he been told?" Although his remark was addressed to Barker, Johnny didn't look at him.

"I'm not sure. I only heard Gifford call the undertaker when he found out that Dr. Herman was the coroner. He told the telephone operator in no uncertain terms what would happen if she listened in on his conversation."

"That must have really got Flossie flustered." Adelaide shook her head.

"I'll stop and tell the sheriff to keep his eye out for Louise Munday. I'm sure Grant will want to talk to her."

Kathleen went with Johnny to the back door. "I feel bad about Dr. Herman killing himself. When we started this we never—"

"Are you feeling guilty? He did it rather than face the music for what he had done. It has nothing to do with you. Now go write your story. It might get picked up on the national news. This is your chance to be famous."

"Will you be back?"

"Of course. I'll not let you go home alone. When your paper hits the street, it might be like seven-thirty on Saturday night around here."

"I love you, Johnny Henry."

"I love you, too."

He kissed her quick and went out.

Adelaide and Kathleen divided the task of writing the story. Adelaide wrote about Doc's background and his involvement in the community. Kathleen wrote of the events that caused him to take his life without giving details of the investigation. She mentioned that a young girl who wished to remain anonymous, had come to town looking for her parents. It had started an investigation that was ongoing.

Paul had the headlines set and locked in place. DOCTOR HERMAN IS DEAD. His subtitle read: DOCTOR TAKES HIS LIFE WHILE BEING QUESTIONED BY STATE ATTORNEY GENERAL. From the file a large engraving of the doctor was placed in the middle of the page.

Judy worked at the linotype. Paul watched over her

proudly. Adelaide pulled bits and pieces of Dr. Herman's biography from the file and put them on the hook for Judy to set while she and Kathleen worked on the current story.

At eleven-thirty, the press began to roll. Adelaide and Kathleen had pored over the proof page and pronounced it as good as it could be given such short notice.

Adelaide called in her paperboys and told them the paper would sell for a dime and they could have a nickel of it. As soon as the cry was heard lights came on in homes all over town.

"Extra! Extra! Dr. Herman killed." Adelaide had told the boys to say no more than that.

It would be a night to remember, but it was not over yet.

Two hours after the paper hit the street, the excitement began to subside. The paperboys had come in, turned in the paper money, and collected their pay. They were elated over their extra money. Judy had gone up to Adelaide's apartment to go to bed. Adelaide and Paul were in his room.

Kathleen cleared her desk as Johnny watched from where he lounged in a chair. He was waiting to take her home.

"This is a night we'll never forget."

"As important as that other night you said you'd never forget?" Johnny teased.

"This night is like ho-hum compared to that night," Kathleen retorted. "But it has been exciting. Nothing like this ever happened in Liberal."

Kathleen reached under the desk and pulled out her typewriter cover. She straightened to see Louise Munday push open the door. Her hair looked as she had just came through an Oklahoma tornado. Dark lines of mascara streaked her cheeks. The look in her eyes was wild. At first her mouth worked, but nothing came out. Then a flood of words burst from her.

"Bitch! You goddamn bitch! You started it all . . . you did it . . . you're goin' to pay . . . for what you did to . . . him. He helped those sinful whores get rid of their brats and you . . . none of you understood how . . . good he was—"

Kathleen stood frozen. Johnny had risen to his feet.

"You'll pay—" Louise screamed. "Doc is gone!" she sobbed. "You killed him!"

"No!"

Kathleen saw the gun Louise drew from under her cape. She held her palm out against the crazed woman, as if to ward off the bullet she knew was coming.

"No!"

Johnny's shout came a second before she felt something slam into the side of her head. Her eyes blurred, her legs turned to water, and she began to sink to the floor. Her hand clutched at her desk. She was vaguely aware that Louise had turned the gun toward Johnny as he sprang at her.

Kathleen came out of a dream where she was riding a dark horse in the sky above the treetops. She first realized that someone was holding her. They were in a car and going very fast. Her head felt as if a thousand hammers were pounding on it. The pain was so severe that she was afraid to open her eyes. Then, a vision of a gun turned toward Johnny flashed behind her closed lids and wild panic consumed her.

"John . . . ny!" She wanted to scream, but her voice was barely audible to her own ears. "John . . . ny—"

"I'm here, sweetheart." The calm, dear voice reached into her consciousness. "Lie still. We're on our way to the doctor."

"Are you . . . are you . . . ?"

"I'm all right. You'll be all right, too. We're almost . . ."

Johnny's voice faded, an inner darkness leaped at her, and she fell back into the dream.

"Can I give him some scraps, Gran? Please—"

"Sure, if you want to."

"He's so skinny and . . . scared."

"He'll be all right."

"Can I keep him? I can't give him a name if I don't keep him."

"What do you want to call him?"

"I'll have to—" Kathleen opened her eyes to see Johnny bending over her. "Oh, Johnny. I was dreaming. Where am I?"

"In the doctor's rooms in Frederick. He stitched your head. I'm afraid you're going to have a bald spot for a while. Would you like a drink of water?"

"Oh, yes." She licked her dry lips, and Johnny put a glass straw in her mouth. She sucked up the water greedily. "That was good. What time is it?"

"Ten o'clock."

"Do we have to stay here?"

"For a while. The doctor said if you woke up and could see all right, talk rationally, and weren't sick to your stomach, we could leave this afternoon."

"I can see all right. So far, I'm not sick to my stomach."

"You were talking kind of silly when you first woke up. I thought uh-oh, she's out of her head."

"I was dreaming about a little dog I found long time ago. Grandma said we had two dogs and didn't need another. Grandpa let me keep it."

"What did you name him?"

"We called him Zack, but he answered to anything. Zachary Taylor was one of Grandpa's favorite men in history."

Barker Fleming's body blocked the doorway. "She's awake," he said, and came to the bedside and held out a small sack to Johnny. "I wasn't sure if you'd had anything to eat."

"You needn't of—"

"It's only a sandwich."

"A lot went on last night that I don't know about," Kathleen said.

"Louise shot you." Johnny placed the paper bag on the bed and took Kathleen's hand. "The bullet grazed the side of your head. I didn't see the gun until it was too late, but I got to her before she could shoot again. Paul heard the shot, came running, and held her so I could get to you."

"Poor Louise—"

"You're too softhearted," Barker said. "She tried to kill you. A half inch to the right, and she would have."

"He brought us here." Johnny glanced at the man on the other side of the bed. "I couldn't have done it alone."

"I wouldn't have wanted to ride with him last night." Barker spoke confidentially to Kathleen. "He hardly knew which end of him was up after you were shot." He laughed at the dark look on Johnny's face. "I'll have the car out front when the doctor says she can go."

After Barker left, Johnny ate the sandwich.

"He had spotted that blue cape and figured it was Louise. He followed her to the *Gazette*. She's a big woman. It took both him and Paul to hold her until the sheriff and one of the marshals got there to take her to jail."

"I like Barker." She chewed on her lower lip and waited for him to say something.

"Not too much, I hope. I'd hate to have to shoot him after he brought us over here last night."

Kathleen sighed with relief when she saw the glint of humor in his eyes. He finished the sandwich, bent over her, and kissed her mouth.

"Do you think that we'd hitch well together, sweetheart? Last night, I almost died when that crazy woman shot you."

"Is this a proposal?"

"Kind of. I've never proposed before. I've never loved a woman before either. I want you so badly that I hurt. But I'm afraid that after a while you may have second thoughts when you really get to know me and . . . how different we are."

"I won't have second thoughts. I know you to be gentle and kind. You face up to your responsibilities. My grandpa always judged a man by whether he was lazy or not. He'd love you. I worry that you'll be disappointed in me. I'm stubborn and fly off the handle. And I'll—have a bald spot."

"Shhhh . . . You're sweet, and beautiful and smart. I love you very much, and I wouldn't care if your head was completely shaved." He kissed her lips lingeringly.

"Does this mean that we're engaged?"

"Hummm. . . . I guess so. I want to do a little work on the house before I bring you home."

"Can I help?"

"If you come out, I'll not be able to keep my mind on my work. I'll be thinking about getting you in bed."

"Well . . . what's so bad about that?" She reached up and pulled his lips down to hers.

Dear Reader Friend,

Instead of writing an epilogue to this novel, I am writing a complete book continuing the story of Kathleen and Johnny. The time is 1945. Johnny has returned after serving in the United States Seabees. He has been in the South Pacific for four years. When war broke out Kathleen left the newspaper in the capable hands of Adelaide and Paul and became "Rosie the Riveter" in a defense plant along with thousands of other women.

All was not well between Kathleen and Johnny when he went to war. Their baby had died. Grief had torn them apart. Kathleen's hope was that the breach could be healed when he returned.

The men who served in World War II came home to America to take up their lives, seldom speaking of the killing that had been forced upon them by our enemies, or the atrocities they had witnessed. Without whining and self-pity, they went to work building their communities.

AFTER THE PARADE, to be released by Warner Books in the spring of 2000, is the story of such men.

Dorothy Garlock

More Dorothy Garlock!

The following is a chapter from

AFTER THE PARADE
(Spring 2000)

The Continuing Story of
Kathleen and Johnny Henry
who met and fell in love in

WITH HEART

Chapter One

October 15, 1945
Rawlings, Oklahoma

> *"Hurrah for the flag of the free.*
> *May it wave as our standard forever.*
> *The gem of the land and the sea,*
> *The banner of the right—"*

The Rawlings high-school band, decked out in full uniform and lined up beside the platform at the depot, played with gusto John Philip Sousa's "Stars and Stripes Forever." A crowd of a hundred or more had gathered to greet the men who had fought to keep them free. When the huge WELCOME HOME banner that stretched across the front of the depot was loosened by the wind, willing hands hurried to hold it in place.

The gigantic engine, belching smoke, its whistle blasting, its wheels screaming against the rails, slowly passed the station and came to a jerking halt. There was a sudden, expectant quiet. The conductor

1

stepped down from the coach and stood with his hands clasped in front of him.

When the first of the weary war veterans, a surprised Marine, came through the door, the music from the band mingled with the cheers of the crowd and the horns of the cars parked along the street. The Marine stood hesitantly before he bounded down the steps, swung the heavy duffel bag from his shoulder to the platform and was soon surrounded by laughing and crying relatives.

At the back of the crowd, Kathleen Dolan Henry watched six more veterans alight from the train. All were greeted by loved ones. She waited anxiously for her first glimpse of Johnny Henry in more than four years. Someone waved a flag in front of her face; she hurriedly brushed it away just as a tall sailor, his white hat perched low on his forehead, a duffel bag on his shoulder stepped down and stood hesitantly on the platform. His eyes searched the crowd. There was a sudden hush, then the band began to play the Civil War song they had practiced for a month.

"When Johnny comes marching home again, hurrah, hurrah.
We'll give him a hearty welcome then, hurrah, hurrah,
The men will cheer, the boys will shout,
The ladies, they will all turn out,
And we'll all be gay, when Johnny comes marching home."

The band stopped playing and the crowd took up the chant: "Johnny, Johnny, Johnny—"

The hero of the small Oklahoma town had come home from the war.

Johnny Henry was stunned. At one time the people of this town had blamed him for bringing disgrace and death to one of their own. Now they were cheering him.

Everyone had heard how Johnny Henry, on an island in the Pacific, had lifted the blade of the bulldozer he was operating, and amid a shower of gunfire, had driven it straight toward an enemy machine-gun nest that was preventing his platoon from building a landing site so the Marines could land. The powerful dozer had buried the Japanese and their guns inside the concrete structure.

Johnny waved to acknowledge the crowd, then walked slowly toward a small group at the end of the platform. His father, Barker Fleming, his black hair streaked with gray, stood with his arms folded across his chest, his Cherokee pride preventing him from showing emotion. The lone tear that rolled from the corner of his eye was seen only by his daughter, who stood by his side.

Kathleen watched as Johnny shook hands with Barker and his young half brother. He said something to his pretty half sister that made her laugh. As proud as she was of him, and as thankful as she was that he had survived the war, Kathleen couldn't force her feet to carry her to the platform and greet him with all the town looking on. Feeling vulnerable, knowing that some in the crowd were watching her, she hurried off down the street to observe the parade from the window of the *Gazette* office.

Kathleen had been working at the Douglas Aircraft plant in Oklahoma City when the war ended two months ago. She had saved the front page of the August 15, 1945, *Daily Oklahoman*.

JAPS QUIT, WAR IS OVER
TRUMAN TELLS OF COMPLETE SURRENDER.

WASHINGTON, August 14. The Second World War, history's greatest flood of death and destruction, ended Tuesday night with Japan's unconditional surrender. From the moment President Truman announced at 6 pm, Oklahoma time, that the enemy of the Pacific had agreed to Allied terms, the world put aside for a time woeful thoughts of cost in dead and dollars and celebrated in wild frenzy. Formalities meant nothing to people freed at last of war.

Tears had filled her eyes, overflowed, and rolled down her cheeks. She had hurriedly scanned headlines. DISCHARGE DUE FOR 5 MILLION IN 18 MONTHS. Another headline had made her smile. OKLAHOMA CITY CALMLY GOING NUTS!

Johnny would be among the first to come home because of the time he had spent in the combat zone. Kathleen thought of the ranch outside of Rawlings where for a while she had been happier than she had ever imagined she could be and where, later, she had sunk into the depths of despair. She had thought that she could never go back there, but she knew that she must . . . one last time.

Kathleen folded the newspaper carefully. This one she would keep to show to her children someday . . . if she ever had any more. The ache that she carried in her heart intensified at the thought of the tiny daughter she had held in her arms that night five years ago while the cold north wind rattled the window and tore shingles from the roof.

The war was over. She was free to leave her defense job, to go back to Rawlings, to tie up some loose ends and decide what to do with the rest of her life. She was still part-owner of the *Gazette*. Adelaide and Paul had kept it going during the war, but they'd had to cut it from an eight-page paper down to six pages once a week.

On this wondrous day that the war ended, Kathleen had volunteered to work an extra shift in the payroll department of Douglas Aircraft. The pay was double overtime for today. The money would come in handy when the plant closed.

Tired after the twelve-hour shift and the long bus ride into town, she had stepped down onto the Oklahoma City street thronged with shouting and cheering people. Cowbells, horns, and sirens cut the air. Hundreds of uniformed airmen from Tinker Airforce Base and sailors from the Norman Naval Base mingled with the crowd. Hugs and kisses were exchanged by total strangers.

"How 'bout a hug, Red?" A young sailor threw his arm across her shoulders and hugged her briefly. "You got a man comin' home, honey?"

"Thousands of them."

"Bet one of 'em can hardly wait to see ya."

The sailor went on to hug another girl, and Kathleen stood back against a building and watched the jubilant crowd. Her eyes filled with tears, and her heart flooded with thankfulness. This celebration was something she would remember for the rest of her life.

Music came from a loudspeaker on the corner.

*"When the lights come on again, all over the world,
And the boys come home again, all over the world—"*

Kathleen stood for a short while and listened to the music. When the next song was, "Does Your Heart Beat For Me?" she felt a pain so severe that a lump formed in her throat. The last time she had been with Johnny before he went overseas they had sat in a restaurant and listened to that song.

Kathleen hurried on down the street to get away from the music. She waited on the corner to catch the bus that would take her to the rooming house where she had lived since coming to the city to do her bit for the war effort. Not many people were leaving the downtown area, and the bus when it arrived was almost empty.

After she was seated, Kathleen looked at her reflection in the window and wondered if she had changed much during the war years. Her hair was still the same bright red. She had tried to tame the tight curls into the popular shoulder-length pageboy style, but had given up and let it hang. Johnny had teased her about the color of her hair, saying that while he could always spot her in a crowd, so could a bull; so she'd better carry a head scarf when she went to the pasture.

Walking up the dark street to her rooming house, Kathleen felt . . . old. In a few months she would be thirty-three years old. It didn't seem possible that seven years had passed since Johnny had saved her from the hijackers on that lonely Oklahoma road outside Rawlings. For a few years she had been extremely happy, then her world had fallen apart.

Why hadn't he loved her when she had loved him so much? He had allowed his suspicion of an affair between her and Barker and the fact that their baby had been born without a chance to survive to come between them. And his stupid feeling of inferiority had deepened the chasm. After this length of time, it could never be bridged.

Kathleen had not filed for a divorce, even though he had asked her to, and had sent every penny of the family allotment money provided by the government to Johnny's bank in Rawlings. He would have a small nest egg to help him get started again.

Johnny would be free to make a new life for himself and with whoever he chose to share it. As for her, she was sure that she would never be completely happy again, but she could, if she tried hard enough, find a

7

measure of contentment in her work. She had kept her connections with her editor at the pulp magazine where her stories had been published.

Johnny had not expected the welcoming party and was embarrassed by it. He wished that he had stayed on the train until it reached Red Rock and avoided all this. In the back of his mind had been the hope that Kathleen would be here. It was a stupid hope. She had probably met and fallen in love with a 4-F or a draft dodger. The last news he had heard was that she was working in Oklahoma City. He wondered if divorce papers were waiting for him.

During the ceremony at the depot, the mayor welcomed the veterans home, gave each an envelope containing gift certificates to be used at various businesses in town, then escorted them to the hayrack that had been decorated with flags and welcome-home signs. Johnny sat with the other returning veterans and waited patiently for the ordeal of being paraded through town to be over. He searched the crowd that lined the street for a head of bright red hair, and chided himself for hoping that she cared enough to be here when he came home.

Two months earlier, Johnny with the rest of his battalion had watched the Japanese plane with the huge green cross painted on the bottom fly over Okinawa on the way to meet with General MacArthur on the battleship *Missouri* and realized that a phase of his life was over. The siren that in the past announced an air raid blew that day announcing that the war was over. The celebration had begun.

The racket was enough to raise the dead!

Lying on his cot, Johnny grimaced at the thought because there were plenty of dead on the island *to raise*.

"Damn fools are going to shoot themselves," he muttered, but the other man in the tent couldn't have heard him over the racket in the camp.

"The war's over, Geronimo! We're goin' home!" The exuberant shout reached Johnny over the sound of the gunfire.

The only Native American in the construction battalion of Seabees attached to the 3rd Marine division, Johnny had of course been dubbed Geronimo.

"Yeah, we're going home."

Four years was a long time to be away from home, yet he could clearly visualize the clear blue sky and the broad sweep of rolling prairies of southwestern Oklahoma. He longed to get on his horse and ride to a place where there was not another human being within miles and miles.

There was no doubt that war was hell. Could he ever forget the bombings on Guadalcanal while they were trying to build an airstrip so Allied planes could land? Could he forget the steaming Solomon Islands, studded with coconut plantations and hut villages of ebony-skinned natives, mostly bearded, short, stocky, and superstitious? He knew that he would never forget the stench of burning flesh as flame throwers drove the enemy out of the caves of Okinawa.

"Ya know what I'm goin to do when I get home, Geronimo?" The excited voice of Johnny's completely bald tentmate interrupted his thoughts. "I'm going to take my woman and my kid in the house, lock the door, and not come out till spring. Do you think my kid will remember me? Hell, she was only two years old when I left. It's hard to believe that she'll be startin' school."

"Sure, she'll remember you, Curly. Goddammit!" Johnny exclaimed as a bullet tore through the top of the tent.

Shortly after that a voice came over the loud-speaker. "Cease fire! Cease fire at once!"

"It's about time," Johnny growled. "Damn officers sitting up there with their heads up their butts!"

He had come through the war with five battle stars for major engagements and had only a few shrapnel wounds to show for it. He was grateful for that. But, hell, he had no wife to go home to. If Kathleen hadn't divorced him by now, she would as soon as he reached the States.

His sister, Henry Ann, had written every week and would be glad to see him, but even she didn't need him anymore. Her life was with Tom and their kids. Barker had sent him a package about once a month. One package had had a camera and film. He'd enjoyed it. Adelaide had sent him copies of the *Gazette*. Sometimes they were a month old, but he had read every line looking for news of Kathleen.

Johnny clasped his hands under his head, looked

up at the bullet hole in the tent, and thought of what he'd do when he got home. He had the land that he'd bought before he and Kathleen were married. As his needs had been few, his pay each month, except for five dollars, had gone back to pay on the mortgage. Keith McCabe had run some cattle on his land. That money, too, had gone toward the mortgage. Considering that he had given almost five years of his life to Uncle Sam, he wasn't in too bad a way financially.

He had stopped looking for mail other than from Henry Ann and occasional letters from Adelaide and his half sister, Marie, after the first six months. The first Christmas he was in the Pacific Theater, he had hoped for a card from the only woman he had ever loved, and had made her a bracelet out of aluminum from a downed Japanese aircraft. Many hours of painstaking work had gone into engraving her name on it. He had been stupid enough to buy a comb made out of trochus shells, from which pearl buttons are made, from a Guadalcanal native.

After that disappointment he had packed away the bracelet and comb and concentrated strictly on trying to stay alive while he raced out of a flatboat onto an enemy-held island and while he drove the big bulldozer to clear the land, or the packer that rolled the coral to make the landing strips.

But, dammit to hell! No matter how hard he'd tried to forget, there was still a vacant place in his heart.

Johnny had been waving automatically to the crowd that lined the street as his mind wandered. He was suddenly jolted back to reality when he saw Paul and Adelaide waving frantically. Behind them a slender figure was standing in the window of the *Gazette* office. Was it Kathleen? Hell, no. If she'd been in town, she'd have been at the depot to get a few pictures and a story for the paper. Now he wished he'd asked Barker if he had heard from her. She and Barker had always been thick as thieves, and at one time he had honestly thought that she was in love with the man.

The truck pulling the hayrack stopped in front of the courthouse. Johnny jumped down and hoisted his duffel bag to his shoulder. Barker was waiting there.

"We'd like for you to come out to the ranch, Johnny."

"Thanks, but I think I'll go on out to the Circle H."

"It's up to you. You know that you're always welcome. The car is just down the street. The kids are down at Claude's."

"That old coot still fryin' hamburgers?"

"He's still at it."

Barker had always driven like a bunch of Apaches were after him. He did that now, dust trailing behind the car like a bushy red tail. Johnny was about to ask about Kathleen, then thought better of it. Instead he asked about the town's main industry, which Barker owned.

"How's the tannery doing?"

"Good. We're getting summer and fall hides and keeping more of the good stuff for our own factory. The government cut down some on their buying when the European War ended, and then almost completely

12

stopped ordering a few months ago. So we must look for another market."

"I'm sure you'll find one."

Johnny's hungry eyes roamed the flat Oklahoma plains, then lifted to the eagle that soared effortlessly in the blue sky. It was good to be home. He noticed things that he had taken for granted before; like the occasional oak or hawthorn tree along the road that was heavy with mistletoe. The whiteberry parasite had become the state flower of Oklahoma. The first Christmas he and Kathleen had been married he had put a clump of mistletoe in each doorway of the house, an excuse to kiss her—as if he needed one.

Thank goodness Barker knew when to be quiet. Johnny glanced at his stoic profile and the hair that was heavily streaked with gray. That had been a surprise. He'd had only a touch of gray when he'd last seen him.

In a few days he'd buy some kind of car and go over to Red Rock and see Henry Ann and Tom. He wondered if Pete and Jude Perry had come through the war. The last he'd heard Pete was in the navy. Jude had joined the army, gone to officers' school and was a captain in the 45th Infantry out of Fort Sill. The Thunderbirds had seen heavy action at Anzio and had taken heavy casualties. God, he hoped Jude had come through. He was the best of the Perrys.

Barker stopped the car in front of the small frame house but kept the motor running. After Johnny got out of the car he lifted his duffel bag from the backseat, bent over, and peered through the window.

"Thanks."

"Don't mention it."

Johnny straightened, and the car moved away. The first thing he noticed after distance had eaten up the sound of the motor, was the quiet it left in its wake. During the years he had been away, there had always been sound coming from somewhere, even on the boat going and returning across the Pacific. He stood still, not wanting to break the silence even with his footsteps.

The small four-room house looked lonely and unloved. Grass was a foot high in the places where Kathleen had planted flowers. The old washtub he had nailed to a stump to serve as a planter was still there, but dried weeds replaced the colorful moss rose that once filled it. He eased his duffel bag down onto the porch and walked slowly around the house. The stock pen was empty, the windmill still.

Johnny sat down on the back steps, rested his forearms on his thighs, and clasped his hands tightly together. Coming back was not as he had imagined it would be. In the jungles of Guadalcanal, New Guinea, and Bougainville he had dreamed of this place. After that first Christmas when he had not heard from Kathleen, he realized that he had lost her. The desire to get back to his ranch was what had kept him sane during the bombings and shellings.

Now that he was back, what was it but just a place? One small lonely spot in the universe.

The following recipe was sent to me by Mary Patchell, Oklahoma City, Oklahoma. It was a favorite of her family during the Great Depression.

CHOCOLATE GRAVY

4 level Tbs. cornstarch (My grandma used 8 Tbs. flour)
2 level tsp. cocoa
1/2 c sugar
dash of salt
2 c milk
1 tsp. vanilla
1 Tbs. butter

Into a pan or skillet, sift together first four ingredients. Add milk slowly. Cook over medium heat, stirring until thick. Remove from heat and add vanilla and butter.

Serve over hot biscuits.

Mrs. Patchell writes: *Sometimes Grandpa butchered hogs and we had bacon, ham, or sausage with our biscuits. And Grandma cooked the best pinto beans, corn bread, and fried potatoes. Even today that is my favorite meal for supper.*